The Dave Brewster Series

THE HIVE

KARL J. MORGAN

CONTENTS

The tekkan star ships floated down noiselessly toward the surface of the planet. Rugged mountain ranges loomed in the distance, while waves danced on a large ocean below the ships. Captain Van Daggamar ordered the colony ship Maxila to remain close behind the cruiser Vanaka in case of any unforeseen danger. The ships approached the mountain ranges which rose out of the sea. Volcanoes spewed ash into the morning air and rivers of lava flowed to the sea, causing massive plumes of steam to shoot into the air far below.

The ships banked to avoid the ash clouds and soon had passed the mountains and crossed over rolling grasslands as far as the horizon. Clumps of dense forest dotted the land. Van ordered the ships to land at the edge of a group of trees standing like sentinels in the center of the rolling hills of grass. The vessels settled down in a barren spot less than two hundred yards from the trees. The mountains were now hundreds of miles behind them, and only a few smoldering peaks dotted the horizon.

"Captain, the atmosphere seems breathable and air pressure is within norms," said Science Officer Nak Gongaleg. "I am reading a number of fauna species in the immediate vicinity. I strongly recommend that our landing party be well armed."

"Very well, Nak. You may signal Lieutenant Fongala that his team may explore our immediate environs," Van replied.

Nan Fongala had graduated from the Don-Makla Military Academy one year ago. He was immediately made a loadmaster on one of the thousands of supply ships ferrying materials to construct the new world at Tak-Makla. He was well respected by all of his superior officers and would likely be doing the same work if he had not met Zon Palaka.

Zon was an almost mythical religious leader on Don-Makla. When the planetary council announced the plan to construct a Hive on the new planet, she was irate. She could not believe they would bring the fury of God onto her people by building a Hive and attempting to elevate themselves to godhood. All the great maklan teachers of the past had insisted that such knowledge was strictly forbidden. The ability to join the spirits and God by uniting with Universal Consciousness was blasphemous. Public sentiment was strongly in her favor at the beginning, but began to waver as the government spent billions to convince the populace The Hive would be used for science and trade and no one had any intention of interfering with Universal Consciousness.

Zon and her allies held rallies all over Don-Makla trying to drum up support for her cause. When the tide started to turn in her favor, the High Council stopped giving her permits for the rallies. It seemed all hope was lost. Don-Makla was to be abandoned in ten years and all maklans were required to move to the new planet. Instead, Zon formed a secret society that acquired four colony ships and four star cruisers. During the final exodus from the planet, her ships would slip away from the thousands of others and make their way to new worlds, where they could maintain their faith. Each colony ship was to establish a home on a different planet with their twenty thousand maklan settlers.

Nan Fogala had been to many of the rallies and believed in his heart that the move to Tak-Makla would bring death and destruction to the maklans there. When Zon herself offered him a spot on her flagship, he agreed happily. His team of ten heavily armed soldiers was now to escort a priest to the surface of the planet to bless it as the new home of their colony. He clipped the two blasters onto his belt. He took a rifle and slung it across his back. After checking his com-link, he left the armory and headed to the landing bay.

As he entered the landing bay, Nan saw that the minor priest for the mission had been replaced by Zon Palaka herself. He knelt in front of her and kissed her hand. "Your Eminence, we are honored by your presence," Nan said.

"Thank you, Nan," she smiled, "it is wonderful to see you again." She addressed the entire group, "Dear friends, on this beautiful day it will be our pleasure to bless our new home planet. I know you must be vigilant for any dangers, but please try to enjoy your opportunity to be the first maklans on this world. In accordance with our tradition, we will kneel at the foot of the ramp when we first touch the soil and give thanks. A few of you may stand guard if needed. Then we will circle this ship three times offering thanks to God for our new home. After a final blessing, we will return on board and our crews can begin establishing a secure boundary." She smiled broadly, and signaled the loadmaster to open the doors and extend the ramp to the surface.

Nan led his team onto the ground of their new home. The grassy surface was soft from recent rain. The air was sweet, clean and ionized from a thunderstorm that left the area as the ships touched down. The security detail formed a twenty foot defensive circle around the landing ramp, with their laser rifles in firing position. Nan and Vak, the other lieutenant leading the team examined the area with their high powered goggles. Nan said, "I see a group of carnivores at eight hundred yards. They appear to be upwind so they should not be a problem. What do you see, Vak?"

"There is a large herd of herbivores one thousand yards downwind, Nan," Vak replied. "There also appear to be some flying creatures circling that herd. I'll contact the captain and have him send two or three flyers to keep an eye on things."

On Nan's signal, Zon descended the ramp and stepped on the planet surface. She dropped to her knees and blessed the planet. Then she rose and walked to each member of the guard blessing them for their role as the first maklans on this world. As they began to walk around the ship, three crew members emerged from the ramp with flying packs strapped to their backs. They launched into the air and began to circle the area from one hundred feet in the air.

"A little help here!" shouted one of the guards who had stepped into a hidden pool of quicksand and was sinking fast. One of the flyers zipped to the area, grabbed the soldier and pulled him free, setting him back on dry land. He brushed off his uniform and rushed back to his position. The flyer used a spray gun to paint a circle around the pool.

"Nak, are you okay?" Nan asked.

"Yes, sir, no problem," the soldier replied as he continued with the group.

"Nan, the herd of herbivores is heading in this direction and the flying creatures are following them," Nin, the leader of the flyers said over the com-link. "They are probably twenty minutes out. My team reports that the carnivores have noticed our activity, but do not seem to be moving yet. I recommend expedience."

Zon and her team had finished the second lap around the ship and they were quickening their pace to be careful. "Nan, it seems our captain has picked a planet brimming with life," Zon said. "The team of guards will have a full time job until this area is safe for our children."

"Don't worry, Eminence," Nan replied. "We've got things under control."

They were nearing the ramp and the final blessing when the flock of twenty flying creatures zoomed quickly toward their group. The flyers flew among them trying to disorient the beasts. A few laser blasts frightened most of them away. One lurched forward and dived toward Zon with two flyers on its tail. They were afraid to shoot as the priest was in their line of fire. The beast reached down and grabbed Zon by the arm and began to lift her off the ground as it flapped its wings frantically. Nan jumped off the ground and grabbed Zon by the legs. He pulled his blaster and shot the animal in the head. The beast fell to the ground dead. Nan grabbed Zon and threw her over his shoulder and ran back up the ramp while the remaining troops formed a tight perimeter at the base of the ramp. Zon was bleeding badly, so Nan ran through the ship to sick bay and laid her on a bed, where the doctors immediately began working on her.

Nan ran back to the landing bay and found all the team had returned and the doors had been sealed. He noticed his uniform was soaked in blood from Zon and the flying beast. Through the windows, he could see the pack of carnivores devouring the dead beast, while the herd of large herbivores moved slowly by.

"Well, what do you think, Dave?" Engineer Nok said as her silver thread of light swirled around his near the dead flying beast.

"This definitely looks like proof that tekkans compromised human DNA," Dave Brewster replied. "At least it is proof that tekkans came to Earth. How far in the past did we come today, Nok?"

"Four hundred million years, more or less," she replied. "The exodus from Don-Makla occurred over a long period, so we don't know exactly when Zon Palaka left. Historical records from that period are sketchy too. Our agent found this by accident and shared it with Zee. Do you want to see anything from your ancient past while we're here, Dave?"

"No thanks, Nok, but this has been great! I could never imagine seeing ancient Earth. This kind of time travel is forbidden using portals," Dave replied.

"Can you imagine the damage any minor change to this epoch would do to modern times?" Nok asked.

"It seems that we are seeing that impact in front of us now. I hope this proves the Paxran never came to Earth and humans are able to join The Hive due to our tekkan ancestors," Dave replied. "We should get back so we can talk to Zee."

The scenery around their strings of light melted away and space-time spun into a blur as they shot forward in time and space. Dave could see his own string of light arching ahead of him as he followed it back to his body deep in The Hive. The silver light of Nok's light was next to him and he was warmed by her presence.

CHAPTER 2

The canopy to the chamber rose and Dave opened his eyes. High Consul Zee Gongaleg, Var Vanadez, Chief Engineer of The Hive, and Mak Andeles, Minister of Internal Affairs were standing over him. Dave and Nok climbed to their feet. "Thank you Nok, that will be all for now," Zee said. Nok shook Dave's hand and left the room. "Let's take a tube to my house to talk."

The four left the room and followed the curving corridor to the nearest tube room. Zee touched the single panel on the wall, which then said, "Destination?"

"High Consul residence, private entrance," Zee replied as he put his face in front of the panel. A green light illuminated his face.

"Security scan approved. Welcome, High Consul, you may enter," the panel replied. On the opposite wall, the maze of lines dimmed and the path to the Consul's home shone brightly. The door on the shuttle opened and the four climbed in and tightened their restraints.

Zee touched the lone panel and said, "Ready." The door on the clear shuttle closed and the wall in front of the shuttle opened to reveal the glass tube ahead. The shuttle shot forward. The four were buffeted form side to side as the shuttle shot upward and switched tubes on its course. "Dave, now you have seen the tekkan contamination of Earth," Var said. "We don't know for certain whether those tekkans were the only reason your neurology and DNA bears a resemblance to ours." The shuttle turned right and the four were pushed to the left. "I have many agents continuing the search since we cannot rule out Paxran influence yet."

Dave Brewster remembered the first time he had taken a tube. It had seemed like an amusement park ride. Now, after dozens of trips, it was becoming a normal way to get around on Tak-Makla. He said, "I would think this evidence strongly reduces the possibility of Paxran influence though." The shuttle shot straight up traveling from deep in The Hive to the planet's surface. Dave felt plastered into his seat. He thought this must be how the first astronauts on Earth felt when they climbed into rockets and blasted into space.

"I agree with Dave," Zee said. "We can't ignore the evidence staring us in the face. Tekkans went to Earth and built a colony. Even if they were all killed by wild animals within a few years, their DNA had an impact." The shuttle leveled off, turned right and slowed to a stop in a tube room. The door opened and they stepped out of the shuttle. Zee led them out the door and up the long passageway into the house. "I've asked our cook to prepare a light lunch for us. Why don't we go to the library while we wait?" The passageway ended near the kitchen of the mansion. The smells of cooking food filled the air. "Var, please take Dave and Mak to the library. I'll have someone bring us coffee and pastries. I'm starving," Zee said.

The next door on the left led into a large library, with volumes of books lining three walls and three levels high. The one bare wall was all glass, looking out on the patio and the beach. Gentle waves slid up onto the sand. A light rain was falling, making trails down the glass. A coffee table was surrounded by four overstuffed armchairs. They sat and looked out to sea. In a minute, Zee came in with two valets carrying trays of coffee and pastries, which they set on the table. The valets prepared cups of coffee and small plates of pastry and set them in front of the four chairs. Then they left.

Zee picked up his cup and savored the coffee. "Aw, this is fantastic. Dave, please tell Darlene and Charlie that the master roasters have done a magnificent job. All of Tak-Makla owes them a debt of gratitude."

"Consul, can we cut to the chase?" Mak asked.

"Mak, you and your type never take time to enjoy life," Zee frowned. "I don't know if you can ever be High Consul with that attitude." Zee turned to Dave and said, "Dave, you may have guessed that Internal Affairs is a diplomatic term for security police. His job is to keep secret that which must be secret, and to protect us all from subversive elements in the population."

"I certainly understand the need for police," Dave replied. "I thought tekkans were very conscientious and tried to fit in?"

"That is almost entirely true, Dave," Mak said. "With a population of twenty billion, even a tiny fraction yields quite a few bad apples. Without any doubt, the lower levels of The Hive are our most important area to control. The bulk of my team work there to make certain security is absolute. Other crimes like theft and assault are extremely rare. The temptation for some to profit from future knowledge is overwhelming. We keep a very sharp eye on any future traveling. While they cannot change the future, they may find something they can use now in their favor."

"We are the same, Mak," Dave replied. "Future travel is controlled by the highest levels of government. We also recognize that the future isn't set and any tiny event between now and then can change the outcome."

"Now it is you and Dave who are wasting time," Zee said to Mak. "This is a very simple meeting, Dave. Since you have agreed to build more Hives, we will need to teach more humans how it actually works. Var has had many agents traversing our territories looking for ideal planets to house a Hive. We have ten candidate planets already. If we start construction soon, the knowledge transfer must also begin soon."

"What do you want me to do, Zee?" Dave asked.

"We believe that teams of maklans and humans would be more trustworthy than just humans," Mak said.

"That's not a good way of getting their support, Mak," Zee said. "Please don't take offense, Dave."

"None taken. It's obvious that maklans are closely related to tekkans," Dave replied. "Your cultures have the same core. Also, the maklans have never tried to take over another civilization. They won't even colonize a planet for fear of affecting indigenous life."

"Exactly, Dave," Zee smiled, "I knew you would understand. So, we are agreed? Lunch will be waiting on the patio."

"I have one question, Zee," Dave said. "You mentioned before that Jake Benomafolays experienced pain when he attempted to join The Hive. I think they need to experience The Hive to be able to actively participate in construction of new ones, don't you?"

"Yes, Dave," Zee answered. "Thankfully, we have already resolved that issue. We discovered the electronic implant that allows them to jump without a portal was the culprit. We were able to create a biological replacement similar to organs in our own bodies. Now maklans can join The Hive and jump much further without the need for teams."

"That's great news, Zee. Let's eat!" Dave said.

CHAPTER 3

A heavy black rain was pouring outside the Governor's Mansion on Nom-Kat-La. Governor Mak-Kal-a entered the main conference room to greet his guests. Following the example of the Io Star Port, a thick glass wall divided the room in two parts. The side he entered had a natural atmosphere. The other side had an atmosphere breathable by humans, Kalideans, Palians and Predaxians. On his side of the glass was the High Commissioner of Greater Gallia, the legendary general Fa-a-Di. Across the glass were Ambassadors Darlene Brewster of Earth, Nominus Malacus of the Kalidean Federation, Kogala of Palus and Zakamar Vondee of Predax.

"My dear friend, Fa-a-Di," Mak-Kal-a fawned, "it is a great honor for you to join our humble negotiation today. My planet is forever in your debt for saving us from the evil of the Alliance."

"It is good to be here, Mak-Kal-a. This is a special day in our relationship with the civilizations gathered here," Fa-a-Di replied. "You have to admit it is a unique group." Unique was not sufficient to describe the races involved. The Galliceans were both fifteen feet tall with lean bodies and bird-like heads. Their skin was pale and iridescent, with no hair or feathers. They had developed on gas giant planets and had relied on flying extreme distances with only small manufactured islands floating in the gas for homes. The Palians were distantly related to the Galliceans. Their home world was Earth-like with forests covering most of the land. On Palus, it had been the birds that became sentient. Kogala, the former warden of the prison planet Localus was ten feet tall with bright red plumage covering his exposed skin. The Kalideans were humanoid, but quite short with bright blue skin and very large, unblinking black eyes. It had been their interdiction in The War that ended humanity's history of self-destruction by proving that humans were not alone in the galaxy. Zakamar Vondee was married to the President of the Predaxian Council which had replaced the empire that had ruled hundreds of worlds through mind control. It had only been a month since the end of the Second Predaxian War and all races were still unsure the Predaxians would give up their ambitions. Predaxians were another maklan race, resembling spiders in some respects, although two legs had grown stronger and longer, enabling them to walk upright and handle tools. This species of maklans were red with small black eyes. The room across the glass had a jumble of levels and seating arrangements to handle the mix of species.

"Brother, it is wonderful to see you again," Darlene said to Fa-a-Di as she pressed her hand against the glass in front of him. "Dave sends his regards, and hopes to visit you on Gallia in the near future."

Fa-a-Di pressed his hand against the same spot on the glass and laughed, "Sister, I cannot wait for that day! I would love to fly Dave around Gallia. I told him before we would have a large audience which would be a spectacle not to be missed. As you know, Charlie Watson and Jon Lake have been traveling through our space looking for planets suitable for human inhabitation. I believe they have found several good candidates."

"Yes, Brother, I have been told. Currently, Dave is on Tak-Makla working on plans to build more Hives. Hopefully, one can be built on one of those planets," she replied.

"Can we please get on with the meeting?" Kogala the Palian asked. "Sitting so close to this Predaxian is very uncomfortable for me. It wasn't so long ago that I was their slave."

"Quiet, Kogala," Fa-a-Di shouted. "You know well that without Zak and Pan, you would still be their slave. I know the wounds have not healed yet, but certainly you can make some allowance for the woman who saved your civilization?"

"It's okay, General," Zak replied. "Kogala, I understand your feelings and you have every right to be suspicious. I hope that over time you will learn that we are changing."

"I will try Ambassador Vondee," Kogala said. "As the first matter for discussion, I think we need to address compensation to Palus for the destruction of our planet."

"No race here was involved in that," Mak-Kal-a said. "Perhaps that issue should be raised with the tekkans?"

"Without the tekkan intervention, the Predaxians may have won the war and taken this planet and more," Nominus said. "Palus would still be enslaved, and all the Galliceans on this world as well, including you. I cannot see how we could ask Tak-Makla to pay."

"The bottom line for us is that all the other races here and the tekkans were deliberate participants in the war," Kogala said. "The Palians were the only race that was forced to fight against their will. Our minds were controlled and we were like machines to be used. Yet, when the war was over, only one planet was gone, and it was our world. Where is the justice there?"

"I hate to admit it, but I agree with Ambassador Kogala," Zak replied. She stood and began to walk around the room slowly. "On the other hand, it had always been a prison world, even before the Predaxian Empire took over. The surface was not inhabitable, and Palus only sent their most hardened criminals there. It is not the same as if Palus itself had been damaged."

"You're right, Zak," Kogala said. "We recognize that Localus was not a vital colony or resort for our people. But it was a planet in our space, and now it is gone, through no deliberate action of our people. It must be worth something."

"Fa-a-Di, have you considered the treaty between us?" Darlene asked. "Could something like that work with the Palians?"

"That's an excellent idea, Darlene," Nominus said.

"You want us to offer a planet in our space to the Palians?" Fa-a-Di asked. "Why not a planet in Predaxian or Earth space?"

Kogala stood and placed his hand against the glass in front of the general. "Dear General, you already know the answer to that question," he snickered.

"Nom-Kat-Un. You want us to give you Nom-Kat-Un, right?" Fa-a-Di said.

"That's preposterous," Mak-Kal-a replied. "I don't want them in my system. This is highly unusual, general. I understand your treaty with the humans. I have flown through the Red Spot there myself. But the humans have never waged war on us."

"Either have we, Governor," Kogala pleaded. "You must remember that Predax was controlling our minds. They were fighting you. We were simply tools they used to avoid dying themselves. My grandfather told me of the great relationship he had with your grandfather, Fa-a-Di, before the Predaxians came. Our cultures are linked by DNA and many generations of trade and friendship. Surely, this gesture is small compared to the opportunity to be friends again?"

"Brother, please allow me to make a proposal," Darlene began. "I recommend a treaty between Palus and Gallia for planet sharing. It will be different because both sides must provide a planet in each exchange. That way, neither gets an advantage."

"That's intriguing, sister, please say more," Fa-a-Di replied.

"Wait a minute," Kogala stammered, "you want us to give a planet to Gallia in exchange for Nom-Kat-Un. I don't have the authority to make such an agreement. Doesn't that mean we get nothing for Localus? How is that fair compensation?"

"It's not about planet A or planet B, friends," Darlene continued. "It is about building mutual trust, friendship and trade. Palus has been isolated for more than one hundred years during the domination by the Predaxians. How much trade has been lost in that time? Nominus and I have been to Nom-Kat-Un. It is a beautiful world with a good atmosphere for Palians. Sixty percent of the land surface is covered with huge forests, many hundreds of feet tall. The oceans are full of fish and many species of fauna inhabit the land. A Gallicean would suffocate in one minute if he was exposed to that air. The planet is useless to Gallia."

"My father told me about it," Kogala reminisced. "His father took him there many times for vacation. He told me about flying through the tree tops and how sweet the air was. I believe there used to be hundreds of resorts there for Palians."

"Nominus and I have also visited Nartang 6," Darlene continued. "It is a massive gas giant, as big as Gallia. There are two Dar-Fas, one in each hemisphere. We took a group of maklans there and they found extensive Ka-la-a and wildlife on a scale with Planet 5 in the Golden Dawn system. No Palian has ever explored that planet. It has done an excellent job of shielding Nartang from asteroids, but provides no other benefit to the Palian systems."

"Darlene, I can really see why Dave loves you so much," Fa-a-Di smiled. "In a few words, you have taken a bad situation and turned it into a great future for Gallia and Palus. I know that Kogala must take this offer to the High Council as I must do as well. I am confident that my council will agree. I must also confess that I visited Nartang 6 just after the end of the war. My grandfather had told me about it too. What a wonderful idea. What do you think, Kogala?"

"I don't know, Fa-a-Di. My orders were to get compensation for Localus. I feel that I have failed. The deal sounds wonderful, except that Localus is forgotten. While the High Council may agree, I feel I will be reprimanded," Kogala whimpered.

Mak-Kal-a stood and pressed his hand to the glass in front of the Palian. "Dear Kogala, perhaps we can upgrade this offer to keep our great relationship. I believe the general would approve adding Nom-Kat-Zuk to the deal. It is a horrible and desolate rock in space at the outer rim of this system. It is twice the size of Localus and there is no measurable atmosphere. In all ways, it seems much like Localus. It may not be pretty, but it could be a replacement prison world for you. What do you think now, brother?"

Kogala stood and pressed his hand to the glass, smiling. "Governor, thank you for that gift. I am certain this new deal can be approved. Let's all toast to our success!"

Var put his face in front of the panel in the tube room. He touched the panel and said, "Hive, level nine-nine-zero-zero-zero, ring fifty."

The green light illuminated his face. The panel responded, "Security scan confirmed. Welcome Minister Var. Ready." The shuttle door opened and he and Dave Brewster stepped in and strapped on their restraints. The wall opened and the shuttle flew into the open tube. Immediately, it turned straight downward and shot into the darkness. There were no other tubes in this area and the walls around glowed light red showing that the security systems were fully activated. After several minutes of flying down, the shuttle leveled off as it approached the bottom of The Hive.

Dave could see that the surface below was solid rock. "Var, is this the surface of the original planet Tak-Makla was built upon?"

"Exactly right, Dave," Var responded. "You can see the curving wall to our left. That is the edge of The Hive. It was built upon the bedrock of the planet for support. Outside this small tunnel, you would find thousands of support columns and mechanical equipment that provides power and light for the underground communities." The shuttle turned sharply to the left and slowed as it entered a tube room and stopped. Waiting for them were two heavily armed guards, who snapped to attention when they saw Minister Var.

"Minister, can we assist you or your guest?" Nik, the guard lead asked.

"No, thank you Nik," Var said as he shook hands with the two guards. "It is very good to see you and Vil again. Let me introduce you to Dave Brewster. He is going to help us build more Hives to protect this region of space." After they exchanged pleasantries, they left the guards and entered another long curving corridor.

"Var, this is the lowest level of The Hive. What happens here?" Dave asked.

"As you know, there are one hundred rings on most of the ninety-nine thousand levels of The Hive. On most levels, each of those rings consists of hundreds of rooms with chambers for our agents to enter the stream of Universal Power. On the bottom fifty levels, there are only fifty such rings. The area outside ring fifty is reserved for the equipment that makes The Hive function. You will note that there are doors on both sides of this corridor. On the left are the circular doors leading to chambers. On the right are normal doors leading to the equipment rooms." He stopped and touched a panel near a door on the right side. The green light again illuminated his face. The door slid into a pocket in the wall, and they stepped in.

The massive room was filled with electronic equipment which rose from the floor several hundred feet into the air above. Metal walkways jutted out from other doors higher in The Hive. Two guards stood by each door. Dave had not noticed them when he walked in, but they were standing next to him. Tekkans walked around checking control panels and hurrying to small rooms constructed in the middle of the equipment. Var led Dave down three steps and onto the rock surface of the planet. The surface had been smoothed and polished until it was as smooth as glass. They walked down a corridor between two banks of equipment that soared over their heads until they reached a room. Var knocked on the door and opened it. Inside were a small conference table and two desks facing one another. The walls of the room were computer screens. Sitting at the desks were a tekkan engineer and what appeared to be a human female. Both wore white scientific uniforms.

"Dave, please let me introduce you to Chief Engineers Nit Valasan and Loni Arrak," Var said as he walked toward the two who rose to shake his hand.

"Hello, my name is Dave Brewster from Earth," he said as he shook the tekkan's hand. He turned to the woman and shook her hand as well. He noticed she was several inches taller than him with very white skin, light blonde hair and startling silver eyes. She was also quite beautiful.

"Hi Dave, I'm Loni Arrak," she smiled. "Var, I don't know why they stuck you with this job." She laughed.

"They say it comes with the Minister's position, Loni," Var sighed. "Let's all sit down and chat. Nit, have someone bring us coffee and biscuits or something."

After they sat, Loni said, "Okay, I'll answer the obvious question in Dave's mind. I am human, but I have never been to your home planet. Well, let me take that back. I have traveled there extensively, but only through The Hive."

"I am completely confused now," Dave replied. "Where are you from, Loni? You can't be from one of the colonies. My ship was the first to discover Tak-Makla. Can you explain what's going on here?"

Loni reached across the table and touched Dave's hand. She smiled warmly at him. "Dave, I am from the Non-Ti civilization. We have been around a very long time, probably three billion of your years. My ancestors saw the rising culture on Ai-Makla. We helped nourish it in hopes they would be our friends one day. When it became apparent their world would die in a nova before they could escape, we dropped some hints to help them discover portal technology. Once they began to build this Hive, we finally formed a relationship that has thrived for millions of years."

"You said you were human, like me," Dave said. "I understand how you helped the tekkans, but didn't humans evolve on Earth?"

"No, they did not, Dave," Loni replied as she sipped her coffee. "As far as we know, humanity originated on the planet Non-Ti which is in what you call the Andromeda Galaxy. We faced a similar problem to the maklans. The sun in the Non-Ti system became a supernova long ago. Fortunately, we had the technology to escape. Since it was so far in the past, we can't be certain whether we developed it, or if some other race gave it to us. Either way, we expanded into our galaxy and others. There are over fifty thousand planets in the Society of Humanity."

"Humans are not like us in that regard," Var interjected. "We are very hesitant to inhabit worlds with other life that may become sentient. We believe those planets should develop on their own."

"Humanity has a different view, Dave," Loni said. "We try to avoid planets with sentient civilizations, even if they are very primitive. However, we have found those to be very rare. In all of the galaxies we have explored, we have only found a few hundred truly unique sentient species. Look at the maklans themselves, Dave. They took over five hundred systems when they escaped from Ai-Makla. Now, some of them have decided to be altruistic, like here and on No-Makla. But remember the Predaxians? That war just ended. I know that Zee has also told you about the Paxran. They have conquered hundreds of worlds to expand their dominance. If we find a suitable planet that none of our friends have the rights to, we view it as fair game."

"What about Earth?" Dave asked. "When did you go there and why did you leave? I studied history and there are no records of any earlier human civilizations."

"Dave, you are sitting here. I think that proves we never left," Loni replied. "Rather than talk about it, why don't I show you the highlights?" They stood and Loni walked over to Dave and took his hand. She led him back into the corridor to an open room on the left side.

Dave and Loni's lights descended rapidly toward the tekkan outpost on Earth. It had been six months since the tekkan ships had arrived and Zon Palaka was attacked on the surface. Security fields were now in place providing a two mile secure radius around the ships. Dozens of structures were either complete or in progress. Half of the colonists had been able to move to permanent homes on the planet. In the center of the newly constructed city center was a government building and a temple. Near the security fields were acres of truck and grain farms producing food to replace the rapidly depleting stores from the ships.

Dave and Loni floated into the center of a group of ten soldiers wearing flying packs. They had assembled on the steps of the Council building. Commander Nan Fongala was their leader. He was promoted quickly after saving Zon's life. "Okay team," Nan began, "this is a normal security sweep of the area. There have seen some odd sensor hits twenty miles to the south. We'll fly in formation in that direction. Keep your eyes focused and report any unusual activity. It is not our goal to engage any targets. You can only respond to attacks on our team. Let's go."

The group of flyers floated up into the air and they headed south toward the security field. As they approached the field, Nan signaled and a small opening appeared ahead of them. They flew through and the hole closed behind them. They rose to five hundred feet above the surface to avoid the frequent clouds of insects and continued southward. They could see small groups of animals foraging for food below them. There were no flying carnivores in sight, which promised an uneventful trip. Ten miles from their encampment, they crossed a wide, slowly flowing river. Clouds of insects could be seen on the surface. Nan was happy to be above them as their stings had proven to be quite painful. Smaller packs of larger insects dove through the clouds to gorge on the smaller prey. A large jungle sprang on the far side of the river. The trees grew two hundred feet tall. They could see flying creatures roaming the tree tops for prey.

"Nan, I see a reflection dead ahead," Nit shouted over the com-link.

Nan looked forward and saw the glint of light on the horizon at tree top level. "Top speed, men," he ordered. The ten flyers accelerated toward the anomaly. It appeared to be the reflection off something metallic. Whatever it was, it turned and shot south at high speed. In a moment, it was gone from view. They continued their pursuit.

After another twenty minutes, Nit said, "Commander, if we don't turn around soon, we won't have enough power to get back to the base."

"Damn it! You are right Nit," Nan confirmed. "Let's get back and give our video feeds to the Captain. Maybe he'll send some shuttles from the Vanaka to search the area more. Let's go home guys." The ten flyers turned in a wide arc and headed back north. Dave turned to follow them.

"Dave, where are you going?" Loni said. "Let's keep going south!" Dave returned to her and they flew southward again. After five minutes, Loni stopped and floated high over the Earth. Dave's light flew up to hers.

"Why are we stopping here, Loni? There's nothing here but more jungle," Dave said. "Shouldn't we keep going south?"

Loni replied, "Things are not always as they appear. Follow me." She flew downward toward the tree tops that were now three hundred feet above the planet. Dave followed behind her. Just as they were going to touch the trees, they slipped through an invisible barrier and found themselves above a vast human colony.

A small town lay below them, surrounded by fields of grain and vegetables. A large roadway led further south past the horizon. People could be seen tilling fields and traveling in glass-like shuttles on and above the roadways. The sky above seemed normal, except for a slight shimmer. Dave surmised this was the security shield which stretched as far as the eye could see. They continued above the roadway for several miles until they came upon a large city. Thousands of buildings surrounded them. Skyscrapers dominated the city center and masses of people walked on the sidewalks hurrying to work or to shop. They floated gradually downward and flew through the roof of a building, stopping in a coffee shop on the ground floor.

Couples sat at small tables drinking their morning coffee and holding hands. Business men sat together arguing about the details of their latest business proposal. Singles sat with their drinks and computers checking the latest news. They stopped at a table where two men wearing ornate robes were sitting.

"Councilor Makan," one said to the other, "we cannot ignore the new settlement to the north. Eventually they will find us. I say we make the first contact and develop some kind of planet sharing treaty."

"Councilor Darta," Makan replied, "surely you must be kidding. We were here first. We have fifty million people here while they have a few thousand. We must expel them. They can find another planet somewhere. Earth 47 is ours!"

"Makan, listen to me. We already have more than a thousand worlds. Can't we share this one? You must remember No-Makla. If we attack these maklans, we might be attacked ourselves. I don't think we can risk interplanetary war right now," Darta replied.

"I hadn't thought about No-Makla," Makan replied. "That's a great idea. Let's send these colonists there with their own kind! Brilliant idea, Darta!"

"That's not what I'm saying at all. I fear the maklans will come to defend their brothers here. This is a new colony, Makan. We could not defeat them and we could all be forced to abandon this planet. Think about the consequences, friend," Darta pleaded.

"Perhaps you are right, Darta. It will take at least ten thousand years to make this settlement fully independent," Makan replied as he sipped his coffee. "If we make an agreement with the maklans, we can be relatively assured they will be peaceful. Okay, friend, I will support your vote at the Council meeting." They stood, shook hands and left together.

Loni wrapped her light around Dave's. "Okay, here you are on Earth. You have just seen a large colony of humans living here millions of years before you were taught humanity evolved here. Now what do you think?"

"This is unbelievable to me, Loni. Thank you for showing me. But if this is true, why was there no evidence in the geologic record?" Dave asked.

"There is evidence, Dave. So far, no one believes it or has found enough of it. To tell the truth, bad luck had a lot to do with it too. Humanity chose to stay in this area through much of this time. A few settlements were built in other places, but this was always the hub of their world. The maklans made the same decision. Once their treaties were in place, trade became their primary business. Over generations, the maklans convinced the humans not to take over the entire planet and allow the indigenous life to evolve. When the end came, most of the evidence of these cultures was destroyed."

"The end? What happened to them?" Dave asked.

"I'm sure you were taught that a large meteor destroyed the dinosaurs. Well, it turns out this region was the epicenter of that collision. Many maklans and humans were wiped out in that cataclysm, along with their cities and infrastructure. During the long winters that followed, the remaining human settlements fell into disrepair and were gradually dismantled for parts and fuel. Their societies failed and people reverted to prehistoric levels. All of their knowledge of space and science was lost. It took many millions of years to rebuild into the human civilization where you were raised."

"I think I'm ready to leave this place, Loni," Dave sighed. "I am getting depressed thinking about how all this was destroyed and all the life that was lost."

"I don't think you understand, Dave. You have to accept when humans decided to fly into space and establish new homes that not every story would end well," Loni replied.

"Loni, I was told I would be remembered as Dave, Founder of a Thousand Worlds. When I think even one would end like this, I wonder if it will be worth it," Dave said.

"Dave, this is what life is about," Loni said. "But you should also know most of the humans and maklans were relocated before the actual meteor strike. A few stayed, believing they would rebuild in other parts of the planet. I suppose they were right, although it took sixty five million years to do so."

"Where did they go when they left?" Dave asked.

"I'm not certain about the maklans, perhaps they went back to Tak-Makla or to No-Makla. You should know this human colony was never very successful. Since this location was so ideal, many different races from the Society of Humanity chose to colonize together. We have found that does not work often. Over the billions of years of our existence, different types of humans have gravitated to specific classes of planets. For example, I am from the Zu species. The people on my home planet are almost entirely Zu, which is why the planet has the name Aranar Zu. When the people left here, they went to other planets of their same race. I know this is confusing, but I don't want you to think we allowed millions or billions of people to be killed by a random asteroid," she continued.

"It is very confusing, Loni. Perhaps we can discuss this back on Tak-Makla," Dave replied.

"Great, let's go have some drinks tonight to forget about what happened here. Remember if everything you just learned did not happen exactly like it did, you wouldn't be here now, or be the guy to establish a thousand more worlds for humanity. Tomorrow, I want to show you more about The Hive and

Universal Power. I think then you may start to understand what's happening in the universe," Loni said.

CHAPTER 6

The morning sun poured through the window, illuminating Darlene's face. She rolled over to escape the light and return to her dream. Her alarm clock sounded and she tapped the snooze button. Her com-link chirped. Resigned to waking up, she climbed out of bed and walked over to her uniform and pulled off the com-link and pressed the contact. "This is Darlene Brewster," she said.

"Ambassador Brewster, this is Consul Zee Gongaleg from Tak-Makla," he replied. "I hope I haven't disturbed you. We need to talk at your earliest convenience."

"Certainly, High Consul," she answered. "Can I contact you in 60 minutes? It is early morning here on Nom-Kat-Un, and I'm just getting started on my day."

"Ah, that is the information I was looking for, Darlene," Zee said. "Please stand by for one moment."

She stood in her pajamas holding the com-link in her hand. She had no idea what Zee wanted. Dave was on Tak-Makla and could handle any issues. She looked at her watch. She was to meet with Ambassador Kogala and Field Marshall Fongula Nokka in two hours to discuss the final arrangements for the planet sharing treaty with the Galliceans. In the early evening, the treaty signing was to take place on the broad beach in front of the resort. Darlene thought signing the agreement on Nom-Kat-Un would be a great gesture of friendship between the Palians and Galliceans.

"Zee, are you there?" she asked.

"Just one more moment, Darlene," Zee said. "Ah, I have your coordinates now, please have a nice day."

"What?" Darlene asked, but the connection was closed. Frustrated and confused, she tossed the com-link onto the bed and turned and walked into Dave. "Dave! How did you get here," she cried as she threw her arms around him.

"Universal power can do some amazing things, sweetheart," Dave replied as he kissed her. "We have a problem with Nom-Kat-Un, Darlene, and we need to fix it before we give this planet to Palus. Get ready and we'll grab some breakfast before your meeting."

As she showered and got dressed, Dave told her about his meeting with Loni Arrak in the lowest level of The Hive and how he had traveled back in time to witness when both maklans and humans colonized Earth hundreds of millions of years ago. She also learned how those settlements were wiped out by a meteor strike sixty-five million years ago. He told her humanity had originated in the Andromeda Galaxy billions of years ago and now inhabited thousands of planets throughout the universe. Dave also confessed that he found Loni to be amazingly beautiful.

Dave and Darlene walked into the large dining hall in the Banganu Resort. Most of the furniture was designed for the much larger Palians, but a few human-scale tables had been improvised for the ambassador's contingent. As they walked toward that area of the room, Charlie Watson stood and waved them over. Charlie shook Dave's hand and hugged Darlene. "Darlene, let me introduce you to Loni Arrak. I'm sure Dave has told you all about her."

Loni rose and shook hands with Darlene, then reached forward and kissed her on the cheek. "Ambassador, it is a pleasure to meet you. Dave has told me so much about you. Please join us," Loni smiled.

"It's great to meet you too, Loni. Please call me Darlene," she said as she sat down at the table. "I hope they have good coffee here. I'm still dead tired."

"It's great, actually," Charlie said as they sat down. "I heard the Palians imported green coffee from Day's End for a long time before the Predaxians took over their worlds. They even began to cultivate coffee plants here on Nom-Kat-Un. The plantations fell into disrepair but are now being cleaned up and repaired for future production."

"It is amazing how much work has been done on this planet since the end of the Second Predaxian War," Darlene began. "Right after the meeting to establish the planet-sharing treaty, hundreds of Palians came here to start the process. Banganu Resort used to be the premiere vacation spot for Palians in this system. Within a month or so, it should be fully renovated. Unfortunately, Dave just told me there is a problem with the treaty. What's the issue, honey?"

"As you all know, The Hive has been looking for planets with strong connections to Universal Power. We hope to build more Hives on those planets to cement our mutual relationships and defense against alien worlds like the Paxran," Dave explained.

"Who are the Paxran?" Charlie asked.

"They are a species of maklans who control more than a thousand planets on the other side of the galactic center," Loni replied. "Zee is convinced they will try to conquer planets on this side of the galaxy at some point. More Hives will provide improved access to Universal Power in this region, enabling us to stop their aggression."

"Just like on Localus," Kogala said as he approached the table. He smiled wryly and continued, "That Universal Power of yours is a powerful weapon. What makes you think the Paxran won't have their own?"

"Our agents in The Hive keep a close eye on them," Loni replied. "We have seen no evidence they have the capability or interest in developing this power. They have been highly successful using star ships and brute force to get their way."

"Let us hope your Hive can protect us if they are indeed that powerful," Kogala said. He turned to Darlene and said, "Ambassador, I will see you in an hour in Conference Room Five to finalize the treaty." He turned and walked to another table where six other Palians were eating.

A short Palian waiter approached the table. He was not happy to serve humans. "I am Nokala and I will be your server today. I have been trained about dealing with humans and want you to know that we do not serve eggs or other avian products. Please don't ask. What would you like?"

"Out of the way, little bird," said Fa-a-Di as he came to the table. He grabbed a large chair and sat next to the group. "I have already given our food order to the chef. You may go now, and please be polite to our guests. This planet is still part of Greater Gallia."

"Yes, High Commissioner," Nokala grimaced as he moved away.

Fa-a-Di was wearing his typical battle uniform with two blasters and three daggers in his belt. He wore a clear globe over his head to provide a breathable air supply. "My dear sister and brothers, it is wonderful to be with you today. Please introduce me to your friend."

"General, my name is Loni Arrak," she said as she shook his large hand. "I am one of the two chief engineers in The Hive on Tak-Makla."

"But you look human to me," Fa-a-Di said.

"Yes, General, I am human. Perhaps later I can tell you the story of how I came to be on Tak-Makla. I haven't told anyone else here that story yet," she replied.

"That would be wonderful," he replied. "Perhaps we can fly over the planet together after the ceremony. Do you like Gallicean whisky?"

"It is one of the best," Loni winked.

A team of waiters brought trays of pastries and meats to the table. They set the trays on stands nearby as the table was too small. Another arrived with coffee and cream and poured for everyone except Fa-a-Di, who waved him off. Fa-a-Di pulled a small bottle of whisky from his belt and set it on the table. A waiter brought four glasses and the general poured whisky into the glasses for the humans. He then put a tube into the bottle which could slip through a small port in his helmet. "Cheers to us all on the day of this great treaty," he shouted. He drank deeply. The humans sipped the whisky gingerly. Gallicean whisky had a reputation of being very strong, and this bottle did not disappoint.

"Brother, there is a problem with this agreement," Dave said. He gratefully drank coffee to get the heat of the whisky out of his mouth.

"A problem?" Fa-a-Di asked. "I haven't been advised of any issues. Darlene, what is Dave talking about?"

"Brother, I have only learned of this issue a couple hours ago," Dave continued. "The Hive transported Loni and me here as soon as we heard the news. We have found that Nom-Kat-Un has very strong connections to Universal Power, perhaps even more than Tak-Makla itself."

Loni jumped in, "We had seen some connections to this planet before, however it seems when Localus was dismantled, the lines of Universal Power touching that world shifted to this one. This planet is the best option of a new Hive for thousands of light-years in every direction."

"Darlene, you made the suggestion for a planet sharing agreement. Are you now telling me to cancel the treaty?" Fa-a-Di asked.

"I'm just learning this information too brother," she said.

Dave stood and walked up to Fa-a-Di. Even sitting down, the Gallicean was much taller. "Brother, I don't think that will be necessary. We need to explain this to all parties involved in this arrangement. A new Hive doesn't require much space, however living arrangements for the billions who work there will occupy a substantial footprint."

"So far, we have found that Galliceans and Palians cannot access a Hive," Loni said. "That doesn't mean they never can. We just haven't found a suitable linking device yet. That means we will need between several billion life forms on Nom-Kat-Un who can access the new Hive. We know that humans and maklans fit in that category."

"I can't imagine the Palians will go for this," Fa-a-Di replied. "This planet is a jewel in their crown. Before Predax, it was a major tourist attraction. I fear Field Marshall Nokka will be irate when we tell him he has to share the planet. There must be another way."

"I think we need to think rationally about this," Darlene interrupted. "When we surveyed this planet, we found the forests and sea shores were the locations where ninety-nine percent of Palians came to vacation. Those areas only occupy about twenty percent of the land surface of the planet. Most of the resorts that used to thrive here were in this immediate area. Doesn't that leave most of the planet available?"

"I don't know, Darlene," Fa-a-Di replied. "This has always been a Gallicean planet. Now we are offering it as a colony site for the Palians. They may have plans to import millions of their own citizens and cover the whole place. I suppose we could negotiate about that though." He grabbed a handful of sliced meats and tossed them in his mouth.

"Dave and I have a plan," Loni said. "Our agents have massive amounts of information on the Paxran and other threats to our security. There have been many movies made on Tak-Makla to show the civilizations in other parts of the galaxy. These are all based on information from our agents. We will be receiving a summary transmission of that data in the next twenty minutes. We would like to make a presentation to the Palians along with some videos of The Hive and its original construction and current operations. Once they see the threat from the Paxran and others, and find out the good a Hive can do for commerce and science, they have to accept this compromise."

"Okay, let's show them and find out what happens next," Fa-a-Di said. "I think I need another drink."

CHAPTER 7

Ambassador Kogala and Field Marshall Fongula Nokka were surprised by the crowd in the conference room. They had expected Darlene, but not Dave, Charlie, Loni, General Fa-a-Di and Governor Mak-Kal-a. After introductions, they all sat with Darlene and the Galliceans on one side of the table and the Palians on the other. The remaining humans sat quietly in a corner.

"Fa-a-Di, this is very unusual," Fongula began. "We were expecting to meet with Ambassador Brewster to understand the final terms of the agreement. We hadn't expected to see you until the signing ceremony at sunset."

"I understand the confusion, Fongula," Fa-a-Di replied. "Some new information has come to our attention just this morning that requires us to make modifications to the treaty. Have you been briefed on the tekkan Hive?"

Fongula laughed. "The destruction of Localus was all the briefing that I needed, friend. What does that have to do with this treaty?"

Loni stood at one end of the table. "Field Marshall, my name is Loni Arrak, and I am the Lead Chief Engineer for The Hive on Tak-Makla."

"But you are human, not tekkan," Kogala said.

"And you are a valakar, Ambassador. I am not sure my physiology is relevant to this discussion," she replied.

"What is a valakar?" Fongula asked. "We are Palians."

"I hadn't planned on this diversion, and I apologize if you feel insulted by the term valakar, sir," Loni apologized. "Perhaps later we can all meet to discuss those matters further. For now, please let us focus on this planet. Since the dismantling of Localus, many lines of Universal Power have shifted from that site to Nom-Kat-Un. This planet is now an ideal location for a new Hive. Our mutual need for galactic security requires that a portion of this planet be reserved for a Hive."

"I have no problem with that," Fongula replied. "We Palians can build and manage a Hive here."

"Unfortunately, Field Marshall, that won't work," she answered. "At this time, we do not have the technology to link a valakar, I mean Palian mind to a Hive. We are actively working on that, but it could take years or decades to find a solution."

"So, Fa-a-Di, do we get the planet or not?" Fongula demanded.

Darlene stood and said, "Fongula, in the updated agreement, you still get Nom-Kat-Un. Your team and ours will chart the entire planet. All of the ideal lands will be exclusively yours. Loni and the tekkans will construct a Hive in an area of the planet that is less desirable to your species. That Hive will be manned by a few billion Beings, who will be citizens of your planet, although they will likely be maklan or human. Besides the tax revenue from them, your people will have complimentary access to the resources of the Hive."

"Billions of aliens sharing this planet seems excessive," Fongula cringed. "There are only ten billion Palians in all of our planets combined! I'm not certain I can agree with such a thing. Those creatures could rise against us and take over."

"That is not possible, sir," Loni answered. "Let us show you some video of The Hive on Tak-Makla and its history. The tekkans are very peace loving. The very nature of a Hive changes those who have been there."

"Do I have to remind you about Localus, Loni?" Kogala laughed. "That wasn't a very peace loving gesture on your part. The Hive on this planet could erase Palus from space. What would stop that?"

"I would," Loni said.

The Palians laughed loudly. Fongula replied, "You would stop it. You are one weak human female. You personally would stop the actions of billions of others madly intent on destroying my home world. You must be insane."

"I have to admit that sounds pretty unlikely," Fa-a-Di said. "Please explain yourself before this entire meeting falls apart."

"The Hive on Tak-Makla did not dismantle Localus," she began. "A single Hive would need fifty billion souls to do such a thing. Eight Hives were involved in that job, including Tak-Makla and the seven human Hives. Each Hive has two chief engineers. All chief engineers must agree, coordinate and fuse with their Hives to complete such a task."

"There are more Hives?" Darlene asked. "Human Hives? I don't understand."

"Let's watch some of the video feed," Loni said. "I fear I've said too much already and am raising the anxiety level. I apologize for that." She sat in the corner as the video wall came to life at one end of the room.

A mechanical voice spoke, "Feed A14C9002, Council meeting, Don-Makla, 50 BE."

"High Consul Gongaleg, I must protest the continued construction of the planet Tak-Makla. This is a violation of God's Will," Zon Palaka said.

"Eminence, I must say your continued complaints are not helping our society deal with the upcoming exodus," Nala Gongaleg replied. "You must have forgotten it was your personal calculations that led us to that planet and the design for The Hive."

"Nala, I have not forgotten," Zon sighed. "It was the folly of my youth. You know how children can be. Age has taught me some things should be outside our power. Universal Consciousness is God's realm, not ours. We must remain here on the home our blessed ancestors on Ai-Makla chose for us."

"Eminence, Consul, please let me intercede," a short, stocky human said. "The Society of Humanity has built many Hives throughout the universe. If God thought they were evil, why do they still exist?"

"Pal Lazar, you are a silly little person," Zon laughed. "You may be evil incarnate for all we know. Where did you get the materials you are providing for the construction? How many billions of slaves have you forced to work on your heinous projects?"

Pal laughed out loud. "Eminence, you should hear yourself speak. I have repeatedly offered to let you enter one of our

Hives and join with Universal Power. Once there you would know it is only a tool for trade and commerce."

"Enough of both of you," Nala demanded. "The construction will be complete in fifty solar cycles. Immediately thereafter, all maklans will move to the new planet and Don-Makla will be abandoned."

"Please Consul, let those of us who wish to avoid God's retribution stay here," Zon pleaded.

"No, Eminence. All of our citizens are required to bring The Hive online and to support our continued growth. If many stay here, it will take generations to make The Hive operational. That is not acceptable," Nala shouted.

"Bide my words, Consul," Zon threatened, "we will not follow you. Some of us do fear God and cannot allow this atrocity to stand. When you and your followers are facing damnation, perhaps we will let you join us."

The mechanical voice spoke again, "Feed C22R0112, Hive inauguration, Tak-Makla, 1 BE."

The screen filled with the center opening in The Hive rising further than the eye could see. All of the windows lining The Hive were illuminated, with thousands of rings of light reaching up toward the planet's surface. The view panned down to reveal a maklan and a human standing on the floor of The Hive. The maklan spoke, "Dear citizens, my name is Val Singalak and I have been chosen as the first Chief Engineer for The Hive on Tak-Makla. We are all very excited about the exodus to begin in one solar cycle. With me today is our Lead Chief Engineer, Vana Listo from the planet Valka Zu. As you can tell, he is from the Society of Humanity." The human looked remarkably like Loni with the same pale skin and silver eyes. "Vana has hundreds of years of experience managing Hives and has volunteered to help us initiate this one. Please say a few words, Vana."

"Thank you, Val," Vana began. "The upcoming exodus from Don-Makla will be a great day for the friendship between our peoples. Our Society has agreed to provide Chief Engineers for Tak-Makla for as long as needed. Those engineers will insure that all Hives can coordinate their activities. The coordination among human Hives has already allowed us to dismantle five dead planets for building materials for Tak-Makla."

"Stop the video," Fongula barked. The screen froze with the smiling face of Vana Listo. "There is that word dismantle again. Loni, you said you dismantled Localus. Does that mean you have all of the material somewhere? I thought that planet disappeared."

"Field Marshall, the fundamental law of conservation of matter means all the matter from Localus still exists," Loni said. "The Society of Humanity includes more than fifty thousand worlds. With our extended lifetimes, we need to have ten or twenty more planets under development continually to keep our people housed and fed. Our goal is to have one Hive for every fifty worlds, so we need to build a Hive every few years. That requires a lot of material."

"Don't you just take the material from the planet where you build the Hive?" Dave asked.

Loni smiled, "Dave, we stopped building Hives like the one of Tak-Makla many years ago. They are too risky."

"What could be more permanent that a planet, Loni?" Fa-a-Di asked. "Gallia has existed for billions of years."

"General, the Society of Humanity has existed for over three billion years," she began. "We have enemies who can attack a planet. Also, suns die. We cannot invest in a Hive that is a target for our enemies or tied to a single planet. The costs and risks are too high."

"You build Hive planets from scratch?" Darlene asked.

"Very perceptive, Darlene. We construct a spherical dome and then fill in the center with our Hive and an artificial planet. Everything is self-contained. It also looks like just a dead chunk of rock floating in uninhabitable space. No other creature would ever expect there to be billions of humans living inside," Loni replied.

"Let me get this straight," Mak-Kal-a interjected. "A big chunk of rock, like Nom-Kat-Zuk in this system could be hollow with a human Hive inside?"

"As a matter of fact, that is exactly what Nom-Kat-Zuk is, Governor," Loni replied. "To be precise, it is under construction at this time. We expect it to be complete in fifty solar cycles."

"That is not possible, Loni," Mak-Kal-a shouted. "Zuk has been in this system for billions of years. We have studied it and sent probes. It is a solid chunk of iron and rock."

Loni frowned, "This is another diversion from the meeting, but what I said is true. Two hundred solar cycles ago, we determined that Nom-Kat-Zuk would be a great candidate for a Hive planet. We removed the interior of the planet and are now building a new one inside. We won't need a new Hive in this region for a while, so we are taking the construction slowly. Once it is operational, it will work together with the Hive here to bring the benefits of Universal Power to this sector of space."

"Your Society of Humanity has commandeered one of my planets?" Fa-a-Di raged. "This is highly unusual. My council will need to discuss this matter."

"General, I apologize for this as well. You must understand that I am only an engineer helping Tak-Makla. The decision to build that Hive was not in my control. Please let us review the final video now. We can all talk about this later," Loni said.

The mechanical voice said, "Feed ZZ02D1001, Galactic security briefing, 400B AE."

Zee Gongaleg, High Consul for Tak-Makla sat behind his desk and smiled at the camera. "Dear friends, Loni Arrak asked me to brief you on the threats facing our galaxy. I pray you will consider this and accept the plan for Nom-Kat-Un. Only more Hives in this region can protect us from those who wish to enslave us. The main threat in my mind is the Paxran Empire. This is a maklan race that inhabits sixteen hundred worlds on the other side of our galaxy. Our agents in The Hive have determined these maklans destroyed a peaceful maklan race called the Maklakar. We had traded and been friends with the Maklakar for many years. At their zenith, they occupied more than two thousand worlds. After some time, our trading relationship slipped away and we lost touch. When we attempted to work with them again, we found their entire civilization had been destroyed and no Maklakars survived. A peaceful civilization of billions of lives had been wiped from history. The Paxran continue to conquer new worlds. They never negotiate and their highly advanced military would overwhelm any of us. Our only hope is to stop them with Hives."

"The only civilization that has resisted the Paxran is the Donnaki Empire, which is a valakar species like the Galliceans and Palians. Their military might is equivalent to the Paxran. While the two races despise each other, neither has the power to wage a winning war against the other. They coexist is a state of constant incursions into each other's space. Planets on their mutual frontier change hands often. Many of those worlds are dead husks where massive populations used to thrive. They must grow in other directions. One of those directions for the Paxran is across the galactic center. The Donnaki might do the same. You can be certain that both of those civilizations have ships and agents exploring our systems for weaknesses. While the Society of Humanity does have a few Hives in our galaxy, that is not enough to stop these threats. Before they could establish more, we might all be killed or enslaved by either enemy. Please think strategically here. The sharing agreement for Nom-Kat-Un is a small price to pay to protect our children in the future."

The video ended and the lights came back to full. Loni Arrak stood and smiled at the group around the table. "Dear friends, let us work together to insure our mutual security in this galaxy. If the Paxran or Donnaki are successful, we humans can simply move to other galaxies. We might lose many lives before we could escape, but the Society of Humanity would survive. Gallia, Palus, Tak-Makla, Kalidus and Earth 47 will not be so lucky. We need each other. General Fa-a-Di and I are scheduled to fly over this beautiful planet now. The signing ceremony will be at sunset on the beach. I hope you will do the right thing and be there. Just as on Tak-Makla, I will guarantee that the Society of Humanity will work with you to build

Hives, learn more secrets of Universal Power and fight any race that attempts to break the peace. General, I will meet you outside in thirty minutes." She turned and left the room.

"Governor Lonk, there are fifty Donnaki cruisers in orbit," Commander Jee Nalta said as he walked into the governor's office.

"Do you think they know what this is, Jee?" Alin Lonk asked.

"They must know something or why would they have so many ships?" Jee replied. "Please bring up the command display, sir."

Alin tapped a button and the command bridge appeared on the wall-sized screen. "General Zilma, what's going on out there?"

"Governor, the Donnaki ships are firing at the surface. So far, they are making small holes in the rock surface. They need to blast through fifty miles of rock to reach the inner shell," General Audy Zilma replied. "That would take days at this rate. I don't think there is much risk yet."

"Perhaps we should signal President Bango on Aranar Zu," Jee suggested.

"The signal could be traced, Governor," Audy replied. "Let The Hive communicate for us."

"Excellent idea, General," Alin said as he pressed another key on his console. The general was replaced by Chief Engineer Lina Aderal. "Lina, our post is under attack by Donnaki cruisers. Have your agents contact Aranar Zu to let them know, and also check out the bridges of those ships. We don't know if this is target practice or if they have discovered that our Hive."

"Yes Governor," she replied. "Give us ten minutes." The screen went dark.

Alin Lonk sat back in his chair. "Jee, there's nothing to do now but wait."

"Alin, I always knew it was a mistake to bring this Hive into Donnaki space," Jee said. "They can feel our presence even if there is no evidence we exist. All Beings can sense Universal Power, but just may not believe it if they can't see it."

"We had our orders, Jee. It's a little late to second guess them now," Alin replied. He tapped a flashing button on his console.

"Governor, we are being hailed by the Donnaki," said the voice of his assistant, Lora Naut. "I'm putting it through."

The thick bird-like head of a valakar filled the screen. "I am Admiral Ski Zan of the Donnaki Empire. We know you are in there, humans. How dare you enter our space without our permission? You will pay for your insolence with your lives. Then we will take over your Hive machine and use it to destroy more of your worlds. By the way, we have a new weapon to try out on your false planet. I hope you enjoy it."

A massive blast from the cruisers shook the entire planet. Lights flickered and The Hive went dark. After a moment, the power returned.

General Zilma appeared on the screen. "Governor, that last blast blew away the rock layer in sector Z975B. I've never felt anything like that. The inner shell is now exposed. I don't know how many more blasts like that we can handle before we have a hull breach."

Alin pushed a button and shouted, "Lina, get more Hives online. We need to evacuate or get this Hive out of here!"

"Yes, Governor, I have seven Hives online now," Lina replied. "Aranar Zu suggests we relocate far outside Donnaki space."

"Do it now!" he shouted as a second blast rocked the planet.

"Governor, the inner hull buckled a bit with that hit," Audy said. "Two more hits and we will likely lose containment."

"Governor, we do not have enough power to jump the planet," Lina shouted. "Should we jump the crews of those ships to their home world?"

"Yes, for God's sake!" he screamed as another blast hit the planet, throwing him to the ground. Jee helped him up and wiped the blood from the governor's forehead. "One more blast like that and we're dead, Jee." Jee helped Alin over to a couch. They sat on the edge of the couch for several minutes waiting.

"What do you think they're waiting for, Governor?" Jee asked.

"Dramatic effect, I imagine," Alin said.

"Governor, the mission is complete," Lina said. "All the Donnaki crews have been jumped to their home world."

"Thank you, Lina," Alin said as he sat back on the couch, holding a cloth against his bloody head. "Jee, get a damage report."

Jee sat at the governor's desk and pressed a button. "General, the governor has been slightly wounded. He needs a damage report."

"We have several hundred cracks in the inner shell, and many are now leaking atmosphere. Approximately five hundred cubic miles of rock have been blow off. One half of the tube network is offline due to the brief power failure. Fifty crew members were burned severely by the last blast and are on their way to hospitals. Several thousand others were hurt by falling objects and other incidents related to the shaking. I recommend that the Governor join them at a clinic as soon as possible."

Alin walked over to the screen to see the general's face. "Audy, what do you recommend we do now?"

"With your approval, I will jump some of my men to the Donnaki ships. We need to understand this new weapon of theirs. When that is complete, I recommend we dismantle the ships and use their material as a temporary fix to our inner core. Once our inner shell is patched, we need to get out of Donnaki space as quickly as we can. I can have our engines online in two hours. With our thrusters, we should leave their space in fourteen days. It would be preferable if the other Hives could jump us out sooner," Audy said.

"Audy, I am declaring a military emergency and putting you in command of Hive 1008. Please do as you see fit. I'm going to take your advice and have Jee help me to the nearest clinic," Alin said as he clicked off the screen.

CHAPTER 9

Loni Arrak sat quietly on the beach in front of the Banganu Resort with her face buried in her hands. A trickle of tears rolled down her alabaster cheeks. Fa-a-Di, Mak-Kal-a and Dave walked down to where she was seated. Dave dropped to his knees and touched her shoulders. "Loni, what's wrong?" he asked. The two Galliceans sat next to her.

"I failed, Dave," she cried. "There was an attack on one of our Hives in Donnaki territory. Without me on Tak-Makla to fuse with the other Hives, there wasn't enough power to protect them."

"What happened?" Fa-a-Di asked. "Were they killed?"

"No, but they could have been. Thousands were injured, many severely. The Hive has been damaged and they are trying to escape before more Donnaki war ships can reach them," she said. "If I had been there, this would have been avoided. I've got to get back."

"Why was there a Hive in Donnaki space?" Fa-a-Di asked. "That seems like an unnecessary provocation, in a way reminiscent of Nom-Kat-Zuk."

"I don't know, General. I frankly don't understand it either," she replied. "The Hives are due to fuse in two hours to jump the planet out of their territory."

"Excellent news, Loni," Fa-a-Di smiled. "That means you still have time for our flight!"

"I don't think I would be good company, General," she said.

"Nonsense, Loni. A change of scenery will do you a world of good," he said as he lifted her off the ground and set her into the harness on his chest. He checked the latches and restraints to make certain she was locked in tightly. "I've asked Mak-Lak-a to fly Dave with us. Usually, I only allow Dave to fly with me, but today you are the lucky one."

Mak-Lak-a lifted Dave into his harness and locked him in. "Dave, I hope you enjoy this trip as much as I have enjoyed the Dar-Fa on Jupiter. This world is probably more to your liking anyway. We Galliceans are not used to trees, calm winds and oxygen atmospheres. I made sure we have a plentiful air supply since we will likely use more carrying you two."

Fongula and Kogala joined them on the beach. "Friends, we were hoping to join you today," Fongula said. "I have seen many videos from the days when this planet was a great vacation spot for our people. I hope to come here myself from time to time."

"Wonderful idea, Fongula," Fa-a-Di said. "This will soon be your planet, so please lead the way."

The Palians took wing and soared along the beach at fifty feet off the surface. The Galliceans followed just behind. Dave could feel the salt spray of the ocean on his face and looked down to see flying fish a few feet above the surface. Kogala dived toward the water and caught one of the fish in his beak. He chewed it up and swallowed it. "Those fish are wonderful, Field Marshall," he shouted.

The group turned back to shore and rose to three hundred feet, just above the tree tops. They could see many small birds flying through the forest as well as other animals in the tree tops. A range of mountains rose far in the distance and the Palians turned in that direction.

"Loni, I hope this view is improving your mood," Fa-a-Di said. "One day you must come to Gallia and fly with me there. That will be an experience you won't forget."

"It would be an honor, Fa-a-Di," she replied. "I have spent most of my life at the bottom of Hives, away from the world. Breathing fresh air and feeling the warmth of the sun is a rare pleasure for me. Unfortunately, the life of a Chief Engineer is lonely. I work with the other Chief Engineer and a few hundred technicians who manage each Hive. I am also the only human on Tak-Makla. While I enjoy the tekkans, it's not the same. That's why I've been so happy to know Dave Brewster."

"Dave and Darlene Brewster are my best friends, Loni," he replied. "You couldn't ask for better friends than them. They have done so much for me and my people. If either one of them needed help, there would not be enough Gallicean colony ships to carry those who would rush to their aid."

"You're making me blush, brother," Dave said over the com-link.

"Must you listen to my every word, brother?" Fa-a-Di asked.

"You set up the com-link, not me," Dave laughed. "But seriously, Fa-a-Di is a great friend. He and his brother-in-law have helped me more times that I can count. Not to mention that he personally ended the Second Predaxian War."

"Not without Loni's help and the billions in the Hives that came to our rescue," Fa-a-Di said. "Where are you taking us, Fongula? We have a limited air supply!"

"We're almost there, General," Fongula said. "My father told me of this spot where he and his father had come for vacation. I heard the story so many times that the location is burned into my mind. Ah, we're here." The Palians spiraled downward and landed at the edge of a cliff. The Galliceans landed next to them.

The cliff loomed two thousand feet over a narrow valley below. The chasm was five hundred yards wide with an equally high cliff on the opposite side. Hundreds of waterfalls plunged off both sides of the cliff walls down to a raging river far below. On both sides, the cliffs backed into forests with trees three hundred feet tall. In the distance, tall mountains could be seen reaching up into the sky. Clouds and snow packs covered the mountain tops. Thousands of brightly colored birds flew between the waterfalls searching for insects or other food. Bright red and orange monkeys howled from among the trees at the top of the cliff.

"My father called this place Zanzanak," Fongula said. "That is an old Palian word meaning paradise, I believe. He said every Palian should see this site once before they die. There are fifty thousand bird species in this forest alone, and they are all our brothers."

"What about the valakars that Loni claims we are both related to?" Fa-a-Di said. "I agree there are some similarities between Galliceans and Palians, but the differences are stark too. My history tells me that we developed from small flying creatures living in the clouds of gas. Neither of our peoples could survive in the other's worlds."

"The valakars are an ancient race," Loni said. "They may be much older than humanity, as a matter of fact. Don't think it is an insult. They are our great allies in this and other galaxies. The valakars and maklans are the only sentient species known to have originated in this galaxy. Even today, the Donnaki have the largest civilization in this galaxy, and they are valakars too. They look more like Palians than Galliceans though with feathers and living in oxygen atmospheres. We haven't spent much time studying history for their origins, but I know there are quite a few valakar Hives working on that."

"If valakars have Hives, then we must be able to join with them too," Fa-a-Di said. "Can we contact them?"

"Yes, but there are no valakar Hives in this galaxy," Loni continued. "From what I have been told, when the Donnaki culture started to gain dominance, the peaceful species scattered around this galaxy and others. We formed alliances to protect each other from predatory species like the Donnaki. It is possible that valakars originated here or on Palus. Only extensive research will determine that. I want you all to know we are adding resources to our research to allow your species to be part of the two Hives in this system. The valakar have been waiting for millions of years for their lost societies to find them again. When we told them about you both, they were very excited. Imagine how the maklans of No-Makla felt when they arrived at Tak-Makla, or how I felt when Dave Brewster walked into my office. Work with us, and the same will happen for you. I guarantee it."

"We shall sign the agreement at sunset," Fongula said. "You have my word on that."

"Well, friends, our air supplies are running low, so we must head back now. You two may stay if you like. Thank you so much for this wonderful experience, my brothers," Fa-a-Di said. After embracing, the two Galliceans took off with their human passengers.

CHAPTER 10

Aranar Zu was a cold planet orbiting at the outer edge of the habitable zone of the Aranar system, ten thousand light-years from Earth. A thin band of warmer climates was located close to the equator. The winters were long in both hemispheres with massive snowfall and temperatures below freezing. The Zu thrived in cold weather and mountain living. They lived in buildings with thick stone walls for insulation. They were avid hunters and gardeners who maintained greenhouses in the coldest areas to supplement their diets. Throughout the Society of Humanity, there were more than eight hundred Zu planets.

Aranar Zu was the first Society of Humanity colony in this galaxy for millions of years, and it marked the beginning of the Society's plan to build a few thousand colonies and to find their lost worlds. The story of Admiral Dave Brewster casually walking into Chief Engineer Loni Arrak's office circulated quickly across the planet. The Zu were the first to connect with the ancient Earth 47 colony survivors. Loni's parents were bombarded with requests for interviews about their suddenly famous daughter.

When it was learned that Loni's Hive paid a critical role is moving Hive 1008 out of Donnaki territory and into orbit around the Aranar sun, the requests for interviews began again. The quiet planet had only been known for ski resorts and beer and cheese production until Loni became their hero. President Jo Bango of the High Council received countless congratulatory messages from other planetary leaders and the Society High Council itself. She sent warm wishes to Loni along with two other Chief Engineers to allow her to return home and enjoy the spotlight she so richly deserved. When Jo learned

Loni would bring the Brewster family with her, a national holiday was scheduled along with events in ten of the largest cities. Aranar Zu had made the big time. Two members of the Society High Council promised to join the celebration in capital city, Sakar.

The visitors were first jumped from Tak-Makla to Hive 1008, which was undergoing final repairs. The only reporters allowed were those who lived on Hive 1008. The Aranar Zu press would have to wait for them to arrive on the planet. Governor Lonk summoned his senior staff to a small auditorium at 1400 local time. They sat quietly discussing the status of the repairs. At precisely 1410, Loni Arrak appeared on the small stage with Dave, Darlene, Bill and Cybil Brewster. The assembled officers stood and applauded their guests. Alin Lonk rushed up onto the stage and hugged Loni.

"Here's our hero!" Alin shouted. "Everyone come up here and meet the admiral and ambassador and their children!" Applause sounded again as the remaining officers came up on stage to meet the group. After the introductions, the governor led the group out of the building and into the artificial sunlight. A large square with streets and tall buildings ringing it surrounded them. Thousands of citizens of Hive 1008 stood in the square or looked out of windows lining it. They applauded wildly. Cameras flashed around them as they made their way up onto a dais to greet the crowd.

The group on the dais stood waving until the crowd noise began to drop. Dave noticed almost the entire crowd had the same complexion as Loni. He realized they must all be Zu. Loni had told him there were fifty official species of humans in the Society. Dave and his family with their twenty-first century stature and color were closer to Pa.

"Dear citizens of Hive 1008, it gives me great pleasure to introduce you to Loni Arrak, Lead Chief Engineer for the Tak-Makla Hive," Alin began to loud cheers. "This beautiful young scientist is the most famous Zu in the Society. First, she found Admiral Dave Brewster, the first connection we have found to our lost colony on Earth 47." Applause rang out again. "Then, with her leadership, our Hive was jumped out of threatening Donnaki space to the safety of the Aranar system! We owe her our lives. Loni, please say a few words." The crowd cheered again as Loni slowly stepped forward to the microphone. Her face blushed bright red and she smiled.

"Thank you Governor Lonk and the citizens of Hive 1008," she said meekly. "I really appreciate your kind words, but I was just doing my job." The crowd cheered again.

Dave noticed that Loni was trembling, so he took Darlene's hand and they stepped forward to support her. "Don't listen to her, she's just shy," Dave said. The crowd erupted with more cheers. "She is a hero to all of us. When I met this young lady on Tak-Makla, everything I thought about humanity changed forever. All humans from my home world have always believed we evolved there and were alone in the universe. My family and I have been very lucky to meet amazing Beings from other cultures, like maklans and valakars. We even found some remarkably human looking species that now turn out to be part of this Society. I had no idea there were thousands of human worlds. I cannot tell you what an honor it is for us to be here with you all today. My wife, Ambassador Darlene Brewster is here to negotiate treaties with your leaders so we can be an integral part of the Society of Humanity again. Thank you, Loni for finding us." He kissed her on the cheek. Loni was crying now and Darlene held her tightly. "And thanks to all of you and all of the Society for allowing us back into the fold."

The group spent the rest of the afternoon taking tubes to various stops to meet the citizens of Hive 1008. They went to inspect the repair operations, where General Zilma showed the repaired inner shell and explained how vast amounts of iron and stone had been pulled from storehouses in space to repair the surface. They took a tour of the Hive and met senior leaders there. They visited hospitals to see the wounded recovering from the incident with the Donnaki. The day concluded with a large dinner party with ten thousand guests.

After dinner, Darlene left the dining hall and stood on a broad balcony overlooking a large park deep inside the false planet. A ring of trees formed the outer edge of the park which was two miles wide and three long. A number of ponds sparkled in the artificial star light, while fountains shot pillars of water into the air. The breeze was slightly cool and felt wonderful after the big meal in the large ballroom. Dave joined her with two glasses of white wine from Aranar Zu. They touched their glasses in a toast and sipped the wine, which was fresh and dry, similar to a sauvignon blanc on Earth. They leaned on the railing enjoying the quiet of the evening. Deep in the park, they could see a small crowd gathered around a large gazebo, where a string quartet played love songs.

"I still can't believe this is a manufactured planet," Dave said. "Tak-Makla took my breath away, and now we learn there are many planets like this."

"I feel the same way, sweetheart," she replied. "Back in our time, people only lived in a tiny ring from just below the surface to a thousand feet or so above. Here, if they need more space for people, they just built a new planet!"

"At least it takes the pressure off of me, Darlene," Dave laughed.

"What do you mean?" she replied.

"I only have to find a thousand planets. These people have fifty times that number already. Now that's impressive!" he said. "Maybe I'll just ask the Society to build a thousand new ones for me, and I'll be done!"

"Very funny, Dave," she said. She pointed to the park and asked, "Dave, isn't that Loni and Bill over there?" The two were holding hands and walking in the park toward the gazebo in the distance.

"I think you're right, babe," he replied. "I noticed those two making a lot of eye contact and flirting today."

"Me too. That's a big relief for me," Darlene said.

"What do you mean by that?" Dave asked.

"I thought Loni was getting a bit too close to you. All that zipping around in The Hive and appearing on Nom-Kat-Un together," she replied.

Dave laughed. "It sounds like someone is a little jealous, Darlene. You have to look at it from her point of view. This young and pretty girl leaves her home world and is stuck as the only human on a planet of twenty billion tekkans. She had to be real lonely."

"I saw the way she looked at you, Dave," Darlene replied. "Even Fa-a-Di noticed the electricity between you two."

"Well, I am flattered that she would like me, but honestly, you know me better than that, Darlene," he said.

"I am happy that she is focusing on a single man now," she said. "Did I just see Bill kiss her?"

"Yes, I saw that too. From where I'm standing, it looks like she kissed him back too," Dave smiled. "That's the old Brewster charm at full speed."

"If you insist, Prince Charming," Darlene laughed. "Did I tell you about Cybil and Rob Watson?"

"No, but then I'm used to being the last person to learn anything," Dave replied.

"Sorry, honey. Bill tells me that they are a real item now. They spend all of their free time together. It's looking like wedding bells may be in their future. What do you think about that?" she asked.

"I think that's wonderful news," Dave said. Dave thought about his future granddaughter, Bea. He remembered meeting her back in the twenty-first when she was a barista at his local Starbucks. The day she came to his room and confessed about her role was a perfect day for Dave. After spending an hour or two with her, he loved her dearly. He smiled broadly and a tear slipped out of one eye.

"What's up with you, Dave?" she asked as she wiped off the tear. "Are you okay?"

Dave pulled Darlene into his arms and kissed her. "Everything is perfect, sweetheart. I just can't imagine how anything could get better."

Chapter 11

Emperor Lok Zul of the Donnaki Empire sat at the center of the high semi-circular bench along with the eleven justices from the Imperial Supreme Court. His bright yellow feathers were immaculately combed in place, and his silver robes flowed off his shoulders. The justices were not happy to have their court commandeered by the Emperor, as their authority was in theory equal to his. They were old men though as attested by their gray, thinning feathers. They knew the Emperor was a popular leader, having grown the prestige of the empire greatly during his tenure. All the justices had been appointed by Lok's father, Zia Zul. While Zia had been a competent ruler, he had continued in his family's tradition of gradually reducing the emperor's power. No new worlds had been settled during the reigns of the last five emperors. Those leaders were convinced the empire had grown too large for a single valakar to manage. They knew authority had to be shared with the regional viceroys or face eventual revolution and the collapse of the empire.

Lok Zul had a different idea. He grew up in military schools and graduated from the Supreme Academy on the home world of Donnaki. He was heavily influenced by the military commanders, who reminded him of the former greatness of the empire. There was a time when vast armadas of Donnaki cruisers dominated this side of the galaxy. Masses of ships would streak into the skies of a new world and destroy the miserable Beings who thought they controlled their destiny. During his father's reign, the hideous Paxrans had begun to attack their frontier. Dozens of worlds were invaded and countless lives lost. The military proved their resolve by pushing the enemy far back into their territory after an offensive that lasted ten years. They then repaid the Paxrans by destroying many of their worlds. The back-and-forth war continued for hundreds of solar cycles. Late in life, Emperor Zia was able to establish a partial cease fire with the Paxran. Isolated incidents continued to happen, but both sides had so heavily fortified the frontier that neither could get a real advantage.

Upon his father's passing, Lok Zul became emperor. He immediately changed the dynamics of the society by increasing support for the military and lessening the powers of planetary leaders. The Viceroys were replaced by regional Field Marshalls, and the Imperial Assembly, which represented the individual planets, was disbanded. When the military leadership told him about their new plasma weapon, Lok knew the time was coming to unleash it on the Paxran. He had no desire to take their planets. He wanted to exterminate them and all other maklan societies. Such nasty insects had no place in a civilized galaxy.

The plasma device required a group of ships to work together. All would fire at a single point in space, where their blasts would form into a ball of plasma which the lead ship would then direct at a target. Testing proved that a single plasma bomb would vaporize any known space ship. Multiple blasts could destroy an entire planet. Unfortunately, the one existing plasma bomb fleet was lost, which was why the emperor was sitting with the court.

The great admiral of the Donnaki fleet, Ski Zan sat at a small table in front of the bench with five attorneys. He looked frail and tired after a week of interrogation following the incident. All fifty captains of the plasma fleet were sitting in the gallery behind him, looking equally worn down. Dozens of reporters and several hundred guests filled the room to overflowing. A contingent of fifty Marines guarded the exits.

"Admiral Zan, I have reviewed all the reports from the High Command on this incident, and frankly, I still do not understand why you chose to attack that planet," the emperor said. "I understand the humans violated our space, but you know your actions led to the loss of an entire fleet and our prototype plasma device."

"Majesty, it was a foolish act, but I did get receive the attack orders from the High Command once they realized it was not a real planet," Ski squeaked. "When we first engaged the planet, we intended to use it for target practice only. Our sensors recorded anomalies after we fired our standard weapons. Those sensors showed the planet was hollow. It was the High Command that confirmed it was a human colony in a false planet."

"Yes, I read that as well," Chief Justice Bon Ika replied. "Majesty, should we have abandoned the fight and let humans continue to violate our space?"

"No, I suppose not," Lok said. "Still we are now without a plasma device and have fifty fewer ships. If the Paxran attacked us today, we could be in very serious trouble. Perhaps you are correct this was just a mistake, but the effects have been very severe. What do you think I should do, Justice?"

"Majesty, a new plasma device is under construction and should be ready within a few weeks," Ski said. "We have enough ships and are already constructing more. In less than one solar cycle this will all be behind us."

"Your Majesty, I concur with the admiral's assessment," Bon replied. "It was a blessing none of our troops were injured. If the enemy had been Paxran instead of human, I shudder to think of the loss of life."

"Do we know how the humans were able to accomplish all of that?" Lok asked. "It is amazing to me that the crews from fifty cruisers could be instantly transported more than one thousand light-years to this planet. The crews we sent to recover the fleet reported no remnants of the ships. They arrived at the scene of the battle within ten hours of the event. This all seems impossible."

"Majesty, we believe this false planet was something called a Hive," Ski replied. "It is rumored a Hive holds billions of humans who can interact with the fundamental essence of the universe, enabling them to do incredible things. Our scientists have no idea how it works, but have been recommending we pursue this technology quickly. If the humans can jump our people long distances, they might show up in orbit here and transport all of our citizens into the sun!"

"Yes, I have heard these requests before," Lok sighed. "Unfortunately, we must balance our competing needs against each other to prioritize. The humans have left our space and have never been hostile to us before this incident. Our first priority must be to rebuild our fleet and get at least ten plasma fleets ready for battle. Our primary enemy remains the Paxran. We must use this weapon on them to push them back from our borders. Once they see our power, they will run like the cowards they are. Perhaps then we can work on this Hive technology. There is still the matter of the lost fleet to deal with." The emperor stood and everyone else came to their feet.

"Shall we retire to consider our verdict?" the Chief Justice asked.

"No need for that, Bon," Lok replied. "I have made my decision." He drew a blaster from his belt and shot Admiral Ski Zan in the forehead, who fell to the ground dead. "Admiral, you are discharged. The officers of the High Command are fired. I will personally appoint a new High Command. The fifty captains here are reduced in rank to lieutenants unless they wish to join Admiral Zan. This court is adjourned." Emperor Lok Zul walked out of the room.

"Clear the courtroom! And get this body out of here!" the Chief Justice shouted after the emperor left. The crowd had erupted in panic at the shot and headed for the exits. The Marines tried to restore calm, but no one was interested in them. They just wanted to escape before more blood was shed. Several of the disgraced captains came forward and carried their leader's body out of the chamber.

When the room was empty, Bon Ika turned to face the other justices. "This is preposterous, gentlemen. This flagrant disregard for the sanctity of this court is totally unacceptable. We must protest and file an action against Emperor Zul. Otherwise, we might as well turn in our robes and run to our homes like frightened children."

"Be careful with your words, Bon," cautioned Justice Nook. "I agree with everything you said, but Emperor Zul has been following this path for years. The Assembly is gone and the Viceroys have been replaced by soldiers. If we push too far, we may join Admiral Zan in death. The court will likely be abolished in time. I don't know if we can affect that eventuality."

"Okay, Nook, what do you think we should do?" Bon asked. "Should we sit in our offices in our robes until the firing squad comes for us?"

"Not at all, Bon," he replied. "We must file a complaint with His Majesty. However, the document must be carefully worded to avoid a confrontation. I believe he will understand our concerns and vow not to repeat such actions in this building again. He is a rational man. That will give us time to allow Fate to intervene. Perhaps these human Hives can one day help us become a freer society that can live in peace with them."

"I think you are dreaming Nook," Bon said. "Why would the humans want to help us? We tried to destroy their Hive. We have never been a peaceful society. And even if they did decide to help, it will take a long time, and the Emperor will have killed us and abolished this court long before that can happen."

"There is much truth in what you say, Bon," Nook replied. "It seems we have two choices in my mind. We can confront the Emperor now and be dismissed or killed today. Or we can soften our complaint and live longer. We are all old men. The Emperor would much prefer us to retire and allow him to appoint a new court. Even if the humans never reach out to us, we will live out our lives with great honor as retirees from the top court in the Empire. I prefer the second option."

The other justices agreed and nodded their approval. They all knew that confronting this emperor would be suicidal.

"Nook, you are correct again. I am assigning you to draft the complaint to the emperor. Please take a few weeks to get that done. Once the memory of today's events begins to fade,

Emperor Zul's anger will subside. He will probably make a weak apology which we will gladly accept," Bon said. "I am too old and tired to try to change the Empire. Let's allow the next generation to fix it for us."

The small star fighter descended quickly through the atmosphere to the planet Tak-u-Baka on the Paxran side of the Donnaki frontier. Tak-u-Baka had once been a garden planet home to five billion Paxrans. Large fleets of Paxran cruisers left from here to invade the Donnaki Empire generations ago. Over the following centuries, it changed hands between the two combatants many times. After the Donnaki were pushed back the last time, the planet became a massive military base with heavy fortifications and hundreds of star ships based there. Five artificial moons orbited the planet. Each was home to sensors arrays, blaster stations and more than a hundred fighters.

After drifting down through a cloud bank, a huge military complex appeared below the ship. Dozens of landing platforms and hundreds of weapon stations dotted the landscape. The ship headed for a small platform near a large building. Laser cannons marked the corners of the building. The craft extended its landing pylons and touched down softly. The engines slowed and stopped. The ship's ramp descended and two Paxran pilots stepped out onto the platform. They pulled off their helmets, exposing their pale blue skin. Rain started to pelt the platform so they hurried to a door leading into the building. One Paxran tapped a code onto a keypad and the door opened.

Two armed guards were waiting on the inside of the door. When they saw the two pilots, they snapped to attention and saluted. The pilots saluted and hurried down the corridor. They entered a lift which shot downward into the planet. After several moments, the door opened and they rushed to the single door ahead of them. They knocked on the door and immediately entered a large control station. The walls were covered with video screens showing different parts of the planet as well as the space nearby. Hundreds of Paxran sat at consoles reviewing the screens and tapping comments on their keyboards. In the center of the room was a single glass-walled office. The two pilots rushed to the office and entered.

"Welcome home, guys," General Abala Konole said. "I'm a little busy now. What do you want?"

"General, we need to tell you what we saw," Captain Ollo Niqir said.

"I'm a busy man, Ollo. I'll read your report in due course," Abala replied.

"With all due respect General, I think we need to talk now," Commander Vi Aku said. "This information is too vital to read in a report."

"You two are the most melodramatic team I have," Abala said as he pulled a bottle of whisky and three glasses from his desk. "Okay, sit down and have a drink. Then you can tell me what is so important."

The pilots had been on a reconnaissance mission deep in Donnaki space, one of several hundred fighters that flew missions daily to keep track of the enemy's actions. Several days ago, they had encountered a large fleet of Donnaki cruisers traveling across the region they were scanning. The fleet was headed away from the frontier so they decided to follow them. After a day of travel, the fleet arrived at a large dead planet around five thousand miles in diameter. They thought the planet must have been hurled away when its sun exploded as there were no nearby stars. The surface was heavily burned and scarred as a planet blasted by its sun would be.

The cruisers began to blast away at the planet. The pilots realized the Donnaki were doing target practice and turned to resume their mission. Their sensors suddenly detected a massive power surge, so they turned back. All of the ships fired at once to a spot miles from the planet. The beams fused into a massive ball of plasma which then shot toward the planet. When the ball hit the planet, a huge explosion occurred and thousands of tons of rock were blasted into space. The cruisers fired two more times and more debris shot into space. Then the ships stopped firing. They scanned the fleet but could not register any life forms. It was as if the crews had disappeared. After an hour, the Donnaki ships began to disintegrate into pieces. The shards fell onto the planet where the blasting had occurred. Within a few minutes, the Donnaki fleet was gone. After another hour, the planet began to move on its own away from the scene. They followed the planet for several hours. They closed on the planet to see the attack site better, but before they could get close enough, the planet simply disappeared.

"You two weren't drinking out there, were you?" the general asked. "You have all of this recorded, I hope."

"We recorded everything, General," Ollo confirmed.

Abala took a long drink of the whisky. "Well, if it's true, that is a very disturbing report. The Donnaki have a new weapon that could destroy our fleet and planets. They also have another enemy who can move planets and melt ships for scrap metal. The planet really disappeared?"

"Yes sir," Ollo replied. "Our sensors recorded it there one minute and gone the next. There was no sound or light or explosion. It was just gone."

"We do have an idea about the planet, General," Vi said. "Shortly before the ships began to crumble apart, our sensors detected humans on board. They were just like the planet though. They were there one minute and gone the next."

"Humans, that's a ridiculous comment, even for you Vi," Abala laughed. "That civilization is too small and weak to do anything. Our agents proved there are only a few human worlds and they are on the other side of the galaxy. You must have misread the sensor readings. Maybe they were valakars too. The Donnaki have plenty of enemies among their own race."

"General, the sensors clearly showed them to be human," Ollo replied. "Perhaps there are other human worlds we do not know about."

"I suppose that is possible. Okay, what is the bottom line of all this?" Abala asked.

"We think the planet was hollow, and the humans were using it a space ship," Ollo said. "There have been rumors around the empire that other civilizations have developed the ability to control matter and energy with a technology called a Hive. It is possible the false planet held a Hive as well. We must find a Hive and capture it so we can learn their secrets."

"We must defeat the Donnaki who can blow up our planets. We must capture a Hive that can magically disappear from space. You have a lot of confidence that our inferior military can beat them, guys. This is becoming surreal. My head is pounding and it is your fault," Abala replied. "You two get out of here and get some rest. Have your report to me by the end of tomorrow. If everything is confirmed, we'll forward it to the Chiefs of Staff and let them decide what to do about it."

CHAPTER 13

The morning sun peeked over the horizon and the light of a new day poured down the streets of Sakar, capital city of Aranar Zu. Six inches of fresh snow had fallen over night and snow plows moved about cleaning the wide boulevards. A large crew was assembled in the central square and park clearing snow and assembling grandstands for the day's events. Snow removal shuttles skimmed the tree tops to clear the new snow. They were followed by crews installing lights in the trees.

On the north side of the park stood the Planetary Council Building, which housed the offices of the two hundred councilors who represented the different regions of the planet, as well as their support staffs. All the buildings in the city were made with thick stone walls. The Council Building was faced with polished white marble. Few lights were on in the building at this early hour. The east side of the park was home to the Military High Command. On the south were the regional and city government buildings along with several office buildings. More commercial buildings were on the west side, including the Aranar Grand Hotel, currently hosting Loni Arrak, her family, the Brewsters and many guests from around the planet and the Society of Humanity.

Bill Brewster felt the sunlight on his face and opened his eyes. Out the window he could see a light snow flurry and the trees in the park, glistening with their fresh covering of snow. He rolled over and looked at Loni Arrak, still sleeping with the bed covers pulled up to her chin. He leaned over and kissed her cheek. When she did not wake up, he climbed out of bed, slipped on a robe and went to the window. He could see dozens of workers raising three flags on each of the line of flag poles in front of the High Council Building. At the top was the standard for the Society of Humanity, followed by the flags for the Zu culture and Aranar Zu itself. As he watched, Loni came up from behind and put her arms around Bill, nestling her face into his back.

"Good morning, sleepy head," Bill said as he turned and kissed her.

Loni yawned. "It's going to be a long day, Billy. I'm so glad that you are here to go through it with me."

"Your planet is awesome, Loni. The one thing I've learned since jumping from the twenty-first is that every day holds something new. And the last few days with you have been the most amazing of all," he replied.

"Thanks, Billy," she said. "I need to ask you a big favor, and I'm afraid you might get upset about it."

"Just ask, Loni," he said. "I'm sure it's no big deal."

Loni held both of Bill's hands. "Can we please keep our relationship from my family for right now? We've only known each other a few days, so who knows what can happen in the future? I don't think my parents will understand."

"Okay, that's fine with me," Bill replied. "I'm not sure why, but if that's what you want, I won't say a word."

"I want you to understand, Billy. Come over here," Loni continued as they walked to the couch and sat down. "Life in the Society has evolved over time. When humans evolved on Non-Ti billions of years ago, the society was very small. Over time, the numbers grew and people expanded all over the planet, much like they did on Earth 47. Within a few hundred generations, dozens of races evolved to best survive in their regions."

"That does sound a lot like Earth," Bill replied. "There were many races in the twenty-first that seem to have blended together by the thirty-second. There was tension and violence among them for a very long time."

Loni smiled, "It shouldn't be surprising that our worlds evolved similarly. We are all human after all. By the time we reached into the stars, our society had become more homogenous again. But just like with early humanity, the climates and conditions on the new colonies were also quite different. By the time the Society reached one thousand worlds, fifty different species had evolved to survive on that many different classes of planets."

"Like the Zu, for example," Bill said. "I suppose that was to be expected."

"Expanding life expectancies led to rapid population growth. We needed to find more planets to give everyone a home and a job. We never found more than fifty types of inhabitable planets though. After many failed attempts to bring wide groups of races to new planets, like on Earth 47, it was decided the races best suited to a planet would get the new one. When Aranar was located, the Society found its climate was best suited for the Zu culture. That's why it's a Zu planet," Loni explained.

Bill replied, "So, humanity reverted to separate races in order to optimize expansion. It is totally logical, but a little cold and sterile."

"We all know that too, Billy," she said. "There are no laws against interracial marriages, but the societal norms are very strong. After a few hundred generations of Zu only marrying Zu, any other marriage seems unnatural to some. My parents are very traditional and proud Zu."

"Loni, I think you are the most wonderful and beautiful woman I have ever met," Bill replied as he kissed her again. "But as you said, we have only known each other a few days. The last thing I want to do is cause a panic in the Arrak family now. If some day we decide to have a permanent relationship, we can cross that bridge then."

"Oh, Billy, thank you for understanding," Loni cried. "I've been so worried about this and The Hive and everything else." She threw her arms around him and hugged him tightly. A tone sounded on her com-link and she rushed over to her clothes, pulled it off and touched the contact. "Loni Arrak… Oh hi Mom, how are you . . . Great . . . Okay, I'll see you then, bye." She came back and stood in front of Bill. "The shuttle with my folks will arrive in an hour. I have to get ready."

"No problem, Loni," Bill said as he rose. "I'll get dressed and clean up in my room." He kissed her again and she hurried off to the restroom. His com-link chirped. "Bill Brewster."

"You old dog," Cybil laughed. "I came by your room and you weren't there. I have a funny feeling I know where you spent the night, Romeo."

"Knock it off, sis," he replied. "Loni is a great girl and we're just getting to know each other. You'd better watch it because I plan to make a full report to Mom and Dad about you and Rob Watson later."

She laughed again. "Very funny, little brother, but I tell Mom everything. I'll keep this secret for you if you like. Hurry up and get ready. I'm dying for breakfast!"

"Okay, Cyb," he laughed. "Give me half an hour and then we can eat. Bye." He closed the contact and pulled on his clothes. As he headed to the door, he knocked and said goodbye to Loni, who didn't hear as she was singing in the shower.

"So tell me everything, Billy, and don't leave out the juicy details," Cybil laughed as they sat together in the dining room of the Aranar Grand Hotel. The room was quite full due to the influx of visitors for the festivities to begin that evening. Almost everyone there was Zu. Loni had told them other races frequently came to the planet to hunt and engage in other winter sports, but it was rare for them to stay permanently.

"Come on sis, you know a gentleman doesn't kiss and tell," Bill smiled. "You know Loni, she's great. We are getting along very well."

"I could tell since you weren't in your room this morning," Cybil replied. "Where is that waiter?"

A woman approached their table. She was well dressed but definitely not Zu. She looked almost as though she had stepped through a portal from the twenty-first. She was about five and one-half feet tall with black hair and gray eyes. She smiled as she approached the large table. "I'm so glad to find more Pa here! This is such a big table. Can I join you?" she asked.

Bill stood to shake her hand and said, "Hi, I'm Bill Brewster and this is my sister Cybil. You can certainly join us, but what is a Pa?"

She looked bewildered. "But you look just like you're from the Pa culture. I'm sorry, I'm Serena Vanatee. I am President of the High Council for the planet Atar Pa, and I'm here for the celebration. Maybe I should find another table?"

"No, please join us," Cybil replied. "You can get a head start on the party by sitting with us. We are the children of Ambassador and Admiral Brewster."

"Really? Wow! I'm so honored to meet you," Serena smiled as she sat across from them. "So, you're descended from the original settlers of Earth 47?"

"Born and raised there," Bill said. "In fact, we were born more than a thousand years ago and jumped to this time not too long ago."

"So you lived on Earth 47? That is really amazing. Do you know Chief Engineer Loni Arrak too?" Serena asked.

"My brother knows her a lot better than I do, Serena," Cybil chuckled.

"Cool it, sis," Bill said. "My dad and I have actually entered The Hive on Tak-Makla with her. She is a wonderful young woman. But tell us more about you and your planet, Serena."

"Well, I am in my first term as President of Atar Pa. My planet was the second colony settled in this galaxy, just after Aranar Zu. We have just over one billion inhabitants now, but we are growing rapidly. There are more than one thousand Pa planets in the Society and many are too heavily populated already. My immigration team handles tens of thousands of relocation requests each week. You two should come there sometime. It's nothing like this freezer," she answered.

"What's it like, Serena?" Cybil asked.

"It's a very lush and wet planet, Cybil. Oceans cover about seventy percent of the planet, so we have become a major exporter of seafood. There aren't many high mountain ranges. Most have worn down over the millennia and are now covered with trees. Our capital city, Pegat is located on the largest continent. That continent has a ring of grasslands and forests on most of the coasts. A ring of mountains just inside that has left the center very arid and dry. The other land masses are much smaller and dominated by jungles in the lower latitudes and forests in the higher ones," Serena said.

"Do you have a Hive there?" Bill asked.

"Oh no, Bill. We don't have the population for that. There are two Hives in our vicinity. The one now orbiting Aranar, and another near Seeka Opa, which is about halfway between here and Atar Pa," she replied. She stood and said, "Hello there, I'm President Serena Vanatee of Atar Pa."

Bill and Cybil turned to see their parents arriving at their table. "Good morning, Mom and Dad. We made a new friend!"

"Good day, President Vanatee, I am Ambassador Darlene Brewster and this is Admiral Dave Brewster," Darlene said as they shook hands. After pleasantries, they all sat again. Two Zu waiters approached the table and offered menus and coffee to the group. After ordering breakfast, the waiters left.

"It is a real honor to meet you both," Serena said. "When the Society decided to repopulate this galaxy, many were skeptical. Things did not work out very well for humanity the last time. It is amazing that the remnants of Earth 47 found us before we could find you."

"As you can imagine, I was pretty shocked to run into a human Chief Engineer on a maklan world, Serena," Dave replied.

"Things have been pretty exciting since then. We are honored this celebration is being held for Loni and our family."

"You can imagine how excited I am to see that you are Pa, like me as well?" Serena asked.

"We cannot deny the resemblance, Serena," Darlene replied. "Unfortunately, there are very few of us from our time and the modern humans look quite different."

"Yes, I have heard that as well," she replied. "But that gives me a great idea! Since you are Pa, I'd love to host you for a visit to Atar Pa. Our population isn't as big as Aranar Zu, and we are not so rich and well developed. But you would have a good time, I guarantee that!"

"It would be an honor," Darlene smiled. "We were feeling a little lonely in a society that looks so different. A little diversion might be good."

"I don't know Mom, I think Billy likes it here just fine," Cybil laughed.

"I told you to be quiet, Cyb!" Bill interjected.

"Don't worry, son, your secret is safe with us," Dave winked. "Serena, just let us know and we will be there. There are a few more folks from the twenty-first who might want to join us, like Cybil's boyfriend. Would that be okay?"

"Of course, that would be wonderful. I'll have my staff work on the details. I am very excited about this," Serena said as the waiters returned with breakfast. "That looks wonderful. I hope they have coffee from Atar Pa. We grow the best coffee in the galaxy!"

Darlene smiled, "We'll let Dave decide. He is a coffee nut!"

They sat quietly enjoying their food for several minutes. The crowd in the dining room continued to grow. The Zu were fascinated by the table of Pa in their midst. The Pa were not great fans of cold weather sports and it was unusual to find many Pa tourists in the winter. After another ten minutes, two well-dressed men approached the table. When she saw them approach, Serena jumped to her feet and shook their hands.

"Consul Arnar, Consul Jeebo, it's wonderful to see you both again," Serena said. "Please let me introduce you to our guests. This is Ambassador and Admiral Brewster and their children. They are part of the surviving colony of Earth 47." She turned to the Brewsters. "Dave and Darlene, these gentlemen are on the High Council for the Society of Humanity."

"Dear friends, we welcome you back into the Society!" Consul Arnar said as he hugged each member of the family. "Serena, I am so surprised to see they are Pa like us!"

Consul Jeebo was not Pa or Zu. He was only four feet tall with dark blue, almost black skin and large piercing black eyes. "I welcome you too, fellow humans. As you can see, I am an Opa. We are one of the smallest species with only five hundred planets. I too am hoping to find more Opa in this galaxy."

Dave stepped up to the Consul and shook his hand heartily, "Consul, I think I can make your day. Hundreds of years ago, the people on Earth 47 were involved in a two century battle among themselves for dominance. The only thing that stopped the war was the arrival of the first sentient species from other worlds. Those Beings, the Kalideans, look just like you."

"What? Can that be true?" Consul Jeebo said.

"It's very true, Consul," Dave continued. "After the war ended, the Kalideans helped Earth 47 with new technologies and medicine so that we could reach out into the stars. When mankind became too enamored with their vacations and studies, a great Kalidean scientist, Mencius, recommended humanity go back in time to find new blood to push us into space. That is where they found us. I also want you to know that Mencius is a good friend of mine and I would love to take you to Kalidus and introduce you."

"Fate has brought you to me, Dave Brewster," Jeebo smiled. "I can't believe this is all true. Please tell me more about the Kalideans."

"Jeebo, we have to get going," Consul Arnar interrupted. "We have a Council meeting in ten minutes. It was wonderful meeting you all and I look forward to the event this evening."

"Dave, I will talk to you more later today! You have my word on that!" Jeebo said as they turned to leave the room.

CHAPTER 15

The skies over Sakar cleared late in the morning and the sun was shining high in the sky as the crowd assembled in the central square and park for the festivities. More than one hundred thousand were expected to witness the Freedom Award being given to Loni Arrak by President Bango and the High Council members present. Large video screens were set up behind the newly assembled stage where the activities would take place. Dozens of food and souvenir stands were set up on the boulevard facing the Aranar Grand Hotel, and the hawkers were busy setting up their goods and preparing Zu delicacies for the crowd. A musical event was scheduled to begin in the early afternoon which would lead up to the presentations. Bands from all over Aranar Zu would compete for the honor of serenading Loni Arrak after she received her award.

Dave and Darlene walked out of the hotel and into the crisp afternoon air. The hotel had provided thick fur parkas and gloves for their guests not accustomed to cold weather. They planned to get some exercise and just blend with the locals, but they were more than a foot shorter than most Zu. They could see hundreds of people sitting in the park already, listening to the musical groups practice for the concert that would begin in one hour. After a few minutes, they stopped at a stand selling local cheeses. The rich smell was very familiar and Dave could not resist. On the counter, they saw an open newspaper with pictures of Loni, Dave and Darlene on the front cover. While their translators were effective for spoken language, they could not read the words.

The shopkeeper was a tall woman with gray hair and slightly golden eyes. She looked at her customers, looked at the paper and back at them. "You are Dave and Darlene Brewster from Earth 47, right?" she said.

"Guilty as charged," Dave laughed. "Your cheeses smell wonderful!"

She extended her hand and shook theirs. "I'm Ipa Nota. It's an honor to meet you. Please, you must sample my goods. Our family makes these cheeses at our ranch five hundred miles south of here. Try this one first. It's called ummu, and it's my husband's favorite," she said as she passed a small plate to them.

The cheese was firm and rich, with a slightly crumbly texture. "Wow, this is very good," Darlene said. "What kind of animal does the milk come from?"

"There are only two animals on Aranar Zu that provide milk, the zolo and the nagli. Ummu comes from zolo milk. Here is a picture of both animals. I keep these for outworlders like you. Those animals are native to this planet and few other planets have anything like them," Ipa replied as she handed a photo to Darlene.

"They look a lot like a cow and a goat from Earth," Dave said. "The ummu does taste like a cow's milk cheese to me."

"If you say so, sir," Ipa replied. "I don't have any idea what those creatures are. Here, this is a nagli cheese called utok. Many people think it is too strong."

"I think I agree with them, Ipa," Darlene said as spat the cheese into a napkin. "What do you think, Dave?"

"I like it," he replied. "I think this would be great with coffee!"

"That's the way I like it too," Ipa said. "There is something about the bitterness of coffee that mellows the flavor of utok. I wish I had some coffee to offer you."

"That's okay, Ipa. It was a pleasure to meet you and thanks for the cheese," Dave said. They turned and continued their walk down the street. They passed stalls selling sizzling strips of meat on skewers and others with small baskets of freshly picked berries. Ipa must have spread the word about their presence because more and more Zu came to welcome them and take pictures.

To avoid the crowds, they walked into the park and sat in the back row of seats, several hundred feet from the stage, where technicians were finalizing the sound and lighting settings. They watched the crowd get larger in anticipation of the musical event but most people sat closer to the stage so their area remained empty. Half an hour later, the musical competition began. After several bands had played, Bill and Cybil came to join them. Bill was carrying a large plate with skewers of roasted meat and slices of cheese. Cybil had a small tray with four hot beverage containers.

"Here Dad, I brought you a coffee," Cybil smiled. "Mom, I brought you a local specialty called zook. It's a lot like hot chocolate, but a bit fruity. I like it a lot."

"I'm glad you guys found us," Dave said. "I'm surprised that Loni isn't with you, Billy."

"Her family arrived and she needed to spend time with them. She hasn't seen them in a couple of years," Bill replied.

"That makes sense. Did you meet them?" Darlene asked.

"Not yet. We just started seeing each other, and I still need to get back to Earth to work on the DNA project. Meeting her parents this soon seemed too much," he replied. "I've only known Loni a few days."

"Don't take us wrong, Bill. Your mother and I just thought you might have run into them," Dave said. "You're absolutely right that it's too early to take a relationship to that level. There's all the time in the world for that."

"Thanks Dad," Bill replied. "I had an idea to knock around with you about the DNA project. Thanks to Loni, we now will have a connection to a human civilization that has been around for three billion years. It seems pretty obvious to me that they must have solved the DNA problem already?"

"So why do the project if we can just copy their results?" Dave asked.

"Exactly," Bill replied.

"There are probably still differences to be taken into account. Earth has been separated from this society for four hundred million years. There may be differences among the races as well," Darlene said. "I certainly didn't think the Kalideans were just another sub-species of humans until this morning."

"Of course, Mom," Bill said. "But ninety-nine percent of the DNA has to be very similar. If we can accelerate our program by focusing on the one percent, we might finish in no time."

"It makes sense. You should contact Chief Engineer Lagerfeld as soon as you can. Once he buys in, it's a done deal," Dave replied. "That's a great solution, son." Dave took a skewer of meat and bit off a large chunk. "This is great stuff too. What a beautiful day to be here with my family." He sat back and listened to the band playing.

Three tall Zu men in a military uniforms hurried up to the Brewsters. They stood as they approached. "Ambassador, Admiral, I don't know if you remember me from your visit to Hive 1008 two days ago. I am General Audy Zilma, head of the military on that planetoid, and these are two of my best guards."

"Yes General, we remember you well," Dave said as he shook his hand. "We're happy to be here today."

"Please call me Audy, Dave. We have had a problem on the station and Governor Lonk wanted me to tell you," he replied.

"What sort of problem, Audy?" Darlene asked.

"Two hours ago, there were coordinated attacks on the Hives on Station 1008 and on Tak-Makla. Both Hives are now down," Audy replied.

"Attacks! How is that possible?" Dave asked.

"We don't have an answer for that yet, Dave. We have heard attacks were also carried out on the two Hive facilities under construction in the Nom-Kat-La system, but they have not been confirmed," Audy reported. "We don't want to panic the citizens here or cancel the events this evening. Security presence here has been doubled in the last hour. I have been asked to escort any non-essential guests out of the area though. Councilors Jeebo and Arnar have already left the planet. A battle cruiser from Aranar Zu is waiting in orbit to take your family back to your space. I'm afraid that Bill and Cybil will have to go with me now. You, Darlene and Loni Arrak will jump to the ship immediately after the award presentation. Jeek and Tho will stay with you until then."

"This seems highly irregular," Dave said. He wondered how it could be true that a Hive in the middle of a giant planet could be penetrated by assailants. The Internal Affairs team on Tak-Makla was huge, and he imagined the one on a military Hive would be even larger. "Perhaps I should contact President Bango's office first," he said as he reached for his com-link.

Audy and the two guards pulled their blasters and leveled them at the Brewsters. Audy frowned and said, "I'm afraid I can't let you do that, Admiral. I was hoping it wouldn't come to this." Before Dave could react, Audy pressed the contact and the blast hit Dave in the chest. He fell backward to the ground. Darlene tried to scream, but the group instantly disappeared, leaving Dave lying on the cold ground. People around the area saw the confrontation and heard the blast. When the soldiers disappeared, they ran over to see what had happened.

Dave had a crushing headache. He was dreaming he was back in The Hive with Loni traveling through space and time looking for his family. Where could they be? He woke with a start and sat straight up in bed, making his head pound even harder. It took a moment or two for his eyes to come into focus. He was in a large white room in what seemed like a hospital. A Zu woman dressed in white turned and saw he was awake. She touched her com-link and spoke in a strange language.

Two more Zu entered the room and rushed over to talk to Dave, but he could not understand them. He asked them about his family, but could not understand what they were telling him. He looked around and saw his translator on a nightstand and reached for it. It was scorched and broken. When they saw the device, one Zu pulled a similar device from a pocket and gently pushed it into his ear.

"Is that better?" the Zu asked. "Can you understand me, Admiral Brewster?"

"Yes, that's better," Dave sighed. "What happened? Where am I? What about my family?"

"I am Doctor Ulu Makak," the male Zu said. "We have notified President Bango that you are awake and she will be here soon. We only know that you took a full stun blast to the chest. You are in Sakar General Hospital, two blocks from where you were injured about an hour ago. How do you feel?"

"My head is pounding like mad, Doctor," Dave replied. "My whole body is tingling."

"Those are normal symptoms of a stun injury. Both will subside in a few minutes. I have been asked to tell you that our police are on the case. Several others in the park saw the incident. One cheese seller told our ambulance crew who you were," Ulu said. "Please try to rest a few minutes. The President should be here very soon."

As the doctors left, President Jo Bango and Governor Alin Lonk entered the room along with two heavily armed guards. "Thank God you are alive, Dave," Jo said. "Alin and I have been reviewing the video feeds from the park and are shocked by what we saw. I am so sorry this happened."

"What happened to my family, Governor? Zilma is your man, isn't he?" Dave asked.

"We all thought he was a loyal soldier, Dave," Alin replied. "Guards, please leave us and do not allow anyone else to come in." The guards left the room and closed the door behind them.

Jo sat heavily on a small chair near the bed. "Dave, what we are going to tell you is very secret in the Society. There are many factions throughout our worlds, Dave. You may have thought we were divided by race, but that is only a small part of the situation. With fifty thousand worlds with an average population of two billion each, there are around one hundred trillion humans. Every culture has subversive elements. If they represent only one tenth of one percent, it is still a hundred billion humans."

"You're not answering my question," Dave demanded.

Alin put his hands on the foot of the bed and looked at Dave. "There are always a few star cruisers around each planet for security, Dave. One of the largest over Aranar Zu was the battle cruiser Vikal, which left orbit shortly after you were shot. We believe your family were jumped to that ship which has now have left this system."

"Why would anyone want my family?" Dave asked. "It just doesn't make sense."

"We believe Councilors Arnar and Jeebo and Loni's parents were also on that ship," Jo replied. "But we don't believe Arnar was a prisoner. There have been rumors that some on the High Council were supporters for the Free Society. Arnar has been very vocal about being more flexible in dealing with them."

"What exactly is the Free Society?" Dave asked.

"There have been discussions for many decades about how best to break the Society of Humanity into smaller groups of planets. No consensus on how to do it has ever been reached," Jo began. "The Free Society plan is to break the Society by region and eliminate the races by actively promoting or requiring interracial marriages. Arnar is a Pa, like you and your family. He believes you are proof that mixing the races can and does work."

"But my family is from the past, when there were many races. As we told President Serena Vanatee of Atar Pa at breakfast, current humans on Earth 47 look nothing like us," Dave replied.

Jo looked at Alin who seemed bewildered. "Serena Vanatee was on Aranar Zu this morning?"

"She joined my family at breakfast. Those two Councilors even stopped by the table to say hello," Dave replied.

"This is most unusual, Jo," Alin interrupted. "We need to contact the Supreme Command as soon as possible."

"What did I say?" Dave asked.

"Dave, Serena is not President of Atar Pa," Jo replied. "She spent her career in the intelligence community. She was recently made head of security for Councilor Arnar."

"Jo, I always had my doubts about her too," Alin said. "She asked to be assigned to Hive 1008, but I personally denied her request. When I heard she went to work for Arnar, I was convinced I had made the correct decision. We need to scan for her too. I bet she's on that cruiser as well."

"The general told me that Hive 1008 and Tak-Makla had been attacked. Is that true?" Dave asked.

"We have heard reports about an attack on The Hive on Tak-Makla and on two planets in the Nom-Kat-La system. We have no information about who may have perpetrated those attacks or if they were connected in any way. The Tak-Makla Hive was severely damaged by explosions on the lowest levels, and several thousand agents died. Fortunately, the Gallicean military destroyed the ships attacking the Nom-Kat-La before they could do any damage," Alin replied. "There has been no attack on Hive 1008 though."

"Can't your Hives jump the captives off the Vikal and put an end to this?" Dave implored. "That's my family we're talking about."

"It would seem the attackers have control of a Hive too, Dave," Jo replied. "They are using that power to shield the ship from our agents. We have no idea where that Hive is."

"What about the Hive near Seeka Opa?" Dave asked. "Serena told us about that too."

"I've never heard of Seeka Opa, have you Alin?" Jo asked.

"That's the name to be given to the next Opa planet located in this galaxy, Jo," he replied. "But no new planet has been located yet."

"Serena said they didn't have enough people on Atar Pa for a Hive, so they used Hive 1008 and another near Seeka Opa," Dave said. "At least that's what my son told me she said."

Jo replied, "Dave, Atar Pa is a massive planet with twenty billion people living there. They have one Hive and there are plans to build a second. The lines of universal power are extremely strong in that area."

"Well, I think we know where the cruiser is headed, don't we?" Dave asked.

"Alin, consult the Supreme Command. We need a fleet and two Hives to go to Atar Pa and find those prisoners. Dave, immediately after the ceremony, we will jump you and Loni back to Tak-Makla. High Consul Zee is frantic since the attack. You two need to get that Hive back online as soon as possible. You also need to find out how the attack occurred," Jo ordered.

"My first guess would be to review the two Chief Engineers you sent there to take Loni's place. The tekkans are not the type to destroy their own Hive. They are more likely to jump two days ahead to get the winning lottery numbers. Can I get out of here now?" Dave finished.

Dave and Loni appeared on the beach in front of the Ambassador's residence next to Zee's home on Tak-Makla. Kally had been advised when they would arrive and he stood on the patio twenty feet away. He ran to them with an umbrella. A cold heavy rain fell about them that night. Local time was 0300 and lightning crackled in the sky overhead. The rain mixed with Loni's tears as they rushed toward the house.

She had been crying almost continually since her parents were abducted. They had been strolling down the aisles of food stands in front of the hotel. They had purchased some zook and meat and were enjoying each other's company. Loni saw Ipa Nota's cheese stand and rushed ahead to see her aunt. The family had spent many summers in the warmth of their farm in the low valleys. As she approached the stand, two soldiers passed by. She smiled at the men she knew were protecting the celebration in her honor. She looked back at Ipa who now had a look of horror on her face. She turned to see the guards manhandling her parents. After a second, they disappeared. At that moment, Loni heard the blaster fire in the park.

As Dave and Loni entered the house, Charlie and Aria Watson and De-o-Nu rushed forward to comfort them. After hugs of affection, Aria sat on the couch with Loni while the three men sat on overstuffed chairs nearby. Kally brought over glasses of wine and whisky for the group and then excused himself.

"Brother, this is an unbelievable change of events," De-o-Nu said. "I cannot tell you how sorry we are at this time. I spoke with my brother-in-law an hour ago and he is distraught as well for both of you. Greater Gallia offers one hundred cruisers to hunt down the cowards who did this act."

"Thank you, brother," Dave smiled. "Your family has always been very generous with mine. Our first priority must be to get this Hive back online. We need that to offset the Hive protecting the kidnappers."

"That's a tall order, Dave," Charlie said. "Almost half the equipment on the lower levels was damaged. Ten thousand agents died when the explosions hit, including Chief Engineer Nit Valasan and Minister Var Vanadez."

"Oh no," Loni whimpered. "This is going to be impossible. We can't do anything without a second Chief Engineer. What happened to the two sent here to take my place?"

"One died in the explosion," Charlie continued. "There is no sign of the other. Mak believes he may have been the culprit. Who else can take the role of Chief Engineer?"

"I can," said Zee as he entered the room. "I was Chief Engineer long ago and I can do it again. This planet needs a Chief Engineer much more than a High Consul right now. We need to get The Hive operational first. Chief Engineers may not matter if we can't get the equipment replaced though." He came to Dave and touched his shoulder, then went to Loni and hugged her. "I am so sorry this happened to you both. Today is a grim day for all of us. Many lives have been lost and souls returned to the Universal Consciousness. I pray tomorrow will be better." He poured himself a whisky and sat next to Loni on the couch.

Loni raised her head and wiped her eyes. "Zee, I just had an idea. Perhaps we can get equipment from the Hive under construction on Nom-Kat-Zuk? That Hive isn't nearly finished and new equipment can be sent there in time."

"I'm sure our Gallicean friends won't mind that either," Darlene smiled.

"Please be our guest," De-o-Nu replied. "We didn't ask for that Hive and dismantling it will only delay it. That's a great idea, Loni." He turned to the admiral and said, "Dave, do you have any residual issues after you were shot?"

"No, after the headache and tingling went away, I feel fine," he replied.

"I must tell you when I learned you were unarmed and had been shot, my mind filled with thoughts of revenge. I honestly considered taking the Kong-Fa to Aranar Zu and shooting the place up," De-o-Nu said.

Dave finished his whisky and went to the bar for a refill. He took the bottle and a bottle of Gallicean whisky and set them on the coffee table. "I'm glad you didn't, brother. The people of Aranar Zu are not the problem."

"Yes, I have seen the reports about the other planet, Atar Pa," he replied. "In the moment when the blood rushes to my brain, as a Gallicean my instinct is to fight now and think later. But the incident did make me think, Dave. You are an admiral who walks about unarmed. That is unthinkable to a Gallicean."

"I understand, brother, but I am more of an explorer than a soldier," Dave said. "I never intended to be in a battle or fight. Remember that in my time I was an accountant."

"True. However, in my youth I wore diapers too. Now I carry three daggers and two blasters wherever I go," De-o-Nu said as he removed his belt. "No Gallicean soldier would be caught without a trusty blade." He pulled the daggers from his belt and laid them on the table. "This curved one is called Nak. It is shaped like a beak to remind us to tear our enemies apart. This one is Falon, which is straight like a warrior's character. Some also say it reminds us of our virility. The wavy one is Ullu which reminds us that flying can be decisive in battle. I have ordered a human size set of these for you Dave. My personal weapon smith is making them now. They will be about the size you see here. As you know, away from this planet, I am more than three times this size, so these weapons are much larger."

"That is very generous, De-o-Nu," Dave said. "I'm not sure I could do anything with them though."

"Yes, but I will personally train you," De-o-Nu said with a large grin. "Each day when you return from your work on The Hive, we will work out with the daggers for one hour, in the Gallicean custom. Afterward, we will eat and drink together. We will use the remaining whisky to clean our blades. That is a sacred Gallicean custom as well."

"I would love to get that training too," Aria said. "I need to be able to protect Charlie here."

"Very funny, Aria," Charlie replied. "Count me in too, brother."

De-o-Nu shrieked with laughter. "This is a glorious ending to a terrible day, friends. We will train and drink together until the day when we free Dave's and Loni's families."

"Don't forget about the ships, De-o-Nu," Zee said.

"Ah, yes, I did forget," he continued. "After the attacks, it has become clear that Tak-Makla needs protection. As long as this Hive is down, the planet is very vulnerable to attack. At Consul Zee's request, twenty star cruisers will be in orbit here within three days. Ten will be from Greater Gallia and ten from Earth. My ship will lead the overall fleet. Captain Jon Lake on the Nightsky will be my second. Nightsky and Kong-Fa are already here."

"Loni dear, I know you've been through a lot," Zee began, "but I still do not understand why my planet was attacked. I was not aware there were such unstable elements within the Society of Humanity. Why would they kill so many and kidnap totally innocent people? Do you know?"

Loni stood and walked to the bar. She poured the wine out of her glass and filled it with ice. She returned to the table and filled the glass with Gallicean whisky and sat down. She took a long drink. "Zee, our Society is huge with fifty thousand planets and more than a hundred trillion people. We have also been segregated into races. Even though it is a tiny percentage, there are billions who believe we are misguided. They think the Society is too large to be one entity and all races should be encouraged to intermarry. If we continue we way we are, they believe the Society will eventually crumble into new societies based on race." She took another drink.

"Is that what you believe, Loni?" Aria asked.

"I never used to, Aria," she replied. "Then I met Bill Brewster, who is definitely not a Zu like me. He is so sweet and wonderful to me." Tears began to roll down her cheeks again. Aria put her arm around Loni's shoulders. "My family would go insane if they thought I would marry someone who isn't a Zu, but I feel like I'm falling in love with Bill. Before today, I never thought about the structure of the Society or the dissidents in the Free Society. I knew my job here in The Hive and that was my life. When I grew up on Aranar Zu, I almost never saw other races, except when we'd go skiing."

"Now I know why I like you so much, Loni," De-o-Nu smiled. "You are a beautiful young girl who likes the Brewsters and Gallicean whisky. Brother, your son is a lucky man to have such love."

"You are right, brother," Dave sighed. "But first we need to find him and get these two back together again. I did have a meeting with President Bango and Governor Lonk while I was recovering in the hospital. The Free Society seems to be led by people from the Pa culture, who look like Charlie and me. They believe that our existence proves that humanity can become homogeneous again. They also think since we look like Pa, that race must be the result of the blending of all the races."

"That seems unlikely, Dave," Aria said. "I am the result of that blending, not you."

"We told them that too," he replied. "We know now that Kalideans and Nanda are also humans. I can't even imagine what would happen if all were blended together. But none of this is about finding the truth. The leaders of the Free Society movement have made their decisions and are looking for any morsel that helps prove their case. Now they have Darlene, Bill and Cybil to prove their point. Loni, I still don't know why your parents are involved."

Loni dropped her head and tears flowed again. She took the glass of whisky and drained it. "I know why," she began. "My parents are old now and were older than most when I was born. When my father was young, he was a soldier and politician. He was President on Aranar Zu two hundred solar cycles ago. He spent four terms on the High Council for the Society. The founder of the Free Society, Wendo Balak was a Pa who was on the High Council at the same time. Both argued that the Society had become too large to manage. You can imagine the bureaucracy for a civilization with a hundred trillion citizens. Over time, they convinced the Council that plans needed to be made to split into smaller groups, with perhaps a small advisory group to liaise among them. Wendo said the division must be along regions of space. That was the only way to insure security within each territory and avoid racial tensions. My father wanted a split based on races to insure domestic tranquility and best utilization of new planets. The Council argued for decades but could never reach an agreement. Finally, both retired from office and new Councilors were elected. My father came to Aranar Zu and built a large farm where his sister and brother-in-law still make cheese. Wendo moved to Atar Pa and kept working on the Free Society."

"Revenge is an excellent motive, and we must move quickly now to save their lives," De-o-Nu said. "But are we certain that the attack here was led by humans? I must tell you the fleet that attacked the Nom-Kat-La system was not human. Our people are still sifting through debris to determine who was behind it. It would be foolish to assume all the attacks were coordinated this soon."

CHAPTER 18

The midday sun baked the desolate landscape surrounding The Hive on Atar Pa. The Hive was located in the center of the vast Pegat Desert that filled the interior of the continent of the same name. The lush coastline with its large cities was thousands of miles away. That distance was filled with rocky mountain ranges, broad expanses of white sand and little else. The life that could survive in the Pegat Desert clung to the first few mountain ranges and valleys that separated this wasteland from the coastal areas. Those mountains were far from this spot and the flat sand stretched to the horizon in every direction. The mile wide opening at the top of The Hive was covered with a mirror-like glass dome to prevent the frequent sand storms was damaging the upper floors, and to repel the temperature extremes common to the area. It was noon now and the temperature was already over one hundred ten degrees.

The bottom level of The Hive was almost two hundred miles below the surface. Outside The Hive, Center City had been built underground to house the billions of agents and their support staff. An enormous network of tubes connected the area to the cities on the Pegat coast. Ten miles north of The Hive, a smaller silver dome marked the landing platform for the space port that served the area. Dozens of shuttles flew in and out of the port daily taking people and goods to other continents and into space. With no bad weather in the forecast, the dome was half open. The opening moved with the sun to keep the bright light out of the port.

A small war ship approached the port slowly and dropped through the opening to land on the designated spot. Dozens of armed guards rushed out to the ship to provide security. The landing ramp descended and several guards stepped off the ship and saluted the troops on the ground. Another group of guards came out of the ship with the Brewsters and the Arraks. They were followed by Councilors Arnar and Jeebo, General Zilma and Serena Vanatee. The prisoners were escorted toward a heavy metal door which opened as they approached. The rest entered the tall glass doors of the terminal building.

"My friends, welcome home," said Wendo Balak. Wendo was an old man now, even more grizzled by his years of self-imposed exile on Atar Pa and unending struggle to build the Free Society.

"Lord Balak, this is a pleasant surprise," Arnar said. "I hadn't expected to see you until we arrived at the capital."

"When you told me you had my old friend Antar Arrak, I took my shuttle here. That man has bedeviled me for my entire career. Now it is time to pay him back for what he has done," Wendo replied.

"It was my pleasure to do so," Arnar said. "I must inform you we were not able to get all the targets."

"Yes, Arnar, I know. Serena here sent me a message when your ship left orbit over Aranar Zu," Wendo said. "Serena, how are you my dear?"

"Very well, Grandfather," she replied. "The operation went smoothly until Admiral Brewster started asking questions. Zilma here was forced to stun him."

"I'm sorry, Lord Balak," Audy said. "The time was very short and I had to act quickly."

Wendo continued, "It seems more like panic than haste, General. Our plans were put in serious jeopardy by your actions. While I do not regret taking the Arraks, it was our plan to invite the Brewsters as guests. Now we will be branded a planet of madmen, who go about the galaxy kidnapping innocents at will. What can we do with you now, Zilma?" Wendo motioned to a nearby guard, saying, "Guard, take General Zilma out of my sight and find a place for him in the brig!" The guard led Zilma away. "This kind of incompetence will be the death of us all."

"Lord Balak, I heard that attacks on the Hive on Tak-Makla and on planets in another system are being blamed on the Free Society," Arnar said. "Now what will we do? If we don't act soon, fleets of cruisers will come here to make us pay."

"Yes, that was very bad news," Balak replied. "I do not regret our actions on Aranar Zu, but I do not understand how we can be blamed for those other actions. We must protest this most strenuously! However, with Zilma's foolishness, no one will believe us now. Our Hive here needs to help find the culprits for the other attacks. We must also determine how to turn the kidnapping of the Brewsters into a simple mistake."

"Grandfather, to find those responsible, we need to complete the second Hive. There are many planets in the Free Society," Serena said. "Certainly there are factories to make parts for our new Hive."

"Yes, but that will take time, Serena. Now that the Society is blaming us for attacks in two systems and kidnapping, I doubt time is on our side," Wendo replied. "Once these stories spread through the Society, we may lose many friends, making our task even more difficult."

"Fate does seem to be aligned against us, Grandfather," she said. "You seem a bit tired, are you well?"

"I am tired, Granddaughter, but I will be fine. I think we should share a meal now and then visit my old friend and our other guests. You may all join me for dinner tomorrow in Pegat City for a small celebration of these events," Wendo concluded.

"So Mom, where do you think we are?" Cybil asked.

"I don't know for certain, sweetheart, but that woman Serena claimed to be from a planet called Atar Pa," Darlene replied. "All the people we've seen here look like Pa to me."

They Brewsters were in a large room with a heavy metal door at one end. The walls were cold stone with no seams. Bright artificial lights were built into the ceiling and made everything look sterile and lifeless. There were three sets of double bunk beds and several small metal chairs scattered about the space. A small pair of dividers offered slight privacy for the toilet and sink on the wall opposite the door. After their group left the ship, guards hurried them into a prison-like facility. Antar Arrak was separated from the rest and taken away. Zina Arrak and the Brewsters were led to this room and the door was locked behind them. They had been waiting here for three or four hours with no other contacts.

Bill sat on one of the beds next to Zina, who had been crying since her husband was forcibly taken from her. His arm was around her shoulders for comfort. "Zina, I'm sure we'll get out of here soon," he said calmly.

"Thank you, Bill," she cried. "Antar is convinced this is the work of the Free Society. If he is correct, there is little hope for any of us." Hearing Zina speak for the first time, Cybil and Darlene came to join them. "Most citizens of the Society know that it has become too large and unwieldy to be managed. At some point it will begin to collapse under its own bureaucratic weight. When Antar was on the High Council, he made suggestions on how to peacefully break the Society into smaller pieces. The founder of the Free Society disagreed and kept the Council from making any decision that was not his own. Ultimately, the Council gave up and my husband retired.”

“Has the Society begun to fracture yet?” Darlene asked. “I haven’t heard about this Free Society or any unrest.”

Zina stood and begin to walk back and forth slowly. “There is always unrest in a Society of fifty thousand human worlds. A few planets declare independence from the Society each year. Fortunately, the lack of trade and insecurity always cause them to return after they get that extra taste of freedom out of their mouths.”

“Isn’t the Free Society a collection of worlds that are independent?” Bill asked.

“Oh no! The Free Society is a state of mind and an opinion about how the Society should change for all planets,” she replied. “There are a few hundred worlds that believe in those ambitions, like this one. The people here work behind the scenes to change public opinion and governmental policies in that direction. For the ideals of the Free Society to work, all the planets have to accept it, or the High Council has to impose it. The Free Society requires all the planets in a region to become a separate federation. Unless the leaders of the Free Society have control of all the planets in a region, they could never do it on their own. That is why Antar’s idea was always superior.”

“What is his idea?” Cybil asked.

"The Society of Humanity should break based on our races. For example, all Zu planets would form one federation, no matter where they were located. The other races would do the same. Since all the federations would be intermingled in space, the Society would maintain responsibility for defense and trade negotiations," Zina replied.

"Segregation by race seems extreme to people from the twenty-first, Zina," Darlene said. "Our Earth has dealt with those issues for all time."

"That is the one failing of the plan and why the Council could never agree to it," Zina said. "Antar recognized that but felt it was a bit different. On your world, all the races lived on the same planet. They were competing with each other. One race might think it was better than another. Here we are talking about entire planets. The Society has identified fifty different types of habitable planets. Each of our fifty races is specialized for one of those types. These races were not manufactured in a laboratory. They evolved naturally over generations. When we left Non-Ti, all humans were homogeneous. Some humans inhabited the first cold weather planet and over thousands of generations became Zu. Others found large hot planets with rich atmospheres and became Pa."

"So, it's evolutionary change," Bill said. "You're not saying one race is better, they are just better suited to a particular environment."

"You can teach your husband's lies well," a voice said on the other side of the room. They turned to see Wendo Balak, Serena Vanatee and ten armed guards just inside the door. "Antar spent much of his political career holding the Society together in spite of itself. We need the Free Society to allow a controlled dissolution before civil war and chaos does the job for us."

"Where is my husband, Wendo?" Zina demanded.

"Don't worry, Zina, he is safe for now," Wendo smirked. "I just want to chat with him in private first. Then I will return him to you."

"Sir, I am Darlene Webster, an ambassador from Earth," Darlene said. "I demand that you release us immediately."

"Please accept my apology, madam ambassador," Wendo replied. "I am Wendo Balak, President of the Free Society. I am shocked that my guards put you in this cell. They had specific orders to move you and your children to a wing of my palace in Pegat City, where you will be my guests."

"Mr. President, what we want to do is leave this place," she demanded.

"I'm afraid we cannot do that yet," Wendo replied. "The foolishness of General Zilma and some unrelated attacks on other systems have put us in a very difficult situation. It was our intention to invite your family here to show our people that the Pa species is a natural state for humanity. Now, we need you and the Arraks to keep the Society at bay while we utilize the Hive on this planet in order to ascertain who made those attacks on the other systems. Be assured we will give you and your children full access to Atar Pa while you are here. However, you cannot leave or contact anyone off this planet until I say so. We also require you to attend certain functions to be held in your honor."

"You are holding functions to honor your prisoners?" Bill asked.

"Don't be insolent son," Wendo snapped. "You are our guests and we will treat you well if you behave. The people of Aranar Zu were honored by your presence, and the Pa here will be thrilled to see their Pa ancestors."

"Your man shot my husband," Darlene interrupted. "You want me to be nice after that! You must be insane."

"Madam, please believe me. General Zilma's actions were wrong, and I have arrested him already. Thankfully, your husband was only stunned. My agents tell me that he and Loni have already returned safety to Tak-Makla. If you accept my hospitality now, in two days I will allow you to enter our Hive and see them for yourselves," Wendo replied. "As soon as it is feasible, I will release you all with our sincerest apologies."

"I don't know whether I believe him or not, but take the offer, Darlene," Zina said. "You have no choice anyway. I'll take care of Antar here."

"Aren't the Arraks going with us?" Bill asked.

Wendo smiled, "Not right now. I need to discuss the Free Society with Antar again. If I can convince him to join our cause, then we will all be together soon," Wendo said.

"I don't want to leave you here, Zina," Bill said.

"Don't be stupid, Bill. Get out of this place. It doesn't matter what happens to Antar or me. Don't worry about us. As long as I have Antar by my side, I will be happy," Zina smiled as a few tears slipped down her cheeks.

A group of guards led the Brewsters out of the room. As they left Bill looked back and saw Wendo and Serena sit next to Zina. One of the remaining two guards closed the door. After walking down a long corridor for ten minutes, they stopped at a door. The lead guard touched a small panel and a blue light illuminated his face. The door opened and the group entered a small tube room. Another guard with a large laser rifle stood inside. The shuttle in the room was much different from those on Tak-Makla or Hive 1008. It was metal with only small slit windows. The guard tapped a panel, which said, "Destination."

"Center City Main Tube Station," the guard said. The blue light illuminated his face again. The door of the shuttle opened revealing ten metal seats. "Please board and buckle yourselves in. This is a high security shuttle area so there is no panel inside. Once you are ready, I will activate the shuttle. It will take you to the tube station where some of Lord Balak's assistants will meet you. They will move you to another tube that will take you to the palace in Pegat City."

"This isn't some kind of trick, is it?" Cybil asked.

"One thing you learn on Atar Pa is that Lord Balak never lies," he responded. "If he said you are now a guest that is the truth. Right now, you are in a secure penal facility. Once you arrive at the tube station, you'll be outside where people can move around as they please. You won't see prison guards out there."

"What's your name, son?" Darlene asked.

"Bolo Narz, madam ambassador," he said and blushed a little.

"Thank you Bolo. Please call me Darlene. I hope to see you again under better circumstances," Darlene replied.

"Thank you, Darlene," he said. "Have a safe journey, and I hope you return home soon." They climbed on the shuttle and it darted out of the room.

Antar Arrak sat on the cold floor in absolute darkness. After he had been separated from his wife, the guards led him down several corridors past multiple security gates with armed soldiers guarding each. They passed through a reinforced steel door into a short corridor with doors along both sides. A door was opened and he was pushed inside. The guard told him to look around and closed the door. Immediately the lights were turned off and he was alone in the dark. He could remember a toilet and sink in the far corner of the ten by eight foot cell, but nothing else. He walked slowly until he could feel the wall and sat down on the floor, which was no simple task at his advanced age. He waited in the blackness for what seemed to be many hours. He wondered about Zina, hoping she was in better conditions than his cell. He could not understand why they had been kidnapped on the greatest day of his daughter's life. He had retired from politics more than one hundred years ago. He ran a small farm raising vegetables and producing cheese for the first forty of those years, until he became too weak to keep up the pace. His youngest sister and her husband took over for him and Antar and Zina moved to a nearby village. It did not make sense to kidnap an old man and his wife who lived simply in a small town.

The lights turned on suddenly. Antar covered his eyes with his hands to lessen the shock of the brilliant light. After a minute or two, he grew accustomed to the light and opened his eyes. Sitting not two feet in front of him was Wendo Balak who had served in the High Council at the same time as Antar. Two guards stood by the door, which stood open. He did not know why guards were needed. There was no risk of Antar trying to escape. He was old Zu on a planet of Pa. He would stick out like a sore thumb wherever he went. "Wendo, what is the meaning of all this?" Antar asked.

"Antar Arrak, I am pleased to see you too. It amazes me that we are both still alive. I'm almost nine hundred years old now," Wendo said. "How about you?"

"Nine hundred and fifteen, Wendo. But why am I here and where is Zina?" Antar pressed.

"Zina is fine, Antar. I just spoke with her not an hour ago," Wendo smiled. "My guards have moved her to more comfortable quarters here for the time being, where she is now waiting for you." He turned to the guards and said, "Please bring a good chair for my friend here. He is much too old to sit on the cold floor." One of the guards left. "Antar, I would like us to discuss the Free Society again. I am hopeful you might change your mind about it."

"You want to talk about the Free Society? Wendo, we both retired so long ago. I became a farmer until I was too weak to continue. Now I live in a small village, tending my garden and reading books of poetry most days. I haven't thought about the Free Society in a very long time, old friend," Antar replied.

"Zina seems to have it on the top of her mind, Antar. If you haven't discussed it, why is she so interested in it?" Wendo asked.

The guard returned with a chair and helped Antar off the floor and onto the chair. "Thank you, young man," he said to the guard. "You and I argued about the Free Society for many decades when we were on the High Council, Wendo. Once I realized the High Council would never make a decision, I gave up and retired. I think Zina could never let it go though. She thought you ruined my chances to be President of the High Council. Perhaps she was right, but after seeing how ineffective the Council was, I began to realize that I didn't want any part of it. Moving onto that farm was the most satisfying day of my life, until the day my daughter was born."

Wendo was looking irate with a flush coming to his cheeks. "Antar, you ruined my chance to be President too! I haven't forgotten or forgiven you for that."

Antar put his hand on Wendo's knee, saying, "Wendo, I am deeply sorry for that. When I was younger I believed all the Society's problems had a perfect solution. Perhaps I believed only my ideas were good enough. But I was a fool. When I recognized that my presence was part of the cause of their ineffectiveness, I knew I had to get out. Looking back on it now, I wish I would have left a term before you. Maybe the Council could have accomplished something."

Wendo looked confused. "So you now agree with the idea of the Free Society? You realize it was the right thing to do all along. Is that what you are saying, Antar?"

"No and yes, Wendo. If I were President of the Council today and could make a unilateral decision about how to split the Society, I would not choose the Free Society model. But that situation could never exist," Antar explained. "Your model is flawed. My model is flawed. There can never be a perfect model when imperfect humans are involved. If I had to choose between the Free Society and the current declining situation where no other options exist, I would strongly support the Free Society. Something needs to be done. If the current mess continues, ultimately the whole thing will fall to pieces."

"Antar, I am not certain how to reply. I have been angry for a long time. My people have been working to convince more planets to join our coalition. It has been slow, but progress occurs every day. We probably can rely on the support of five hundred planets right now. Unfortunately, they are spread throughout the Society, and they represent only one percent of the total," Wendo replied.

"I apologize again for your anger, old friend. Some days I wish I still had the fire to do things like that. Being President of Aranar Zu and on the High Council were wonderful days. Now, I like being a humble retiree living far from the spotlight," Antar said.

"Would you consider adding your voice to mine on this?" Wendo asked. "If we both speak positively about the Free Society, perhaps we can make real change happen now in our golden years."

"I don't think it will do any good, Wendo. It's been so long since I've been in the public eye. I doubt anyone remembers me any more. But if I do this for you, can we put the old animosity behind us?" Antar asked.

"Of course, old friend. I think you have more strength in the Zu community than you think. Please, will you and Zina come to my palace in Pegat City? I am holding a celebration tomorrow night, and that would be an excellent opportunity to showcase our new alliance," Wendo replied.

"There is the issue of the kidnapping to be considered, Wendo," Antar stated. "I'm not sure how that can been turned into a positive."

"True. Hopefully, Councilors Jeebo and Arnar can come up with a solution," Wendo said. "Kidnapping you and Zina was their idea. Thanks to the incompetence of General Zilma, I'm now being blamed for the shooting of Admiral Brewster and kidnapping his family. I don't know why, but the Free Society is also being blamed for attacks on two other systems."

"Friend, I will gladly speak favorably about the Free Society, but those other issues are over my head," Antar said.

"Let us leave this place together, Antar," Wendo said. "My shuttle will take us to Pegat City much quicker than tubes. I will have a suite of rooms prepared for you and Zina. After you both freshen up, perhaps we can dine with my granddaughter and the Councilors and pass that assignment on to them."

"Speaking of Admiral Brewster, whatever happened to the Brewster family, Wendo?" Antar asked.

"They are already on their way to Pegat City. I have set aside a wing of my palace for them. Somehow, we must get them to support whatever story we come up with," Wendo replied.

Antar put his arm on Wendo's shoulder. "That will be a difficult job, old friend."

Arto Umbly was delighted to help out the tekkan Hive while Loni Arrak visited her family and received an award for finding the lost human tribe from Earth 47. Arto had rarely meet non-Zu humans, no less a completely alien culture. He had been briefed about tekkans by Chief Engineer Lina Aderal of Hive 1008 who joined him on this mission. He was a bit shocked when he met a tekkan face to face though.

Arto and Lina jumped directly into the office of Chief Engineer Nit Valasan, at the base of The Hive. Nit greeted them warmly and offered them some food and drink. One by one, the engineers who worked behind the scenes of The Hive came in and were introduced to the two who would take Loni's place for a few days. After shaking more than a hundred insect-like hands and learning their names and faces, he began to view them more as coworkers than tall translucent spiders. The control panels were refreshingly similar to those on human Hives so his confidence in his ability to handle this assignment rose.

After the meet and greet session and a leisurely lunch, the three Chief Engineers took a tour of the power systems of The Hive. The huge towers of computer banks and HVAC equipment were modeled after human Hives. The control panels were similar to others he had seen, but were modified to allow the tekkans to use more than two arms and hands. As with all engineers working in Hives, Arto had been taught about the building of the Tak-Makla Hive many generations ago. The friendship between the cultures continued to the current day. The tekkan Hive was a crucial tool to help mankind stretch back into this galaxy. It formed an anchor point for Universal Power in the galaxy so other Hives could pinpoint jumping locations. While planets were being settled, the Hive was an important reference marker between this galaxy and the home galaxy. The value of The Hive had declined in recent years since other human Hives were now online, but the bonds of friendship and trade remained as strong as ever.

After the tour, Nit took the human engineers to the Earth 47 Ambassador's residence on the surface. That site had become a comfortable and convenient gathering spot for non-tekkans who visited the planet. One wing of the mansion was set aside for Ambassador Brewster and her close associates. The rest of the residence was open for others. Before he left for his home, Nit told them he would return at 0700 tomorrow to put them to work in The Hive. Kally Karsen welcomed them to the embassy and showed them their rooms. He invited them to share dinner with the other guests in the residence in one hour.

An hour later, Kally led Arto and Lina into the library of the residence. Already in the room were three humans and one tekkan having cocktails and conversing happily. Kally introduced the two engineers to Charlie and Aria Watson, Mencius the Kalidean and High Consul Zee Gongaleg.

"My dear friends," Zee said, "it is wonderful that you have come to take Loni Arrak's place for a few days. I must warn you that you have big shoes to fill. She has been the rock of our Hive for many years. Lina, I heard you were running the Hive on Hive 1008 when the Donnaki attacked it with their new weapon system. That must have been a frightful experience."

"Yes, Consul, it was shocking they could have developed such a weapon system," she replied. "The technology we found seemed far beyond their level of development."

"Lina, do you have any idea how they developed it?" Aria asked. "Does the Society of Humanity have similar weapons?"

"No, but we will soon," Lina said. "If we want to continue growth in this galaxy, we need to be able to face those weapons as some point. At least they don't seem to have Hive technology since they were unable to stop my agents from jumping their crews off the ships. I shudder to think what an enemy would do if they could jump a ball of plasma like that onto a planet full of people."

"We have worked on similar devices in the past," Mencius remarked. "We were never able to create a stable plasma ball and ultimately had to cancel the project. Fortunately our alliance was able to stop the Predaxians with normal weaponry."

"Mencius, I was not aware of any Opa systems in this galaxy," Arto said.

Mencius laughed, "Well, I wasn't aware that I was an Opa. I am from the Kalidean Federation which covers ten thousand planets in this galaxy. What exactly is an Opa?"

Arto blushed, and continued, "I didn't mean to offend you sir. The Opa are one of the fifty species of humans in the Society of Humanity. You look exactly like them."

"Please don't be concerned, and do call me Mencius. My friend, Dave Brewster has told me that humanity came to this galaxy long ago and established planets," Mencius continued.

"If Kalidus was originally populated by Opa from your galaxy, we will need to correct a lot of our history records. How many Opa worlds are there in the Society?"

"Around five hundred, Mencius," Lina replied. "They are one of the smallest groups in our galaxy. If your culture has ten thousand, the Opa have gone from bottom to top in the few minutes I've known you."

Kally interrupted the group and asked them to follow him to the dining room as dinner was to be served momentarily. The group rose and headed out of the room. After the last person left, Kally returned to close the door. For a moment, he thought he saw some movement, but when he looked again, the room was empty. He closed the door and walked away with his guests.

Three maklans appeared on the ceiling of the room. They were quite different from the other species known, with slightly green glass-like skin and bright blue eyes. They had two sets of legs that had developed into arms with hands and opposable thumbs. One set of legs was heavy and long to allow them to stand on two feet. Their bodies were elongated and three feet in length. They had large dragon-fly double wings which shimmered in the light in a range of hues. They moved together until they were touching each other in a tight circle.

"Okay team, give me your reports," Awl Porto thought.

"Captain, we have managed to relocate our devices into The Hive," Ensign Eel Valak reported. "We will be ready at the appointed hour."

"Captain, I have heard that our fleet is approaching the valakar system. They should launch their attack on schedule,"

Lieutenant Oul Zeel said. "Our ship is fully shielded and will be ready to jump us out five seconds before detonation."

"Eel, how many troops do we have in The Hive at this time?" Awl thought.

"Nearly two thousand sir. It will take another three hours before we are ready to act," Eel replied. "Most of our troops will evacuate one hour before detonation."

"That's great news! It looks like we will be right on time." Awl looked around the room quickly. "I keep getting the feeling we are being watched. How about you two?"

"Don't worry, Captain, it's just a case of nerves," Eel said. "We'll be off this world soon and headed back to Maklakar space. We'll all be sleeping in our own beds in a few days. We should all get medals for this mission! By deactivating this Hive, we can keep these maklans from surpassing our technology."

"I know. I was raised to remember Paxran too. When those traitors destroyed our society, we learned our military and technology were the only things that could keep us safe from others in our species. We all saw the video of that planet this Hive destroyed. Even our plasma bombs can't compete with weaponry like that!" Awl thought.

"Captain, I'm getting that funny feeling about being watched too," Oul said. "We'd better get out of here just in case!" The three maklans glowed brightly and disappeared.

The ribbons of light from Bill and Cybil Brewster spun around each other in the room. A third from Serena Vanatee pulsed nearby. "You saw all that right?" Serena said.

"So, the Maklakar were behind the bombing on Tak-Makla?" Bill asked. "I thought they were wiped out long ago."

"Apparently some survived and built new worlds. It looks like their military technology is far beyond ours," Serena replied. "I think we need to see the whole event though. Follow me and we'll go a few hours forward." Their lights twisted about each other and fell into a black tunnel. After a few minutes of blackness, they reappeared deep inside The Hive.

The clock on Nit Valasan's desk read 0330. The door flew open and Nit, Lina and Arto entered the room. "I'm sorry for interrupting your sleep, but I have been getting odd readings from the core since around midnight," Nit began. "The power levels are jumping around all over the place. I've called in some agents to help check things out. I've never seen readings like these before."

"Wow!" Lina agreed. "The Hive is in sleep mode, isn't it?"

"Of course, Lina. At this hour only the maintenance crew is here. Let me contact their supervisor to get a report," Nit replied. He pushed a button on his control panel to summon the shift leader. After a minute with no response, he pressed the contact again.

"This looks like a power imbalance to me," Arto said. "They are very rare and usually occur when other systems are accidentally tied into The Hive's grid. I'll go check it out." Arto ran out the door into the darkened maze of machines.

"We may be forced to take The Hive offline, Nit," Lina said.

"That should be a last resort, Lina. The Hive is our only defense system for Tak-Makla. Until we can be certain we are not being breached in some way, The Hive must stay on," he replied.

"Perhaps some agents should enter The Hive and check nearby space for intruders? If you think there might be a threat, it's the logical thing to do," Lina said.

"I've already summoned fifty thousand agents to do that. They should be here in the next few minutes. I'm stationing them at the top of The Hive in case there is more trouble down here," Nit replied.

"That's wise, Nit." Lina noticed motion on one of the monitors. "I thought I saw something moving in the dark on this monitor," she said.

"Probably just Arto or one of the mechanics," Nit noted as he continued to watch the system monitors.

Arto used his lantern to light the area in front of him. The Hive was very quiet when the systems were in sleep mode, and that made the power fluctuations seems even stranger. He thought he sensed motion just out of the range of his light, but as he moved forward, he found only the machines. He was nearing the central core now and raced toward it. He quickly turned a corner and tripped, falling to the ground. He sat for a moment to catch his breath and rub his shoulder and hip that had taken the brunt of the fall. He turned to look where he had tripped and saw a maklan leg sticking out from beneath a computer rack. He crawled to it and pulled the dead body out into the corridor. He recognized the body as one of the engineers he had met earlier that day.

"We've got a big problem out here," Arto said as he clicked on his com-link.

"What is it, Arto?" Lina asked.

"I just tripped over the body of one of Nit's engineers. It looks like he was suffocated. Send some agents over here to investigate," Arto replied.

"Just wait there, Arto, help will be there soon," Nit said.

"I can't wait. I just heard more noises just ahead. It sounded like a door closing. I'll go investigate," Arto said as he climbed to his feet. He held his lantern in front of him and ran toward the sound. After he turned another corner, a large metal door blocked his path. He knew this type of door should mark the edge of The Hive. Typically, these doors are heavily secured, but this one stood slightly ajar.

He tried to look through the open slit, but could see only darkness. He pulled the door open slowly and stepped through. He was in a small hallway about twenty feet long. A second door with several magnetic locks was at the other end of the hallway. He moved forward quickly. He raised his lantern to examine the locks. All of them were badly burned. He pulled slightly on the door which cracked open slightly. There was no alarm although this was the most sensitive part of The Hive. He heard movement on the other side of the door and closed it softly. He whispered into his com-link, "Lina, there's been a breach on the exterior wall of The Hive. I can hear activity on the other side, but no voices. Whoever did this has already killed at least one maklan. I have to imagine that the Hive may be hit very soon. Please have Nit evacuate."

"Understood, Arto. Nit insists that some agents review nearby space first in case there is an invasion fleet. This Hive is their only defense. Get back here quickly, Arto," she pleaded.

"There's too much at stake for that, Lina. I've got to check out what's happening out there. The Hive could be full of explosives set to go any second," Arto said. "I'd rather die out here trying to stop it rather than sitting helplessly there. Send as many guards as possible to my coordinates!"

Arto turned off his lantern and sat quietly until his eyes were more accustomed to the darkness. He set his com-link to send sounds from his side but not accept inbound sounds. He pulled the door open very slowly, trying to avoid making any noise whatsoever. Pale greenish light partially illuminated the exterior of The Hive. He stood with his back flat against the wall of The Hive and moved slowly in the direction of the light. After twenty feet or so, the wall was blocked by massive bundles that seemed to rise a hundred feet over his head.

He stood with his back against the bundles and moved forward. After another thirty feet, he could see a group of several hundred Beings standing in formation. When he saw them, his first instinct was to see spiders, but these creatures were bipedal and wearing military uniforms. The group of soldiers closest to him glowed brightly and disappeared. Suddenly, he could see his badge start to glow bright red. He turned his back to the soldiers to shield the badge. The red light was a signal that explosive material was nearby. He had to warn the others and started to move back to the door. He reached the door to open it when it flew open and Arto was face to face with one of the spiders. Before he could think, the spider pulled a blaster from his belt and shot Arto in the chest. He fell back onto the hard floor. Several other troops saw the shot and rushed to the scene.

"How did this human get this far?" Captain Awl Porto said as he returned his blaster to his belt.

"I have no idea, Captain," Lieutenant Oul Zeel replied. "Someone was supposed to guard those doors."

"It doesn't matter, Oul," Awl said. "Almost everyone has jumped back to the ship and nothing can stop the countdown now. Let's go."

"Captain, I have an idea," Oul said. "The human is only stunned. Why don't we take it with us?"

"We don't need any humans, Oul. Don't be ridiculous," Awl laughed.

"Captain, since our agents have been on Tak-Makla, we've learned that humans helped them build the device," Oul reasoned. "Perhaps this human can be convinced to teach us the secrets of this machine. This is one technology where humanity is far ahead of us."

"Well, you might be right, Oul. If we leave the human here, it will die in the explosion. If we take it and can convince it to help us, we could surpass all races in the galaxy. And if it doesn't help us, we can kill it anyway," Awl said.

"Exactly, sir," Oul smiled. "I'll have a couple of my men jump it to our brig."

"On the double, Oul. The whole thing will blow in two minutes," Awl said as he walked away. Two soldiers rushed forward and carried Arto with them to their formation. Immediately the last group of maklans disappeared, leaving the exterior of the Hive lifeless.

"Okay, Serena, you were right," Bill thought as Serena's light twisted about his. "We will support Lord Balak's evidence that Maklakars attacked The Hive."

"Thank you both," Serena thought. "The idea that my grandfather would do such a horrible thing is ridiculous. Now, we should leave before the explosion since that will have a serious impact on Universal Power." The three lights sped out of space-time and back to The Hive on Atar Pa.

A few seconds later, the wall of explosives detonated, vaporizing the outer layers of The Hive. The core was breached and a rocket of molten radioactive material shot through the control rooms and into the lower levels of The Hive, killing anyone in the area instantly.

When the blast reached the center of The Hive, it moved straight up toward the sky, destroying most of the chambers in the first two rings and damaging more. By the time the blast reached the surface, most of the energy had already been spent. The dome covering the opening was shattered and the pieces plunged downward into the toxic smoke and fires that now filled The Hive.

The areas within a hundred miles of The Hive felt violent earthquakes. Hundreds of buildings shook and groaned under the impact. The footings of several failed and entire blocks of businesses and residences crumbled and fell toward the center of the planet. Tsunamis surged across several oceans and rock and snow avalanches filled the mountains. Ten minutes after the initial explosion, an eerie calm descended on Tak-Makla, followed immediately by the sirens of first responders.

Charlie Watson was flying across the room, tumbling head over feet. He landed on the stone floor and groaned in pain. Aria jumped onto him and slashed at his throat with her Ullu. She stood victorious and raised her arms over her head.

De-o-Nu laughed, "Very good Aria! But you are supposed to use your Nak for slashing. The Ullu is for throwing and the Falon is for stabbing. You've got to remember the details if you want to be a Gallicean warrior."

Charlie sat up where he was and added, "And try to throw me onto a mat next time, sweetheart. The stone floors here are hard on my old back."

She bent over and kissed Charlie on the forehead. "I'm sorry Charlie. I guess I just got carried away by the excitement." She helped him to his feet and they walked over to a bench against the wall of the gymnasium and sat down. "Okay, De-o-Nu, show us how to do it right!"

De-o-Nu and Dave Brewster circled each other in the middle of the mat. Both held their Nak and Falon blades in their hands, and made threatening gestures to each other. "Remember, brother, no flying," Dave said.

"There are no rules in battle, brother," De-o-Nu laughed. "But you remember how to tell if I am about to fly, don't you?" The Gallicean stepped back slightly and stood very straight.

"You will step backward and stand up straight," Dave replied, hunching over slightly more. "Then you will switch from the Falon to the Ullu."

"Very good, brother," De-o-Nu smiled. After a movement almost too quick to see, De-o-Nu now had his Ullu in his right hand. He jumped up and extended his wings and began to circle the room at fifteen feet off the ground. "Now what do you do, friend?"

Dave tumbled across the floor to gain some separation from De-o-Nu, while switching the Nak in his hand for his Ullu. He crouched down and then launched himself toward De-o-Nu and threw the Ullu. The Ullu hit De-o-Nu in his forehead and he tumbled to the ground. Dave jumped onto the Gallicean's chest and stabbed him in the chest with the Falon.

"Ah, you got me, Dave," De-o-Nu laughed. "That was really excellent! Unfortunately, the hilt of the Ullu hit me in the forehead. If I had been wearing battle armor, it would have bounced off. You are supposed to have the blade strike my wings to knock me out of the sky. But for three days of practice, I must say you are all doing wonderfully."

Dave helped De-o-Nu to his feet. "Thanks for the vote of confidence, brother. Of course, on any other planet, you'd be more than three times this size, so I doubt I could have done that well," Dave replied.

"That's true, Dave, but you will never face a Gallicean in combat anyway," De-o-Nu said. "We are your most loyal allies. The tools you are learning will help you if other species try to attack. I imagine you could have defeated the three humans who attacked your family on Aranar Zu with these blades, if they were sharpened, of course."

"Well, I don't know if I could have beaten them all, but I wouldn't have been taken by surprise so easily," Dave replied. "This has been a wonderful distraction from that event, old friend. Thank you for that."

De-o-Nu patted Dave on the back, "You are quite welcome, brother." He walked to another bench and picked up a golden tray with four glasses, a large gold basin and a bottle of Gallicean whisky and returned to the group. He set the tray on the bench next to Charlie and Aria. "Glory to Greater Gallia." He set the four glasses in the basin. "Glory to Earth and her colonies." He opened the bottle and poured into each glass until it overflowed into the basin. "May God bless our friendship." He took a glass and raised it. The others took a glass and raised them to touch De-o-Nu's. "And may God bring Dave's family back to him soon." They drank as much of the whisky as they could and poured any remnants into the basin. "Though we pray we will never need them again, may God bless our weapons." Each of them placed their daggers into the pool of whisky, with the Nak first, the Falon second, and the Ullu last. De-o-Nu held the basin over his head and moved it around in a circle. Then he placed it back on the bench. Each took a towel from the tray and wiped the weapons of the others. Tonight, Dave cleaned Aria's daggers; Charlie cleaned De-o-Nu's; De-o-Nu cleaned Dave's; and Aria cleaned Charlie's.

After the blessing ceremony, the group returned to their rooms to clean up and then joined Consul Zee at his residence next door for dinner. Each of the last three days, large memorial services had been held around the planet for those who died in the attack on The Hive. Zee was traveling around the planet continually and consoling his people. He had not returned until late this evening. Since there had been no notification, Dave believed tonight would be a quiet dinner. As he approached the

Consul's residence, he could see several hundred humans and tekkans mingling by the beach.

As he saw them approaching, Zee left the crowd and rushed toward Dave's group. When he reached them, he threw his arms around Dave and hugged him. "Dave, the most wonderful things have happened. Come on all of you and join our dinner celebration." As they joined the crowd, they saw a long table with dozens of whisky bottles near the beach. Behind the table, Minister of State Fak Mondoka was pouring drinks for the guests. De-o-Nu left Dave and went to greet Fak. She smiled broadly when she saw the Gallicean approach. Dave thought about joining them, but Zee pulled him in a different direction.

As Zee and Dave approached, two Zu turned to face them. "Dave, it's good to see you again," said President Jo Bango of Aranar Zu. "I'm certain you remember Governor Alin Lonk of Hive 1008?"

"I must say you look much better than the last time I saw you, Admiral Brewster," Alin smiled as he shook Dave's hand.

"This is quite a surprise to see you two on Tak-Makla," Dave said. "What is the occasion?"

"Not now, Dave," Zee interrupted. "We will explain everything in a minute after the crowd is seated. But I can tell you again that it is wonderful and shocking news! Please, my friends, let's find our places at the table." After Dave's team had arrived, the waiters began directing the crowd to their seats. By the time Dave and Zee arrived at the head table, everyone else was seated. Zee motioned for Dave to sit next to him. Dave was surprised to see several empty chairs across the table. De-o-Nu hurried to sit between Dave and Loni Arrak.

He brought three glasses full of ice and two bottles of Nanda whisky. He opened one and poured into their glasses. He placed the second on the floor.

"My fellow tekkans and human friends," Zee began, "It is my distinct pleasure to welcome you all to my humble home. As we all know, this week began with a great tragedy for our planet and for our dear friends, Admiral Brewster and Chief Engineer Arrak. These attacks not only devastated this planet, but also threatened to break the Society of Humanity into pieces. I am happy to report tonight that the Society is safe and our relationship with mankind is as strong as ever." The crowd erupted in applause.

Dave touched Zee on the arm and said, "I don't understand Zee. What has changed?"

Zee whispered, "Please trust me, Dave. This speech has a very happy ending, but I must be on schedule." Zee turned back to the crowd and continued, "Early this morning, the human planet Hive 1008 entered the Tak-Makla system. Based on a communication from the planet Atar Pa, several human and tekkan agents used Hive 1008 to visit our Hive in the hours and minutes before the explosions. We have conclusive evidence that humans did not cause the destruction on this planet. Humans also did not attempt to attack the Hives in the Nom-Kat-La system in Gallicean space."

De-o-Nu grabbed Dave's arm and said, "Dave, what is this all about? I haven't been advised about any of this."

"I don't know either, brother," Dave replied. "We better just listen and see what happens next."

"Our agents have seen firsthand that a maklan species called the Maklakar were behind this heinous act. Many of you know the history of the Maklakar. They traded fairly with us for millions of solar cycles until the dreaded Paxran destroyed their civilization. Until today, we thought they had been eliminated from history. Now we know they have found other planets and still exist, although we do not know why they have chosen to attack us." The crowd murmured about the change in events. Confusion was taking over the evening. "Quiet please! Quiet please!" Zee shouted. "I need to complete my remarks quickly now." Relative quiet returned. "I have also spoken to Lord Wendo Balak of the planet Atar Pa. His planet has one functional Hive and a second under construction. He has offered to give us as much of the equipment in their second Hive as we need to rebuild ours." The crowd cheered. "He has also told me about the mistakes made by some of his people that led to the kidnapping of Admiral Brewster's family and Chief Engineer Arrak's parents. He has incarcerated General Zilma who shot Dave and took his family. He will turn the culprits over to Society authorities for punishment. He has also recommended that two High Councilors of the Society be terminated due to their actions in this matter."

"What does this all mean?" Dave asked Zee again.

"Just a few more seconds, Dave," Zee pleaded. He looked at his watch and waited. Time seemed to slow to a near stop. After ten more seconds, Zee said, "I give you our guests for the evening," and pointed to the stairs to the beach. Without a sound or flash, Wendo Balak, Serena Vanatee, Antar and Zina Arrak, and Darlene, Bill and Cybil Brewster appeared on the beach. The crowd jumped to their feet cheering and applauding. Dave and Loni rushed to the stairs to greet their families, followed closely by De-o-Nu, Charlie and Aria.

"Thank God you're safe," Dave cried as he held his family. "Were you treated well? Did you hear about the Maklakars? I've missed you so much."

"We're fine now, honey," Darlene replied. "I'm so glad you're okay too. When I saw General Zilma shoot you, I thought you were lost to me forever."

High Consul Gongaleg's office was crowded. He opened the wall to the shuttle ramp to let more fresh air into the room. Dave and Darlene Brewster sat holding hands next to Zee. Across the table sat Wendo Balak, Serena Vanatee, Governor Lonk and President Bango. Antar and Loni Arrak sat on the other side of Zee. Two of the Consul's assistants roamed the room providing coffee and refreshments to the group. The door opened and High Commissioner Fa-a-Di and Ambassador De-o-Nu entered along with Mencius of Kalidus and Minister of State Fak Mondoka.

"Good morning to you all," Zee began. "It appears that everyone is here now. For those of you who were able to join us for dinner last night, I hope you enjoyed yourselves. I can tell you that the arrival of the Brewsters and Arraks was a magical moment for me. Since the devastation of the Maklakar attack, I had wondered if I could ever be happy again. When they appeared, my heart was filled with joy."

"It was a perfect evening, Consul," De-o-Nu responded. "You and Minister Mondoka were gracious hosts. But let us get to the matters at hand."

"Ah, yes," Zee sighed, "we are here to discuss how to deal with the Maklakar. As I have told Admiral Brewster, we tekkans are not militaristic. We built Tak-Makla so that we would learn more about Universal Power and expand our trading networks. That is why we formed the alliance with your federations. We can provide intelligence through our agents in The Hive, while you provide security for us. Given that, I don't think I should be leading a discussion on possible actions against the Maklakar."

"Your point is well taken, Zee," Mencius replied. "All of our races have had violent pasts, but we have changed too. It is only when we are attacked that our old instincts come back and violent actions may be required. Wouldn't you agree, General Fa-a-Di?"

"Of course, Mencius," Fa-a-Di said. "We all want peace, but sometimes others will not accept it. We can all remember the Predaxian wars. Although Emperor Zendo was a fool to attack us, I could understand his motivation. The Predaxian leadership had become paranoid about other species attempting to depose them. They came to believe the only way to avoid an attack was to attack others. These Maklakar have me stumped. We don't know where they are or what they want. They caused incredible damage to The Hive here and we can't understand how they were able to do it. They launched a tepid attack on Nom-Kat-La that had no chance of success. It's very confusing."

"Brother, perhaps I can help out," Darlene said. "While we were guests on Atar Pa, Lord Balak allowed Bill, Cybil and me to join The Hive on that planet. We saw the attack on Tak-Makla first hand. At our request, Wendo had his agents focus on finding Maklakar worlds. Serena here is the Chief Engineer on the Atar Pa Hive. Perhaps she can provide more details."

"It would be a pleasure, Ambassador," Serena answered. "Once we resolved the issues of the apparent kidnappings of the Brewsters and Arraks, I ordered all agents in our Hive to work solely on finding Maklakar worlds. It turned out to be a simple task. Cybil Brewster suggested that a large number of agents view the attack on this Hive. They followed the

Maklakar when they jumped out to their ships. Then they simply rode those ships back to their bases. Frankly, what they found was terrifying."

Serena rose and began to walk around the table. "The Maklakar inhabit fifty planets on the outer fringe of this side of the galaxy, probably twenty thousand light years from here. When the Paxran invaded their space and began to destroy their worlds, they vowed to find a safe place to rebuild where the Paxran could never find them again. The Maklakar had always been great merchants and manufacturers of high quality goods. Now they were too afraid to form alliances with any other species. They believed any trading relationship could expose their location to the Paxran. Instead they focused only on internal and military development."

Zee asked, "Serena, when we traded with the Maklakar long ago, they told us they were developing a technology similar to our Hives. Did your agents see anything like that?"

"None, Zee. However, it was clear they kidnapped Chief Engineer Arto Umbly in order to learn more about that technology," Serena replied. "Fortunately for all of us, Arto attempted to escape and was shot dead while the ships were still near Tak-Makla."

"Not so fortunate for Mr. Umbly, I'm afraid," Loni sighed. "I trained to be a Chief Engineer with Arto. I can't believe they did that to an unarmed man."

"Loni, I know how you must feel," Serena replied. "But Arto did not die that way. He actually disarmed one of the Maklakars and killed ten others before they shot him. He was a brave man for facing impossible odds like that. Clearly, he knew what they wanted from him and he would never have allowed that to happen.”

“What did your agents learn about the Maklakar's military capabilities, Serena?” Fa-a-Di asked. “I'm still stunned by the strength of the attack here and the feebleness of the attack on Nom-Kat-La.”

“My team put together a video on that, General. We are able to record much of what we see on our trips in our Hive. It might be more helpful to see rather than listen to my words,” Serena answered. Zee tapped a button on his control panel and the open wall closed and a large screen slipped from its place in the ceiling.

“Team 157 report, Atar Pa Hive, Agent Volli Naza speaking,” said a voice. “Our team has been examining the planet Oti-Makla for several days.” The screen showed a large terrestrial planet with one large continent surrounded by large oceans. Dozens of large star cruisers were stationed in orbit. “This planet serves as the hub for the Maklakar civilization. The current leader, Supreme General Ulon Porto runs the society from his residence in the capital city of Oti-La. We have learned that the General's grandson, Captain Awl Porto led the raid on Tak-Makla. Much of the success of that raid was due to the advanced Maklakar shielding technology. Those ships updated with this technology are almost invisible to sensor detection. This technological advance is new and only about ten percent of their fleet has it. Pay particular attention to this ship in your view.” A pointer was aimed at a large cruiser in the middle of a group of five others. After a moment, the ship began to fade and completely disappeared from the screen after five seconds. Fifteen seconds later, it appeared again. “You have just seen the Maklakar testing a new installation of this shielding system.”

"That is amazing," De-o-Nu gasped. "How can they do that? Is there no heat signature at least?"

Serena stopped the presentation. "From what we've seen, the sensor block is almost perfect," she replied. "The level of detection is well below the noise level that our systems currently ignore. If we tuned our system to detect them, every bit of space debris or a random gamma ray would set them off continually. These ships are invisible."

"What else have you learned, Serena?" Fa-a-Di asked.

"General, have you been briefed on the plasma bomb technology found on the Donnaki fleet by Hive 1008?" she asked. He nodded. "The Maklakar invented that as well. It seems they gave that technology to the Donnaki."

"Why in Heaven's name would they do that?" Fa-a-Di shouted. "Those crazy creatures can take over half the galaxy with that."

"The Maklakar know the Donnaki and Paxran empires are rivals. What better way to weaken the ones who destroyed the Maklakar civilization than to give a superior weapon to their worst enemy?" Serena responded. "Now it is possible for the Maklakar to get their final revenge without doing any fighting. The Donnaki will kill the Paxran for them."

"But won't the Donnaki attack others and perhaps even the Maklakar with that technology?" Dave asked.

"Unfortunately for us, the Maklakar don't care about us," Wendo said. "They yearn only to be left alone. If that weapon is used to kill trillions of others, they say so be it."

"The plasma bomb is not new technology for the Maklakar, Dave," Serena interrupted. "It has a serious weakness the Maklakar discovered long ago. They have rectified that problem and now have better systems."

"What weakness?" De-o-Nu asked.

"When we were attacked on Hive 1008, our first reaction was to flee," Governor Lonk said. "We were in their space and did not want an intergalactic incident. To his benefit, General Zilma figured out the weakness shortly after we disabled the Donnaki fleet. The plasma bomb is very unstable until it is launched toward its target. If your ship is being attacked by such a weapon, you only need to fire at the ball while it is developing. That will cause it to explode with the force traveling backward to the attacking ships. Audy calculated that if we had done that, the explosion would have disabled or destroyed half of the Donnaki fleet."

"The weapon is as dangerous to the shooter as the target," Fa-a-Di laughed. "Still, the Donnaki could destroy hundreds of Paxran ships before they figure that out. How did the Maklakar correct that problem?"

Serena walked around the table and stopped behind Zee. She touched a button and said, "Advance to stop 15." The picture changed to a longer distance view of the planet Oti-Makla. A small metallic moon orbited precariously close to the planet. "This is their solution. It is a manufactured moon, approximately one thousand miles in diameter. It is basically a battle station. It houses two hundred thousand soldiers, ten star cruisers and five hundred star fighters. It also contains ten plasma bomb systems. The plasma balls develop completely within the planetoid. They only fire out when they are stable. If you were to shoot at the plasma bomb after it is launched, there is a chance it would explode. However, even if it did, there would be no pulse back into the station."

"My God," Zee said. "That is the most horrifying weapon of war I have ever seen. How many of those systems do the Maklakar have?"

"We have found only five," Serena replied. "However, we heard plans to have a total fleet of twenty. The good news is their plan is to use them to protect their frontiers only. The bad news is they would be unstoppable if they chose to invade."

"I'm not clear how they penetrated to the heart of The Hive without us knowing. Couldn't our agents see their ship or their actions on our planet?" Fak asked.

"The Maklakar ships were stationed ten light-years from Tak-Makla," Serena said. "Apparently, they have the technology to jump troops and other materials from that distance. So, we have a sphere with a radius of ten light-years. That's over four thousand cubic light-years. With the smaller agent force during the night, the odds of finding a few ships in that much space is very small. Also, the ships were shielded. It is possible the Maklakar have a portable shielding system that accompanied their soldiers."

"But why attack us?" Zee asked. "We were their friends for a very long time. We have never done anything to hurt them."

"I don't know for certain," Serena said. "It seems clear the Maklakar are frightened of the technology in a Hive. This Hive is the closest to their space. They may also know of your relationship with these other Beings who are not as passive as the tekkans."

"That brings us back to Nom-Kat-La," Fa-a-Di said. "If these Maklakar are afraid of Hives, then why did they send an inferior force to attack my planets? We have two Hives under construction, and I must admit we Galliceans are not the most friendly-looking creatures."

"We haven't found that out yet, General," Serena admitted. "I believe they underestimated the Galliceans. Remember that the Maklakar are xenophobic. Your race has never had any interaction with them. Their fear of the Paxran probably extends to other maklan races like the tekkans. To them, your species is another race of inferior valakars, like the Donnaki."

"They know better than that now!" Fa-a-Di exclaimed. "Even though I am proud of my military, our victory now frightens me. Perhaps the Maklakar will try to attack again with one of those battle stations. I don't know if our civilization would survive such an attack."

"Clearly, the danger level for all of our societies had been ratcheted up several notches," Mencius said. "None of us are in a position to oppose such a threat. It's astonishing to me that the Maklakar would attack without provocation. I suppose I can understand their desire for vengeance against the Paxran and their fear of Hive technology. But that does not excuse them for attacking Tak-Makla, Nom-Kat-La or any other peaceful planet."

Antar Arrak rose and stood behind Wendo Balak. "Dear friends, we want you to know the Society of Humanity is behind you. Wendo and I will be traveling to the home galaxy soon to meet with the High Council. We have already advised them about this threat and the weapons available to the Maklakar. The Society has committed to retrofitting ten Hive planetoids to have weapons and shielding systems similar to the Maklakar battle stations. Those planetoids will be moved to this galaxy to provide protection."

Wendo rose and said, "As you may know, we are about to change the organization of the Society into what I have always called the Free Society. All of the Society planets in this galaxy will form a new federation. The Society will still survive, but it will have a much more limited role. We have discussed the possibility of adding all of your worlds to the local federation, regardless of species. If that happens, our first priority will be to build an additional twenty battle-ready Hive planetoids. We believe that will be enough to stop the Maklakar, Paxran or Donnaki from attacking any of us."

"That is an interesting idea, Wendo, but how can a federation of humans expect to manage Galliceans or Predaxians or Palians?" Fa-a-Di asked.

"I understand your concern, General," Wendo replied, "but I think you miss the core values of the Free Society. Each planet has its rights and its society. The Gallicean worlds can maintain almost full autonomy. Even though the Kalideans are human, they can do the same. That's why it is called the Free Society. All worlds have a voice in the overall management of the federation. Votes are based on population. Each individual gets to vote. If the majority of Beings are human, it is likely a human would be elected President of the federation, but not necessarily. As of now, I would say the first President would likely come from the Kalideans, since they have the largest group of worlds."

"The federation is more about defense, intercultural relations and trade," Antar said. "I encourage many of you to join us on this trip. Representatives from each group of planets need to decide how they wish to run their societies, as part of the federation or not. If Greater Gallia or the Kalidean Federation chooses not to join our federation, we can still have mutual defense treaties and trade."

Wendo continued, "This is an opportunity to put our divisions behind us and join together. Our federation will provide security and prosperity for thousands of generations. Darlene told me about the treaty Earth 47 made with Greater Gallia for planet sharing. I thought that was marvelous. That type of thing would become the norm in our federation. We would all be brothers."

"I don't know if my old body could survive traveling to another galaxy in a pressure suit," Fa-a-Di said.

"General, we can take care of that," Alin Lonk replied. "We don't have the technology the tekkans use to let you survive here. However, Hive 1008 is a space ship, and therefore has many sections that can be closed off in case of hull failure. We can isolate one small section and provide the correct atmosphere for your team. When you wish to travel to other parts of the ship, you only need a facemask to provide air. Do you think that will be acceptable?"

"That will be fine, thank you. How long will all of this take?" Fa-a-Di asked. "I wouldn't pass such an important assignment to anyone else, but I have my own civilization to run."

"It will take a few days to organize enough Hives to transport Hive 1008 back to the home galaxy," Alin said. "We will stay here until that time. We will also prepare quarters for all the teams during that time. You can arrange for your teams to come here in the next three or four days. I am guessing the meetings there will go on for a week or two. Once that's over, we'll come right back."

"But how long does it take to make the trip?" Darlene asked. "It's two million light-years away, after all."

"It really takes no time at all, Darlene," Alin replied. "The trip is just another jump into a wormhole. It will seem longer inside the wormhole, but in universe time, it's instantaneous. It might feel like a while inside the hole, but that's just the effect of the quiet and darkness."

CHAPTER 24

The twin suns of the Oti-Makla system crawled slowly above the horizon, casting the first light of a new day on the dark streets of Oti-La. Streetlights began to switch off as the light level rose. The broad boulevards of the capital city were almost deserted at this hour, with only a few taxis and military transports floating along. The massive Oti River flowed slowly through the city, crossed every few blocks by massive stone and steel bridges. As daylight flowed into the center of the city, the cavernous walls of skyscrapers attempted to push it back. Sunlight illuminated the tall walls that separated the Central Government Compound from the remainder of the city. Just inside the walls, the treetops were lit with the light of the new day and birds chirped and flew among the branches.

Unlike the city outside the walls, all of the buildings in the Compound were limited to three stories tall and were constructed from cold gray stone. Only the Supreme General's residence was clad in bright white marble, which is why it was named the White House. Central Lake in the middle of the Compound was alive with dozens of fountains. The lake was surrounded by a park and wide walkway all around the five mile circumference. Central Boulevard separated the lake from the long rows of governmental office buildings. Hundreds of troops were marching around the lake and preparing for the new day. A single light could be seen from a window on the first floor of the White House.

Supreme General Ulon Porto looked out that window on the new day. His office was not large, with room for a desk and a conference table with twenty chairs. One wall was decorated with memorabilia from his long reign. The opposite wall was lined with bookshelves containing reports from the other forty-nine planets and the various military leaders. He turned from the window and sat at his desk again. The report on the attack on Tak-Makla lay in front of him. He flipped through the pages, half reading the words and then slammed it shut.

There was a quick three knocks on the door, and his chief of staff, General Udu Bora entered. Udu had worked for Ulon for fifty solar cycles, the entire time Ulon had been Supreme General. Together, they had come up with the idea for battle stations, which would finally give their people some assurance that the Paxran could not return.

"General, good morning," Udu said. "I see you read the report on the action at Tak-Makla. You should be very proud of your grandson."

"Thank you, Udu, but I'm not so sure," Ulon replied. "The attack went as planned, but the decision to take that human prisoner did not turn out well."

"I think he had the right idea, sir," Udu said. "We need to know what these Hives are before they are used in battle against us. It is unfortunate our troops underestimated human strength and treachery."

"I understand the concern about the Hive technology, Udu," Ulon replied. "However, the tekkans used to be our friends. They have always been a very peaceful society. If the Hive was a weapon, why would it be there and not on a Paxran world?"

"I don't know General," Udu replied. "The tekkans appear to have an alliance with the humans though. They come from another galaxy and may be using the tekkans to provide critical intelligence about other civilizations for them to conquer."

"I have thought that too from time to time, Udu. The humans frighten me more than the Paxran to tell the truth. I cannot imagine the technology to travel from another galaxy. If they decide to take over this galaxy as well, we may meet our match a second time, only now we will have no place to run," Ulon said.

"They are definitely more advanced than we are, General," Udu replied. "That is a serious risk to our security. But they are far from our space and don't seem to be moving in this direction."

"Yet," Ulon said. "They may choose to do so anytime. We must be prepared. If we can stop them now, they might reconsider their decision to come to this galaxy. There are hundreds of billions of galaxies to choose from. Why this one?"

"Our spies tell me they originated in the nearest galaxy," Udu continued. "That makes us the closest target."

There was a single knock at the door. Udu opened it and General Ava Liko joined them. She had been with the Supreme General longer than anyone else, having met in the military academy more than one hundred solar cycles ago. Her job was Minister of State and was charged with maintaining relations with the other planets in the federation. Ulon went to her and hugged her. "Ava, what a pleasant surprise," he said.

"General, it is good to be back on Oti-Makla," she smiled. "My ship just returned from Zia-Makla, where I met with General Valoo."

"That old fool," Ulon snarled. "His troops botched the attack on the Nom-Kat-La system utterly. They are lucky to be dead. What was his excuse this time?"

"He put his faith in a fast-rising colonel under his command," Ava said. "That man, Colonel Valik assured Valoo that the Galliceans were weak and timid. He led ten of our older cruisers there to their deaths."

"We cannot have fools like Valoo around. What are we going to do with him?" Ulon said.

"We have to be careful, Ulon," Ava said. "Valoo has many friends in his sector of our federation. I am told that ten planets follow his orders, even over yours."

"Those fools want us to sue for peace with other civilizations," Udu spat. "He believes they can be our friends and help us avoid the Paxran. None of them helped us when the Paxran almost destroyed our entire society!"

"Udu, calm down," Ulon said. "Ava is right. I don't plan to negotiate with anyone for peace. We tried that and are now relegated to the extreme edge of the galaxy. Trillions of Maklakar died at the hands of the Paxran. But we cannot afford a rift in the fabric of our federation either. We need Valoo and his ten planets to help maintain safety for all of us. Thankfully, his planets are the closest to the other societies. When aliens attack, they will hit him first."

"General, Valoo is also an old man," Ava interrupted. "You and I took classes from him back in the academy. He can continue to do his job until his passing. Then we can try to get a bit more control over those planets."

"You are both right. I'm sorry for reacting that way," Udu apologized.

"Don't worry, Udu, I understand completely," Ava replied. "Ulon and I feel the same way about him. In fact, I may be crazy for saying this, but perhaps it is time to start talking to some other societies."

"You are crazy," Ulon said. "That goes against everything we have been raised to believe for many generations. None of them can be trusted. Any of them could tell the Paxran where we are. I hope you can explain yourself in a way that will convince me that you are still sane."

"General, it's just a thought," Ava replied. "First, we need to accelerate our program to build battle stations. No matter what else happens, that has to be the top priority. While we do that, if we can start some negotiations with our closest neighbors, we might gain some critical intelligence. We are all deathly afraid of the Paxrans. We even gave the filthy Donnaki our plasma bomb technology, hoping they would attack them. Also, we have no idea what this Hive technology is all about. We failed to learn anything from the information we gleaned from Tak-Makla before the explosion. The human captive chose to die rather than work with us."

"But what about disclosing our location? That would be a disaster," Ulon replied.

"Clearly, we would have to be careful not to do that," Ava said. "It is possible the tekkans have used that Hive technology to find us already. If we choose to do this, we could send one battle station on a circuitous route into the galaxy to disguise our location. The ambassadors there could then begin the process of meeting new civilizations. We may learn nothing. We might learn about the Paxran and Hive technology."

"So, it's like spies out in the open," Udu said. "I had never thought of that. I like the idea."

"There is significant risk," Ava replied. "Even if we learn no new technology, we might convince some others that we are not a threat. They may even help us fight the Paxran when they come looking for us. What do you think, General?"

"Your idea has a lot of merit, Ava," Ulon said. "But who do you think could pull it off?"

"The leaders of the expedition would have to be one hundred percent convinced they were establishing treaties with friendly civilizations. I was thinking about Ambassador General Valoo. This is exactly what he has wanted to do for a long time. He could take a team of assistants and other ambassadors with him, probably a contingent of five hundred or so. We would also have at least a thousand more who would act as helpers and office workers for any consulates we set up. They would be spies loyal only to you, General," Ava replied.

"I don't know about you, Udu, but I think it might work," Ulon smiled.

"I'll start working on the text of the edict now, General," Udu said. "And I'll get General Valoo on the com-link so you can give him the good news."

"This is Nightsky," Lia Lawson said. "We will reach your position in ten minutes and are ready to land." The view screen showed the vast sphere of Hive 1008 growing rapidly as the ship approached. Hive 1008 was in a high orbit over Tak-Makla. The two worlds were almost the same size and the orbit of Tak-Makla had to be managed carefully to avoid a permanent shift due to its large companion.

Two massive doors began to open on the surface of the planetoid. Inside a deep cavern lined with landing lights dropped hundreds of miles below the surface. The Nightsky maneuvered itself directly over the opening which was several times larger than the star cruiser. All motion stopped and the ship hovered in place five hundred yards over the opening.

The view screen image split in half, with a smiling Zu face on the left side. "Welcome Nightsky. This is Major Arthun Nikka, and I will now assume control over your ship and bring her into her holding bay. When you feel our tractor beam attach to your ship, please turn off any maneuvering jets."

"Aye-aye, Major," Captain Jon Lake said. The ship shuddered as the tractor beam grabbed the ship. "We are turning over all controls to you now."

The Nightsky slowly descended toward the opening. The ship moved slightly to align more perfectly with the shaft below. As the ship dipped below the surface, the doors above began to close. Being several miles thick, the doors moved very slowly until the sky was blacked out. Nightsky passed several open bays. As they continued to drop, Jon recognized the Kong-Fa sitting in one bay. The large ship barely fit into one of the largest bays on Hive 1008. Nightsky stopped on the same level with Kong-Fa and began to move into the open bay across the tunnel from the Gallicean ship. Flood lights illuminated the bay as the ship inched forward. Men in pressure suits entered the bay and began to prepare for the ship's arrival.

"Nightsky, you may now extend your landing struts," Major Nikka said.

"Aye-aye, Major," Jon replied. "We are deploying our landing gear now."

The three bay doors opened on the bottom of the ship and the landing gear extended. The Nightsky descending very slowly until the metal struts touched down. "Your ship has landed, Captain," Arthun said. "Welcome to Hive 1008. Governor Lonk sends his warm regards to you and your crew."

"Thank you for piloting us into position, Major," Jon replied. "What do we do now?"

"Please just relax for a while, Captain," Arthun said. "Our crew is now attaching landing blocks to keep your ship from moving. Then we will attach pressurized tunnels to allow your crew to exit the ship. Our staff will let you know when you can open your ship and exit. Finally, we will attach power systems to keep your ship operational without using her engines. We have assigned quarters to all of your crew in our Balthazar community. You can keep as many on your ship as you deem necessary for security."

"Thank you, Major," Jon replied. "I think most of our crew will stay on the ship. We will offer shore leave on your planetoid to all crew. Of course, the Admiral and Ambassador and their entourage will accept your hospitality."

"Very good then, Captain," Arthun said. "You and your officers are invited to join Governor Lonk for a dinner celebration to be held this evening at 1800 local time. It will be in the Governor's Hall in Central City Square. I look forward to meeting you there later. Hive 1008 out."

Dave Brewster entered the bridge. He sat next to Jon Lake. "Wow! We're really inside the planetoid, Jon. I never could imagine that."

"It's pretty amazing, Dave," Jon replied. "We're parked across from the Kong-Fa. That ship barely fit into the landing berth. And this whole planet is going to jump to the Andromeda Galaxy tomorrow! I just can't believe the Hive technology involved to make that happen."

"Jon, you and I have similarities in our backgrounds. When you were back on Far Sky, you didn't live that differently from me in the twenty-first. Now that we are explorers in space, reality seems to bend and twist more than I could have ever dreamed," Dave said. "Sometimes I could swear I'm sleeping and will wake up in my old bed on Earth and find I still don't have a job to go to."

"Sorry, Admiral, but I think you are stuck with us here," Jon laughed. "But I know I made the right decision to join you and Charlie. Then I thought I'd travel around our region of the galaxy and find new planets for our population. I could never have dreamed about the Society of Humanity and fifty thousand systems across multiple galaxies."

"Pardon me, Captain," Lia interrupted. "The ground crew has attached the exit tunnels and power to the ship. They are requesting that we power down and open our doors."

"Confirm the atmosphere outside the ship and then open the doors, Lia," Jon replied.

"Lia, what are you still doing here," Dave smiled. "I thought you'd be on Golden Dawn with your mother. Isn't she still waiting for you?"

Lia laughed. "Admiral, since we visited Tak-Makla the first time, I knew my place was here with you and Jon. I've asked my mother to select another secretary of state for now. Maybe I'll join her in a few years when all of this becomes normal. Right now, every day is too breath-taking to give up."

"Thank you, Lia," Dave said. "I hope you don't regret your decision someday. You've always been the best communications officer in the fleet, so I'm very happy you are here."

"Thanks, Dave," Lia replied. "I'm getting a signal that the Kalidean research vessel Manila in entering the Hive. Mencius is leading their team and offers his best wishes. He is looking forward to joining you at the dinner celebration this evening. Also, Governor Lonk is in the terminal near our ship and is waiting to escort your team to your quarters in the Balthazar community."

"Great. Please contact Darlene and Charlie and have them meet me at Door One," Dave said. "Arrange to have our things moved to our new quarters." Dave stood and shook hands with Jon Lake. "Jon, I will see you and your team at dinner later. Is your crew staying on board or moving into Balthazar as well?"

"Dave, I think we'll stay here. No need moving all of our people and their baggage when our own quarters are here. I'll be offering as much shore leave as they want though," Jon replied.

"Understood. I recommend that you all spend as much time off the ship as possible though. This ship looks just like a planet and there are billions of people to meet," Dave answered. "We'll have plenty of time on this ship in the future."

"Aye-aye, Admiral," Jon smiled. "I'll be sure that everyone gets off the ship when they can. I don't feel comfortable taking everyone off for security reasons."

"I know. We haven't known about these people for long. But I have a special incentive for you personally to stay in Balthazar for a few days," Dave said.

"Okay, Dave, what incentive is that?" Jon asked. "Is an armed guard going to escort me off?"

"Not at all, Jon. As you know, the Society of Humanity has very advanced military technology that they are now willing to share with us. I would like you to work with them on understanding their systems and figuring out how to upgrade our ships," Dave smiled. "I even have a weapons expert arriving on the Kalidean ship to help you."

"That would be great! Since the Nightsky is right here, perhaps we might be upgraded while the ship is docked," Jon laughed. "I know the Kalideans will want to see that technology too. Who are they bringing?"

"For their own purposes, I don't know who they have. Mencius has likely brought a few engineers. The Manila is bringing one of our best officers to help you," Dave said. "And I assume you won't mind working with Captain Lauren London?"

<h1 align="center">CHAPTER 26</h1>

The Balthazar community in Hive 1008 reminded Dave of the old brownstone neighborhoods of New York City. The buildings were only a few stories tall with ornate moldings and small windows. Wrought iron balconies overlooked the broad streets. Potted trees dotted the wide sidewalks and hedges filled the open space between the sidewalks and the buildings. The ground floors of most buildings were home to small shops and cafes. It was early afternoon local time, and the Brewsters and Watsons strolled along the streets near their residence passing the time and being amazed they were inside a planet-sized space ship. The sky was mostly cloudy and intermittent drizzle dotted the streets. Everyone knew the sky was artificial, but the effect was so real they forget to think about it.

As the rain picked up a bit, Aria and Darlene escaped into a small women's clothing store to shop. Next door was a coffee shop, so Dave and Charlie told their wives they would meet them there. A bell jingled as Dave opened the door, with the first scents of coffee and cinnamon filling his head. A woman in a tight uniform rushed toward him with a coffee in one hand and a com-link in the other, forcing Dave to step back. As she passed, she noticed the non-Zu holding the door and stopped short.

"Excuse me," she said, "aren't you Admiral Dave Brewster?"

"Yes, I am," Dave replied with spots of rain hitting his shoulders and face.

"Oh my goodness, let me get out of the way, Admiral," she blushed as she stepped back. Dave and Charlie gladly stepped out of the rain and into the small store. "I am Lieutenant Alda Nackly, sir. I work in The Hive. It's a pleasure to meet you."

"Thank you, Alda, it's nice to meet you too. This is my best friend, Commodore Charlie Watson," Dave said.

"Hello, Alda," Charlie said. "For a second there, I thought you were going to tackle both of us."

"I'm sorry for that. I'm rushing to get back to The Hive. We're trying to prepare for the jump tomorrow. Lots of coordination for that, you know," Alda replied.

"We don't mean to keep you if you're in a rush," Dave said. "Perhaps after the jump, you can tell us more. We've been in The Hive on Tak-Makla, but we don't know much about how they do what they do."

"It would be an honor," Alda blushed. "I'll contact you the day after tomorrow. Thanks again. Bye." Alda shook their hands and rushed out into the rain.

They sat at a table near the front of the café so the wives would find them easily. A waiter took their order and went back to the counter. The counter was a large glass case filled with traditional Zu pastries, which were all shapes and flavors. The Zu loved chocolate and cinnamon, so everything had to be good. Dave asked the waiter to bring them a selection of the best and two cafe lattes. The rain was pouring down now, and the streets were running with water. They could hear distant sounds of thunder and what appeared to be flashes of lightning. People were rushing up and down the street. Now and again, a taxi shuttle would zip by full of wet Zu workers. After a few minutes, the waiter returned with a tray of pastries and two coffees.

"Here's to us, Charlie," Dave said as the two touched their cups together in a toast. The coffee was hot and rich with just the right level of sweetness. "Man, I needed that!" The two men sat back watching the scene in the street outside.

After a few minutes, Alda Nackly reentered the coffee shop and took off her rain coat and hung it on a coat rack near the door. Then she came up to their table. "Admiral, when I told my boss about running into you, she told me to get back here and get to know you better. Apparently, they don't need my help as much as I thought they did."

Dave laughed. "Please sit down, Alda and have some pastry. I know how you feel. Half the time, my crew is doing too many things and I feel I'm just along for the ride. And please call us Dave and Charlie. We're all friends here."

She sat and sipped her coffee. Alda was yet another stunningly beautiful Zu woman. Her silver-blue eyes matched well with her blonde hair. She was tall as were most Zu, at least six foot three. "Thanks, Dave. You two really came from eleven centuries ago?"

"That's absolutely true," Charlie said. "Apparently, Dave's family will accomplish great things in this time. I think I'm just his side-kick."

"You're much more than that, Charlie," Dave smiled. "You're in charge of finding good coffee and chocolate croissants too!"

"You guys are so funny," Alda said. "Most admirals around the Society are very serious people. I don't think I ever heard General Zilma crack a joke when he was here."

"Well, we're not real military men," Dave confided. "Charlie and I were business men back in our time. In fact, I was an accountant without a job."

"I've never met a funny accountant either," Alda laughed.

"Very true, but somehow Charlie brings out the devil in me," Dave replied. Looking out the window, Dave could see the rain had stopped. "Alda, I was surprised to see the rain pouring outside with lightning and thunder. We're inside a space ship, right?"

Alda said, "When this station was built, they knew the residents would spend many years here, so they tried to make it as much like a real planet as possible. If we were all in a traditional ship with small rooms and corridors, we'd all go nuts after a while. The rain was real enough, but the thunder and lightning were sound and light effects. We have rain to provide realism, but it also refreshes the air and cleans the buildings and streets. All the water is reclaimed and used again and again. With the five billion people in this station, we need lots of water. Almost fifteen percent of the interior space on Hive 1008 is water storage."

"So you have a lot fewer people in this Hive compared to Tak-Makla," Charlie said. "I believe they have ten billion in their Hive."

"We've found that a Hive needs at least two billion minds to function well," Alda replied. "There are three billion in our Hive. Another billion manage the station itself, like running all of these stores and making rain and performing maintenance. The rest are either part of the military command or the dependent children of other residents." She took a knife and cut a small pastry with red icing in half. She took one half and popped it in her mouth. "Oh, these are my favorites. They are called Uluk Zu, which is also the name of the planet where they were invented. They are buttery with the flavor of the Uluk berry."

"Alda, I don't want you to give us any secret information, but even though I've experienced being part of The Hive on Tak-Makla, I still don't really know how they work or where they get such amazing power," Dave asked.

"Whether you know it or not, Dave, you and Charlie have the highest security clearance levels I've ever seen," Alda said. "They are much higher than mine, and I work in the secure area of this Hive. So, there's nothing I know that would be a secret from you. I assume you've heard of Universal Power?"

"The tekkans have told us a bit about it, but please put it in your own words," Dave replied.

Alda said, "Universal Power is the engine of the universe. Everything is made from it. It is the basis for the matter and energy we all see and use every day. The tekkans like the term Universal Power, but in our Hive command, we just call it the Source. It flows through everything constantly. Like the background radiation from the Big Bang, it is not uniform though. The Source is strongest inside of galaxies where part of it manifests itself as matter and energy."

"That's where the lines of force come in, right?" Dave asked.

"Exactly right, Dave," Alda smiled. "But we don't know if they are lines of force or just a pattern caused by some other means. The Source does tend to flow along those lines, and where the lines are most abundant, the Source is the strongest. A strong force tends to go along with heavy mass, so most of the lines are not accessible, as they are inside stars or black holes. But there are other less powerful junctures of lines that we can access. Here near Tak-Makla is a great example."

"Okay, so the Source is the root of all matter and energy in the universe," Charlie said. "But how does a Hive interact with it?"

"Each Hive has massive computer banks and a powerful electric grid. The Chief Engineers use the computers to manage the electricity, which flows through the chambers in the Hive and out into the central column. When the electricity reaches a juncture of the lines of the Source, it pulls the Source down into the column and into each chamber. Our brains are electro-chemically based, so our own energy combines with the Source and our mental energy is pulled out of the Hive and becomes one with the Source," Alda replied. She took a long drink of coffee. "Yikes, my tongue is getting tired."

Dave said, "Alda, please catch your breath. Let me guess now. Once the minds in a Hive are connected to the Source, they can access the power of the Source to travel in space or time. If enough minds are connected through multiple Hives, they can even jump an artificial planet to the next galaxy! Is that right?"

"Bravo, Dave," Alda cheered. "I think you're ready to teach this stuff now. For the jump tomorrow, we'll be coordinating thirty Hives, which is not easy since they are spread across space. That's where the Chief Engineers come in. They have so much experience in Hives and with each other that they can almost instantly locate each other within the Source. All the minds in each Hive connect to their Chief Engineers for such a mission. Once the Chief Engineers find each other, all of those minds move in the same direction and almost anything can happen. That reminds me of the story of Balthazar Opa, the planet this community is named after. Balthazar Opa is the planet where the Opa civilization originated. The residential neighborhoods in its capital city look very much like this part of the ship. Fifty million years ago, the sun in the system became unstable. It happened too quickly to safely move all eight billion Opa to other colonies. The High Council of the Society was frantic. A young Zu engineer named Alda Condil brought a plan to move the entire planet to a new system. Back then, there were only thirty Hives in the Society and thirty thousand worlds. It took a year to find a dead planet of similar size in a system with a good star. Alda coordinated the Hives to recycle the dead planet. Then all the Hives in the Society worked together for the first time and relocated the entire planet."

Dave gasped, "That's amazing! It worked and everyone survived the move?"

"There were some problems, Dave," Alda continued. "Once the planet moved, they had to get it spinning again and revolving around the sun in a safe orbit. It took five Hives a couple years before everything became normal again. I have been to Balthazar Opa on vacation, and it's a wonderful place. Perhaps you can visit there while you are in the home galaxy."

"Let me ask one last question, Alda," Charlie said. "Some of the tekkans believe that our life energy joins with the Source when we die. What do you think?"

"I think that's a matter of faith, Charlie," she replied. "To anyone who has been in a Hive and been connected with the Source, it's hard to believe anything else. Being part of the crew in our Hive, I get to spend a lot of free time just being part of the Source. When you are on assignment, you only think about your job and getting finished. When you can just be there, it is a powerful feeling of peace and connectedness. I've never sensed the soul of any others, but the sense of unity you feel is overwhelming. Personally, I hope I do join the Source when I die. There are no limits there."

"What about the edge of the universe?" Dave asked. "That's a limit, isn't it?"

"No, I don't think so," Alda smiled. "There are those in our Hive who travel beyond this universe. Much of their work is top secret, but we've been told there are multiple parallel universes that have been visited. Some of them are similar to this one and many are very different. Most of those universes have no matter or energy, but are still filled with the Source. I'm sure you've heard that more than ninety percent of the stuff in this universe is the Source. If you include just the universes the Society has visited, that number is well over ninety-nine percent. It's really everything there is."

"Thank you, Alda," Dave said. "This has been an amazing chat. Charlie and I need to go find our wives who have been out spending our fortunes. Will you be at the celebration tonight?"

"Yes, Dave, I will," she smiled. "But I'll be far from the dais where you will be. I'm not very important here."

"I disagree with you on that," Dave replied. "I know more about Hives and the Source now than I ever thought I would. I'll come looking for you tonight. I'd like you to meet Darlene and Aria." All three stood and shook hands.

"Thank you, Dave and Charlie," she said. "That would be amazing. None of my friends will believe it." The men left the shop and stepped into the bright artificial sunlight. Small groups of birds sang and flew among the trees.

It was 1730 when the Brewsters and Watsons left their brownstone to go to the celebration. The weather was sunny and warm now. There would be no rain on Hive 1008 tonight. People were coming from all over the planet and no one wanted to arrive wet and cold. Half a block from their residence a staircase led down to a large tube station. At the bottom of the stairs, the Balthazar One tube station stretched several hundred yards. The shuttles were larger here with a capacity for twenty people. Since more than half of the planet's population worked in The Hive, many people needed to commute there continually. The back ends of shuttles faced the throng of people. Signs above said the destination of each shuttle. At this time, most shuttles were headed to the celebration and the signs read "Center City Square." The four stood in a line with others headed to the party. When it was their turn, they climbed into the large transparent shuttle and strapped themselves in. They waited while the shuttle filled. Many people recognized the Admiral and Ambassador from the frequent news coverage about them. People would wave at them or shake their hands. When the shuttle was full and everyone was secure, the doors slid shut. A door opened in front of the shuttle and it dashed out into the tubes. As soon as it left, another shuttle backed out of the tube to take its place. The riders who were headed to Balthazar exited and more people headed for the celebration entered.

The shuttle hurtled forward through the tube. Center City was located near the center of the planetoid, so the shuttle switched into a downward tube and dove into the planet. Hundreds of tubes surrounded them. Dave could see others in their finest clothes headed to join them at the party. The size of the shuttle was disconcerting to Dave Brewster. It seemed like a small bus hurtling through the planet. He looked out the side and saw another shuttle passing them. There were only six chairs in that shuttle, and the six Galliceans filled the entire space. As it passed, he could see General Fa-a-Di looking back at him through the face mask of his breather. Ambassador De-o-Nu sat near him and was clearly crammed uncomfortably in the limited space. Dave waved at his friends just as their shuttle shot ahead.

"What are those things?" a voice said in front of him. Dave looked forward and saw a young Zu boy staring at him. The child must have been ten years old. "I saw you wave at those things. Are they your friends?"

Dave smiled, "Yes, the two Galliceans I waved at are like my brothers. My name is Dave, what's yours?"

"Zak. My name is Zak, and this is my mom," he said.

"I'm sorry, Admiral, Zak is a curious boy. Never mind him," the mother said.

"Curiosity is a good trait. He doesn't bother me at all," Dave replied. "Please call me Dave, and this is my wife, Darlene."

"Thanks Dave. I am Colonel Aneel Louk and you've met Zak," she replied. "It's nice to meet you both."

"Please, we're just Dave and Darlene," Darlene said. "Your boy is very cute."

"Thank you Darlene," Aneel blushed. "I'm a section manager in our Hive. I believe Dave met one of my team leaders today, Lieutenant Alda Nackly?"

"Yes. Charlie and I had a nice discussion with her about your Hive," Dave said. "Thank you for sending her back to talk to us. I hope that won't affect the jump tomorrow."

"Alda is great. She always knows what to do, even before I do," Aneel said. "We will all be ready on schedule." The shuttle leveled off and slowed. "I think we're almost there now." The shuttle entered a circular room with a diameter slightly larger than the shuttle. It spun around and backed into the Center City Square Tube Station and stopped. The doors opened, and people began exit the shuttle. "I hope we didn't ruin your trip, Dave."

"Not at all, Aneel," Dave smiled. "This is the first time I have forgotten the moving and twisting and just relaxed. Thank you and thank Zak for that!"

Dave and Darlene stood and turned to Charlie and Aria. They were both asleep with Charlie's head against the wall and Aria's on his shoulder. "Now that's relaxed!" Darlene laughed. "I almost don't want to disturb them, but I know the shuttle won't leave as long as they are here." She shook their shoulders and they looked up sleepily. "Time to go, sleepy-heads."

The Center City Square station was flooded with people. Everyone was headed up to the Square where the festivities were due to begin soon. Most people were in their uniforms which were every color of the rainbow. Hive agents wore white. Hive engineers wore light blue. Soldiers wore green. The crew flying the planetoid and her war ships wore dark blue. The senior leadership wore silver or gold, depending on rank. Other less common roles had their own colors. As they reached the stairway up to the street, an exceptionally tall Zu wearing silver held up a sign reading "Dave Brewster." Dave walked up and introduced himself.

"Hello, Admiral and Ambassador. I am Mak Aloop. Governor Lonk asked me to bring you to the dais," Mak replied.

"Great, let's go," Dave said. "You certainly are tall, Mak."

"That's why I get these jobs, Admiral," Mak laughed. "If I hold the sign over my head, anyone here will see it. I just met the Gallicean team and they make me look like a child."

"They are pretty big, Mak," Charlie said. "You should try flying with one of them holding you in a harness against his chest. We've all had that experience, and it is amazing. Fly with them once and the memories will be with you forever. Isn't that right, Dave?"

"That's for certain," Dave replied. "But you have to do it on one of their worlds. When you see one of them again, ask them about Ka-la-a."

"I'll be sure to do that, Dave," Mak replied. They climbed to the top of the stairs and out into Center City Square. Dave remembered this park from the last time he and Darlene were here. Much of the large open park had been transformed into a giant banquet hall. The tables reached from near the small gazebo to the large balcony where he and Darlene stood and watched their son Bill kissing Loni Arrak. Dozens of portable bars were set up along the edges of the park and lines of people waited for a drink.

"Mak, can you give us a minute?" Dave asked. "There's someone here I want Aria and Darlene to meet."

"There's not much time, Admiral," Mak said, but the rest had already started toward one of the bar lines. Mak followed them sheepishly.

As they approached the line, Dave tapped a woman on the shoulder. Alda Nackly turned and blushed bright red when she saw who it was. "Admiral, what a surprise!" she giggled. "I didn't think I'd see you this evening."

"I'm a man of my word, Alda. Please let me introduce you to my wife, Darlene and Charlie's wife, Aria," Dave continued. "Alda is the Hive agent who spent some time with Charlie and me this afternoon. I practically feel like a Hive genius now."

"If you made my husband into a genius, you really are a miracle worker," Darlene laughed. "It's a pleasure to meet you."

"I'm glad to meet you too, Alda," Aria said. "Charlie didn't tell me how beautiful you are. I wonder why?"

"You are all too kind. I'd like to introduce you to my boyfriend, Captain Lons Macu, and my baby sister, Ilsa Nackly," Alda said. After introductions, Mak touched Dave on the shoulder and hurried them to the dais, where several tables of dignitaries were already seated.

At precisely 1800 hours, a series of tones sounded to quiet the crowd. Governor Alin Lonk strode to the podium and stood smiling as the crowd applauded him. He waved to the crowd and then motioned for quiet. "Fellow citizens of the Society of Humanity and cherished guests, it is my pleasure to welcome you to this celebration of the coming together of new cultures and civilizations to join us on this voyage back to the home galaxy." The area was filled with thunderous applause. "Our arrival in the home galaxy will mark the beginning of a new era for our universe. This will be an era of brotherhood among different Beings to create the Free Society in this galaxy. Tonight, you will hear from several new civilizations that have lived in this galaxy forever. They join us now to cast a new vision of the galaxy where race or species is irrelevant. Those of us who were born in this galaxy know we cannot always count on day to day support from the Society. The effort required to move ships and people between galaxies is taxing on our Hives. The fifty thousand worlds of the Society all have needs, and we are but a small percentage of the total. We need to learn to support ourselves as well. Only then will we be able to defend ourselves from those civilizations that want to enslave or destroy us. Just a few days ago, forces of the Maklakar culture mounted a ruthless attack on the peace-loving tekkans of Tak-Makla. Tonight, I can tell you that High Consul Zee Gongaleg and his Minister of State Fak Mondoka are here to join us on this trip and in our new alliance. The evil Maklakar also attempted to attack two Hives in the Nom-Kat-La system. They were easily dispatched by the forces of Greater Gallia. Tonight, the legendary general and High Commissioner of that culture, Fa-a-Di, and his brother-in-law, Ambassador De-o-Nu are here as well. We are honored by the presence of all of our guests. But I don't want to talk all night. This is a party, after all. After dinner, I will ask a few others to speak, but for now, I raise my glass and offer a toast to our new Free Society!" Shouts and applause reverberated around the buildings edging the park.

Hundreds of waiters worked the tables, bringing bottles of beer and wine and an array of foods to the hungry crowd. The Brewsters and Watsons sat at the end of the main table, with the men on one side and the women across from them. Next to them were a number of senior leaders from Hive 1008. Much of the food was from Tak-Makla, especially the seafood and fresh vegetables. There were large farms and livestock yards inside Hive 1008 as well, but new items and cuisines were always relished.

Dave was getting very full after the main course, and yet more food kept coming. He told the waiter not to bring him anymore and he sat back feeling content. The lighting level had gradually decreased as though there was a sun that was setting. By the time the dessert courses arrived, the sky was dark with artificial stars twinkling above. Dave was resting his eyes and knew he was in danger of falling asleep right here at the table. A massive hand touched him on the shoulder. He opened his eyes and looked up to see Fa-a-Di smiling at him through his breather mask. "Brother, can we talk privately?" the Gallicean said. Fa-a-Di turned and walked away. Dave rose and hurried to catch up to him.

Fa-a-Di found a quiet corner of the balcony fifty yards from the tables. He sat on a small bench, and stretched out his legs. Dave said next to him, but the Gallicean was well over his head. Dave then sat on the rail of the balcony and could more or less look at Fa-a-Di in the eyes. "Is there a problem, brother?" Dave asked.

"Probably not, but all of this seems useless to me," Fa-a-Di sighed. "We have big problems, like the Maklakars, the Paxran and the Donnaki. All of this love fest is not setting well with my team. I had to force De-o-Nu to leave the Kong-Fa for this dinner. He wants his crew ready to fight at a moment's notice."

"We should just write our own defensive pacts and get back to life," Dave suggested.

"Exactly! Obviously, the opportunity to visit another galaxy is amazing. That's probably the only reason any Galliceans are here tonight," Fa-a-Di confided. "If there is to be an alliance, that's great. We want that too. Like the treaty Darlene made with us for planet sharing. That's a wonderful opportunity for our cultures. But all of this seems too fake to an old soldier like me."

"I think this is more about the Society that it is about any of us," Dave said. "The Society has been around a very long time. I've been told that planets drop out every year. Also, they have disintegrated into fifty fairly distinct sub-species that don't really like each other. Now all they want to do is find an acceptable way to break it into smaller pieces. But they are steeped in billions of years of tradition. And the government for more than a hundred trillion people must be monstrous."

"So, all the nice talk and cocktails keeps them from tearing each other's throats out?" Fa-a-Di asked.

"Basically, I think that's right," Dave smiled. "But this Free Society thing is the best thing that could have happened for all of us, brother. In their home galaxy, they will end up with many new Free Societies based on regions. So they will still be dealing with the same animosities and resentments they have now. In this galaxy, the largest human group with be the Kalideans. And we both know and trust them, right?"

"Of course, they have always been fair with all of us," Fa-a-Di said.

"The next biggest group with be Greater Gallia. After that will be the maklans, including the Predaxians, Tak-Makla and No-Makla. The non-Kalidean humans will be far down the list," Dave replied.

"So, we will pretty much be the same as we are today, except with a few dozen new human planets and Hive technology," Fa-a-Di reasoned. "You know, Dave, I think you are exactly right. This is going to be very good for us."

"Whether we love these people or not, they want to be our friends. The tekkans have trusted them for a long time. You will have two Hives in the Nom-Kat-La system alone. If we can put up with a few dinners in our honor, we will be well rewarded," Dave finished.

"You know, brother, I have some good whisky at my table. After dinner, you, Darlene and the Watsons must come over and toast our good fortune together," Fa-a-Di smiled.

"It would be our pleasure, brother," Dave agreed. "I have an odd question, brother. How did you eat with that breather on?"

"These humans are pretty clever," Fa-a-Di replied. "It's the most amazing thing. When I bring food or drink up to my beak, it passes right through the shield without compromising my atmosphere. I need to talk to them about that technology. It's a wonderful improvement. If you had one of these on Jupiter, you could have tried that moss like me. It is much better raw, Dave."

"I'll take your word for it, brother," Dave laughed.

Alin Lonk came to join them. "Friends, could both of you join me at the podium? I'd like each of you to say a few words about our new alliance and the trip, if you can?"

"We would be honored, Governor," Fa-a-Di laughed. "Please lead the way."

CHAPTER 28

Dave and Darlene sat in the coffee shop where he had met Alda Nackly the previous day. Dave sipped his cappuccino and looked out at the sunny morning inside Hive 1008. Darlene was sampling the Uluk Zu pastries Alda had recommended to Dave. It was sweet and fruity, tasting of strawberries and orange. It was mid-morning local time, and the jump was scheduled for noon. All non-essential residents had been advised to return to their residences by 1100 hours to prepare for the jump. If all went as planned, the jump would be just another moment in time. At 1200, Hive 1008 would be one hundred thousand miles from Tak-Makla at a key intersection point of Universal Power. A couple seconds later, Hive 1008 would be one million miles from Earth Prime, in an outer arm of the Andromeda Galaxy.

Fola Untor, the shopkeeper of the coffee shop came up to their table. "Just to let you know, I'll be closing in twenty minutes, folks. I've got to get home before the jump, you know."

"Of course, Fola," Darlene said. "We understand. Our place is just around the corner, but we'll get out of here soon."

"Please come back after the jump though," Fola replied. "I've prepared some special chocolates for the arrival party."

"Arrival party, what's that?" Dave asked.

"It's an old tradition, from the days before there were as many Hives," Fola replied. "The effort to move this planetoid is huge. If it succeeds, everyone celebrates!"

"If it succeeds? That doesn't sound very comforting, Fola," Darlene said.

"There hasn't been a failure in millions of years, Darlene. Please don't worry. But it is a great excuse for a party, isn't it?" Fola laughed.

"We'll be back," Darlene said. "Dave and Charlie don't pass up the opportunity to eat chocolate."

"I can't argue with that," Dave said as he finished his coffee. "We're headed to our residence now, Fola. You should close early if you can."

"Thanks you two and I'll see you in a couple hours. I reopen at 1300," Fola said as Dave and Darlene headed out into the morning sunshine.

The sidewalks were full of people returning to their homes before the jump. While everyone seemed calm, there was a tension in the air. Even for such an advanced culture, the thought of relocating a seven-thousand mile diameter artificial planet two million light years in the blink of an eye was disconcerting. Dave could remember how nervous he felt when he rode in an airplane back in the twenty-first. The idea of flying thousands of feet over the ground in a metal tube was unnerving. He imagined that was the same anxiety the billions of residents on Hive 1008 felt right now. As they walked up the short stairway to the door of their residence, Dave heard a tone in his ear. He tapped the com-link and said, "Dave Brewster."

"Admiral, Jon here. I strongly recommend that you and the ambassador return to the Nightsky for the jump," he said. "In case something bad happens, you will be safer inside the ship. Charlie and Aria are already here."

"Understood, Jon. I can't really argue with you. That does seem like a reasonable response to a truly unbelievable thing that will happen soon. We're on our way. Out," Dave replied as he clicked off the com-link. "Darlene, let's go back to the Nightsky for the jump. Jon recommends that as a precaution."

"Good. To tell the truth, this whole jump has me on edge," Darlene said as they went back down the stairs. They hurried to the tube station. A mass of people were flooding the tube station and they had to wait their turn to go down to the entrance. Dave held Darlene's hand as the crowd pushed them down the steps.

Inside the station, long lines led to each shuttle. Many of the lines reached all the way to the stairway into the station. Dave led Darlene over to a monitor on the wall. He touched the panel and said, "Space Port." A line of light traced the tube to the Space Port, and the words "Shuttle Sixty-Four" appeared above the line. He and Darlene moved through the crowd toward the higher numbered shuttles. It took almost ten minutes to reach a small shuttle numbered sixty-four. Dave glanced at his watch, which read 1110. The tubes would run for another thirty minutes, so they would have no trouble reaching their ship. They entered the small shuttle and buckled themselves in. There were ten seats in the shuttle and only four people on board so far. The shuttles were timed to leave every five minutes or less if they were full. High Consul Zee Gongaleg and Minister Fak Mondoka entered the shuttle and sat behind the Brewsters.

"Dave and Darlene, we are happy to have found you both," Zee said. "Your Captain Lake suggested we join your crew in case of any emergency."

"Zee and Fak, it would be our pleasure," Darlene said. The doors on the shuttle closed and it launched out into the network of tubes. The space port was on the opposite side of the planetoid near the surface, so the shuttle shot upward at incredible speed. The web of tubes was full as shuttles took all the residents to their homes. "Where's Zak when you need someone to distract you?"

"I wish he was here talking to me now," Dave replied. "I'm not crazy about tubes and I have no idea what to expect during the jump. It's like time is racing ahead and I'm powerless to do anything but sit here and wait." The tube shot through the planet. Now it was above a large sea of water that was completely enclosed. "Alda told me that fifteen percent of the ship's interior is full of water."

"That's why we prefer our external world, Dave," Zee commented. "It seems much more natural to us. I don't know why you don't like tubes. The shuttles here seem quite slow to me."

The shuttle shuddered as though the entire planet was being shaken by a giant hand. It slowed and stopped with the vast water pool below them. Waves were splashing against the walls of the container. Several more tremors hit the shuttle and the water seemed to be boiling. After several minutes, the tremors stopped and the shuttle began to move again. It increased to full speed, and left the water storage behind. A giant cylindrical shape was directly ahead and the shuttle slowed as it approached. When the shuttle was within fifty feet, a circular door opened and the shuttle entered the Space Port Tube Station and stopped.

As they exited, a Zu soldier approached them. "Admiral, I'm Captain Bol Nessor. Governor Lonk asked me to escort your team to the Nightsky. He also asked me to apologize for the problem in the tube. When each Hive connects to our planetoid, there are waves of Universal Power that flow through. It can feel like an earthquake, but it is normal for this kind of operation."

"Thanks, Captain," Dave smiled. "I feel better knowing that! For a second, I thought our shuttle would drop into that giant water tank."

"That's very unlikely, sir," Bol replied. "Follow me to the lift." They entered a large elevator and the door closed behind them. Bol pushed a button and the elevator lurched upward. After two minutes, it stopped and the door opened. Lieutenant Lia Lawson was standing by the door smiled.

"Thanks, Bol," Lia said. "I've got it from here. Follow me, everyone." She turned and began to walk down the long tube connecting the Space Port to the Nightsky. After they entered the ship, Lia tapped her com-link and said, "Captain, our last four guests are on board. You may close the doors at your discretion." After tapping her com-link, she turned to the group and said, "Consul and Minister, would you prefer to go to your quarters or join the Admiral and Ambassador on the bridge?"

"It would be an honor to share the bridge," Zee said.

"Very well, follow me. We need to step up the pace though. It is now 1145 hours," she said. They followed her into the lift and it shot upward toward the top of the ship.

"It's good to be home," Dave said. "Our residence on Hive 1008 was too nice. It's great to be inside one of my ships."

"I don't know, honey," Darlene said. "I was getting used to living like I was on a planet again." The door opened and they entered the bridge. Lia led the tekkans to seats that had been prepared for them. Then she returned to her communications station. Dave and Darlene sat in their command chairs next to Captain Jon Lake. Charlie and Aria sat on the opposite side of the captain. Dave glanced at his watch, which said 1155. He took Darlene's hand and squeezed it.

The voice of Governor Lonk came over every speaker on Hive 1008 and on all the ships in the port. "Friends, I am pleased to report that all Hives are now locked onto our coordinates. Acting Chief Engineer Loni Arrak is now coordinating the actions of all Hives and she reports everything is progressing according to plan. I apologize for any discomfort during the first part of this process. Please relax and know we will soon be in the home galaxy. The actual jump can be somewhat troubling for some. Any symptoms, such as headache, nausea or the like should be short-lived. If not, please contact your doctor. Thank you and we'll start our arrival celebration at precisely 1300 hours. I wish you all the best."

Dave glanced at the ship's chronograph. It read 1200. A searing pain surged through the back of his head. He could see his vision narrowing into a tunnel and becoming fuzzy. Tremors rocked through the ship and warning lights and buzzers sounded all over the bridge. Ali Bai, the helmsman leaned back and fell to the floor. Lia tried to go to him but could not stand. Dave could feel Darlene pulling on his arm and saying something to him, but he could not understand her words. Her face seemed distorted like an impressionist painting. Jon Lake was shouting to his crew for calm, but everyone seemed to be in their own world.

"Dave, are you okay?" Darlene said. "Dave, wake up!"

Dave opened his eyes and found he was still sitting in the same chair. Darlene was standing over him wiping blood from his nose. "What happened? Where are we?"

"Dave, it looks like you passed out," Jon Lake said. "Ali, Charlie and Aria all passed out too. But everyone is okay. Ship containment is secure. We're waiting for confirmation from Hive 1008."

Dave glanced at his watch, which read 1202. He looked up at Darlene and could see a few tears streaming down her cheeks. He took her head in his hands and kissed her on the lips. "I'm okay now, Darlene. I just hope it's over. How do you feel, sweetheart?"

"Much better than a minute ago, honey," she replied. "I felt like I would throw up or pass out, but then it just went away. I'm feeling lucky."

Dave turned to Lia. "Lia, try to get the Galliceans or Kalideans and find out if they're okay."

"Dave, all communications are out," Lia said. "We were told that would be normal for a few minutes after the jump. We also have no external visual. All sensors are also off-line. We could be floating in space and not know it."

"Zee and Fak, how are you?" Dave asked.

"Just fine, Dave. Thank you for asking," Zee said. "The jump doesn't seem to have affected us at all."

"You're lucky. I felt searing pain in my head and passed out. I feel okay now, but I hope I don't have to do this very often," Dave replied.

The speakers came alive with Governor Lonk's voice. "I'm glad to report the jump has been completed safely. Earth Prime sends regards and welcome to the home galaxy. All electronic systems should be back online within the next ten minutes. As with any action of this magnitude, there have been minor issues. Approximately ten percent of our non-Hive personnel report some discomfort during the jump, with symptoms like headaches, nausea and fainting. We also had a hull rupture near the space port. There were no injuries from the incident and the rupture has already been sealed. There have been reports of damage to buildings in the Balthazar neighborhood. Teams will be sent to begin repairs within a few hours. As you can imagine, due to the shaking and movement, there is a lot of dust and debris in many streets. We will begin a heavy rain simulation to clean things up. It will take two days until all areas can be cleaned. Thank you for your help and patience during this exercise. A number of leaders from Earth Prime are already on their way here to join our arrival celebration. Thanks again and good-bye."

CHAPTER 29

One hour after the jump, the tube system was fully operational again. Governor Alin Lonk contacted Dave Brewster and asked to meet at the building serving as his residence in the Balthazar community. Traffic in the tube network was very light which was unusual for the lunch hour on Hive 1008. Most non-Hive residents had been given the day off to prepare for the jump and to celebrate the success afterward. The success celebrations tended to be local to each neighborhood, leaving little reason for people to travel around the planetoid. Dave asked Charlie to join him so they could stop at the coffee shop after the meeting.

The shuttle backed into the Balthazar Tube Station at 1325. A few dozen Zu were boarding and exiting shuttles from different parts of Hive 1008. Dave remembered the mob that filled the station the previous evening. A cleaning crew swept debris off the floor. Some wall and ceiling tiles had fallen during the jump, and Dave could feel bits of tile and sand under his boots. As he and Charlie approached the main exit, they could see several broken steps had been barricaded, leaving only room for one person at a time to ascend to street level. Fortunately, with the sparse crowd there was no need to wait.

The street was littered with more debris, as bricks had crumbled from some buildings. Two mangled wrought-iron balconies lay in the street. Several workers were using plasma torches to cut the metal into smaller pieces to be hauled away. Another worker was using a lift device to attach metal sheets over the broken walls where the balconies had been attached. It seemed to Dave that Alin had understated the damage to this part of town. Charlie touched Dave on the shoulder and pointed up. The overcast sky seemed almost real, except for a large section where a square hole seemed out of place in the gray cloud layer.

Through the opening, they could see a maze of pipes and conduits. Several electricity lines were arcing where the connections to the fallen panels had been severed. Two workers were approaching the broken section in a floating vehicle. Further up past the pipe and conduit, they could see several tubes from the tube network. They continued toward the brownstone and turned the corner. Now Dave knew why Governor Lonk was so interested in meeting Dave here. The broken piece of ceiling had fallen onto the building where the Brewsters and Watsons had been staying. The section was fifty feet square and several feet thick. The top two stories of the building were crushed. Charlie and Aria had been staying on the third floor while Dave and Darlene were on the second. As they moved closer, they could see Governor Lonk and several others in gold suits standing in the middle of the street waiting for them.

"It looks like we owe our lives to Jon Lake," Charlie said.

"I guess we're even with him now!" Dave exclaimed. "This is unbelievable. Now I do wish I was back in the twenty-first."

Alin Lonk saw the two approaching and rushed forward to greet them. He grabbed both men and hugged them. "My dear friends, I am so glad you and your wives are safe. This kind of thing never happens during a jump. The last tragedy like this was recorded more than a thousand years ago. Please come with me." They joined the others in front of the building. "Admiral Brewster and Commodore Watson, please let me introduce you to Senator Aon Nardu and Councilor Nola

Balee. They have just arrived from Earth Prime and wanted to meet you."

"Gentlemen, we are so proud to welcome the descendants of Earth 47," Aon said. When Dave first saw her, he was certain she was Kalidean, with the same blue skin and large black eyes. "We are horrified by the damage here and what might have happened to you. There will be a full investigation and inspection of the entire planetoid. I guarantee you of that."

"I certainly concur with the Senator," Nola said. Nola was a Pa and looked remarkably like the barista Bea Watson, only thirty or so years older. "The inspection process could take several weeks though, but after our business is concluded, we can certainly jump you and your ships back to your own galaxy. I assure you we have no problems like this when we move an individual ship."

"Thanks to all of you for your concern," Dave began. "We don't want a random accident to color our stay here, so don't worry about that. It is a pleasure to be here in the home galaxy with all of you."

"Thanks for your understanding, Dave," Alin said, "but I must also tell you this was probably not an accident. Our Hive has calculated the odds of this happening randomly are less than one in one hundred million." The others nodded their agreement.

"You're saying someone did this on purpose?" Charlie asked. "Why would they do that?"

"We don't know at this time," Alin replied. "Immediately after the jump, I sent several security teams here to access the damage. They saw evidence of tampering with the struts that connected that portion of the ceiling. They also checked other nearby panels and found everything normal."

"So they were trying to kill us specifically," Dave said. "That's chilling. Who would want us dead?"

"Well, we can't be sure it was aimed at you. The panel could have fallen in a number of directions. However, I've committed the Hive to find out what happened and why by checking the past for activity in this area. It may take a few days to complete," Alin said. "Also, they may not find anything."

"How can that be?" Dave asked. "Won't they view every moment of time? How could they not find anything?"

"Dave, we will do our best. Space and time are not as simple as we might think. There are those who can cloud the past to avoid detection," Aon said.

"I've think we've said enough already, Senator," Nola interrupted. "There will be time for this later. Dave, I have recommended to Governor Lonk that all foreign space ships leave Hive 1008 for the time being. You are all welcome to orbit Earth Prime. That is where our meetings will take place. It will also give the crew here time to make repairs and finish their investigation. When you arrive there, contact my office and I will finalize the meeting dates and times."

"Again, I am very sorry about this, Dave and Charlie," Alin said with genuine concern in his voice. "We will figure this out and bring those responsible to justice. Let me know when your ship arrives at Earth Prime so I'll know you are safe." Everyone shook hands and the three walked toward the tube station.

"Let's get that coffee, Charlie. I really need it now," Dave said as he headed down the street. "Aria and Darlene are not going to be happy about this."

"I just don't get it, Dave," he replied. "If they tried to kill Wendo Balak or Antar Arrak, I might understand it. Those two are central to the whole Free Society thing. You and I are just along for the ride."

"Darlene is the ambassador here to help in the negotiation. But she has no dog in this fight. We only want the federation in our galaxy," Dave said. "None of us care what happens here."

The fragrance of chocolate and coffee rushed at them as they opened the door. The shop was crowded with patrons celebrating the jump. Fola Untor saw them and waved. He was busily placing trays of chocolates and pastries on top of the counters where the patrons eagerly filled small plates. Fola pointed over to a small table near the back of the store and they moved toward it. Sitting at the table was Alda Nackly, who had been crying. Her eyes were puffy and red. She smiled broadly as Dave and Charlie approached. She stood and hugged them both.

"I'm so glad you are safe," she cried. "When I heard about the damage here, I rushed home to check on my baby sister. My place is only a couple blocks from where the ceiling collapsed. I overheard that some visitors from Earth 47 had been staying there and I immediately knew it was you."

"Don't cry, Alda," Dave said. "We're all fine. We rode out the jump on our ship. How is your family?"

"My sister is fine," Alda smiled. "Lons and I were in the Hive, so we're both fine too. It's unbelievable that the sky could fall from a jump. When I was in college, we were told such a thing was practically impossible. I'm so happy you are safe."

"Is it possible that someone would do this on purpose, Alda?" Charlie asked. "Are there people against the Free Society or who might have a grudge with us personally?"

"The Society of Humanity has plenty of problems," she began. "Every race thinks they're better than the others. Except the Opa, of course. They are always level thinking and kind. When I was a child, the other kids said the Opa were that way since there were so few of them. They had an inferiority complex as a race. At the university, many of my professors were Opa, and they were great. I think that's when I realized that many of the things I was taught as a kid were just wrong."

"I'm also surprised that there is a Society of Humanity, Alda. Didn't anyone ever try to include other species?" Dave asked. Fola came to their table with a tray with four coffees and a sampling of the chocolate goodies.

"Can I sit with you?" he asked. They welcomed him and each took a coffee. "I overheard what you were talking about and just want to warn you," he whispered. "There are lots of agents around all the time who frown on these discussions. Dave and Charlie are okay, since they are not from the Society. Alda, you know the trouble you could get into. Hold on a minute." Fola stood and went to the counter. "Okay folks," he shouted. "I'm out of chocolate and the big celebration starts in one hour. Time to go!"

The crowd hooted and complained but then quietly left the shop. Fola locked the door and returned to the table. He took a chocolate and chewed it. "Alda, you should probably tell the guys more about me."

"Dave and Charlie, Fola used to be the Chief Engineer for the Hive on Earth Prime," she began. "He also taught at the Earth Prime Engineering University, where I received my degree. Ten years ago, the High Council received a report identifying Fola as an operative for the Free Society. He was fired and disgraced."

"Were you an operative?" Dave asked.

"Never, Dave," Fola replied. "I'm sure you've heard about the arguments in the High Council about breaking up the Society. They never accomplished anything, and I didn't really care. Being a Chief Engineer and university professor was more than a full time job. I had no time to worry about politics."

"Apparently, a senior official with the Free Society group was apprehended with a list of names, including Fola's," Alda said. "It was just a list of names. The High Council assumed it was a list of members and everyone on it was fired. Fola and the others on the list complained and denied the charges, but the decisions had already been made."

"After that, I moved to Aranar Zu in your galaxy and became a farmer," Fola continued. "I had no desire for Hives or college or anything else. Time can play funny games on a person though. My farm was next to another that raised livestock and made cheese. The animals there loved my feed, and I became close to them for a long time."

"Let me guess," Dave said. "The cheese maker was Ipa Nota."

"How could you know that?" Fola asked.

"I've had the opportunity to try her cheese," Dave smiled. "I still remember talking to her about having utok with coffee."

"That's an amazing coincidence, Dave," Fola laughed. "That is a great combination. I wish I had some here for us to share. Anyway, after a few years, I had the chance to meet her brother, the former High Councilor Antar Arrak. He and his wife had nothing good to say about the Free Society. I learned a lot from him. It was Antar Arrak who convinced me to take a job on Hive 1008. My son is now running the farm."

"What about the danger of talking here, Fola," Charlie reminded him.

"Yes, the agents. The Society has seen better days. Since the High Council was never able to find a way to peacefully break it up, they have become more and more paranoid about dissent. I'm amazed that Antar Arrak and Wendo Balak were allowed to make the jump here at all. Planets declaring independence is on the rise again. Two years ago, a group of ten planets formed an alliance and declared independence. It used to be the Society would wait a few years for them to crawl back when there was no trade or security. But this time there were Hives on two of the worlds. Four planetoids like this one were dispatched with hundreds of war ships. The Hives were destroyed and countless lives were lost. Finally, the alliance collapsed and the Society regained control."

"If the Society knows it can't last, why do they fight it?" Charlie asked. "Let the ten worlds live in peace. It seems like a natural way to let the Society move forward."

"You'll see when you arrive at Earth Prime, Charlie," Fola replied. "It's no longer about how to break up the Society. It's all about power. The government is so big that it behaves almost like a living organism fighting for its life. No one in government really cares about the folks anymore, only their jobs and holding on to power."

"Aren't you afraid they may be spying on you now, Fola?" Dave asked. "With your past, it seems logical to check on you too."

"The Chief Engineers are an exclusive club, Dave," Fola smiled. "Each of us has a sacred responsibility to safeguard the others, even when we leave the service. Also, we have developed certain abilities that others do not possess."

"Fola can see the strings of light of others even when he is not in the Hive," Alda replied. "Very few agents can do that, but all Chief Engineers can."

"There is more, but this is not a safe place to discuss that," Fola said. "I have spoken with one of your maklan friends here. He said his name was Jake. He offered to jump me to your ship later. Would that be okay?"

"Of course, Fola," Dave replied. "Just be sure to bring some of these chocolates for our wives."

"It would be my pleasure," Fola said. "I'm sensing several agents entering the room." He stood and took the cups and tray from the table. "Okay folks, thanks for coming, but I've got to get ready for the celebration myself." He walked over to the door and unlocked it. He turned and looked into an empty corner of the room. He smiled and waved. Turning back to Dave and Charlie, he said, "They hate it when I do that."

The Nightsky slowed and cruised into a high orbit over Earth Prime. The planet was unlike anything Dave Brewster could have imagined. The planet itself was close to Earth size, however only the land within ten degrees of the equator was visible, with large forests, windswept plains and rivers coursing toward a single sea. Outside that band in the middle, the remainder of the planet was covered with a giant city to both poles. Dozens of star ports were suspended in orbit around the equator with hundreds of star ships arriving and departing every day.

"Earth Prime Central Command, this is the star cruiser Nightsky requesting berthing instructions," Lia Lawson said.

The view screen image split in two and a smiling face said, "Welcome to Earth Prime, Nightsky. Councilor Balee has advised us of your imminent arrival. I am Lieutenant Silva Odeen and I will be your main contact until you have berthed. Unfortunately, due to some over-scheduling of the ports, it may be a day or two before we can find a spot for you. Do you have any emergency needs in the meantime?"

"Not at this time, Lieutenant Odeen. I am Lieutenant Lia Lawson, Chief Communications Officer of the Nightsky. Please contact me if you need anything from us. We are carrying the Ambassador from Earth 47 as well as the ambassadors from Tak-Makla and No-Makla. We are expecting Antar Arrak and Wendo Balak to join us via shuttle in the next few hours as well. Please coordinate with your people there so they can attend any meetings in the meantime. We may require some stores after a couple of weeks, but so far we are in good condition. Silva, you can also just call me Lia," she replied.

"Thank you, Lia. I hope we can meet sometime during your stay here," Silva replied. "If I may be indelicate, which species are you, Lia? I've never seen anyone who looks like you."

Lia blushed bright red as the rest of the bridge crew chuckled. "I'm sorry, Silva, I don't know how to answer that. On Earth 47 at this time, we all look like this."

"I'm sorry, Lia, I didn't mean to be disrespectful," Silva replied. Silva was a very handsome man with dark brown skin and piercing black eyes. He smiled and said, "I am an Ela. There are more than a thousand Ela planets in the Society."

"Lieutenant Odeen, this is Captain Jon Lake of the Nightsky," Jon laughed. "I will make certain that Lieutenant Lawson meets you in person later so you can chat. Nightsky out." As the image of the planet filled the screen, the bridge crew began to laugh. "Looks like you have a hot date, Lieutenant."

"You all are terrible!" Lia shouted. "Or maybe you're just jealous." She joined them in the laughter. Dave and Charlie walked onto the bridge and were surprised by the crew bent over laughing.

"What did we miss?" Dave said. "I could use a good laugh too."

"It's nothing Admiral," Jon replied. "We were just having a little fun at Lia's expense. No hard feelings, Lia?"

"Never, Jon," she replied. "We were just laughing because the berthing officer we contacted was hitting on me."

"Wow, in front of the bridge crew?" Charlie asked. "He must have been really smitten. That's my little girl." The laughter broke out again.

Fola Untor appeared suddenly on the bridge with Jake Benomafolays clinging to his chest. "I hate it when you do that, Jake," Dave said. "I preferred it when you made the flash of light. At least then I knew what was happening."

"They call it progress, brother," Jake said as he flew off Fola's chest and landed on a command chair. "I heard there would be a delay getting off the ship, so I thought it would be a good time to bring Fola over."

"Good call, Jake," Dave replied. "Welcome to the Nightsky, Fola. I'm glad you could come." They shook hands. "Let's go to my ready room. Lia, please signal Darlene and Aria to join us there."

"Aye-aye, Admiral," Lia replied. "I'm happy to do anything to stop the teasing."

Charlie, Fola, Jake and Dave left the bridge and sat at the conference table in the ready room. "Thanks for the invitation, Dave," Fola said. "Are you certain that the ship is secure?"

"As far as we know it is," Dave replied. "I know maklans like Jake are very sensitive to life energy strings like you are. The ship has been manned during our entire stay on Hive 1008, so I have no reason to doubt it."

"Dave, my team has monitored the ship the entire time," Jake said. "There is no chance any tampering has occurred." Darlene and Aria entered the ready room with a crewman who brought a cart with refreshments. After placing the cart, the crewman left. Fola was introduced to the women and everyone sat again.

"Fola, Charlie and I have shared what you told us with Jake, Darlene and Aria. We're here and we are listening. Please tell us what you want us to know," Dave said.

"In the few hours since your ship left, there have been major discoveries about the ceiling failure in the Balthazar community," Fola began. "I've seen the new evidence, and I now believe that you were not the target of the collapse."

"But it hit directly where we were staying," Darlene said. "Who else was it meant for?"

"The struts were partially cut, but not evenly," Fola replied. "The perpetrators assumed that the weakest parts would fail first, but the opposite happened. Whoever did this underestimated the forces in a galactic jump and must not have been very familiar with Hive activity. The waves of space-time and Source that buffet the planetoid are unusual and related to the strengths and weaknesses of the various Hives involved. In this particular jump, the smallest cuts failed first causing the panel to fall on your residence."

"Where would the panel have fallen if it fell where they wanted it to?" Aria asked.

"On my shop," Fola said. "I suppose I should have guessed that."

"So, they were after you," Dave replied. "But who lives over your store?"

"My apartment is on the third floor over my shop. The flat on the second floor was reserved for the High Consul from Tak-Makla," Fola responded. "Fortunately, he never stayed there. He asked for his group to stay in the Alcazar community near the delegation from No-Makla just after he arrived on the planetoid."

"That means the perpetrators damaged the struts before we arrived on the planetoid," Aria reasoned. "Or at least did not know about the change of plans. But why would they target the tekkans? I thought the Society had been friends with them for hundreds of millions of years."

"I think Dave already knows the answer to that question, Aria," Fola replied. "He asked Alda Nackly a question that caused me to close my shop and join them. Do you remember, Dave?"

"I asked why there was a Society of Humanity and why no other races were ever added," Dave said.

"That's exactly right!" Fola shouted. "Believe me that the variety of life in the home galaxy is no less full than in your own. The Society trades with thousands of other worlds representing dozens of highly advanced societies. As you may know, the valakar started here, like humanity. Now they stretch to your galaxy with peoples like the Palians and Donnaki."

"And the Galliceans," Dave said.

"Actually, you will be surprised to know that the Galliceans are not valakar at all," Fola said. "I believe they originated on Gallia in your galaxy. I mentioned that Chief Engineers have some unique abilities and some are even more advanced. I am able to see differences in the light strings of different species. There are similarities among all human species as well as all valakar. The Galliceans are very different though.”

“So, why is the Society closed to non-humans?” Darlene interrupted.

“Call it racism or ethnocentrism or lack of trust, I don’t know,” Fola said. “Since the Society is so big, it doesn’t need others. Every sentient species evolves to be the top of the food chain on their home world. All other species are seen as inferior or even as dinner. When a new and very alien sentient species is found, there is great ambivalence about how to deal with them. Should we conquer them? Should we trade with them? Should we eat them for lunch? It’s complicated and hard to work on level terms.”

“In my time, the Earth was divided into hundreds of countries and many races of humans,” Charlie said. “It was very difficult to handle race relations. Relations between different countries were ever more difficult, even if they were the same race!”

“So, you understand,” Fola said. “Now imagine if the zolo and nagli munching grass in the field demanded equal rights and payment for their milk? There are limits to what a human mind can accept. Since the Society is so large, it becomes the norm and acceptable. We don’t need to work with them, so we don’t. If we can trade goods and agree not to attack each other, then that’s enough.”

“Where do the tekkans fit in?” Dave asked.

“Long ago, the Society reached out to them and give them key elements of Hive technology,” Fola continued. “Back then, we thought it was good to form bonds with other species as we entered a new galaxy. Their Hive could help us move our people and ships into your galaxy where we could build new worlds. But the experiment backfired. The tekkans were able to do much more with their Hive than we ever could. They offered to exchange technology, but by that time the Society had begun to distrust aliens. Rules were put in place to prohibit the transfer of any Hive technology out of human hands."

"So the entire Society is out to get the tekkans," Charlie said. "They are such a peaceful race. That hardly seems plausible. Aren't there other civilizations with Hives? Didn't Loni Arrak tell us that?"

"Loni? I'm not surprised. You have to remember that she is a young Chief Engineer and was born in your galaxy," Fola replied. "While she received excellent training, she and the others in your galaxy are not as closely linked as the Chief Engineers here. The only Hives we know of are either human or on Tak-Makla. But it's not the whole human population that is the problem. It is a few at the top of the Society who are trying to hold it together. They want to keep Hive technology a secret by keeping one Society and all Hives human."

"What does that mean for the Free Society?" Dave asked.

"Good question, Dave," Fola laughed. "The leaders of the Society know that if we break into Free Societies, eventually one or more will include non-humans. That's the main reason you are here now. But even if there were a few hundred Free Societies in this galaxy, a few would invite non-human to join and the lock on Hive technology would be broken. They will not allow that."

"So we are all wasting our time here," Dave replied. "We came here for nothing."

"Not at all, Dave," Fola smiled. "You are here to do the greatest thing in the history of the Society of Humanity. You are going to get approval for a pilot of the Free Society in your galaxy. Our councilors will see how humans, maklans and Galliceans can live together in peace. Lord Balak is also here with Lord Arrak. When they talk about the Free Society, the public will hear and yearn for it. Whether the government wants it or not, a new day is coming to the Society. And I am so happy you are here to help us now."

"You believe they will allow the pilot?" Darlene asked. "They could just say no and send us home."

"That won't happen, Darlene," Fola said, "because you have Balak and Arrak on your side. Those men defined the difference between the Society and the Free Society clearly. Now both are on the same side. The High Councilors cannot ignore that without serious trouble in the Society. But this is not about a meeting on Earth Prime. You need to travel around and take your case to other key worlds. Off of this planet, everyone will treat you like the saviors you can be. I guess you can tell that I'm very excited."

"I hope we can match your expectations, Fola," Dave said. "My goal is to get the Free Society in my galaxy. We need that to counter our enemies like the Donnaki and Maklakar. If we accomplish that, I'm happy. If we need to travel around with Wendo and Antar to do it, that's what we will do. But if the High Council gives us the green light tomorrow morning, I'm petitioning for a jump back in the afternoon."

Fola laughed out loud. "Dave, you haven't dealt with our bureaucratic mess yet. You'll be lucky to have the first meeting in a week. I would recommend not spending too much time orbiting this planet waiting. Get a schedule and coordinate with Wendo and Antar. They can pick the planets you should visit. Then get out of here and don't come back until the day before your meetings."

"Okay, Fola, I understand," Dave replied. "We'll do our best. Before you go, there's one thing I don't understand. Do you think they were out to kill High Consul Gongaleg only, or you too?"

Fola laughed again. "Whoever arranged for the consul to be in my building had a sense of humor. You know I've been wrongly marked as a member of the Free Society. If they could get me too, that would have been a nice bonus. Of course, what they didn't know was that I wasn't there anyway."

"You weren't there?" Dave said. "Where were you during the jump?"

"I was baby-sitting Ilsa Nackly, Alda's sister," Fola said. "She usually spends time in my shop when she's not in school. I went over to Alda's house to help her through the jump. It's good that I did with all the damage and commotion. The poor little thing was scared to death!"

"Thanks for the update, Fola," Dave said. "If you think of anything else, please let me know. I hope no one finds out you were gone."

"Don't worry about that, Dave," Fola said. "It's another of those Chief Engineer skills. I leave traces around the station that confuse any agents from the Hive. If they come around my shop physically, my staff tells them I stepped out. And if worse comes to worst, and they know I was gone, I'll just change what they see in the Hive."

"That's not possible, is it?" Charlie said.

Fola just winked and smiled. Jake landed on his chest and the two disappeared.

CHAPTER 31

It took a day to get meeting schedules from Earth Prime. Fola had been correct. The first meetings were not scheduled for eight days. Antar and Wendo arrived on Nightsky and provided a list of planets to be visited during that time. The farthest planet was Narta Ela, which was several days away at maximum velocity. Fortunately, most planets had orbiting portals to expedite passage. Earth Prime had five portals which were in use constantly to support the traffic. Given the noted passengers on board, Nightsky was given priority usage of a portal. After waiting in line for five hours, the ship slipped out of space and time and arrived at the Narta Ela portal.

Narta Ela was a large planet, with a diameter of eleven thousand miles. Oceans covered one-half of the surface and three massive continents covered the rest. The planet was very green with forests and jungles covering two-thirds of the continents. All the mountain ranges were low and tree-covered. Only a few peaks were high enough to have a permanent snow cap. The non-forested lands either clung to the coastlines or were in islands surrounded by trees. The bulk of the eight billion people on the world lived in ten major cities. A single Hive was being built in the outskirts of Tanman, the capital and largest city on the planet. Narta Ela was surrounded by a thin ring, similar to No-Makla and eight small moons. A single yellow-white sun was ninety-five million miles away.

Rainor Prebow was the current president of the Planetary High Council. He eagerly agreed to meeting with the dignitaries on Nightsky and scheduled celebrations around the planet to commemorate the visit of Wendo Balak, Antar Arrak and the descendants of the settlers of Earth 47. He also approved shore leave for any crew members and heartily recommended the seaside city of Boolea or the hunting centers in the Baala region.

A single shuttle dropped out of the bay doors on Nightsky toward the thick atmosphere. Dave Brewster and the rest of the group were strapped in and watching the planet grow as they approached the atmosphere. In exchange for an invitation to the celebration, Captains Jon Lake and Lauren London piloted the shuttle. The chemistry between them remained very strong, even though Lauren had been assigned to a desk job on Earth since her release from the Predaxians. Jon repeatedly asked Dave to help her join their team, but all of Dave's ships had full crews and excellent captains, and neither Jon nor Lauren were prepared to resign. Dave knew they were both young and that fate would provide an opportunity at the right time. The shuttle slipped through some cloud cover and emerged over a vast jungle stretching to the horizons.

"Admiral," Lauren reported, "the Kong-Fa and Manila have made the jump to Narta Ela. General Fa-a-Di and Ambassador Mencius send their regards and request a team of maklans to jump them to the surface in time for the celebration."

"That's great news," Dave said. "Please contact Jake and ask him to handle that. Be sure to send them the coordinates for the landing site."

"Aye-aye, Admiral," Lauren replied.

It had not taken much effort to convince the Galliceans and Kalideans to leave Earth Prime and join them. The prospect of sitting in their ships for eight days while the bureaucrats stalled was enough to convince them alone. Dave had also told them about the sabotage on Hive 1008 that could have killed him, and everything that Fola Untor had told him about life and conspiracy in the Society of Humanity. It became obvious to Fa-a-Di they could be targets as well, due to human contempt for other Beings. Everyone knew it would be better to stay together for security. Since their passengers did not have the recognition factor of Antar and Wendo, they were not able to get an expedited jump. The two ships opted to travel to the closest planet with a portal, which was eight hours away as top speed. That extra delay caused them to arrive just now at Narta Ela. With the help of the maklans, they would arrive at the celebration before the shuttle.

The jungle receded and vast farmlands lay below the shuttle. The people of Narta Ela were determined not to spoil the wilds of their planet, so agriculture had to be very efficient to feed the eight billion from a small portion of the land. Even with that, the planet was a net importer of food. The only resource they had in abundance was seafood, given the large oceans. Narta Ela was the home world of the Ela race. As such, the Planetary High Council served as the leaders for the twelve hundred Ela worlds. To make up for the lack of food, they became expert traders, handling almost one-quarter of all Society trade. The home world became a center of science and culture, with hundreds of the best universities and museums to be found anywhere.

The capital city peeked over the horizon. Tanman was vast, with a non-Hive population of eight hundred million. There was a narrow ring of suburbia on the outskirts of the city, forming a break between the farms and the center city. The city was more than one hundred miles across with countless skyscrapers stretching from suburbia to the center of the city. The tall buildings were in ten different clusters, defining the major neighborhoods of Tanman. The buildings stopped suddenly, leaving a five mile diameter park in the center. Only a few marble structures marred the gentle rolling hills in the center. As the shuttle descended more, they could see a large area set up for the evening's festivities. Rainor had told Darlene that more than ten thousand citizens of the city had been invited to the party. The roof of one large marble building opened revealing a landing area for the shuttle. Jon Lake maneuvered the shuttle to align with the markings and was guided down to the ground by ten soldiers. As the engines stopped, a group of dignitaries came toward the ship. Dave could see Mencius, Fa-a-Di and De-o-Nu at the back of the group. "The show is on," Dave laughed.

The ambassadors exited first and were introduced, followed by Antar Arrak and his wife Zina, Wendo Balak and his granddaughter, Serena Vanatee and then the rest. Dave was at the back of the group and helped Jon secure the shuttle. They were adjusting the security panel when a voice behind them said, "Admiral Brewster, I presume."

Dave turned to see President Rainor Prebow standing with his right hand out. Dave shook his hand and replied, "Mr. President, it is a pleasure to be here on your world. This is Captain Jon Lake, master of the star cruiser Nightsky and my dear friend."

"It's great to meet you too Jon," Rainor smiled as they shook hands. Rainor had the same dark color and black eyes as Lieutenant Silva Odeen, which should not have been a surprise since this was an Ela planet. What Dave could not have known from seeing the Lieutenant on the screen was the Ela were very tall. Rainor was more than seven feet tall and towered over Dave.

"I have heard so much about you, Dave Brewster," Rainor laughed. "I am astounded that descendants from our early settlers in your galaxy have come home to us. This is a wonderful experience for me. I have been speaking to your friend, General Fa-a-Di and he tells me you enjoy a nice whisky from time to time. You must join me after dinner to sample some fine Ela whiskies. The general says he has some Gallicean whisky with him and I am thrilled to try that too. I may be prejudiced, but I think the Ela make the best in the Society. Please come with me."

The group walked toward the doors as the roof closed over the shuttle. As they stepped outside onto the grass, the throng of guests burst into applause. There were ten glass circles in front of them on the ground. Each had a handrail all around. Rainor stood on one and motioned Dave and Darlene over. Once ten people were standing, Rainor said, "Please hold the rail." The disk slowly rose into the air and moved over the crowd, who continued to cheer. More dignitaries moved onto the other disks and moved toward the dais, until only the Galliceans and maklans were left. They extended their wings and flew around the crowd to wild hooting and applause, with the maklans flying in circles around the Galliceans.

Special tables and seats had been provided for the giant Galliceans and the tiny maklans at one end of the table. Rainor sat in the center, with Antar, Wendo, and the ambassadors flanking him and his ministers next to them. Dave sat next to Fa-a-Di with Jon, Lauren, Aria and Charlie. Hundreds of waiters moved around the tables, pouring brown liquor into small, crystal glasses. Rainor stood and clipped a small microphone onto his black and golden robes. He raised his glass to the crowd and said, "This is a great day for Narta Ela and the entire Ela race." Thunderous applause filled the area. He motioned for the crowd to be quiet. "Tonight we will celebrate the presence of two of the Society's greatest leaders, Antar Arrak and Wendo Balak, who have come to give us their solution to the overwhelming problems of the Society. We also celebrate the presence of the descendants of our Society in the Ulagong Galaxy. And we will meet new friends from that galaxy who are not human, but not that different from us. In accordance with our tradition, all such celebrations must begin and end with a taste of Ela whisky. To our visitors and each of you here tonight, I bid you welcome." He drank the whisky and shouted, "Now, let's get this party going!" Applause and cheering broke out again.

Fa-a-Di bent over to Dave and said, "This whisky isn't bad, brother, what do you think?"

"Pretty tame stuff by our standards, brother," Dave smiled.

Fa-a-Di and De-o-Nu broke out laughing. "Now you are becoming a Gallicean warrior, Dave Brewster. I'm proud of you," Fa-a-Di said.

"I want you both to know that I argued for hours with Darlene about my daggers," Dave said. "She told me I either left them behind or I couldn't come. Can you imagine that?"

"I know, Dave," Fa-a-Di replied. "My brother-in-law had a fit when we were told not to bring any weapons."

"Can you blame me, General?" De-o-Nu said. "I feel naked without them."

"We are naked without them," Fa-a-Di replied. "But we are ambassadors now, not soldiers. Let's just enjoy dinner. President Prebow has promised us more whisky after dinner. Let us hope it is better than this."

The dinner was wonderful with new foods unlike any from the Ulagong Galaxy had ever seen. Much of the meal was seafood, but the textures and flavors were more like beef and veal than fish. The greens were spicy and reminded Dave of the Gallicean style greens harvested on Jupiter. Several different wines were served, all of which were full bodied and rich. As the plates were being cleared, De-o-Nu pulled a large flask of Gallicean whisky from his uniform and set it on the table.

"Ah, dessert has arrived," Fa-a-Di laughed as he opened the bottle and poured for the group. "I hope you have more of this, brother-in-law, or we won't have enough to get drunk!"

"Don't worry, General," De-o-Nu replied, "I have two more bottles hidden in this suit. It helps to be big!"

Rainor approached and put his hand on Dave's shoulder, saying, "I saw that bottle and had to come right over. What are you drinking?"

"This is the best Gallicean whisky, Mr. President," Fa-a-Di smiled. "Please give me your glass." Fa-a-Di filled the glass and handed it back. "Be careful, it's pretty potent stuff. Dave can hardly stomach it."

A broad smile crossed Rainor's face as he swirled the whisky around in his mouth. "This is fantastic. I have a few rare Ela whiskies which we can try after the speeches. Don't worry. I have arranged accommodations for everyone after the party. No drunk shuttle flying allowed! May I have some more, please?"

De-o-Nu pulled another full bottle out of his suit. "Please, Mr. President, take this one and share it with your other guests," he said. "I will have our ship send you a case later. We always carry a lot, especially when my brother-in-law is along for the ride."

"You are too gracious, Ambassador," Rainor replied. "I appreciate the formality in this setting, but when we retire to my den for drinks, please call me Rainor." He smiled and returned to his seat, where he offered small amounts to those around him.

"Jake, come over here," De-o-Nu said as he pulled another bottle from his suit. "I know you maklans don't like much of what was served, but take this for your friends."

Jake fluttered over and was flickering between pink and blue. "Thank you so much, brother," he said as he took the bottle. "The food was pretty much inedible for us, however the wine was great." He looked at himself changing colors. "I think it's affecting me though." He flew back to the other maklans and opened the bottle. They each extended a narrow tendril into the bottle and drank.

"Great!" Fa-a-Di shouted. "Now we're out of whisky!"

De-o-Nu pulled out a fourth bottle and laughed. "I would never disappoint the High Commissioner of Greater Gallia!"

After a few short speeches by various ministers, Antar Arrak and Wendo Balak took the podium. Once the applause quieted, Wendo began, "Thank you for the wonderful welcome. I'm sure Antar agrees with me that it is great to be back in the home galaxy. Neither of us has been here since we left the High Council a hundred years ago. Back then, we could never agree. Unfortunately due to our stubbornness, we allowed the Council to remain deadlocked on the future direction of the

Society as a whole. Nothing much has changed since then. We are sorry."

"But today is a new day," Antar began. "As I worked my farm and tended my garden later, I began to understand this deadlock would ultimately cause the collapse of the Society. Hundreds of planets have declared independence since we left the Council. I was horrified to find the last group of such planets was brutally put down by the military. We are all human and we cannot allow ourselves to descend into civil war."

"There is another way," Wendo took over. "For too long, two small words have been taboo, but now must be said. It is time for the Free Society." The crowd erupted into concerned murmurs. "Don't fear those words. They are just two small words that have no power to hurt anyone. We are here to petition the High Council to establish a Free Society in the Ulagong Galaxy as a pilot. If it is successful, as I know it will be, it may well become the model for this galaxy as well."

"But there is more, dear citizens," Antar said. "This will not be a Free Society limited to the fifty-one human species. All sentient Beings will be able to join. Tonight, we are joined by three such species: the Galliceans and two maklan species." Wild cheering filled the area again. "And there are others too. All of the peace-loving societies of the Ulagong Galaxy will be able to join. It is time for our human-only racism to end." The audience became very quiet.

"These are difficult words to hear, I know," Wendo said. "But we already have strong relations with dozens of other species in this galaxy. Think of the power we would have together if our enemies attack. Think of what we can learn from each other if we have a true partnership. This is the way of the future. Would Dave Brewster, Fa-a-Di, Zee Gongaleg and Jake Benomafolays please join us?" The four crossed the floor to the podium. "High Consul Zee Gongaleg of Tak-Makla has taught me much over the last few days. These four individuals come from very different worlds. Zee and Jake are both maklans, but their sub-species are very different. They have overcome their differences and now are the best of friends. Admiral Dave Brewster, please say a few words about this amazing friendship." Applause rang out again as the four took over the podium.

"Thank you, Antar and Wendo," Dave began. "I honestly had no idea I would be asked to speak, but if I know anything, I know what it means to have brothers and sisters. I was born more than eleven centuries ago on Earth 47." He pointed to Charlie Watson. "Charlie, please stand up. This man, my closest friend, was recruited to get me and my family to jump to this time and help mankind rekindle the spirit of adventure and discovery. Fate smiled on us, and I am here today with my beloved wife, Ambassador Darlene Brewster." The audience applauded. "The first thing Darlene did in this time was to negotiate a treaty with the Galliceans to share planets. The Galliceans are a native species in my galaxy, and they live on gas giant planets that are totally useless to humans like me. Likewise, they have terrestrial planets in their systems they cannot inhabit. In order to build our relationship with the Galliceans, it made sense to offer them our gas giants in exchange for their terrestrial planets. With that one agreement and a flight over a gas giant in the Earth 47 system, strapped to the chest of High Commissioner Fa-a-Di, the greatest general in the history of Greater Gallia, we have become brothers." More applause sounded as the Galliceans stepped forward and hugged Dave. "Shortly thereafter, I needed help to apprehend a pirate ship in our space. I asked for their help, but they did not send a ship to help us. They sent thirty ships!" The audience cheered and clapped. "That led me to a forgotten human colony planet where I found Jacomofledes Benomafolays, a maklan from No-Makla, another gas giant in the Earth 47 system. The partnership among the Galliceans, maklans and humans then stopped both the senseless slaughter of innocents on No-Malka, but also an enemy invasion of Greater Gallia. Together, all of us followed a trail that led us to Tak-Makla, and Zee Gongaleg. Zee introduced all of us to the technology of a Hive. The Hive on that planet was instrumental in our victory in the Second Predaxian War. That war could have caused billions of deaths and unknown destruction. None of us could have accomplished any of that alone. Alone, our galaxy would be a very dangerous place. Together, we did it all. Now, we are here to petition to form a Free Society in my galaxy. Everything Antar and Wendo have said is true. We can form true multi-species societies because they benefit us all. I can no longer imagine my old life in the past. To think I could have lived my whole life never knowing any of these great people is sad. These have been the best years of my life. Let us try this experiment. When you see it working, you will know you can do it too. Thanks for listening. After the speeches are over, all of us will be happy to meet you personally. Even though they don't have their harnesses, I'm sure my Gallicean brothers would love to fly some of you around. Also, Jake and the maklans from No-Makla can fly some around as well. May God bless us all."

The entire crowd jumped to their feet applauding and cheering. Fa-a-Di and De-o-Nu extended their wings while the maklans flew around the crowd. Wendo walked up to Dave and said in his ear, "Antar and I are not needed here Dave. If you keep selling the Free Society like that, we can go back to our gardens. Thank you so much." He grabbed Dave's hand and thrust their arms into the air. Antar took the other arm and did the same.

The Nightsky, Manila and Kong-Fa left Narta Ela at 0900 on course to Bantar Zu, which was ten hours away at top speed. Bantar Zu was the hub of the Zu culture and housed the Zu High Council that set standards for all Zu planets. Antar and Zina Arrak were born and lived there until his retirement from the High Council.

Dave Brewster sat at a corner table in the coffee shop closest to the bridge, savoring his first cappuccino of the day and nursing a hangover from the whisky the night before. After the celebration, he and others joined Rainor in his study for more whisky. While he could not remember completely, Dave thought they must have tasted more than a dozen varieties from different Ela planets. By the time the party ended, everyone was desperate for sleep. Dave could see Narta Ela quickly shrinking from view as Nightsky accelerated. He hoped there would be less whisky on Bantar Zu.

"Excuse us, Admiral, may we join you?" Wendo Balak said. Dave turned to see Wendo and Serena standing by his table. "I would like to discuss a change of itinerary."

"Please sit down," Dave said, motioning to two empty chairs.

"You sit Grandfather," Serena said. "I'll go get us some coffee." She turned and went to the counter.

"Lord Balak, I don't understand. You want to change the itinerary you gave us yesterday?" Dave asked.

"Dave, please call me Wendo," the old man smiled. "I have a small confession. The itinerary Antar and I wrote was more for the High Council than us. You don't know any of these planets, but the ones on the list are the cream of the crop of Society worlds. If we stick with that schedule, you'll have four more nights of giant celebrations in big, chic cities populated by happy people. While you would not doubt be impressed by each one, none of them will help you understand why I brought you and your friends here."

Serena returned and set a cup of black coffee in front of Wendo. "Here you go, Grandfather." She sat next to him.

"I thought we were here to petition for a Free Society in my galaxy," Dave said. "Isn't that it?"

"Of course, son," Wendo replied. "But did you ever wonder why planets declare independence from the Society? If all the worlds are like Narta Ela, why would anyone want out?" Wendo sipped his coffee. "This is wonderful coffee, Dave. You must share the source of your beans with us later. Let me ask another question. Did you ever wonder why I named my idea the Free Society?"

"I thought it meant each smaller group of planets had the freedom to set their own course and choose their destiny," Dave replied.

"That is only partially true, Dave," Wendo said. "You've heard how there are fifty classes of terrestrial planets and fifty human species that have developed over time to live on them, right? Perhaps you jumped to the conclusion that all fifty are equal and have the same wonderful planets like Narta Ela or Bantar Zu. Unfortunately, that is a false assumption."

"So, some of the races are subordinate to the others. Is that what you are saying, Wendo?" Dave asked.

"That is correct Dave," Wendo replied. "But I don't want you to believe it because I said it. You and your friends need to see it for yourself. That is why we need to change course for the Lagamar system. It is actually closer than Bantar Zu."

"What planet are we going to see there, Wendo?" Dave asked. "What species lives there?"

"I chose Lagamar because there are three human worlds there, one for each of the most downtrodden races in the Society," Wendo stated. "Normally, you would have to travel long distances to see any one of these races, but in this case they share a system. There is also a gas giant in that system of interest. I need the Galliceans to visit there and make a report for you. I think they are going to be shocked at what they find." Wendo finished his coffee. "Serena, could you please get me another cup?" She smiled, took the cup and returned to the counter. Wendo placed his hand on Dave's knee and leaned close to him. "Dave, the Lagamar system will show you everything you want to know about the Society. You'll learn why it is failing, why the races don't get along, and especially why the High Council has been fighting both Antar and me on how to move forward. Unfortunately, you will also learn some terrible things about humanity." Serena rejoined them.

"Okay, how do we get to Lagamar?" Dave asked.

"I have the course and coordinates, Dave," Serena said. "If I can go to the bridge, I will provide them what they need. Which planet should we visit first, Grandfather?"

"Lagamar Opa, I think," Wendo said.

Dave touched his com-link to activate it. "Jon, I'm sending Serena Vanatee to the bridge now. We're changing course to Lagamar Opa, and she has the course."

"Aye-aye, Admiral," Jon replied. "Why the change, Dave?"

"We'll discuss that later, Jon. Don't worry, it's for the best. Also, please advise Kong-Fa and Manila of the change. I'm sure Mencius will be pleased to finally see another Opa planet. Brewster out," he said as he closed the connection. "Okay, Serena, you can go to the bridge now. Jon's expecting you." Serena left the room. "Wendo, you mentioned that the High Council was fighting both you and Antar. I thought it was an ongoing argument between the two options."

Wendo chuckled softly. "That's what we thought too, Dave. Ultimately, we were pawns. As long as the people thought we were working on a plan, there was peace and relative tranquility. The news was constantly filled with the arguments in both directions. Everyone was thrilled that progress was on the horizon. When Antar and I finally gave up and left, the balloon burst. Suddenly, all hope was lost. Antar and I had to flee the home galaxy to save our lives. The hopes and dreams of trillions of people had been crushed by our inability to succeed. Looking back on it now, there never could have been a choice. The High Council would not accept that."

"I don't understand," Dave said. "You were on the Council. There were only two options being discussed. If one was selected, wouldn't that be it?"

"Let me explain, Dave," Wendo began. "If we broke the Society by races, there would be fifty or fifty-one new societies. If we broke into regions, there would be fifty or so new societies. Either way you get the same result, basically. Who stood to lose if either choice was made?"

"The High Council would lose," Dave answered. "They would lose power and control over fifty thousand planets."

"You see, Dave, it's simple really," Wendo said. "Earth Prime would no longer be needed. All of those billions of bureaucrats would be out of work. Many would return to their new society and lead there, but leading a thousand planets doesn't pay as well as running the whole Society."

"It's always about power, isn't it, Wendo?" Dave asked.

"That has always been the case," Wendo sighed. "Dave, the Lagamar system will open your eyes. You have been on Aranar Zu and Atar Pa in your galaxy, and they are nice places, but not like Narta Ela. Those planets are more humble and people lead simple lives in comparison. So Narta Ela is on one extreme. Lagamar is the opposite. You said your friend Mencius would be pleased to see another Opa world. Don't count on it. Did you ever wonder why Consul Arnar, Consul Jeebo, and General Zilma risked their careers to get you and the Arraks?"

"I thought you wanted us to support the Free Society," Dave replied.

"That's true, but going to such extremes is unusual, wouldn't you say?" Wendo asked. "The Society is crumbling around us even now. I was prepared to stay retired on Atar Pa, sulking over my lost opportunity, but Arnar and Jeebo convinced me that we had to act now and do whatever was necessary to repair things before the entire Society falls into civil war. Antar and I had held the imagination of trillions of people with our ideas to help the poorest races and give atonomy to regions. We failed all of them when we gave up. We were desperate to get the Arraks on our side again. And when we found you and the other humans from Earth 47, we knew that would be the opportunity of a millennium. Here is our chance to elevate all humans to the same level. Here is our chance to let regions succeed because Earth 47 has proven that smaller regions can thrive. But let's leave it at that for now, Dave. I don't want my words to change your opinions. I will let the Lagamar system do that for me."

"That's a phenomenal story, Wendo," Dave gasped. "I guess we'll see in a few hours. Can I ask you one last question?"

"Certainly, Dave," Wendo smiled.

"I heard it first from Antar last night and now you said it too," Dave said. "I've heard fifty or fifty-one human species. Which is it?"

"There are fifty types of terrestrial planets and fifty-one species of humans in the Society," he responded. "I'm glad you noticed that. The last planet we'll visit before returning to Earth Prime is Nan, the home world and only planet of the Nan culture. Since they have only one planet, they don't count to the Society. But that is not the end of their story. Their story is something most humans know almost nothing about, and it is perhaps the greatest tragedy and miracle of the Society of Humanity. Outside their home world, the Nan are known as the invisible people. You will love their planet, I guarantee that. We will discuss them at length when we return to Earth Prime. In my heart, the Nan are the reason for the Free Society. I must leave you now," Wendo said as he stood up. Dave stood as well and they shook hands. "Thank you so much for taking this journey with Antar and me. I spoke to him recently and we compared ages. Then, I thought I had ten or twenty years left in my life. Now, with the opportunities in front of us, I feel like a young man. Thank you Dave and I will see you later."

"Captain, Lagamar Opa Central Command is hailing us," Lia said.

"Put them on the screen, Lia," Jon Lake replied. The right side of the view screen was filled with a bright blue man with large black eyes. "Lagamar Opa Central, this is Captain Jon Lake of the Nightsky. We request permission to establish an orbit over your planet."

"Permission granted, Nightsky," the Opa said. "Lord Wendo Balak advised us you would be coming a few hours ago. I am Major Ulan Makwee, and I've been asked to schedule your dignitaries to meet with some members of our council. I am now transmitting coordinates for your orbit. I will pilot a shuttle to your ship in two hours to escort our guests."

"Thank you, Major," Jon smiled. "We have received the coordinates and will lay in a course to match."

"Very good, Captain," Ulan replied. "We don't get many visitors in the Lagamar system. It's amazing that both Lord Balak and Antar Arrak are coming here. Thank you for fulfilling this dream for all of us."

"It's our pleasure, Major," Jon said. "By the way, we are also carrying a delegation from the Kalidean Federation in our galaxy. The Kalideans are descendants of Opa settlers in our galaxy millions of years ago. They certainly will be joining the group, I trust."

"Absolutely," Ulan smiled. "Frankly, I wasn't aware of them, but that is wonderful news. I will forward that information to our Council immediately. Thank you, Jon. Lagamar Opa out." The screen switched back to a full view of the planet.

Nightsky settled into a high orbit. The vast expanse of the planet lay below the ship. Lagamar Opa was twelve thousand miles in diameter. Only twenty percent of the surface was covered by oceans. The large continents were covered by hundreds of tall mountain ranges with permanent snow caps. Narrow bands of forested hills separated the mountains from the wide grass plains that stretched to the coastlines. The plains were marred by giant pit mines which were partially obscured by clouds of sand and dust. Very few cities could be seen, and those mostly clung to the coastlines, far from the mines.

Dave and Darlene Brewster were waiting for the rest of the guests in the pressurized section of the shuttle bay. The doors had already been opened for the shuttle. Through the open doors, they could clearly see a large sandstorm moving across the plains, rapidly approaching a large pit mine. As they watched, the large shuttle flew slowly into the bay and landed. The shuttle was more than twice the size of the shuttles used by the Nightsky. Its surface and windows were badly scarred as though it had been through too many sandstorms. The bay doors closed and flashing lights indicated the area was being repressurized. After five minutes, the lights stopped flashing and the shuttle opened her doors. Five Opa walked off the ship. Two wore military uniforms, while the three others wore suits, not unlike those of twenty-first century Earth.

Dave and Darlene left the antechamber and joined the group. "Good day, I am Ambassador Darlene Brewster from Earth 47, and this is my husband, Admiral Dave Brewster," Darlene said as she shook hands with the Opa. "Welcome aboard the Nightsky."

"Ambassador, welcome to Lagamar Opa. I am Orlo Vance, the President of the High Council. These are my associates, Aon Falon, President of Lagamar Opa Minerals, and Baty Makal, Ambassador to the Regional Council. This is General Mali Nook, head of our Armed Forces, and Major Ulan Makwee, who is acting as our shuttle pilot today."

After the introductions, Dave said, "We're just waiting for the rest of the party. They should arrive any minute."

"Dave, Major Makwee advises you have a group of Opa from your galaxy on board. Is that true?" Aon asked.

"That is what I'm told," said a voice from behind them. They turned to see Mencius of Kalidus with two assistants entering the bay. "This is amazing for me," Mencius continued. "When I was told there were people like us in another galaxy, I didn't believe it. We always believed we originated on Kalidus. I guess I know how you felt when you met Loni Arrak now, Dave."

After a few minutes, they were joined by Zee Gonaleg, Jake Benomafolays, Antar and Zina Arrak, Wendo Balak and Serena Vanatee. Major Makwee led everyone back onto the shuttle. As Dave entered, he saw another man cleaning the seats. When the dignitaries started to enter, he slipped behind a small door. The man was quite short with light brown skin, narrow blue eyes and white hair above his tall forehead. He had seen people like that before, but couldn't quite remember where.

Wendo and Serena were sitting in front of Dave. After they were strapped in, Dave tapped Wendo on the shoulder. He whispered, "Wendo, did you see that other person cleaning the shuttle a minute ago?"

"Yes, Dave," Wendo whispered back. "You have seen an invisible human. We should not talk of this here." He turned his head to the front.

General Nook touched a button and his chair turned to face the guests. "As soon as the bay is depressurized, we will descend to the planet. Lord Balak sent us a list of places he wanted you to see. President Vance has added a small dinner celebration at his home afterward where we can show you our gratitude for your visit. It is uncommon for us to entertain visitors, especially of your stature. I personally am very interested in learning more about the Opa culture in the Ulagong Galaxy. For now, just sit back and enjoy the trip. We are very informal here, so you may call us by our first names if you so wish." The bay doors opened and the shuttle lifted off the deck. "Ah, here we go now."

The shuttle left the Nightsky, which shone like a giant silver bird above them. As they slipped down into the atmosphere, the shuttle creaked and shook. "Sorry about that, everyone," Ulan said. "We don't get replacement shuttles very often. This is actually our best one at the moment." After a few moments of shaking, the shuttle ride softened and they flew down toward the surface. They leveled off at around five hundred feet over one of the great plains. The land rolled very slightly with grassland stretching to the horizons. Where the rolling hills met, a few tufts of scrub trees often stood. They flew over grain farms covering tens of thousands of acres. Massive combines moved across the land harvesting the grain. Every few minutes they would pass over reservoirs full of water to irrigate the land. Finally, they began to approach a cliff that stretched beyond the horizon. It reminded Dave of the huge cliff he flew over on Tak-Makla. The shuttle slowed quickly as it approached the edge. A number of buildings were huddled a mile in front of the cliff. The shuttle landed on a pad near those buildings and the engines shut down.

"Okay everyone, you can call me Aon from now on," the Opa said as he stood. "This is our first stop. Outside you will see the Alcala Strip Mine. It is the second largest strip mine on Lagamar Opa. As President of the Lagamar Opa Mineral Consortium, it is my job to make sure all the mines on the planet are operating at top efficiency. We have recently replaced our mining equipment to gain a twenty-two percent efficiency gain, which we are all very proud of. It's a bit warm today, but not too bad. I think we can walk for a while without a problem. Major Makwee will give each of you a respirator mask in case we encounter too much dust. Please follow me." He stood and walked to the open door where the Major handed him a mask. The others quickly followed and stepped into the warm Lagamar Opa afternoon.

Dave was the last to exit. As Ulan handed him a mask, he glanced back. The small man was adjusting the bolts securing the seats to the floor. When the man saw Dave looking at him, he smiled meekly and rushed back behind the small door at the back of the ship. Dave Brewster stepped onto Lagamar Opa. This part of the planet reminded Dave of Kansas. Slightly rolling hills stretching as far as the eye could see. The group had already moved off toward the buildings and he rushed to catch up to them. As he went ahead to catch up to Darlene, Wendo grabbed his arm and pulled him aside.

"Dave, please do me a favor," Wendo whispered. "I know how you are, but do not try to make contact with the Nan. You have a good heart, son, but the rest of our Society will not understand. If anything, you will make it worse for the man on the shuttle."

"I don't understand, Wendo," Dave whispered back. "But I will do as you ask. It just doesn't make sense to pretend a whole race of people doesn't exist."

"You're right, Dave. It doesn't make sense, but that is the way it is here right now. The Free Society can fix this. But we can't be so obvious. When Antar or I make reference to the fifty-one races of humanity, everyone knows what we're talking about. But neither of us would ever demand equal rights for the Nan. They are humanity's dirty little secret. All we can do is talk about equality and justice for all races. Once people accept that, the Nan win by default."

"Are they slaves, Wendo?" Dave asked.

"Of course not! That would be barbaric," Wendo replied. "And don't feel sorry for that man on the shuttle. The people on the three Lagamar worlds treat the Nan almost as equals. Everyone here is poor compared to the other planets. Come on now before we raise more suspicions." They hurried to catch up again.

The buildings that looked so small from the shuttle were gigantic. Aon opened the doors of one building to reveal an earth-moving machine that rose more than one hundred feet above them. They stepped out of the sun and into the shadow of the truck. "This is one of our new loaders. These are built on Lagamar Ulu. It has three times the capacity of our earlier version and travels almost twice as fast. It looks like the crew is coming now." Three gray men came toward them through the doors. They heads and bodies were coated in heavy sand

and dust. Their blue faces could be seen through the glass of their helmets. They walked right past the group and entered a small lift that carried them upward to the cab. Two minutes later, the giant machine began to move toward the doors. Aon hurried his guests out of the way and it rolled by them very slowly and out into the bright sunlight. It turned and moved out of their line of sight.

The group left the building and headed toward a smaller one nearby with two metal doors piercing an otherwise blank wall. "This is one of the dormitories," Aon began. "These doors are for the workers after their shifts. They led to showers and their rooms. We'll go around front for the visitor entrance." After five minutes, they arrived at two large glass doors, which opened automatically as they approached. Aon led them inside and the doors slid closed behind them.

The air conditioning was a relief. The lobby was very large with dozens of couches and small tables scattered about. Many workers were sitting and talking together before their shifts or on their days off. Their uniforms were neat and clean, totally unlike the three who took the loader. Mencius walked away from the group and began introducing himself to the miners. They were amazed to meet an Opa from another galaxy. Four Nan workers moved quickly through the room cleaning tables and collecting glasses. Dave had to focus to even see them. It was no wonder there were called invisible people. Dave tried not to look for them and maintain the ruse that they were not even there. Aon sent Ulan to keep tabs on Mencius and led the rest deeper into the building.

The left the lobby and walked down a short hallway. At the end, other hallways led both left and right, while in front of them was a large dining hall. Hundreds of miners were enjoying a meal before or after their shifts. Laughter filled the air. The far wall of the dining hall was all glass with many doors. Aon led the group through the dining area. Dave could feel his mouth water from the aroma of the food. They walked through a glass door and into a huge garden. A large glass dome separated them from the heat of the afternoon. A variety of exotic plants filled plots of land representing many of the Opa planets. The largest was in the center, representing Lagamar Opa. A pair of hundred foot evergreen trees filled the center, reaching almost to the dome.

President Orlo Vance said, "We are very proud of our dormitories. Our miners travel long distances to find work here, leaving their families behind for weeks at a time. Providing decent food, lodging and diversion is the very least we can do. Can I answer any questions?"

"Are all Opa planets filled with mines?" Mencius asked.

"Well, that's who we are, Mencius. In the Society of Humanity, we Opa carry the load for finding and harvesting natural resources," Orlo responded. "When a new planet is found with rich resources, we are the first to be selected. This is where we excel."

"But what about science and the arts?" Mencius added. "In my galaxy, we lead in many disciplines. I'm just a bit surprised."

"Really? I just learned today that there are Opa in your galaxy," Orlo said. "What else can you tell us?"

"We are the largest civilization in the galaxy that we are aware of," Mencius began. "We have ten thousand worlds. I believe Greater Gallia and the Kalidean Federation are the leading societies there."

"I would agree with Mencius," Dave said. "Without him, I would still be in the twenty-first century looking for work. The Kalideans also helped humanity when we were at our worst."

"This is a startling revelation, I just tell you, Mencius," Orlo replied. "We will speak more of this at dinner, I assure you. Aon, you can continue the tour now."

"Thank you, Orlo," Aon said. "I too am at a loss for words. I wish we were off to dinner now to find out more. I think we should return to the shuttle now. We will fly over the pit to give you more perspective of the scope of this operation. Then we will head to the Mount Naglamar Deep Mine."

As they headed back to the shuttle, Antar and Wendo held Dave back a bit so they could talk to him in private as they walked. "Wendo, I think today is going to be a resounding victory for us," Antar said quietly.

"Yes, it will," Wendo replied. "Bringing Mencius to an Opa planet was brilliant. For millions of years, the Opa have worked the mines for the Society. Now they see a glimmer of hope that there are other possibilities. I had no idea how advanced the Kalidean Federation was. I can hardly wait for dinner either. It will be an amazing conversation among the Opa. What do you think, Dave?"

"I must be stupid," he replied. "I still don't understand completely. I understand why the Zu like cold planets and the Pa like warm ones. But mining is not a state to be adapted to, it is an occupation. Don't all planets have mines?"

Wendo put his hand on Dave's shoulder. "I think you understand more than you realize, Dave Brewster. The five hundred Opa planets are incredibly rich in mineral resources. It will take millions of years to extract them all. When they are finished, the planets will either be abandoned or given to other races. This planet would make a wonderful Pa planet then, for example. But you never visited any mines on another planet, did you?"

"You're telling me those mines are filled with Opa?" Dave asked.

"That's very likely, Dave," Antar responded. "In some cases, the dominant race will do their own mining, although most will hire Opa teams to extract the minerals and then leave."

"So, in those cases, the Opa are just like the Nan," Dave whispered.

"That's close, Dave," Wendo replied as they approached the shuttle. "The Nan are a unique case, but essentially you are correct."

After they were strapped in, the shuttle lifted off and headed for the edge of the mine pit. As it crossed over the edge, the ground dropped a thousand feet below them to the bottom of the pit. The pit was so large the other edges disappeared over the horizon. "The Alcala Strip Mine is approximately two hundred miles in diameter," Aon said. "The veins we are working are quite deep here, so we expect to keep mining here for another one hundred and fifty years. Fortunately for us, most of the land in this area has similar veins, so we will be in this region for a very long time. Now we are going to head to the moutains to see our richest mine. Please enjoy the ride."

The shuttle climbed out of the pit and headed back toward the mountains. After ten minutes, the snowy peak of Mount Naglamar dominated the view. Smaller mountains formed a range that ran beyond the horizon. The shuttle flew over a small mountain covered with tall trees like the ones in the dormitory they had just visited. A large river rushed through the valley below carrying snowmelt to the plains and thirsty crops there. A few hundred feet above the river, a large landing area had been cut from the lower levels of the mountain. Ulan leveled off and landed the shuttle near ten others stationed nearby. New fallen snow had been cleared and formed mounds around the pad.

"It's going to be cold outside," Aon said. "But we only have to cross over to those doors." He pointed to two glass doors a hundred yards away. "Let's keep together this time." The shuttle door opened and the brisk air rushed in. Dave could feel himself shiver as it washed over his thin uniform. They moved quickly and arrived in the heated terminal building after only a minute or two.

A smiling Opa wearing a silver jumpsuit was waiting for them with two racks of similar suits. "Good afternoon, distinguished guests," he said. "I am Pak Makwee, and I manage the Mount Naglamar Deep Mine. I have jumpsuits to protect the clothing of our human guests, but unfortunately we don't have anything for the others. I apologize for that."

"Please don't be concerned," Zee said. "Jake and I will be doubly careful." Everyone laughed.

After donning the suits, Pak led them to an elevator. The car was very different, with twenty chairs bolted to the floor. "Please take a seat and strap in," Pak said. "This is a different kind of elevator." Dave sat next to Darlene and strapped himself down. He took her hand as Pak pressed a button on his seat. The car shot downward. Dave could feel himself lifting off the seat. Fortunately, the straps held. The downward trip seemed to last forever. It began to slow and Dave could feel the seat beneath him again. It came to a stop without a sound or motion. The outer doors opened and they stepped out into the brightly lit cavern. "We are now ten thousand feet below the landing pad," Pak continued. "The elevator ride can be uncomfortable for some, so we'll wait here a moment to catch our breath. This is the largest precious stone and mineral mine in the Society. It was built more than two million years ago, and the quality and quantity of product kees improving. We are very proud of the work we do here. Let's continue now."

They walked through the cavern for ten minutes and turned into a narrow tunnel cut through stone. The tunnel sloped slightly downward and Dave could feel the temperature rising as they moved forward. At the end of the tunnel was a closed metal door. Pak placed his com-link against the door and it slid open. "This is what we call the crystal cave. I hope you enjoy it." He switched on lights and they stepped in. The room was magnificent. The ceiling was two hundred feet over their heads, and the room was more than three hundred yards across. The walls, ceiling and floor were completely covered with crystals of different shapes and colors.

"What are these crystals, Pak?" Dave asked.

"Diamonds, mostly," Pak replied. "We have found many rooms like this, only smaller on this level. This one has been left as we found it."

"Why would you do that?" Dave asked. "These stones have to be worth a fortune."

"You are quite right," he answered. "I'm sure you are noticing the heat rising as we move through the room. Less than one hundred feet beyond the far wall is a massive magma pool.

There is no way we can remove these stones without risking a horrible, searing death."

"Pak, that's an excellent reason," Dave laughed. "I agree and think we should leave in case Nature picks this minute for an earthquake."

They returned to the surface and boarded the shuttle again. The sun was sinking toward the horizon as they lifted off and rose above the trees and headed away. Dave was more confused than ever. The Opa seemed to relish this work, but they did not choose it. He thought about the ancient caste system in India. Was that what was happening here? He began to realize why Antar and Wendo could never change the Society. The races had been put in roles so long ago they had become happy with them.

Darlene leaned over and kissed him on the cheek. "Dave, you're a million miles away again."

"I'm sorry, sweetheart," he replied. "There's too much going on for my mind to cope."

"Did you see that other guy in the back?" she whispered. "What's he doing?"

"I can't talk now," he whispered back. "I'll tell you when we get back to Nightsky."

He looked out the window to see the shuttle settling down in front of a large home on a beach. Several other large homes followed the curve of the sand. The doors opened and Orlo said, "Welcome to my home, everyone. Let's have a drink and some dinner now."

After spending a lot of time at the beach residence on Tak-Makla, the surroundings seemed familiar and comfortable to Dave. The President's home was not an official residence like the one Zee Gongaleg enjoyed on his planet. This was Orlo's home, where he and his family had lived since he took his first job at the Mount Daglamar Deep Mine almost two hundred years ago. The house was about three thousand square feet, and it was clear that multiple additions had been made over that time due to growth in the family. All the Vance children had long moved out to begin their own lives, and the interior had been updated again to a more open great room look. Several conversation hubs were marked by overstuffed sofas and coffee tables. One wall was a bookcase with hundreds of worn books packed onto the shelves. Orlo led the group through the house and out the glass doors where a large stone patio reached from the house to the beach one hundred feet away.

Several Opa were working feverishly setting the tables that had been set up in a U shape to enhance conversation. Strings of lights mounted on poles gave the area a warm and cheery feel. Orlo led them to a small bar where a smiling young man was waiting for them. "My dear guests, this is my son, Umbly, and he will be our bartender tonight," Orlo said as he hugged his child. While everyone was introducing themselves, Orlo slipped away to the outdoor cooking area where three grills were working to cook fish and vegetables. The smoke had a unique fragrance unlike anything from Earth. Dave wondered if that was the wood from those tall trees on the mountains. There certainly were not many trees in this area. He looked carefully to see if there were any invisible people in the area, but could not see any.

"Here you go, Dave and Darlene," Zee said as he approached from the front of the line. "Having more than two hands comes in handy on occasions like this." He held out a glass of red wine to Darlene and a glass of whisky over ice to Dave, while sipping his own whisky. "Let's find a place to chat." The three of them walked to the end of the patio and stepped into the soft sand. Zee led them to the edge of the water and then down the beach fifty feet to be away from the crowd. "So, what do you think of Lagamar Opa, Dave?"

"It's a beautiful planet, Zee," Dave replied. "Why do you ask?"

"I was surprised to see Opa being treated as a lower caste," Zee frowned. "I've known Mencius and other Kalideans for some time now, and they are an incredibly talented people. All of that seems to have been wasted here." He looked around to see if anyone was listening. "And did you see that other race of humans working as cleaners? Who are they? Everyone, including them seems to behave as though they are invisible."

"You're absolutely right, Zee," Dave said. "But please, those people are a very delicate issue in the Society. Wendo asked me not to talk about them here and I think we need to respect that. He said we would visit their home world on this trip, and then he can tell us more."

"I suppose that's acceptable," Zee replied. "And it's not that different from the experience of the maklans if I think about it."

"How do you mean," Darlene asked. "There are many maklan species and you know them better than we do, but I wasn't aware of a case where some were held down by others?"

"As you may remember, we have relationships with over three hundred and fifty maklan societies in our galaxy. Virtually all are single planet cultures like Tak-Makla, following in the footsteps of our ancestors on Ai-Makla. Some live quite closely with others, and there are some cases where stronger ones dominate smaller ones. Anymore than that, I don't know. You'd have to ask Fak, as she keeps closer tabs on our trading partners. But we did have one case that makes the Society look like saints," Zee continued. "We know the Galliceans, maklans and Kalideans have been investigating the planets in the Don-Makla system. I don't know what they have learned."

"That was your home world after the Great Rebirth, right?" Dave asked. "Wait, now I remember something. That invisible race looks just like the people of Nanda!"

"You are right, now that I think of it," Zee smiled. "But what have your scientists found about the other maklan worlds there?"

"They found a planet where the Predaxians lived for a few million years, and another planet that had a race of giant maklans that went extinct, as I recall," Dave pondered. "I'm not certain, but I think they chronicled the evidence and gave up."

"The giant maklans were descendants of Don-Makla, like me," Zee said. "You have seen the story of Zon Palaka in The Hive, correct?" Dave nodded. "Well, there were others who followed her plan to settle other planets. One of those ships had a critical engine failure shortly after leaving Don-Makla. They had intended to go to another system, but had to crash land on that other planet. Agents in The Hive have seen that many of their leaders and scientists died in the landing. The remainder did what they could to build a sustainable culture, but it couldn't last. The size of the planet and the thick atmosphere were too much for the people. Over generations, they adapted to the circumstances by becoming much larger. Unfortunately, they began to devolve until they lived in crude shacks trying to survive."

"Until they went extinct themselves," Dave said.

"If only it were that easy, Dave," Zee sighed. "That culture finally began to advance again after millions of years. They started to build villages and discovered agriculture and animal husbandry. That was about two hundred and fifty million years ago, which was the same time the Predaxians moved to the other planet."

"So the two species knew one another?" Darlene asked.

"That may be an over-simplification, Darlene," Zee frowned. "The Predaxians who came there were outcasts from Predax. They were the first to develop mind control over other maklans. The leaders felt it was an abomination and exiled them. As fate you have it, they ended up in the Don-Makla system on that one planet." He turned and saw the rest of the group taking their seats at the dinner table. "Let's walk slowly back now before they come looking for us." As they walked, he continued, "The planet they chose was dying. Its thin atmosphere and high solar radiation forced them to enclose their cities in giant domes. Still, the radiation changed them into monsters before it sucked the life out. When they found the giant maklans on the next planet, they began to harvest them for food."

"They became cannibals?" Darlene said aghast. "That's horrible."

"Horrid but true, Darlene," Zee said. "Unfortunately, the giant maklans were not enough to keep the Predaxians fed. Once they were all dead, their society broke into warring factions. Whoever lost the day's battle became the evening meal." Zee dropped his head. "It was the most horrible thing I've ever seen. Eventually, insanity brought on by the radiation and starvation killed them all. The only positive thing is that they died before they encountered the Nanda. I shudder to think what would have happened to them. At that time, the Nanda were also just finding their civilization."

"We were beginning to think you were lost," Orlo said as the three joined the group. "You three don't look so well. Is something wrong?"

"We're fine, Orlo," Dave said. "Zee was just telling us some history that did not have a happy ending." He smiled. "Where do we sit?"

All the Opa ministers huddled around Mencius and his assistants. Stories of the greatness of the Kalidean Federation were the talk of the night. Dave and Darlene sat with the maklans, while Wendo and Antar sat at the opposite table with the Opa military leadership. The meal was simple but very tasty. They started with toast with a spicy green salad on top. That was followed by a rich fish soup with seaweed. The main course was an odd crustacean with four claws. The meat was dense like beef with a strong aroma of the sea. As a worker class, the Opa did not indulge in fancy desserts and pastries. Large plates of nut-flavored cookies and strong coffee completed the meal.

Mencius recounted the history of Kalidus as he had been taught. He told them of the time he stood before High Consul Palidus and advised them to go back in time to find the best of their adventurers to restart their journey into the stars. He talked of bringing Dave and Darlene Brewster into the future to do the same for the humans of Earth 47. The group was overwhelmed when Mencius spoke of the ten thousand worlds in the Federation and the thousands of major universities and the advanced state of Kalidean science. Tears pooled in the eyes of the Opa when they learned how advanced their meager culture had become in another galaxy.

The waiters cleared the plates and three small glasses of whisky were given to each guest. Orlo stood and cleared his throat. "My dear friends, this has been a magnificent day for me, and I hope you feel the same way. I can assure you that the five hundred Opa worlds of the Society are one hundred percent behind your application for the Free Society in the Ulagong Galaxy." Everyone applauded. "The glasses of whisky are a traditional closing to an Opa feast such as this. Each Opa world makes many different whiskies. We say that a working man needs a working man's drink. The three before you are from Lagamar Opa. Traditionally, we start from left to right, which is to say from sweet to bitter. This reminds us that the sweetness of our celebration will be followed by hard work when the sun rises again. In honor of our Kalidean guests, I want us to break that tradition right now!" He picked up the far right glass and held it out to the group. "After this night, we know there is something better for all Opa in this universe. While our lives here are hard and bitter, we can now look forward to a day when we join with our Kalidean brothers and find a sweet future for ourselves and our children. Please drink with me!" He drank the bitter whisky and said, "Today was hard." Everyone followed suit and said the same phrase, then applauded. He drank the center whisky and said, "Now there is hope for tomorrow." The group copied again. He picked up the last glass and looked at the whisky swirling about. His eyes filled with tears again as he drank the liquor. "And tomorrow will bring sweetness to us all."

CHAPTER 35

Lagamar Vol lay beneath the Nightsky. The terminator moved slowly across the planet as a new day dawned in New City, the capital of the planet. Dave Brewster stood in his ready room, looking out the window at the planet below. Lagamar Vol was Earth-sized with forty percent water surface. There were almost no mountains and the planet seemed like a giant farm. The few visible mountains were heavily worn down and covered with forest. Small ice packs clung to the poles. Dave sipped his first coffee of the day and contemplated what they would find on this planet. A tone sounded and he returned to his desk. He tapped a button and the face of Fa-a-Di filled the screen. "Good morning, brother," Dave said.

Fa-a-Di did not look happy. "I'm sorry, Dave, but I have to tell you I am very upset at all humanity right now."

"What's wrong, Fa-a-Di?" Dave said, puzzled by the words. "Whatever happened? Was it something I said or did?"

"No, of course not, brother," Fa-a-Di said with a forced smile. "You and I are not from this galaxy, so how could we have anything to do with this abomination?"

"There's been an abomination?" Dave asked. "What happened?"

"The only humans from this galaxy I can stomach today are Wendo and Antar," Fa-a-Di, "They sent me to Lagamar 7 to see what is happening there, and I am thoroughly disgusted by what we are seeing."

"Please tell me, brother," Dave said. "I know nothing of this."

"I know you don't Dave. But I need to get the anger out of my system, and it's too early to start drinking whisky. Please don't take it personally," he replied as he put his beak close to the glass of his screen. "Yesterday, we visited the first location on the planet that Wendo Balak suggested. That planet you saw yesterday is a mining world, right?"

"Yes, and it's horrible how the Opa have been reduced to servants to the other races," Dave started.

"Whatever," Fa-a-Di scoffed. "That planet and those Opa send ten freighters to Lagamar 7 every day to dump slag."

"What!" Dave shouted. "They're using the planet as a dump?"

"That's right, Dave," Fa-a-Di replied. "Ten freighters every day dump tons of slag from high orbit onto the planet. My brother-in-law and I flew over that area of the planet and saw what has been happening there. Dave, there are Ka-la-a on this planet and many species of gas giant life. Imagine that Ka-la-a we stood on when we visited Jupiter, with the moss and giant beasts lumbering around innocently."

"I remember, brother," Dave smiled. "I'll never forget that day."

"I won't forget yesterday either Dave," Fa-a-Di scowled. "Imagine those animals feeding peacefully when thousands of tons of slag fall from the sky. The Ka-la-a are being destroyed along with the life. Then the slag finds its way to the Dar-Fa and rains down on the planet again. It was horrifying. Those poor Opa. What a bunch of garbage. They could care less what they are doing to life on that planet. It sickens me."

"I don't know what to say, Fa-a-Di," Dave replied. "I'm sure this is part of the story that Wendo and Antar are weaving for us. I believe we will all understand by the time we return to Earth Prime."

"If I could, I would fly the Kong-Fa back to our galaxy right now," the Gallicean said. "Without the jump, that would take thousands of years, so I suppose I have no choice. Wendo has selected another part of the planet for us to examine today. I can only imagine what horrors we fill find there. Where are you now?"

"We are orbiting Lagamar Vol," Dave answered. "From what I've heard, it is an agricultural planet. That seems simple enough and there would be no need for dumping on Lagamar 7 for that, but I suppose we will both learn more today."

"You know Dave, this trip is not helping our ambition to form a Free Society," Fa-a-Di started. "Seeing what humanity has done is angering my entire crew. Hopefully, there will be good news today."

"We have to remember that the humans in our galaxy are not the same as the ones here in the Society, brother," Dave replied. "Wendo and Antar brought us all here to show us the truth of the Society so that we learn from their mistakes and not repeat them."

"I know, Dave." He sat back in his chair and sighed. "It has taken these humans billions of years to devolve into the Society we see before our eyes. I spoke with Zee earlier today and he told me about the invisible people and the plight of the Opa. I must admit the Galliceans have plenty of dark shadows in our past. I just assumed that sentient Beings like us would improve over time." Fa-a-Di's characteristic grin crossed his beak. "Thank you, brother. Getting this anger out of my system has helped a great deal. We will continue through this journey together and return home soon. Kong-Fa out." The screen went dark.

Another tone sounded and Dave pushed the flashing button. Lia Lawson looked back at him through the screen. "Admiral, Commander Adamsen and the away team are waiting for you in the shuttle bay," she said.

"Tell them I'm on my way, Lia," he said as he rose and dashed out the door. After walking down two corridors and taking a lift, he found himself back in the shuttle bay. The people of Lagamar Vol had no shuttles capable of carrying important passengers, so Dave asked Avery Adamsen to fly them down to New City. Dave noticed that everyone was already strapped in when he came inside the shuttle. "I'm sorry for being late, everyone," he apologized. He sat next to Avery and strapped in. The shuttle bay doors opened and the ship slipped off the platform and into space. Dave looked up and saw Nightsky shrinking away as they dropped toward the atmosphere. He turned and said, "Wendo or Antar, is there anything you want to tell us about this planet? I also want you both to know that the Galliceans are furious today."

"As well they should be, Dave," Antar replied. "Fortunately, they will have a better day today, I can guarantee that! Lagamar Vol is a food basket for the Society, as are all fourteen hundred Vol planets."

"Doesn't that make them the largest group in the Society, Antar?" Darlene asked.

"In number of planets, yes," Antar replied. "However, in number of residents, they come in a distant eighth. Lagamar

Vol is pretty typical with about two billion people. Virtually all of them are in the food business. The land surface is practically one giant farming cooperative. The lakes and seas are rich with seafood as well. No race can compete with the Vol in agriculture and fishing."

"And they are experts in sustainable agriculture and fishing as well," Wendo interrupted. "What you will see today is a marvel of science and raw talent. This one planet can provide enough food for one hundred other planets. We want you to notice the people most of all."

The shuttle shuddered slightly as it encountered the atmosphere. Dave remembered the shaking and shuddering of the old Opa shuttle the previous day. It was quite cloudy near New City today. Rain was abundant all over the planet which helped the crops grow and moved nutrients from sea to land and vice-versa.

"Remember what you learned on Lagamar Opa," Antar said. "You found a planet where everyone loved to do their jobs and were damned good at it. The Opa are well paid for their minerals and are without a doubt the wealthiest planet we will show you this trip. You noticed their wealth was very modest compared to Narta Ela though. But even with all of that, they had no idea they could do so much more with their talents."

The shuttle moved below the cloud deck and flew two thousand feet over the vast farmlands below them. Heavy rain pelted the ship and some lightning was visible on the horizon. The edges of New City began to show on the horizon as the shuttle continued to drift downward. The shuttle moved ahead of the rain and the sky cleared as they passed over the edge of the city. New City was small for a capital with only half a million residents. All of the buildings were squat and wooden.

The tallest buildings in the city were stone structures only three or four stories tall. A small landing area was adjacent to a park in the center of the city. Avery aligned the shuttle with the landing marks and gently settled the ship to the ground. A group of Vol came out of one of the stone buildings and approached the shuttle. The Vol were between five and six feet tall with medium brown skin, black hair and bright green eyes that were just a bit too big for their heads. They wore green suits that looked like overalls and straw hats. When the shuttle doors opened, Wendo and Antar led the group out into the cool morning air. Dave was the last to exit the shuttle and stopped with Avery who was still at the command station.

"Avery, I think we will need this shuttle today," Dave said. "I don't have a schedule yet, but why don't you stay here."

"Aye-aye, Admiral," Avery smiled. "Please let me know the schedule when you have one, sir. I can smell breakfast cooking out there and if I'm going to be awhile, I might go get some."

"You've got it," Dave laughed. "Come with me for a minute." The two went to the door and stepped out. "Wendo!" Dave called out. "How long before we need the shuttle?"

"We'll be here at least two hours, Dave," Wendo shouted back. The Vol had almost reached him.

"There you go, Avery. Have a nice meal," Dave said as he hurried to join the others.

The group was introduced to Mulwi Deka, President of the High Council, Norwa Senda, Minister for Agriculture, Onlo Borka, Minister of Fisheries, and Bola Deka, the President's wife and Minister of Trade. The entire group then returned to the stone building, which turned out to be the Capitol Building, where a large breakfast banquet had been set up for their guests.

Mulwi led them to the large table and Nan waiters moved around the tables pouring water and coffee for everyone. He stood at the head of the table and said, "It's an honor to have you with us today. It is especially wonderful to have Lord Balak and Lord Arrak on Lagamar Vol again. They know that we Vol are simple farmers and fishermen. We know the value of a good breakfast before a long day of work. To us, this is more common than a large dinner and drink. While we do love our wine and whisky, our primary meal is what you see here. A drink before bed is great, but clear minds are needed to do our work well. I welcome you all and I hope you enjoy."

Dave was happy he had not eaten breakfast already. The Vol food was exceptionally good. Everything tasted very fresh and satisfying. The coffee was the best he ever had. It was like a traditional farm breakfast with eggs, meats, potatoes, bread and more. "This is fantastic, sweetheart," he whispered to Darlene.

She smiled and replied, "I know. It tastes so fresh. I guess it is all right off the farm."

Mulwi stood and tapped his glass with a spoon to get everyone's attention. "Before we forget, let's have a round of applause for our Nan brothers who have cooked and served all of this wonderful food." Everyone applauded and the Nan smiled and waved happily.

Wendo sat across the room from Dave and was staring at him. When Dave noticed, Wendo only smiled broadly. He motioned for Dave to come over, so he stood and walked to the other table. Dave bent down to the old man. "Not so invisible here Dave, are they?" Wendo chuckled.

"Why the difference, Wendo?" Dave whispered.

"Dave, it should be somewhat obvious to you by now," Wendo frowned. "You tell me why it's different here."

"The Vol are simple people, people of the land and the sea. They have no need for pretense and are grateful for anyone who helps them," Dave guessed.

"You see, I told you it was simple," Wendo laughed as he clapped Dave on the back. "But you missed one thing. The Nan may be on the bottom rung of the Society, but the Vol are only one or two steps above them. When you are at the top, it is simple to look far below and discount the humanity of those at the bottom. When you are right next to them, it's much more difficult. Now go finish your breakfast. It's going to be a long day for you."

After the meal, the group took a small tour of the center of the city. The rain had arrived during breakfast and each guest was given an umbrella. The Vol did not mind the rain as it brought life to their crops and was as natural as they were. Most of the buildings in this area were for the government of the planet. Those offices were generally on the two upper floors, leaving the ground floors for small businesses and restaurants. Dave counted ten coffee shops in the five blocks they walked. He hoped to bring Charlie here one day to try them all. As they were headed back to the shuttle, they passed a small restaurant just as Avery was walking out. Dave invited him to join them on the short trip.

"The food here is amazing, Admiral," Avery said. "If I lived here, I'd gain a hundred pounds in no time."

Bola Deka overheard the comment and joined them. "No chance of that here, son," she said. "After breakfast, we spend the whole day in the fields or at sea working hard. By the time the day is done, you are lucky not to have lost weight. By the way, my name is Bola, what's yours?"

"I'm Avery Adamsen, the shuttle pilot, Bola. It's a pleasure to meet you," Avery replied.

"It's very fortuitous that we meet, Avery," Bola smiled. "I was hoping that you and the Admiral here could help us on a mission of mercy later this evening. It would require another shuttle with room for cargo, if that is possible?"

"We'll do what we can," Dave said. "Can you give us any more details?"

"This is all part of the trip," Wendo interrupted as he joined them next to the shuttle. The others climbed aboard and began to strap in. "You two will also need pressure suits, since your trip will take you to Lagamar 7. This is something you have to see for yourselves. Please trust me on this, Dave."

"We're in deep already, so we'll do it," Dave said. "Avery, have another shuttle sent down when our tour is finished. That pilot can take this shuttle back, and we'll take Bola wherever she wants to go."

"Bless you, Admiral," she said as she hugged him. They joined the rest on the shuttle and strapped in. Dave wondered if this was going to be a mistake.

The shuttle rose through the rain and flew out over the endless farmlands. They could see large combines harvesting grains out to the horizon. Mulwi turned to face his guests and said, "Lagamar Vol is one of the most productive food baskets in the Society. Our gentle climate and vast resources allow us to grow and harvest food year round. I think you get the best view of this area from the shuttle. The scope of our farming operation is pretty evident. This region grows grains. Lord Balak has told us that many of you love coffee, so we are heading to our primary coffee growing region now." The shuttle accelerated and continued through the rain. After ten minutes, the clouds broke and bright sunshine filled the air. The ground had become hilly and groves of trees clung to the hillsides. Fruit hung heavy on the stout trees. Groups of workers and trucks moved among the trees collecting the ripe fruit. They crossed over railroads that stretched out in all directions to get the food to the cities and star ports. The grain fields were far behind them now. The hills became steeper and coffee trees began to dominate the area. A large warehouse sat in the middle of the hills. The shuttle slowed and landed near the building which covered a square mile. A Vol and Nan stood outside waiting for them. After the doors opened, the group left the ship to meet their hosts.

"Good day to everyone. I am Orpa Nang and I am in charge of the coffee crop in this area of Lagamar Vol. This is Iku Ont, our master roaster. Come along and let's see the facility." It was warmer here than in New City and the sky was clear and sunny. Small flying insects buzzed around the group as they walked the hundred yards to the giant building. As they crossed the threshold, they could see the ceiling towering a hundred feet over their heads. There were very few posts to support the ceiling so it seemed to float almost magically above them. This section of the building was open, but storage racks could be seen a hundred yards or so further into the building. Those racks rose to the roof. Large lift devices strolled along the aisles placing and retrieving pallets of product.

Orpa led them through another doorway and the smell of roasting coffee was overwhelming. Twenty large roasters filled the large room and dozens of Nan workers ran around checking the product. "Most of the planets in the Society prefer to roast their own beans," Iku began. "However, the people on some worlds like knowing their coffee was roasted at the plantation. That's where my team comes in. We roast fifteen percent of the coffee grown here. The rest is shipped green."

"Thanks, Iku," Orpa said. "Personally, I think Iku is the best roaster in the Society, but no one listens to me."

"I think I had his coffee this morning," Dave said, "and I agree with you." The group clapped and Iku blushed.

"Okay, folks, let's let Iku get back to work and go see the shipping area," Orpa said as he led them out the door. They walked down the mile-long aisle to the other end of the building. The racks seemed precariously high and were heavily laden with bags of green and roasted coffee.

Wendo put his hand on Dave's shoulder as they walked. "Dave, that was a great gesture back there," he said.

"It wasn't a gesture, Wendo," Dave replied. "That was the best coffee I've ever had. But the Vol seem to appreciate the Nan here. It shouldn't be too surprising for them."

"You are right about the Vol, Dave, but you are not a Vol. All Iku knows is you are a visitor from another galaxy that looks like a Pa. Unfortunately, we Pa are not as accepting as the Vol. We treat and pay them fairly, but they remain servants and janitors for us too. Here it is a unique partnership. The Vol are incredible farmers and fishermen, however, preparing the food and keeping the equipment running are not their strengths. The Vol know their profit comes from the partnership, not just their hard work. So what do you think about the Society now."

"It has a lot of flaws, like all civilizations, Wendo," Dave replied. "I was horrified by what Fa-a-Di told me this morning. I could never imagine the Opa doing something like that."

"That's why I want you to go with Bola later," Wendo smiled. "You'll learn many answers when you are away from the group, and from me."

The exited the building and stepped into the warm afternoon air. Before them was a large star port with ten freighters lined up on the tarmack. Nan crews rushed containers of coffee from the building and out to the waiting ships. As soon as a ship was filled, it would lift off and move off toward the heavens. Within a few minutes, another would fly out of the scattered clouds to take its place. There was a rail spur at the far end of the port where more crews loaded roasted coffee to be sent to the cities and towns across Lagamar Vol. While they watched, a burly Pa rushed out of the building and bumped into them and turned suddenly. "Oh, I'm so sorry, but my ship is late," he said as he straightened Wendo's robes. He looked closely and tears began to fill his eyes. "Lord Balak, I had no idea. I am so sorry, sir."

"Don't worry son," Wendo said. "It was an accident."

"Lord Balak, my name is Wendo Othee. I am a simple trader from Molta Pa. It is an honor to meet you. As you can tell, my mother gave me your name," he said.

"I am happy to meet you Wendo," he replied. "As one Wendo to another, you need to relax and let things happen. Stress is a killer."

"Yes, sir, my wife tells me the same thing constantly," the trader said. "Unfortunately, I don't get home very often anymore. In fact, I'm headed there now, which is why I'm in such a hurry."

"Before you go, let me introduce you to my dear friend, Admiral Dave Brewster," Wendo said. "He and I have come from the Ulagong Galaxy to meet the High Council."

"It's an honor to meet you sir," the trader said. "I hate to chat and run, but my crew is expecting me. Have a blessed day." He turned and raced to the closest ship. After a couple minutes, it rose into the air and flew away toward the stars.

Serena Vanatee came up from behind them and took their arms. "Grandfather, you missed the discussion on the tonnage that travels through here everyday. Lucky you," she smiled. "We are headed back to the shuttle and the next location, gentlemen and we are falling behind again."

The shuttle traveled northward through the driving rain. The fields below were full of vegetables drinking in the water. Crowds of Vol workers moved through the fields removing weeds and checking the progress of the crops. The fields ended in rocky terrain, marking one of the few areas with no agriculture. After a few minutes, the rocks gave way to the sea. A small town with a large sea port clung to the rocks. Outcrops reached out into the sea to form an aritificial harbor, holding hundreds of ships and fishing boats. By the time the shuttle landed near the harbor, the rain had stopped, but clouds were hung low in the sky. The shuttle had landed in another star port where several freighters were waiting to be loaded. It was gray and cold when they left the shuttle and walked to the large market next to the harbor. Salt spray and the smell of the sea filled the air as they walked into the market building. Just inside the door, twenty refrigerated containers from the freighters waited to be filled. Each was guarded by a crew member. Three of the guards were Ela. Dave remembered the Ela were master traders, so it made sense they would be here. The rest was a mix of human races that Dave had never seen before. He remembered there were fifty-one, so he thought no more of it and hurried to catch up to his group. He passed through an air curtain into the main auction area of the building.

Boxes and glass cases of seafood seemed to stretch for ever. Dave had almost caught up to the group when a pair of odd eyes caught his. He turned to see a large glass box filled with water. Inside were two large crustaceans thrashing about in the water. Each was six to eight feet long with eight legs. They had small claws that looked almost like hands. One of the beasts stopped moving and stared at Dave with its large blue eyes, which were on stalks protruding from its head. The creature seemed very frightened and its eyes seemed to be begging for release from this box.

Wendo noticed Dave was missing and hurried over to him. He grabbed Dave's arm and pulled it. "Dave, we've got to go now," Wendo said. He pulled harder but Dave did not budge. "Dave, for the love of God, let's go." Dave relented and walked away from the crate, glancing back one time. The creature was still looking at him.

"Wendo, what was that animal?" Dave asked. "It looked sentient to me, was it?"

"Dave, we cannot talk about that here," Wendo demanded. "When we are safe on your ship again, I will come to your ready room and tell you about the Zula. Please don't say anything more now. This is like the invisible people, only worse."

They caught up to the group and Dave grabbed Darlene's hand. She looked at him and knew at once something was wrong. "Tell me, Dave. What's wrong?" she asked. Dave said nothing, but squeezed her hand tightly.

Mulwi was discussing the tonnage of seafood that leaves Lagamar Vol each day and the treacherous conditions the fishermen live with. He showed pictures of some of the oddest creatures that were sold here. Dave hardly heard the words. He turned back and the crate of Zula was gone. Tears started to pool in his eyes and he fought them back. Darlene could see the battle in his face and placed her head against his shoulder. Mulwi and the others talked about how the sea accounted for forty percent of the revenue of the planet and how their success relied on the partnership with the Nan. Hearing that word again, Dave looked back and saw many Nan rushing around the floor, pushing crates and boxes toward the waiting containers. Dave heard a tone in his ear and tapped the com-link. "Yes, Avery, what's up?"

"Admiral, the other shuttle has arrived," he replied. "A team of Nan has loaded some crates on board under orders from Bola Deka. I've exchanged control keys with Lieutenant Aldo, and she is ready to ferry our guests back to Nightsky."

"We'll be there soon, Avery, and thank you. Brewster out," Dave said as he closed the connection. Darlene had slipped out of his hand and was thanking the hosts for the wonderful adventure. Dave joined her and thanked them heartily, although his mind was still full of thoughts about the Zula.

"Thanks again to all of you for visiting," Bola said. "Admiral Brewster will be traveling with me for a while this evening on another shuttle. Commander Adamsen will make certain he gets to the ship safely. Come along, Dave."

"What's all this, Dave?" Darlene asked. "You're not coming with us now?"

"Sorry, sweetheart," Dave said. "This is all part of Wendo's master plan. Don't worry, Avery and I will be fine." He kissed her on the lips. "The two shuttles are next to each other. Let's go." The group walked back through the auction room. Dave looked at the spot where the Zula had been sitting. A large tray of fresh fish replaced that crate. Ten men of various races were standing around the tray arguing about the price. When they reached the shuttles, Dave kissed Darlene again and wished everyone a safe trip back. Wendo smiled and waved.

Dave and Bola climbed on board the shuttle where Avery and five Nan were already strapped in for the ride. Several large crates were secured in the bay. Dave strapped himself into the seat next to Avery. The shuttle lifted off and started to climb rapidly.

"Hold on there a minute, Avery," Bola said. "We need to take a short detour and drop off some precious cargo. Just head due east about one hundred miles out to sea."

"Is this necessary, Bola?" Dave asked.

"Just trust me on this one, Dave," she smiled.

"Okay, Avery, take us out to sea," Dave replied and the shuttle moved eastward. It took fifteen minutes to get a hundred miles out to sea. The shuttle slowed and hovered a thousand feet over the calm ocean.

"Avery, take us down to no more than five feet off the water," Bola said. "Don't worry, the sea is calm tonight." Avery looked at Dave, who shrugged and the shuttle slipped downward. Within a few minutes, the shuttle hovered a few feet above the sea, which was unusually calm this far from the coast.

"Come on, Dave, I want you to see this," Bola said as she and several Nan unbuckled themselves and moved back into the crates. One of the crates was covered with a large brown tarp. One of the Nan pulled the tarp off, revealing the two Zula swimming in the crate of water.

"Oh, my God," Dave said. "They're safe. You're going to let them go?"

"Of course, Admiral," Bola laughed. "This is what we do, when we can." She told the Nan to prepare the crate. They worked on the bolts that held it together. Water began to leak onto the deck of the shuttle.

"Avery, open the cargo door," Dave shouted. As the doors began to open, he saw the two Zula looking at him. Their eyes blinked and seemed to smile at him. Suddenly, the side of the crate opened and the water and Zula rushed out of the door and into the ocean. The Zula stuck their tails in the air and seemed to be waving goodbye. A lump formed in Dave's throat as the cargo doors closed. "I don't understand, Bola. What just happened here?"

"Come on Dave, let's go strap in now," she replied. "We're going to be late getting to Lagamar 7 due to this detour. But I'll tell you on the way."

The shuttle shot up into the sky and shuddered slightly as it left the atmosphere and entered open space. Dave could see the Nightsky and Manila far in the distance and hoped everyone had arrived safely. His com-link chirped and he touched it. "I was just thinking about you, sweetheart," he said, recognizing Darlene's signal.

"Are you sure you're okay, honey?" she asked. "You looked like you were going to fall apart there in the auction house."

"It's okay now. Everything turned out well," he replied. "I'll be there before too long. I love you."

"I love you too, Dave. Nightsky out," Darlene said.

"Okay, Dave, let's talk about the Zula," Bola said. "First of all, I want you to know that we would never hunt them ourselves. But Earth Prime requires us to offer all products from our planets. We've tried to fight it, but some of the Councilors have acquired a taste for them."

"They seemed to be sentient to me, Bola. Could that be true?" Dave asked.

"Yes, they are very intelligent and we know it," she replied. "But we cannot fight the High Council. We are only Vol and Nan here. Our votes mean nothing to them."

"So the High Council wants to eat sentient creatures," Dave winced. "That seems very barbaric."

"It is, but we are a poor people, made poorer by the Zula," she said. "By law, we must offer all foods from this planet. We try to limit our catch of Zula. But every few weeks, we have to catch some to avoid scrutiny from Earth Prime. Most of the time, no one buys them because they are very expensive. Once in a while, someone buys one. Then we take most of the profit we have earned and use it to buy the poor creature back, like tonight. However, there are times when we cannot buy it back. Usually that happens when the top chefs from Earth Prime want to cook Zula for the High Council. Then our hands are tied. We are all horrifed when that happens."

"Tell the whole story, Bola," one of the Nan said. "Admiral, you have been so good to us, but the Zula situation is our fault. It brings great shame on all Nan."

"Whatever do you mean? And please call me Dave," he said.

"Thank you, Dave, and my name is Ilu. The Zula are native to Nan, our home planet," Ilu said. "We share our world with them and they are our friends. We would no more eat one of them than our own brothers. The Zula bring us great luck and good fortune. The Vol have been our best friends for many generations. We wanted to share our luck with them and brought a few Zula to this planet. We could protect them on Nan because no one wants to go there. We have taken them from a safe place and turned them into a delicacy."

"How many Zula live on Lagamar Vol?" Dave asked.

"Around five hundred, I believe," Ilu answered. "That is the number that comes to me when I see them. That is how they communicate with us."

"Avery, when we get back to the ship, I'd like you and Jon Lake to work on a solution to this problem," Dave said.

"Aye-aye Admiral," he smiled. "My mind has been working on that since this conversation started. By the way, Lagamar 7 is dead ahead and we're closing fast." Dave could see the large planet growing quickly through the main window. A dense set of rings circled high above and several moons orbited silently. The Kong-Fa was far away and appeared as a dot above the planet.

"Avery, there is a platform at twenty-six degrees north latitude and fifty-five degrees west longitude at three hundred thousand feet," Bola said. "We can land there. We have some pressurized buildings there, but will need our pressure suits to get there."

"Aye-aye, Bola," Avery said. "The platform is sending me their coordinates and I'll lay in a course. We should land in less than ten minutes."

"Your shuttles are a lot faster than ours," Bola laughed. "It takes us hours to get here, and we do this several times a week."

"Admiral, the Kong-Fa is signaling us," Avery advised.

"Send my regards to Fa-a-Di and De-o-Nu," Dave replied. "Tell them I can't talk now but will brief them both tomorrow."

The shuttle was buffeted by the strong wings as it sank lower into the atmosphere. Avery moved around the highest wind areas and the large platform loomed ahead of them. The shuttle approached the platform and settled onto the deck next to two other shuttles. Everyone donned pressure suits and checked each other's readings. Confident they were correct, the cargo doors opened and the Nan quickly began removing the crates and pushing them toward an open storage building. Several others rushed from the building and helped with the goods as Dave and Bola entered the antechamber of a large building. The air was quickly changed to a breathable mix and the inner door opened to reveal a hallway. Bola led them down fifty feet to an open door. Inside were an Opa and a man of a race Dave had not yet encountered.

"Bola, you're early," General Mali Nook of Lagamar Opa said. "It's good to see you again too, Admiral Brewster. Dave, let me introduce you to Minister Vee Ondi of Lagamar Ulu." Dave had never seen an Ulu before. Vee was very thin but muscular. He was about Dave's height with extremely white skin, almond shaped silver-blue eyes and red hair. Everyone shook hands and took seats at the large table. The two Nan poured hot coffee for everyone and placed trays of snacks on the table.

"We're heading out to the ward now," one of the Nan said.

"Okay, Ola," Bola said. "We'll meet you there soon." The two Nan left and closed the door after them. She waited a moment to make certain the Nan were out of earshot. "What do you think you're doing Mali? Dumping slag on Lagamar 7 again! Are you insane?"

"Calm down, Bola," Mali begged. "It's not like it seems. We were trapped by the Brotherhood. We had no choice. Please try to understand."

"The Brotherhood is on Lagamar Opa?" Bola asked. "When did this happen? Who tipped them off?"

"What's going on here?" Dave asked. "What is the Brotherhood?"

"Where in the galaxy did you come from, Dave?" Vee asked. "You don't know what the Brotherhood is?"

"Calm down, Vee," Bola said. "Dave Brewster came with Wendo Balak and Antar Arrak from the Ulagong galaxy. He's a descendant of the Earth 47 colony."

"Wow, that's amazing!" Vee said. "Welcome to our little galaxy of fun, Dave. The Brotherhood is an arm of the High Council that insures we comply with all rules."

"They're spies, Dave," Bola replied. "The High Council has become so convinced that regions are about to declare independence that they created the Brotherhood. They were recruited from our intelligence agencies that used to spy on other civilizations. Now they are looking inside the Society for behavior that might signify pending revolution."

"And now Balak and Arrak have brought them on us," Mali complained. "That's why there came to Lagamar Opa. I'm sure there are agents crawling all over your planets too! We didn't want to dump slag here, but the Brotherhood agents confronted us when they found evidence of dumping at old strip mines."

"Can we just hold on for a minute or two," Dave said. "There's someone else who really needs to hear this." They stared at Dave as though they couldn't believe their ears. "I promise you this is very important."

"Well, Dave, you did help us save the Zula," Bola said. "I think we can give you a few minutes." The others just looked down. Clearly, Bola led this group.

Dave tapped his com-link, and said, "Avery, please get a hold of Jake and ask him to get Fa-a-Di and jump him to these coordinates. He can tell the general that this is a big favor for me. He'll need to bring a breather. Also, ask him to stoop over when they jump. The ceiling is high here, but I don't know if it's high enough."

"Aye-aye, Admiral," Avery replied.

Dave sat with the others and sipped his coffee. "My brother, Fa-a-Di should be here any minute." He took a cookie and bit it. "These are great."

Mali was squirming in his chair. "We don't have all night, Bola. If the Brotherhood finds out we're here together, we'll all be in big trouble." He stood. "Maybe I'll take a walk, this is driving me crazy."

Without any sound, Fa-a-Di suddenly appeared in the room. Jake was clinging to his chest. Mali fell back into his chair and the others flinched at the surprise. No human in this galaxy had ever seen anything like the fifteen foot tall winged Gallicean. As usual, Fa-a-Di was wearing his black battle armor. The golden handles of his three daggers glistened in the harsh light. "Hello, brother," he said. "It is good to see you in person again. I suppose you brought me here to tell me which of these three people are dumping on this planet."

Vee pointed to Mali, saying, "That would be him."

"That is your brother?" Bola said with disbelief. "He's is mighty big for a human."

Fa-a-Di laughed out loud. "Your friends are hilarious, Dave. Now tell me, why am I here?"

Mali told them about the visit of the Brotherhood. Groups of their agents visited each planet every few years, looking for signs of unrest and conspiracy. They had been discovered on

Lagamar Opa a week ago. There are no Opa or Nan in the Brotherhood, and finding other races sneaking around was not difficult. Society law requires the Opa to dispose of waste materials off the planet, so that other cultures to move there later would not find a polluted mess. Even though Lagamar Opa was the richest planet in the system, they had no money to acquire a freighter capable to sending the slag into the sun or a garbage planet in another system. An edict from the High Council required the Opa to dump their waste on Lagamar 7 until they could afford a better method.

Orlo and Aon did not agree with the order. Lagamar Opa had many exhausted mine sites that sat as empty pits or abandoned deep mines. They ordered their people to dump the slag there. They had to keep a wary eye on everyone foreign to the planet because anyone of them might turn them in to the Council. Some one apparently did. The Brotherhood agents arrived and went immediately to the site currently being used. The planet was fined six months of profits and ordered to use Lagamar 7 for their dump site or face imprisonment far from their planets. The previous day, Brotherhood agents traveled with the freighter crews to Lagamar 7 and supervised the dumping.

"This is really horrible, Dave," Fa-a-Di said. He faced the others. "I owe you an apology, friends. After seeing the results of the dumping, I told Dave I was ready to kill whoever was responsible. When I saw Mali here, the blood ran cold in my body. Now I understand it was not you, but the High Council and the Brotherhood who caused this. My race evolved on planets like Lagamar 7. I am High Commissioner of Greater Gallia, a civilization with many such worlds. But what can we do to end this madness?"

"We have another problem, brother," Dave said. "But I think we may have solutions for both, if I can get more help from you."

"Dave, you know that you do not need to ask," Fa-a-Di smiled. "Just tell me what to do."

"Boys, we're not done here yet," Bola said. "Dave, I'm going to trust you on finding solutions. But arguing is not what we do here. We need to put our pressure suits back on to leave this building. General, you probably just need to take off your breather when we go outside."

After donning their suits, the group moved across the platform toward the largest building. They opened the large doors and proceeded inside. They were in a vast room with lines of cages on both sides. Inside the cages were different animals from Lagamar 7. Most were bandaged and asleep.

"What's the meaning of this?" Fa-a-Di asked. "Is this some kind of zoo?"

"Don't be silly, General," Bola said. "This is a hospital. The ones in cages are too injured to fly on their own. Once they can fly, we move them to the open ward. We don't want an injured Boley falling to its death off the platform."

"What is a Boley?" Dave asked.

Bola stopped and walked to the cage on her right. "Here's one now, Dave, and he's awake." At first glance, the creature looked a lot like a Gallicean, although it was only five feet tall. It lay quietly on the floor and stared at the people outside the cage. A heavy layer of bandages covered its chest and stomach area. It tried to back further into the cage until it saw Fa-a-Di approach. It turned its head from side to side wondering where this giant Boley had come from. Fa-a-Di saw the beast looking right at him, and instinctively he stood very tall and outstretched his wings. Then he bowed his head. The Boley climbed to its feet and approached the bars. It stood very straight and tried extending its wings too, but squealed in pain and fell down again.

Jake flew off Fa-a-Di and landed on the bars, looking at the Boley. Jake turned his head from side to side and looked very confused. He glowed red and the Boley moved backward. He glowed blue and the Boley approached him.

"What are you doing, Jake?" Dave asked.

"This is crazy, Dave," Jake replied, "but I'm talking to this Boley. He says his name is Fanon and wants to know who the giant is. I told him he was General Fa-a-Di, and he asked me if the General would allow him to touch his hand."

"The Boley can talk?" Mali said. "Is that possible? Bola, what's going on?"

"Damned if I know, Mali. Damned if I know," she replied.

Fa-a-Di stepped forward and smiled at Fanon. Bola opened the cage and Fa-a-Di got on his knees and crawled inside. There was no room to sit up, so he lay on his side next to the Boley, who reached out and touched his hand. Two Nan noticed the commotion and joined the group. All stood transfixed as the sight of the two gas giant animals inside the cage with the winged glass spider clinging to the bars. After ten minutes, Fa-a-Di crawled back out of the cage. The two Nan went inside and examined the Boley's wounds, which were improving very slowly.

"Let's see what else you have, Bola," Fa-a-Di said as they walked away. He looked back to see Fanon smiling at him. After the cages, they entered an open ward where several other Boley and other creatures were being treated. Fa-a-Di looked around at the other creatures. There were more than twenty injured Boley and a dozen other smaller creatures in various states of mending. Dave could see tears in the general's eyes.

"Are you okay, brother?" Dave asked.

"Yes and no, brother," Fa-a-Di replied. "Friends, I sincerely thank you for what you are trying to do here. Frankly, I'm amazed at your generosity and kindness in the face of such abomination. No matter what happens here, I want you to know that Greater Gallia stands with you. You are doing your best here, I know. If it is acceptable, I'd like to send the doctors from my ship here tomorrow morning along with some medical equipment more suited to these creatures." He turned and shouted, "Jake, come over here please!" Jake flew across the room and landed on the general's chest.

"Are you leaving now, brother?" Dave asked, seeing the pain in his friend's face. "I'm sure Bola has more to show us."

Fa-a-Di put his hand on Dave's shoulder. "That's okay, brother, but Fanon has already told me much more than I wanted to know. I sincerely hope and pray there is a solution for the problems in this system." He turned to the rest. "My medical team will arrive at 0900 local time. Okay, Jake, get me out of this place." The two disappeared.

"All of you provide doctors and medical supplies to help the injured on this planet, right?" Dave asked. "But did all of this happen due to one day of slag dumping?"

"Let's head back to your shuttle, Dave," Bola said. "I think we're finished here for tonight. Good night Vee and Mali." They waved as she and Dave walked away. "We try to come here whenever we get enough money to buy supplies. I probably come two days a week. It's expensive too. We have to buy all of our medical supplies from other systems. We have to pay fines for every rule they say we break. The Opa do better than the Ulu or us, but all imports are very expensive. We've started pooling our profits to make life better for all, but then expenses like this hospital and buying Zula back hit us." They arrived back at the shuttle and climbed aboard. Avery repressurized the cabin and they pulled off their helmets. The shuttle slowly lifted off the platform and headed back to Lagamar Vol.

"Admiral, Captain Lake advises they are waiting for us to depart for Lagamar Ulu on our arrival," Avery said. "We will arrive on Lagamar Vol to drop Bola off in twenty minutes."

"Thanks Avery," Dave said. "Bola, thank you. This trip was amazing. I've learned a lot of good and bad tonight. Hopefully, we'll find a way to keep the good and stop the bad."

"Admiral," Avery interjected. "I have an idea on the Zula problem. We need a big favor from one of your friends though."

"I knew you would come up with something, Avery," Dave replied. "I'm guessing you're suggesting De-o-Nu."

"I can never keep a secret from you, Dave," Avery laughed.

Bola grabbed Dave's arm. "Your friend is having a rough time now, Dave. He, Jake and Fanon were able to talk, so there are no secrets anymore."

"What do you mean, Bola?" Dave asked.

"First, you have to know that we might control our planets, but the system belongs to the Society. That's why they can dictate to the Opa to use Lagamar 7 as a dump," Bola said.

"I guess that makes as much sense as anything I've seen so far," Dave replied.

"Lagamar 7 is much more than a dump, Dave," she said. "The Opa have a very limited area where they can dump. The rest of the planet is a hunting preserve."

Lagamar Ulu was a mysterious planet. From the forward view screen, Jon Lake saw a planet covered in a dense brown-yellow cloud bank. Only small patches of blue in the center of oceans and the peaks of dozens of mountain ranges avoided the cloud cover. Lagamar Ulu was a manufacturing center for this sector of the Society. Raw materials were sent from mining planets like Lagamar Opa and other worlds to be converted into the goods that the Society relied on for everyday life.

"Jon, Lagamar Ulu Central Command is hailing us," Lia said. "Shall I put them on?"

"Yes, thanks Lia," Jon replied. The screen split and the face of a beautiful Ulu woman filled the right side. "This is Captain Jon Lake of the Nightsky requesting orbital clearance at your convenience."

"Welcome to Lagamar Ulu, Nightsky," she replied. "I am Major Voa Maroo of Lagamar Ulu Central Command. I am transmitting orbital coordinates to you now. I spoke with Minister of State Vee Ondi earlier today and he offers his regards to Admiral Dave Brewster."

"Thank you, Voa," Jon smiled, "but Admiral Brewster will not be joining the away team this morning. He hopes to catch up with them later this afternoon."

"Thanks for the update, Jon," Voa said, smiling sweetly. "I'll let the Minister know after we disconnect. Our team will be awaiting your dignitaries outside our capitol building in Porto at 1000 hours local. I will send those coordinates shortly. I have also been advised to let your dignitaries know that our atmosphere can be disturbing to some and we recommend that every person has a breather. Lagamar Ulu out." The full screen was filled with the planet again.

Ali Bai turned from his helm and looked at Jon. "You'd better watch out or I'll tell Lauren," he laughed.

Lia laughed out loud. "Thank goodness! Turn about is fair play!" The entire bridge crew laughed.

"Now this is supposed to be respect for your captain?" Jon shouted, and then laughed as well.

The Kong-Fa hovered ten feet over the ocean on Lagamar Vol, in the same location where Bola had freed the Zula the previous evening. Five of her fighters circled the area to watch for anyone who might notice the massive Gallicean star cruiser sucking tons of ocean water into her sealed hold. A set of shuttle bay doors were opened and several crew members wearing breathers managed the hoses and checked the water level in the hold. Ambassador De-o-Nu supervised. He touched his com-link and shouted, "No-ka-De, watch the controls! We're starting to roll to the port and we're losing altitude. You have to compensate for the weight of the water, fool!"

"Sorry, Ambassador," No-ka-De answered. "I've got it stabilized now. It won't happen again."

A shuttle from Nightsky pulled up next to the Gallicean ship and hovered. Gradually, it moved forward and landed inside the shuttle bay next to the working men. Dave Brewster and Jake Benomafolays exited the shuttle and came over to the

Ambassador. "Brother, I'm so happy to see you here," Dave smiled as he shook his friend's hand. "This is a wonderful thing you are doing today. How is it going?"

"This part is easy, Dave," De-o-Nu said. "We should have sufficient water in ten or twenty minutes. But I am very concerned about my impetuous brother-in-law."

"Where is Fa-a-Di?" Dave asked. "I thought he would be here."

"What he saw last night was too much for him. He took a contingent of Marines with him to the platform to guard the doctors," De-o-Nu replied. "I know he can take care of himself, but the anger in him is too high. I'm afraid he might do something we will regret later."

"Unless a stupid hunter shows up today, I don't think there should be a problem, brother," Dave said.

"My instinct tells me differently, brother," De-o-Nu sighed. "I just have a feeling in my gut that things are going to get crazy soon."

"Captain," one of the Galliceans said, "we have enough water now. I'll start retrieving the hoses now."

"Thank you," De-o-Nu said. He turned to Jake. "I guess it's up to you now, friend."

"I'll do my best, but I'm not sure what I'm looking for," Jake said. "Wish me luck." Jake dived into the water and disappeared from sight.

"Nothing to do now but wait, brother," Dave said as he sat on the deck.

De-o-Nu pulled a flask of Gallicean whisky from his suit and offered it to Dave. "It is going to be a very long day for all of us, brother. Before going into battle, it is customary for us to share a drink. You first." Dave took a drink from the bottle and began coughing. De-o-Nu shrieked with laughter. "You need to learn to love this stuff if you are going to be a warrior, Dave Brewster!"

A small black shuttle slipped downward through the atmosphere of Lagamar 7. Twelve humans in black pressure suits were strapped in as the ship was pushed about by the driving winds on the gas giant. The ship followed the coordinates provided by Bola and Mulwi Deka who were handcuffed and chained to the last row of seats. The platform came into view and they approached it rapidly.

"What is going on down there, Igol?" the pilot said.

"I have no idea, Ordo," Igol replied. Two massive shuttles filled most of the open space on the platform. Ordo maneuvered the black shuttle to the edge of the platform and landed. Igol walked down the narrow aisle to the Dekas. "Thanks for the information, you two," he said. "I hope you don't mind if we leave you here for your own safety." He laughed and said, "Okay men, it's time for the Brotherhood to investigate and deactivate this facility. Let's go."

The ten agents of the Brotherhood left the black shuttle and secured the door so the Dekas could not escape. They were shocked by the size of the other two shuttles. Each was five times larger than their own. The markings on the ships were unlike anything they had seen. All the agents were armed with two blasters. Each held one in their hand, ready for any eventuality. Five agents entered the smaller building while the others maintained the perimeter. After a few minutes, the agents left the building with three Nan in handcuffs. They were dragged along with the group toward the second building. Two agents stayed outside with the prisoners while the rest entered the hospital.

They passed the rows of strange creatures in cages quickly and entered the open ward. Three giant winged creatures in white coats were tending to other injured beasts while three more Nan ran about assisting them. "What is going on around here?" Igol shouted, as he fired a blast into the ceiling.

Doctor No-o-Ka spun around to see what was happening. "Get out of here!" the Gallicean physician shouted. "Can't you tell this is a hospital, you fool?"

"Who and what are you and who gave you authorization to set up a hospital on Lagamar 7?" Igol asked as he and his agents aimed their blasters at the doctor.

"I am a medical doctor, son," No-o-Ka replied, "and I don't need anyone's authorization to help the wounded and sick."

"Let me make this clear, Doctor," Igol laughed. "This is a Society of Humanity planet and you clearly are not a human, so you have no jurisdiction here. Either you leave this room with us now, or I will kill all your pets here, then I will kill the Nan, and if I need to, you will be last."

"Let's not be rash now, son," No-o-Ka said as he raised his hands. "My team will go quietly. We are here to save lives, not end them. Please let the Nan stay here for a few minutes to make sure these patients are stable. You can leave guards with them."

"I guess that's fair," Iglo said. "Let's go now."

The three Gallicean doctors left with six guards, while the remaining two kept an eye on the Nan who were frantically closing incisions and checking on their patients.

CHAPTER 38

The shuttle drifted through the dense smog layer over Porto, capital city of Lagamar Ulu. At three hundred feet, the cloud layer ended and the huge city spread out beneath them. Other than the small center where the buildings of government sat, the city was divided into dozens of zones with large industrial complexes in the center and housing and commercial property radiating outward until they met the next zone. The windows of the shuttle were covered with dust and grime from the clouds as the ship settled down on the landing marks provided.

"Please remember your breathers," Wendo said. "This is not a pleasant place without them." He pulled a breather over his head and smiled. The group donned their masks and exited the shuttle. Avery Adamsen stayed on board to guard the ship. He breathed some of the local air while the dignitaries exited and had no desire to wander about this dirty place. A single Ulu man with no breather approached their group. When he saw Wendo and Antar, he hugged them both and led the group into a large stone building, which was stained from years of exposure to the smog. They strolled through the large rotunda and into a legislative chamber that was empty. Rows of wooden desks surrounded a central podium where the President would suggest new laws for consideration.

As they stood in the large chamber, Vee Ondi said, "Good morning and welcome to Lagamar Ulu. I am the Minister of State for this planet. Unfortunately, most of the ministers who wish to meet you are not in the city today. As you may know, we Ulu work three weeks with no breaks and take every fourth off. Our President and Minister of Economy are currently taking their week off on Mount Alila. We will catch up to them this afternoon. Now if you will follow me, we will visit the foundry in the Neko Zone and the assembly plant in the Oplo Zone. We have provided the coordinates for all sites to your shuttle pilot who has offered to take us around. As we are going outside again, I suggest you replace your breathers."

Though it was still morning, the sky over Porto was dark and dreary. Black rain drops stained the outide of the shuttle as it moved to an even darker area. Hundreds of chimneys pierced the skyline belching smoke into the air. They landed in a small pad near the Neko foundry. They could see a line of freighters hovering over the huge planet. One at a time, each freighter would drift down over a massive grate over a hole in the roof of a building and open its cargo doors. Ore would drop from the ship and pour through the grate and into the plant. That freighter would head back to the stars to be replaced by the next in line. The shuttle moved to the far end of the plant where pallets of freshly poured metal ingots were loaded onto other freighters for export or trains to be sent to local factories.

No-o-Ka and the two other Gallicean surgeons walked out onto the platform with the Brotherhood agents. After a few minutes, the final agents brought the Nan assistants out of the hospital and they secured the door. All the Nan were chained together and secured to the door of the hospital building. Agents Igol and Ordo walked over the No-o-Ka. "Okay, doctor, I suppose I know whose shuttles these are now," Igol said. "Where are you from and why are you here?'

"I am chief physician for General Fa-a-Di. The general is the current High Commissioner of Greater Gallia in the Ulagong Galaxy," No-o-Ka explained.

"I heard about you guys," Igol laughed. "You've come with the traitors Balak and Arrak to request a Free Society in your galaxy, right? You have to know that will never happen, don't you?"

"Little man," No-o-Ka said. "You can put away your weapons. I am no danger to you. But why do you say the Free Society will never happen?"

"Sorry about the blasters, doctor, but rules are rules. Until I find a way to secure you three, we have to be ready for an attack," Igol replied.

"That is probably wise, little man," said a voice behind them. They spun around to see Fa-a-Di land on the platform. He was wearing freshly polished black armor which gleamed in the sunlight. He wore a black and silver battle helmet and war boots with long metal talons. His blasters and daggers were secured to his belt.

"Let me guess," Igol said as he aimed his blaster. "You are Fa-a-Di."

"Very good, little man," the Gallicean said. "But to filth like you, I am General Fa-a-Di, High Commissioner of Greater Gallia and hero of both Predaxian wars. In my galaxy, it is an act of war to aim a weapon at a head of state."

"But this is not your galaxy, general," Igol laughed. "You and your doctors are under arrest."

Fa-a-Di screeched with laughter. "Silly little bug, do you think I came here alone?" Two Gallicean Marines landed on both sides of Fa-a-Di. Their dark red battle armor was the color of human blood. Each had two blasters in their hands and four daggers on their belts. As the agents watched, more than forty more Marines landed on the platform, each carrying a laser rifle aimed at them. "As I see it, you have two choices, little man," Fa-a-Di smiled. "You can shoot me or you can surrender. I have been shot by better weapons many times. You might hit me or you might not. Either way, my Marines will kill you all and feed your remains to the Boleys in the hospital. What will it be?"

The agents dropped their weapons and a Marine quickly retrieved them. "Okay, general, you are in charge now. What are you going to do with us?" Igol asked.

"Although you do look delicious, I have already had my breakfast today," Fa-a-Di laughed. "I suppose we will let you leave. We do not want war in this galaxy. Let me take a look at your ship first." The Gallicean walked over to the black shuttle and looked through the windows. He could see Bola Deka and another Vol chained inside. He waved and smiled at Bola, then turned to Igol again. "You are a very naughty boy. What is your name, son?"

"I am Agent Igol Vart of the Brotherhood, general," he replied. "You are in desperate trouble for detaining us. Those people in the shuttle are our prisoners and we won't give them to you."

"I am in desperate trouble," Fa-a-Di pointed at himself and laughed. The Marines began to laugh as well. "I have dozens of heavily armed Marines here and you have nothing. If any of you accidently fell off this platform, no one would ever know. You, your friends and your shuttle would drop into the gas until you are crushed by the pressure below. Perhaps bits of you would rise again in the Dar-Fa to fertilize a Ka-la-a. And I am in trouble. Please open the shuttle, Igol."

"I can't do that general," Igol replied. "You have no jurisdiction in this galaxy."

"I'm glad you said that, Igol," Fa-a-Di said. "By the way, you are going to love this." He turned to the Marine on his left and said, "Um-de-Bo, may I borrow your baloo?" The Marine pulled a large sickle shaped dagger from his belt. "You see, Igol, only our Marines carry this blade. Very few can learn to use it properly. Um-de-Bo, if I break it, I will buy you two more. Please give it to me."

The Marine threw the blade away from Fa-a-Di. It flew fifty yards and then started to curve. It zipped around the exterior of the platform and continued to curve. Fa-a-Di held his right hand in the air and grabbed the baloo from the air as it approached. "Pretty impressive, right?" the general smirked. He walked over to the shuttle and plunged the baloo through the side of the ship. Then he sawed a giant tear in the vessel and ripped a large section of fuselage off and dropped it on the platform. He used the baloo to cut through the chains securing the two Vol and helped them out of the ship and led them back to the Marines. "Um-de-Bo, thank you," Fa-a-Di said as he handed the weapon back. "You sharpened it well, and I am proud of you. Please chain these agents together and take them and the rest to Lagamar Vol."

"Yes, general," Um-de-Bo replied as the Marines began unchaining the Nan and cuffing the agents.

Fa-a-Di stood next to Igol Vart as he was handcuffed. Before he was chained, Fa-a-Di grabbed him around the waist with one hand and held him high in the air. He walked over to the edge of the platform and suspended him over the gas giant. "You know, son, if I accidently dropped you here, you would fall for five or ten minutes through the gas until the external pressure overwhelmed your pressure suit. After another minute or so of falling, you would be crushed to death by the pressure. It would be an agonizing death, little man, as your body compressed and the air and water was squeezed out of your system until it collapsed into a lump of dead meat jerky and bones." He carried him back to the rest of the agents where he was quickly chained to the rest. "If I find that you or any of your agents return to this planet or take any revenge on the people of these planets, you will pray that your death could have been that easy." He thumped the human's chest hard so that he stumbled backward. "I hope you understand that, Igol."

Dave and De-o-Nu still sat near the open bay doors on the Kong-Fa, watching the smooth water below the ship. Three Zula popped their eye-stalks above the water. It felt like they were smiling at them. Jake flew out of the water, shook the water off his body and landed next to Dave. "I'm sorry it took so long, but these guys aren't easy to find," Jake said.

"Could you understand them?" De-o-Nu asked.

"Pretty much," Jake replied. "They are quite skeptical, but I told them a friend was here with me and these three came to see. Jake flew down and landed on one Zula that was looking at him. "This one says her name is Ulook and she remembers Dave from the fish market and when he helped release her. She wants to know what you want with them. Can you come down here, Dave? If I can touch you both, you might be able to communicate with her."

At De-o-Nu's order, the ship dropped to five feet over the water. De-o-Nu dropped a small rubber raft into the water and lowered Dave onto it. Ulook swam over to Dave and touched him. "I can hear her thinking, Jake," Dave said. "Come over here so I can get a better connection." Jake connected to both of them. "Hello Ulook, my name is Dave," he said.

He could hear her in his mind saying, "Hello Dave. Thank you again for helping us last night. I was so terrified in that market. When I saw you, I felt your pain at seeing me in that box. Bless you for releasing my brother and me."

"Ulook, you and the rest of the Zula are in danger on this planet," Dave said. "I want to take all of you back to Nan where you will be safe."

"What is Nan, Dave?" Ulook thought.

"It's the planet you come from, isn't it?" Dave asked, suddenly confused.

"Oh, now I understand," she thought. "Those humans on our home world call themselves Nan, so you call the planet that. Dave, interestingly enough, we call that planet Zula. Won't the other humans follow us to Zula and try to eat us there?"

"I hope not, Ulook," Dave said. "No other races visit Nan because they are seen as second or third class people. Also, we don't intend to tell anyone where you went, not even the Nan on this planet."

"They will become suspicious when we are gone, won't they?" Ulook asked.

"Perhaps, but the people here will believe the Zula just died off and they will fish for something else, I believe," he replied.

"But how will we get there, Dave?" Ulook asked. "How do we travel through space without the Nan to take us there?"

"My friends on this star cruiser have filled their holds with sea water," Dave began. "Once you are aboard, they will fly at top speed to Nan, where they will release you."

Ulook looked up at the massive ship and the odd creature looking down at them. "I don't know, Dave," she thought. "That creature looks very dangerous. What if they eat us themselves?"

Dave looked up and said, "De-o-Nu, you need to come down here too. You have to explain that you won't eat them when you take them home." De-o-Nu laughed and removed his boots and weapons belt. He lowered himself from the deck, slipped into the water and swam over to the raft. Ulook seemed very afraid, but she and Jake managed to touch the Gallicean too.

"Ulook, I know we Galliceans are fierce looking, but that is only because we are warriors from an exotic planet," De-o-Nu said. "Dave is like my brother, and if he asks me to transport you all back to Nan and deliver you there safely, that is what I will do. I would not hurt you any more than I would hurt my own children."

"Thank you, De-o-Nu," Ulook said. "I have touched your mind and know your words are true. Can your ship carry us all?"

"How many Zula are here, Ulook?" Dave asked.

"Five hundred and eleven at last count, Dave," she thought. "We are a very close community and do not wander far from this spot. The water is calm here and the food is abundant."

"Let's try to fit everyone," De-o-Nu said. "This is a big ship and I think we'll be okay. It will take a several hours to reach Nan from here at top speed due to the added water weight.

Make sure you bring enough food for a day. We have oxygen stored to refresh the water during the trip. Just bring everyone here and we'll be on our way."

"Thank you both for this," she thought. They could feel the warm and gratitude in her heart. "Our people have lived in constant fear of the fishermen. I know the Vol have done what they could do to save us, but we have lost many of our people over the years on this planet. Bless you both."

CHAPTER 39

Avery Adamsen flew the shuttle out of Porto and toward Mount Alila, two hundred miles away. As they traveled away from the city, the clouds became less gray and almost white. A driving rain washed most of the grime off as the altitude increased. At five thousand feet above sea level, the clouds gave way to brilliant sunshine. The peaks of a mountain range were twenty miles ahead. The green peaks ended in white snow caps that glistened in the light. As the shuttle approached, small villages could be seen dotting the sides of the mountains, carved into the dense forests.

"The tallest peak here is Mount Alila," Vee said. "All the mountains on Lagamar Ulu that rise above the clouds are used for our monthly time off. Villagers provide meals and lodging for tired factory and government workers like me. You may have noticed that we had no Nan workers in the factories or cities below. Their lives are difficult enough without having to deal with the pollution. There are many here where it is safer for them. Also, we are machinists and engineers and cannot manage the many things they do for us."

A large landing area sat outside a dense village near the treeline on Mount Alila. Avery settled the shuttle down on the landing marks and shut down the engines. Dave Brewster was standing out on the landing pad with two Ulu men. The shuttle bay opened and the guests filed out to meet Fao Konki, President of Lagamar Ulu and Roe Bala, Minister of the Economy. Dave hugged and kissed Darlene, then shook hands with Vee and led him away from the group.

"Vee, it's good to see you," Dave said, "but you need to know there was an incident on Lagamar 7 this morning."

"What happened, Dave?" Vee asked.

"The Brotherhood captured Bola and Mulwi Deka and forced them to tell where the platform was. Their shuttle went there and they tried to shut down the hospital," Dave replied.

"That's horrible, Dave. What happened to the Dekas?" he asked.

"This is where it gets interesting," Dave began. "General Fa-a-Di and a squad of Gallicean Marines arrived and took the agents captive. He personally ripped their shuttle apart. Then he sent the agents and the Dekas back to Lagamar Vol. Before he released them, he told them to stay out of this sytem or they would be killed."

"This is terrible news, Dave," Vee replied. "Now thousands of agents will come. What has Fa-a-Di done?"

"Let's not overreact just yet, Vee," Dave said calmly. "The Galliceans only went to that planet because Wendo and Antar wanted them to. I know there is a plan in there somewhere, but we have to be patient while it plays out." A tone sounded in Dave's ear. "I'm sorry, Vee, but I have to take a call. Please keep everyone talking about something else." After Vee walked away, Dave said, "Okay, Jon, what's happening?"

"Dave, we've moved most of the crew and their baggage from the Manila," Jon replied. "I've spend most of the morning re-labeling the control systems for the Opa. On your orders, I turned command of Nightsky over to Lauren. The remaining crew and I are leaving orbit now and heading to Lagamar Opa."

"Fantastic job, Jon," Dave said. "I knew your experience on Far Sky and with that ship would come in handy one day. Did you hear about the situation on Lagamar 7?"

"Yes, Dave. Bola Deka contacted me from the Gallicean shuttle on its way to Lagamar Vol," he replied. "I was thinking about relieving them of the Brotherhood agents."

"Don't do that, Jon," Dave cautioned. "Right now, only the Galliceans are caught in this issue. We will figure a way out. Anything else new to report?"

"I spoke with De-o-Nu a few minutes ago, and he advses that all the Zula fit into his hold easily. He kept Ulook in a small tank on the bridge with him. He will need her to help pick out a site on Nan when they arrive. He has left Lagamar Vol and should reach top speed soon. He said he would contact you when he arrives. It sounded like Fa-a-Di was with him at the time and it seemed like they had a few drinks to celebrate the victory on Lagamar 7," Jon said.

"Okay, Jon, thanks," Dave replied. "Please keep an eye out for more agents on Lagamar Opa. Once word of the incident with the Galliceans gets out, all of these planets will be crawling with them. Brewster out."

Darlene found Dave standing alone and took his arm. "Dave, you're being rude to our guests," she said as she pulled him along. "Jon and the Galliceans can take of themselves for now, sweetheart."

"You always know everything that's going on, Darlene. How is that?" Dave smiled.

"You talk in your sleep," she laughed.

The group walked slowly through the streets of the town named after the mountain. Fao was telling them about this village where thousands of workers came every month to relax and get the stench of the city out of their lungs and minds. The buildings facing the cobblestone streets held small shops and restaurants, while the upper floors were either rented or partially owned by Ulu from the cities for their monthly rest periods. The city blocks were arranged so there was never more than three blocks without a park. All the parks were crowded with families enjoying a picnic lunch or simply basking in the warm sunlight. Fao told them families tended to use the same villages for many years. If certain members moved to another city far away, they could still be with the rest of their family once a month. Dave thought about his own children and wondered what they were doing now in the other galaxy. He stopped walking suddenly, almost causing Darlene to fall over. "What's wrong, Dave?" she asked.

"Just wait here a second, sweetheart," he said as the rest of the group continued up the hill toward the next park. He tapped his com-link.

"Aye-aye, Admiral," said Lauren London.

"Lauren, please get a hold of Loni Arrak and Governor Lonk on Hive 1008," he said. "I need them to get Bill Brewster here as soon as possible if they can. Then contact General Fa-a-Di and tell him I need No-o-Ka's help again."

"Yes sir," she replied. "I'll do that immediately. Anything else, Dave?"

"Please ask Jake to come here as soon as possible. Oh, and how do you like commanding Nightsky, Lauren?" he asked.

"She is a wonderful ship, but she'll always belong to Jon as far as I'm concerned. Nightsky out," she replied as the line went dead.

"What's going on in that brain of yours, Admiral?" Darlene smiled. "I miss Billy too, but why bring him here?"

"Darlene, you remember how Bill and No-o-Ka helped us translate Jake's thoughts for the Galliceans, right?" Dave asked.

"You want them to translate the Zula and Boley for the High Council," Darlene replied.

"You're very smart, you know that. That is one of the many reasons I love you, Darlene," he replied as he kissed her gently.

"I'm already on it, Dave," Jake said.

"Where did you come from?" Dave asked, startled to see the maklan on the ground next to them.

"I was on the bridge with Lauren when you asked for me," he replied. "I'm not sure what your plan is, but I'm beginning to like it a lot. Just like old times, huh?" Jake disappeared into thin air.

Dave and Darlene rushed to catch up to the group, which had entered a large restaurant with an outdoor seating area which was reserved for them. Dave and Darlene were led to seats between Wendo Balak and Antar Arrak. Zina and Serena sat next to them. Waiters moved through the crowd pouring local beer for the group. It was cold and bitter from the herbs. Small plates of salami, cheese and pickled local vegetables were placed in the middle of each table. Fao was telling the group how all the ingredients come from the region above the smog, where the fresh air and water produce Vol quality produce. He began to tell the story of the temple at the top of the village and how it was built millions of years ago when the planet was fresh and young.

Wendo put his hand on Dave's shoulder and leaned toward his ear. "Dave, how is your visit going so far?"

"This is a unique system, Wendo," he laughed. "I hope it is not the death of us all."

"Don't worry about the Brotherhood, Dave. They are cowards who will slink back into their caves to hide from the Galliceans," Wendo replied. "I heard what Igol told his supervisors when he was released." The old man laughed. "He asked for a six week vacation to begin immediately on the other side of the galaxy."

"Fa-a-Di will be happy to hear that, I'm sure," Dave smiled. "You and Antar are planning all of this for a reason. Did you know the Galliceans would react like they did?"

"Honestly, Dave, you already know the answer to that. Put yourself in his shoes. If this was the Society of Gallia and we were hunting your ancestors, you'd do the same thing," Wendo answered.

"I thought the Galliceans evolved on Gallia. Didn't you tell me that?" Dave asked.

"Probably, but our civilization is so old that the stories often change when new facts are uncovered," Wendo said. "I had no idea the Boley were relatives of the Galliceans until Fa-a-Di communicated with the wounded Boley last night. If the two species evolved independently, that would never be possible. Back in the time when we first traveled to and begin to settle the Ulagong Galaxy, we hunted the Boley's ancestors, which I can tell you were not sentient. When many gas giants were found in your galaxy, I imagine some hunters moved those creatures to your galaxy, hoping they would thrive and be worth hunting some day. Over the millions of years, those here became Boley and in your galaxy, they became Gallicean. At least that's my theory. Yes, Antar?"

Antar Arrak was leaning across Darlene. "I agree, old friend. There can be no other way it could happen. Dave, I want to tell you I just heard from Loni. She is working on getting Bill here soon. I'll let you know whatever I hear. I think that is a brilliant idea, by the way."

"What idea, Dave? Who is Bill?" Wendo asked.

Darlene put her arms out to hold all three of them close. "We are being rude, so let's pay attention to our host. So you know, Bill is our son. He, Jake and No-o-Ka worked on a team that translated maklan mind patterns into human and Gallicean languages. That stopped the attack on No-Makla and led to victory in the Second Predaxian War. No more talking!" After lunch, the group started back up the hill toward the Alila Temple that sat at the edge of the village where the trees stopped and the rocks and snow cap began.

The street became increasingly steep. After five blocks, the street ended and a long stairway reached higher still. There were benches every fifty steps or so for older citizens to rest. As Dave and Darlene climbed, they passed Antar and Wendo sitting on the first benches and waved. The two men were deep in conversation and did not notice them pass by. At the second landing, Minister Vee Ondi was sitting and panting. Dave and Darlene sat with him.

"I've been in the city for three weeks," he weazed. "It takes a day or two to build lung capacity here. That's why we sleep so well up here. Cold nights and thin air keeps you in bed. What do you think of our planet, Ambassador?"

"Every planet I've visited is a contradiction, Vee," Darlene said. "The people work very hard in often terrible conditions to make a meager living. Through it all, they seem to be quite happy. The Ulu seem to have the worst possible circumstance. The pollution is terrible and the factories seem ancient and in desperate need of repair."

"Well Darlene, we do what we can and what we know," Vee replied. "The Ulu, Nan, Opa and Vol have been living this way and doing this for too many generations to count. If there is another way, we've forgotten about it. The sun comes up in the morning and we trudge off to do our jobs. When evening comes, we wander back home to spend a few hours with our families. You know, I think we Ulu have the best circumstance of all of the lower caste races. We have our mountains to escape from our lives. I suppose that makes us like the Nan."

"How so, Vee?" Darlene asked.

"The Nan only have one world," he said. "They work for many months on planets around the Society. A typical Nan is given two months a year to return to their planet. They go there like we come here, except we come every month and don't have to travel long distances on overcrowded freighters to get here. After that short break, they climb back on rusted ships and return to work for another year. Many of them are separated from their spouses and children, not unlike here. At least we can communicate while we are separated."

"But why don't you try to do more and be more than underpaid factory workers?" she asked. "You met Mencius of the Kalidean Federation. The Kalideans have long ago outgrown their mining ancestors. Every race can do that too."

"The Opa of the Kalidean Federation were lucky, just like the Pa on Earth 47," Vee smiled. "They lost touch with the Society and had to create their own new reality. We never had that chance. They never let us go and never allowed us to be any different than we are. We have learned to make the best of the world and the lives we can. That is why the Opa pride themselves on their mining prowess using machines built on this planet. The Vol produce more food than any other race and want everyone to know that. Our factories are the most efficient in the Society, and none of the other races could survive without the goods we provide. Without the opportunity to be different, we accept what we have and learn to love and take pride in it." He rose to his feet. "Let's continue on to the temple now. I feel much better. When you see the temple and meet the priests, you will feel renewed as we all do." They continued walking up the steps toward the temple.

The final step ended on a broad stone patio two hundred feet square. In the center, a large fountain bubbled and splashed water into a shallow pool. A narrow band of thick grass separated the patio from dense groups of trees on two sides. Beyond the trees, the other peaks in the range loomed far away. On the fourth side, a tall brick wall formed the outer gate to the Mount Alila Temple. That wall was pierced by a single arch shaped entry way. The mountain continued to rise higher into the sky behind the temple. Just outside the entry, ten monks in brown robes formed a line. Each person approaching the entry was asked to remove their foot coverings, as only bare feet were allowed to pass through the gate. Dave removed his boots and socks and handed them to a monk, who gave him a small token and dropped an identical one into one of his boots. "Enter in peace, Brother and Sister," the monk said. At the entry, a small stream of water flowed through a channel in the stone patio. Dave noticed each person stepped into the water with both feet for a moment, and then passed through the entry. Dave and Darlene held hands and stepped in the water, which was icy cold. They quickly stepped out on the other side.

Another monk came to them with a towel and wiped their feet. He then handed them leather thongs to wear inside the compound. "Reflect in peace, Brother and Sister," the monk said as they passed by.

The interior courtyard was very large, and several gardens and at least five large temples could be seen from this vantage point. Serena Vanatee and Zina Arrak joined them and took Darlene's arms. "Darlene, please let us show you the temple,"

Serena said. "It is traditional for men and women to be separate inside the gardens and smaller temples. The areas to our right are for women and those to the left are for men." Wendo and Antar joined them and stood on either side of Dave. "My grandfather and Zina's husband will show Dave around. We will meet again in the main temple later."

"It's okay, Darlene," Dave said as she was led away. "I'll see you in a few minutes." The two old men led Dave off to the men's section of the temple. They walked through a meticulously groomed garden with many fresh blooms. The scent of the flowers was hypnotic. A few short wooden steps led up to the first temple, which was no more than twenty feet square. The back of the temple was open and Dave could see a number of men walking around a large garden with a reflecting pool in the middle. The next mountain stood high in the background. The other sides of the temple were lined with candle-filled niches. Both men picked up fresh candles. Wendo gave one to Dave. They lit the candles and placed them into empty niches. Wendo and Antar stared at the lights for a few moments and then led Dave out to the garden. To his left, the outside wall of the temple stood. On his right was a second, larger temple. Past the garden and reflecting pool was a structure like the temple but much smaller.

"Come on, Dave," Antar said. "We've got to pick up the pace. The High Priest is waiting for us. Try to move quicker but act calm. We are supposed to be at peace in this holy place." They tried to move fast and slow at the same time around the others examining the garden and pool. Several men sat on benches and seemed to be communing with nature. Small, brightly colored birds flew around the compound singing. Many would land on worshippers and sing to them. As they approached the smaller structure, Dave could tell there were four men sitting facing the opposite direction, looking toward the next mountain. One was wearing bright blue robes, while the others wore normal attire. Wendo and Antar led Dave around to the other side to meet the men.

Wendo said, "Of course you already know Mencius and Orlo Vance. This is Odo Pak, Elder of Nan and our beloved High Priest, Obu Neela. Gentlemen, may I present you to Admiral Dave Brewster of the Ulagong Galaxy." Both men hugged Dave tightly and asked him to sit down.

"Dave, we have heard so much about you and your wonderful friends," Odo said. "I am told you will be visiting my world next. We are honored. In light of this happy coincidence, I was hoping you could escort me home."

"Of course, Elder," Dave said. "The Nightsky is pretty full now, but we always have room for distinguished guests."

"Thank you very much, but please call us Odo and Obu," the Nan replied. "We are all just men after all, are we not?"

"Dave, I have told everyone about your act of generosity in giving us the Manila for slag dumping," Orlo said. "That is an amazing gift."

"Thank you, Orlo, but it was a gift from Mencius," Dave replied. "It was his ship to give. I just had the kernel of the idea."

The High Priest began to chuckle. "I'm so sorry, everyone. I know it is not priest-like to laugh about the plight of another, but I was just remembering what we were told about the Gallicean encounter with the Brotherhood. You and Mencius have very brave and powerful friends."

"As Wendo told me earlier," Dave said, "any of us would have done the same if we were in that situation. Fa-a-Di is a great friend and I would do anything for him."

"That offer may be called soon, my son," Obu said. "Those agents have been scared to death, but there are too many thousands more who may be out after all of our blood."

"Why do you say that, Obu?" Dave asked.

"Orlo, could you please bring us some strong refreshments?" Obu said. "The rest of us need a few moments alone."

"Of course, Your Excellency," he said and quickly hurried away.

"Orlo is a great patriot, Dave Brewster," Antar said. "However, there are too many things that no one outside this circle can know. Wendo, it's your plan, go ahead and tell us what comes next."

The right side of the temple was a mirror-image of the men's section, with a few exceptions. The gardens were more lush on this side and the reflecting pool was replaced by a line of fountains spraying water high into the air. Along the outside wall of the temple were twenty separate bathing chambers where women could bathe before heading to the larger temples. All Ulu women took a ritual dip in the water here when they first came to the temple each month. All Ulu were expected to bath in their residences before coming up the hill. Instead of the single small temple where Dave now sat with the others, theirs was an open grass lawn reaching out to the edge of the mountain where a short wall stopped them from falling over the cliff. Many small benches were placed to provide a perfect view of the mountains. The three women sat on one bench near the cliff's edge.

"May I ask you two a question?" Darlene said. "If we have to bathe after we enter the temple, why do we wash our feet at the door? Is that just another ancient custom?"

"Actually, it is not," Serena smiled. "That custom began shortly after the establishment of the Brotherhood. The priests learned that all agents have tattoos on their feet to show their allegiance to the group and to identify dead agents. Our temples are sacred places and it would be unthinkable to have agents checking on honest citizens while they commune with nature and pray. The monks at the gate are checking everyone's feet for tattoos going in and coming out. It's pretty clever, right?"

"Very clever, Serena. Thanks for letting me know," Darlene smiled. "Why are we here and what are we waiting for?"

"Darlene, Dave is meeting with a closed group. You know that things are going to get very complicated now," Zina said. "So many gears are now in motion that cannot be stopped."

"I know," Darlene said. "This may not end well for any of us. Do you think Wendo's plan can succeed?"

"Of course, it can," Zina said. "Antar and I have pledged our lives to this very moment. If we are very smart and extremely lucky, we will survive and the Society will progress."

"But if things start going wrong, then none of us will leave Earth Prime again," Serena interjected. "The actions of the Galliceans have put all of us in jeopardy. I still don't understand why my grandfather sent them to Lagamar 7."

"I disagree, Serena," Darlene said. "I believe the Galliceans are the key to our success."

"I agree with you, Darlene," Zina said. "At the appropriate moment, the Kalideans, Nan, Zula, Boley and Galliceans will bring the High Council to justice. I can feel it in my old bones."

"I don't understand, Zina," Serena said. "What's going on?"

"Now is not the time or place for this," she replied. "We don't know who might be listening to us."

CHAPTER 41

"Greetings, star cruiser," said the voice over the speakers on the bridge of the Kong-Fa. "I am Apa Engu of Nan. May I know the purpose of your visit?" The view screen split and the horrified face of the Nan stared back at De-o-Nu's beak.

"Don't be afraid, little man. We come in peace. We are on a mission for Lords Balak and Arrak, Apa," the Gallicean replied. "We need your approval to approach your oceans."

"Ah, you are the Galliceans, correct?" Apa said, quite relieved.

"That is correct. I am Ambassador De-o-Nu of Greater Gallia. Do we have your permission?"

"Of course, sir," Apa replied. "I'm sorry but we get very few visitors and I've never seen a non-human."

"Don't worry, son," De-o-Nu said. "Perhaps after our mission, some of my crew can visit your world?"

"Of course, sir, it would be a pleasure. Welcome. Nan out," Apa said as the screen went back to the full planet view. The bridge crew began to laugh out loud. Two of the crew fell out of their chairs and could not stop laughing.

"Captain, I thought the little human was going to jump out of his skin when he saw you," the helmsman laughed.

"I know. My wife tells me I've very handsome, so I can't imagine why," De-o-Nu chuckled back. He reached into the glass tank and touched Ulook gently. "Do you know where on the planet you want to go?"

"I'm sorry, De-o-Nu. I was born on Lagamar Vol. However, we have many older Zula in the hold. Perhaps we can go swim with them," she thought.

"Take the comm," De-o-Nu shouted to the helmsman, "I've got to put on my swim trunks. And have two men take Ulook and place her gently in the hold with the others. And when I say gentle, I mean gentle! If anything happens to any Zula, I'll eviscerate you all!" He stormed off the bridge.

The two crew members carried the glass case down to the hold, where they were too confused to continue. They were deathly afraid of hurting the poor creature, but would have to lift her out of the case to drop her into the hold. They squatted next to the tank and thought but couldn't come up with an answer, and they knew the captain would be there soon. Each imagined the De-o-Nu's Nak cutting through their skin and watching their entrails drop to the floor. As they sat there, Ulook swam next to them and touched them with her hand-like claws. "Don't be afraid, you two," she thought.

They looked around to see who was talking, but they were alone. Then they noticed the Zula touching them. "I don't bite," she thought, "and I'm not made of glass. One of you just pick me up and lower me into the water."

Um-lu-Ka had just left the academy and was on his first mission. He thought about this quandary for a moment. He realized that De-o-Nu wouldn't really kill his own troops and would likely take pity on him since he was just a young man. He cautiously reached into the pool and found places to put his hands. He pulled her slowly out of the water and held her in the air next to him. Her blue eyes seemed to smile at him. "Very good, Um-lu-Ka. Now just lower me into the tank." He reached over and lowered her into the water. When her tail was touching, she said, "That's good. Thank you so much for your gentleness, Um-lu-Ka. You can release me." He let her go and she swam around with other Zula.

De-o-Nu marched into the room and pushed the others aside. He looked in the tank and saw Ulook gazing up at him. He turned to his men and said, "Very good work, soldiers. This will look good on your record, if we survive this trip." He pointed to the other soldier and told him to get out, and he rapidly obeyed. "Um-lu-Ka, I'm going to put on this harness and attach a cable. I want you to secure the cable to the wall and to your body. If something goes wrong, you need to pull me out, got it?"

"Yes, Captain," he replied and assisted De-o-Nu into position and gradually lowered him into the hold.

"That's enough," De-o-Nu said as he held the outer rim of the hatch. "I don't want to go any lower than this. Go over to the screen and start scanning the oceans of Nan slowly. The Zula will touch me and hopefully tell me where they want to go."

"Aye-aye, sir," Um-lu-Ka replied. The oceans of Nan began to be displayed on the view screen.

"Argh! Oh my god!" De-o-Nu shouted.

"Should I pull you out sir?" the other replied.

"No, that's okay," De-o-Nu said. "There are hundreds of cold claws all over my body and I'm afraid to look down. My wife will be disappointed if they snip off the wrong parts." Both

Galliceans laughed. "Come to my ready room after this, son, and we can share a glass of whisky."

"It would be an honor, Captain," the young man beamed.

"Stop there!" De-o-Nu shouted. "A litte north, now a little east. Good, now zoom in. Perfect, send those coordinates to the bridge and get me out of here."

Several hours later, Nightsky began to approach Nan. Dave could see Kong-Fa in orbit high above the planet. De-o-Nu had contacted him after the Zula had been released. At least those creatures were safe for the time being. Nan was a large planet with a diameter of twelve thousand miles. Thirty percent of the surface was covered by three large oceans. There were few tall mountains, similar to Lagamar Vol, but most of the planet was covered by forests and jungles. Rain was common and the vegetation on most of the planet was very lush. Although there were fifty billion Nan in the galaxy, only six or seven billion lived on Nan permanently. The population consisted primarily of the young and the old. Anyone who could work would find better paying jobs on other planets and send extra money back here to their parents who generally cared for the smaller children.

The face of Apa Engu filled half the view screen. He said, "Greetings, star cruiser, may I know your business on Nan?"

"We are bringing a number of dignitaries, including Elder Odo Pak and Lords Balak and Arrak. I am Lauren London, acting captain of the Nightsky. May we have permission to orbit?" she said.

"Certainly Captain, it is an honor for your ship to bring our dear Elder back to us. I am transmitting coordinates now. Will you require shuttles, or do you have your own?" Apa said.

"We have enough shuttles, Apa. Thank you for the offer," Lauren smiled. "Please let us know where we should deliver our dignitaries."

"I am sending coordinates now for our landing station near the Elder's residence," he said. "They are expected in two hours. May I tell you that you are not so fearful looking as the crew of the other ship."

Lauren smiled. "Yes, our Gallicean allies can take a little getting used to. Nightsky out."

CHAPTER 42

The shuttle landed at the coordinates given. The Elder's residence was on the outskirts of Nan City, which served as capital of the planet. Nan City was the only city on Nan with a large permanent population, consisting primarily of government workers. Half of those workers coordinated the travel of other Nan to their work planets and back. The city consisted of stone and wooden buildings along narrow roadways. The center was very compact as the Nan preferred to live close together and be able to walk to work.

The residence was one story and very open to the environment. There was no fence or gate and residents were encouraged to stop by and visit with the Elder and his family. Nan culture was very relaxed and informal, although they worked very hard here and across the galaxy. After a long day's toil, they loved to sit outside with a cold drink and their loved ones and watch the evening slip by. The residence included hundreds of small suites where visitors could spend the night if the drink and conversations lasted too long. The dignitaries from Nightsky were provided with accommodations in those suites.

Dave and Darlene were led to their suite which was at the far end of the compound, almost at the edge of a forest. It included a ten foot square bedroom with a large soft bed, a sitting room of the same dimensions, and a small but adequate restroom. They were told to relax and enjoy themselves and that dinner would be served in two hours. Dave walked out to the small patio where two chairs and one sofa sat invitingly. A gentle rain began to fall and puddles of water began to form on the stone walkways that led through the dense lawn. Darlene joined Dave on the large sofa and held his hand. "Dave, this is a beautiful place," she said. "I don't know why, but I've been feeling very energetic since we got here. Perhaps it's the ozone in the air or the rain, but it sure feels good."

"I know, sweetheart, I feel it too. Even the sound of the rain splashing into the puddles seems so different and alive here," Dave replied as he put his arm around her shoulders. She snuggled her head against his chest. The rain was pouring down now and thunder could be heard in the distance.

Two Nan exited the building across the broad patio and headed toward them through the driving rain. Darlene sat up and watched them getting drenched by the rainfall. The first was carrying a large covered tray. Water poured down his face, but he was smiling happily. The second wore a hooded robe and his face was obscured by shadows. They crossed the lawn and walked onto the porch next to the Brewsters. The first Nan placed the tray on the short table and removed the cover, revealing small dishes of food and several chilled beverages. The second Nan removed his hooded robe. It was Elder Odo Pak, who bowed slightly and sat on a chair next to them.

"Dave and Darlene," he began, "it is my pleasure to welcome you to my home and offer you some refreshments. My assistant here is Alo Pak, and he is also my youngest grandson."

Dave stood and shook the young Nan's hand. "It is a pleasure to meet you, Alo."

"Thank you, Dave and Darlene Brewster," he smiled back. "It honors our home to have you with us. Grandfather tells me that you come from the Ulagong Galaxy. That is amazing."

Darlene stood and hugged Alo. "Not only that, Alo, but we also come from more than a thousand years in the past," she replied.

"Thank you, Grandson for helping me with the tray," Odo said. "I need some time to talk with our friends now. Please help your grandmother with the arrangements for dinner. With this rain, we may have to move the feast indoors."

"Yes Grandfather," Alo said as he hurried away. The Brewsters sat on the couch again as he disappeared into the driving rain.

"Dave and Darlene, I know many people have high expectations for the coming days," Odo said. "You may be feeling excessive stress from the pressures placed on both of you. Such feelings are natural but also destructive."

"The meetings on Earth Prime may well determine the fate of the Society and our own lives, Odo," Dave replied. "I'm not sure how to relax with that day coming soon."

Odo put his hand on Dave's knee. "Dave, you do not hold the fate of the Society in your hand. Our lives are also not that important in the greater scheme of things. After dinner, I usually take a walk in the forest with my guests. It helps to calm our nerves and prepare for bed. During that walk tonight, I would like to take the two of you to another place. It is a temple that will help you understand what I am saying now. Is that okay with you both?" They nodded their consent. "Good! I know this experience will change your perception and then you will begin to understand." Odo picked up a pickle and bit it. "You must try these pickles and other delicacies. Everything is locally grown and produced. These drinks may be potent, but they are also quite nutritious."

Darlene asked, "Odo, we have been feeling very energetic and alive since we arrived on your planet. Why is that?"

Odo smiled and sipped his drink. "Darlene, do you know why this is the only world for the Nan in this galaxy?"

"No Odo, I do not," she replied. "It does seem very odd, though."

"This was one of the first planets settled when the people of Non-Ti moved into the stars, long before the Non-Ti sun died," he began. "After a few generations, the people of this planet became powerful and threatened Non-Ti for supremacy in the infant Society. A major war raged for decades until the forces of this planet were defeated. That victory came at a horrible price, and the Society languished for thousands of years. Only the impending death of the Non-Ti star forced the people of Non-Ti back into the stars. At that time, there were only fifty-one planets in the Society, and all but Non-Ti had developed into the fifty races we have today. The people of Non-Ti were deathly afraid one of the other races would inhabit this planet and become powerful again, so they gathered the Nan people from all over the Society and sent them here. They knew we are not fighters or aggressive, and by making this planet the exclusive property of the Nan, the others would not come here."

"I'm sorry, but I thought the Nan originated here," Darlene said.

"No, Darlene," Odo smiled. "We originated on Non-Ti, along with the ancient race currently called by that name. Even in those days, we were second class citizens, forced to travel across the planet to find work and send the money back to our families. Not even the passage of billions of years had changed that."

"But why did the original settlers of Nan get so powerful?" Dave asked. "It seems like an ordinary planet to me."

"Really, it seems ordinary to you," Odo scoffed. "First, no planet is ordinary, Dave, and Nan is exceptional. Please come with me, you two." Odo stood and walked out into the rain. Water poured over his head and ran down his face and body. The Brewsters stood and walked off the porch, trying to shield their heads with their hands. "Stop blocking the rain, you two. Come stand here next to me." They walked to the center of the patio and let the water wash over them. "Now, form a circle and hold my hands, close your eyes and turn your head upward," Odo demanded.

The water drops splashed all around and soaked through their clothes. Darlene felt the warmth of Dave's and Odo's hands in hers and smiled. In her mind, she saw Beings of light dancing around them. She could not tell what kind of Beings they were, but they danced about and seemed to be laughing. She saw one of the Beings stop and run toward her. She flinched and the Being flew right through her body. She felt a rush of heat and then an inner warmth unlike anything she had felt before. She opened eyes and found herself standing in the rain with Dave and Odo. The Beings were gone. She felt cold and alone and longed for the Beings to return. Dave and Odo opened their eyes and smiled.

Odo asked, "Darlene, what did you see?"

"It was so surreal, Odo," she smiled. "There were Beings dancing around us. I couldn't tell what they were and they seemed to be lit up from inside, shining like suns. One of them ran through my body and made me feel warm and happy. When I opened my eyes, they were gone and I missed them." Dave was squeezing her hand tightly.

"That is very good Darlene. Frankly, most people who first experience this see nothing and only feel the rain. I'm impressed. And you, Dave Brewster, what did you learn standing here in the rain?" Odo asked.

"This planet is a natural Hive," Dave said, staring into space. "I could see lines of Universal Power surging through the planet unlike anything I've ever seen. There were so many strings of light passing through this patio and our bodies that they would be impossible to count. For a moment, I felt my light string joining them and flying off into space. Then Darlene squeezed my hand and I was back here, surrounded in light."

"Excellent, son," Odo said. He put his hands on their shoulders and led them back to the small porch. "Now you know everything about Nan and our people. You know why they chose us to settle this planet. They knew we wouldn't have enough work here and most of our people would have to travel to other planets. That kept the local population too small to take advantage of the Hive. All the other races look down on us and would never come here and learn this secret. But they miscalculated."

"What do you mean?" Darlene asked.

"It is true that a constructed Hive requires several billion people to make it function. Our permanent population is mostly young children and old people who would never work in a Hive," Odo smiled. "But as Dave noted, this is a natural Hive, created by God. It functions whether we are here or not.

A single man can join with this planet and do all the things the billions can do in a constructed Hive."

"So, just sitting here, I could send my light string across space and time?" Dave pondered.

"Well, not exactly here, Dave," Odo replied. "The Source is very strong everywhere on Nan, which is why you felt what you did in the rain. However, we have temples across the planet where our citizens can enter the Hive. Our entire group will be going to one of them tonight as I mentioned earlier." He hugged Dave and then Darlene. "Well, I must be off now. You two should probably change out of your wet clothes and prepare for dinner. My wife must be frantic moving everything inside." He pulled on his robe and stepped back into the rain, which had lightened considerably. "I'd better go help or I will be in trouble, again." He laughed and walked back across the patio and disappeared into another building.

A large tent had been erected in the patio next to the Elder's private residence. Several tables were set with simple settings of stone plates and plain glasses. Several buffet tables were loaded with trays of local specialities. Dave and Darlene wore their dress uniforms as they joined the others coming into the tent. Everyone had been given umbrellas to protect them from the rain, which was spotty now, and the three moons of Nan were peeking through the clouds. Alo Pak welcomed them, took their hands and led them to a table, where they joined Mencius, Zee Gongaleg, Fak Mandoka and Jake Benomafolays.

Everyone was feeling the energy of the planet and they were talking and laughing among themselves. The food was wonderful and the drinks were better. Dave could feel the heat in his face and decided to avoid any more drinks. Zee, Fak and Jake were giggling uncontrollably and slurring their words. Darlene had gone to the dessert table and was chatting with Zina and Serena. He sat back in the chair and closed his eyes for a moment, basking in the warmth of the gathering. He felt a hand on his shoulder and looked up to see Wendo Balak standing next to him. "Let's get away from the crowd for a minute, Dave. I need to talk to you," Wendo said. Dave rose and they walked out of the tent into the bright light of the three moons.

"Is something wrong, Wendo?" Dave asked.

"Yes, I'm afraid there is, Dave," Wendo said as he looked around to be sure no one was listening. "The High Council has been stonewalling our request to have Bill Brewster jump here.

Of course, we can't tell them why we want him or they would deny the request immediately. I've discussed this with Elder Pak and he needs your help to resolve this. He will tell you more later. Please keep this from everyone tonight." Wendo patted Dave on the back, smiled and walked back into the tent. Odo Pak was talking to the crowd as Dave entered the tent. He could see that Serena Vanatee had taken his seat, so he stood in a corner by the entrance.

"Dear guests, I hope you have enjoyed this evening meal," Odo said. "It honors our home and our planet to have you with us tonight. We are especially honored by the presence of Admiral Dave Brewster. Dave and his dear friend Ambassador De-o-Nu of Greater Gallia have returned our beloved Zula to us. I was saddened that the Ambassador could not join us tonight. I am told he had pressing business on Lagamar 7." The group applauded. "It is our custom to walk in the nearby woods after dinner. Any of you who would like to join me are welcome. If you have had too much drink, you may retire to your rooms if you prefer. In the woods, we will find two small temples where you may meditate and relax. You may return here at any time. My sons will set up some drinks here in the tent for anyone when they come back. You are also welcome to stay here and continue your conversations. Thank you."

Most of the guests either stayed in the tent or returned to their rooms. Odo and Alo Pak led Dave, Darlene, Wendo, Serena, Antar and Zina away from the party. A stone path led through the trees deep into the forest. After a few hundred feet, the trees became less dense and many rose hundreds of feet over their heads. They crossed several small stone bridges that crossed streams swollen from the rain. They walked more than a mile until they reached two small open wooden temples. Odo explained that men and women meditated separately here as on

Lagamar Ulu. As everyone moved toward the structures, Odo held Dave back. "Come with me," he whispered.

A second narrow stone path led into thick underbrush. Odo led the way and strode confidently in the darkness. After another hundred yards, they came upon a small waterfall splashing onto a large flat stone. The water rushed off the stone into a small pond. Odo stood in front of the waterfall and bowed deeply. The water stopped. "Hurry, Dave, it will start again soon." They moved through an opening behind the waterfall and went down a long set of stone steps that ended in a circular room hewn from the stone. Ten stone slabs radiated from the center of the room. Each had a rolled, heavy blanket on top. Odo unrolled a blanket and laid it across the stone. He sat on the blanket. "Come on, Dave. Do what I'm doing. We don't have much time. The others will be looking for us after a while."

"What exactly are we doing, Odo?" Dave asked.

"You aren't trying very hard are you?" Odo asked. "Please just do it. Lie down and close your eyes." Dave followed the orders, but took a second blanket as a makeshift pillow. He sat on the cold blanket and adjusted the pillow until he felt a little more comfortable. Knowing it would not get any better, he closed his eyes.

Dave could feel his light string rip out of his chest and fly though the hill over the stone temple. He looked down and could see Darlene sitting peacefully with her eyes closed. His light flew into space and through the hull of Nightsky. He stopped in Lauren London's quarters and noticed her sitting on the bed looking at a picture of Jon Lake on her dresser. He shot back into space and joined countless trillions of other strings flying around him. A single silver string of light raced at him and seemed to merge with him. "Hello Dave, it's good to be with you again," said the voice of Nok, the tekkan engineer.

"Nok, how are you?" Dave replied. "I guess The Hive on Tak-Makla is functioning again. That's great."

"I guess you didn't know, Dave," Nok said. "My body was destroyed in the explosion in The Hive. But that Hive will be working again soon."

"You died? I am so sorry, Nok," Dave said. Tears filled his eyes back in the stone temple.

"Don't be upset, Dave," she replied. "I'm not sad at all. I've joined the Source again. I've never felt happier. Dave, I made a star today! How wild is that?"

"How did you do that, Nok?" he asked.

"Well it wasn't just me," she replied. "Many of us went to the stellar incubator, which is really just a cloud of gas. We spun the gas around and it began to collapse under its own weight. Finally, it shrank down until fusion began in its core. It was a miracle."

"Excuse me, Dave," Odo said as his string joined the others. "I'm glad you found an old friend, but we have work to do. Bless you, Nok."

"Bless you too, Odo and Dave," Nok replied. "I will see you again." Her string untangled from them and shot away.

"I'll show you one thing to warm your heart and then we have to go to Earth 47," Odo said as they shot away through the stars. They reached Lagamar 7 in a few seconds and raced toward the surface. Dave could see a Gallican shuttle on the platform next to Bola's shuttle, but Odo raced right past it into the gas.

They stopped on a Ka-la-a deep inside the planet. There were five Gallicean Marines and De-o-Nu standing in front of several hundred Boley. Fa-a-Di sat nearby watching the rest. They gave belts and daggers to each Boley and began teaching them how to fight. "Your friends are great men, Dave," Odo said. "De-o-Nu and Fa-a-Di could not let the violence continue. I pity the next person to come here and try to shoot one."

"This is amazing," Dave smiled as he watched the Boley throw each other around and work with the daggers. Odo streaked back into space and Dave followed him. Odo was going so fast that Dave could barely keep up. He knew if he got lost, he could just return to his body, but felt he had to keep trying.

After several minutes, they approached Earth. They shot through the atmosphere and landed in a small bedroom. It was the middle of the night here. Dave's light could read the clock which said two thirty in the morning. The man sleeping rolled over and Dave recognized his son, Bill. "Dave, this is the hard part," Odo said. "Very few can do what I'm going to show you. If you can succeed, we can take Bill back with us. Either way you need to try as though all of our lives depend on it."

"What do I need to do?" Dave asked.

"You need to reach into your mind and concentrate every bit of it on this place and your son," Odo said. "You need to want to be here with all your heart and soul. Watch me and then you try." Dave's string of light watched as Odo's string became a blob and started to morph. After a few seconds, Odo was standing in the room. But it wasn't the real Odo; it was a shimmering light version, like Darlene had seen dancing around her. The shining Odo reached over and touched the sleeping figure and said, "Bill?"

"Whoa!" Bill shouted at the sight of the Being of light in his room. He pulled away to the other edge of his bed and pulled the covers around him. "Who or what are you?"

"I am a friend, son," Odo replied. "My name is Odo and I have your father with me. Please help me and think of how much you love him to help him appear like me."

Bill was half-asleep and dazed and did not know what to think or do. Out of the corner of his eye, he could see another form taking shape. "Dad!" he shouted. He thought about his dad and how much his parents needed him in the Andromeda Galaxy. He remembered them playing catch when he was a young boy and the nights he pitched a tent in the backyard and his dad would sleep with him there.

Dave's body of light stood in front of his son. "Thanks, Billy," Dave said. "I don't think I could have done this without you." He sat next to Bill and put his arm around his shoulders. "What do we do now, Odo?"

"Stand up, both of you," Odo said. "Now, Bill, you stand between us. Dave, you and I are now going to grab onto Bill and each other as hard as we can. Then we will think of our wives back on Nan and pray the Source can help us. Bill, if we fail, you'll just be standing here alone. But your prayers for our success are greatly appreciated." Bill could feel the warmth as the two lights fused around him. He closed his eyes and could see billions of strings of light flooding through the walls, ceiling and floor of the room. He was immersed in intense light and it seemed to burn through his skin and eyelids. He was frozen in the spot, unable to move any part of his body. Suddenly, he felt his body dissolving into the light and passed out.

"Billy, wake up!" Darlene said as she shook her son. He was lying on the stone bed with Dave and Odo, who were still holding him. "Dave, Odo, Billy, someone wake up please!" she begged with tears flowing down her cheeks.

"Geez, don't be so melodramatic, Mom," Bill said as he opened his eyes. He shook the other two men and they woke as well. "Odo, I think it worked."

Odo stood and stretched, "Yes, I think it did. Welcome to Nan, Bill Brewster."

Darlene grabbed Bill and pulled him to his feet so she could hug him. "If I knew your father was going to attempt this… I don't know what I'd do."

Dave stood and stretched too. "Odo, that was the most amazing experience in my life. I've never felt so at peace. What happened in the room with all those strings of light?"

"Dave, why don't you guess?" Odo asked.

"Okay, those strings were like Nok. They were the souls of billions of others who are not in physical bodies at this time. They felt the love and desperation in us and came to help us. They kept coming and coming until there were enough to bring us here," Dave said.

"Very good, Dave," Odo replied. "I think it must be time for breakfast. I am starving after that adventure. My wife makes the best coffee and pastries on all of Nan, although my opinion might be prejudiced. There is still much work to be done and very little time. Come along everyone." The climbed back out of the stone temple and walked slowly back toward the home as the morning sun crept over the horizon. "By the way, let us please keep what happened in the temple between us. Very few people know about the power of the natural Hive and we would invite more problems if we discuss it," he finished as they left the small clearing and headed back into the woods.

CHAPTER 44

Major Ulan Makwee was the last officer to be trained to command the Manila. He sat confidently in the command chair watching his crew and the image of the Lagamar sun directly ahead. Captains Jon Lake and Theodus sat on either side of him. Their goal was to train ten pilots from Lagamar Opa to fly the Manila before turning over the ship to them officially. The training had gone quite well, and Ulan was proving to be a masterful ship's captain.

Few modifications had to be made to convert the pride of the Kalidean research fleet into a garbage truck. Most of the ship was left untouched so it could be used for other purposes as well. The major changes occurred in the large hold, where the external doors had been adjusted to open quickly and a large ram was installed. Some of the controls had been modified so a crew of twenty could manage the ship designed for a crew of one hundred.

"Major, we are approaching optimal distance to the sun," said the helmsman, Balik Namm.

"Very good, Balik," Ulan replied. "On my command cut all thrusters and transfer the helm controls to my panel."

"Aye-aye, Major," he replied.

Even with the full defensive array projected in front of the ship, the temperature was rapidly rising on the bridge. Jon could feel a trickle of sweat running down his face and brushed it away. The sun loomed very large in the view screen as they grew within a few million miles of its dazzling corona.

"Cut thrusters now!" Ulan shouted. He took the joystick with his right hand and turned hard right, causing this ship to yaw one hundred and eighty degrees. Ulan pressed a button on my control panel under his left hand and the hold bay doors flew open. The stern of the ship was heating very quickly as streams of radiation hit the unprotected metal. Ulan pulled a large red lever and the newly installed ram shot backward and pushed the hundreds of tons of slag out into space. He pressed the same button again and the hold doors slammed shut. "Move the defensive array to the stern and get all thrusters up to full power!" Manila fought against the massive gravity of the sun for a moment and then shot away from the star. "Balik, I'm giving you control again. Get us out of here."

Theodus and Jon Lake stood and applauded. "Ulan, that's was a great run. Good job," Jon said. "What do you think, Theodus?"

The Kalidean captain laughed. "I never thought I'd say this, but Manila is your ship now, Ulan," he said as he shook Ulan's hand. "Hey, Jon, can I get a ride from you? It seems I no longer have a ship." Several million miles away, the tons of slag raced toward the Lagamar sun, trapped by the intense pull of gravity. At two million miles away, the material glowed red and then white hot. A million miles later, the slag vaporized and was absorbed into the solar atmosphere.

"I thank both of you for training me and our crews," Ulan said with a broad smile. His black eyes glistened with joy. "I never could have imagined that other Opa lived in the Ulagong Galaxy. And it is a miracle that you came to my planet and gave us such a wonderful gift that will keep the Society off our backs. I know there will be a big celebration back on Lagamar Opa in honor of this day. I hope you can attend."

"I'm sorry, Ulan," Jon said. "I have to travel to Nan to retrieve Bill Brewster. He has a lot of work to do on Lagamar 7. Theodus, you should stay for the party. I'll pick you and your men up when I return with Bill."

"I have a better idea, Jon," Ulan smiled. "Your shuttle would take two days to go to Nan and come back here. Manila can get there in a few hours. Then you and the admiral's son can be at the party and he can be on Lagamar 7 a day earlier."

"That's a great idea," Theodus said. "Come on, Jon, it makes perfect sense, and I know you are not the type to excuse yourself from a party."

"I can't argue with logic like that, guys," Jon smiled as he sat down again. "Okay, Ulan, show me what this ship can do with an Opa master."

Wendo Balak and Antar Arrak were sitting together at the large table in Odo Pak's kitchen when the Brewsters emerged from the woods and approached the house. Ila, the Elder's wife and her daughter Uli were arranging freshly made pastries on trays and setting them on the table when Odo walked in with Bill Brewster and his parents. Bill was introduced to the group and offered a seat between his parents. Uli poured hot coffee into large mugs and set one in front of each guest.

"Odo, this is wonderful," Antar smiled. "Which Hive did you convince to help jump Bill here? Wendo had told me there was a problem with that."

"Sorry, Antar, but that is a trade secret," Odo laughed. "We wouldn't want another planet to get in trouble with the High Council, would we?"

Dave put his hand on Bill's shoulder. "There is a lot for you to do here, Bill. I need you, Jake and No-o-Ka to repeat the job you did with the maklan telepathy with two new species. And it has to be done within seven days."

"Dad, I don't think that's possible," Bill replied. "You remember it took Jake a hundred years to learn to communicate with Horace Hildebrand."

"We have a big head start here, son," Dave explained. "The Boleys on Lagamar 7 can communicate with Jake and the Galliceans telepathically already. And the Zula on this planet can communicate with anyone they can touch. But we need them to be able to communicate through translators on Earth Prime in a week. I hate to say it, but the stakes this time are even higher than before."

"I don't believe that is the case, Dave," Odo said. "Have you forgotten what I told you just yesterday on the porch of your suite?"

"You said that I don't hold the fate of the Society in my hands and that an individual life was not that important in the scheme of things," Dave replied.

"Very good, Dave," Odo smiled. "I'm sure you recall everything you saw last night as well, especially the blessed Nok and those blessed others who made Bill's presence possible."

"Of course, Odo, I could never forget any of that," Dave answered.

"Excellent. Do you now understand my words from yesterday better?" Odo asked.

"I do not control the fate of the Society because it has already collapsed. The High Council's efforts to hold it together cannot succeed because it is hopelessly broken," Dave said. "All I can do is my best to love and protect my family and friends and do my small part to make the dissolution of the Society peaceful. Whether that happens or not depends on the efforts of every person in the Society."

"Spoken like an Elder, my son," Odo replied. "But why is your life not so important?"

"I am just a man, Odo," Dave said. "I can only carry the burden that these two shoulders can bear. I could spend my life trying to fix the Society or my own planet. But then I would have neglected my greatest responsibility, which is to be happy and to love and care for my friends and family."

"Perfect!" Odo laughed. "I must contact High Priest Obu Neela later today. You could be taking his job any day now."

"Wow!" Darlene said. "Where did all that come from, sweetheart?" Antar and Wendo were staring at Dave and wondering what was going on.

"I'll tell you about last night later, Darlene," Dave smiled. "Right now, I'm still a bit overwhelmed by the experience." A tone sounded on his com-link and he touched it. "Yes, Lia, what's up?"

"Admiral, the Kalidean ship Manila is entering orbit over Nan," she replied. "Correction, the Lagamar Opa ship Kalidus is entering orbit."

"That's odd," Dave replied. "What are they doing here?"

"Dave, Major Makwee advises that he is here to take Bill Brewster back to Lagamar Opa for a celebration and then to Lagamar 7 tomorrow. Captains Theodus and Jon Lake are also aboard and give you their warm regards," Lia answered.

"Thanks, Lia," Dave said. "Please let them know we are just having breakfast now, but we will take Bill there in an hour or so in our shuttle. Nan out."

CHAPTER 45

"Earth Prime Central Command, this is the star cruiser Nightsky requesting berthing instructions," Lia Lawson said. The city-planet filled the entire view screen. Long lines of star ships queued for permission to land on the surface or berth at one of the massive star ports.

The view screen image split in two and a smiling face said, "Welcome back to Earth Prime, Nightsky. I don't know if you remember me, but I am Lieutenant Silva Odeen and I will be your main contact while you are here. Your ship will berth in bay E2 at Star Port 27. I am sending you the coordinates at this moment. My team and I will board your ship once she is connected to our systems. It is a standard security sweep and nothing to worry about."

"Yes, I do remember you well, Silva. Why is a security sweep necessary?" Lia asked.

"I assure you this is a standard procedure on Earth Prime, Lia," he replied. "The High Council, Supreme Court, and Military High Command are all in session now and we need to review all ships for problems. I'm sure you understand. And my offer to share a coffee still stands. Earth Prime out."

"Well, he seemed a lot calmer this time, Lia," Ali Bai said from the helm. "Too bad, I could have used a good laugh at your expense."

"Shut up, Ali," Lia laughed. She touched a button on her control panel.

"Yes, Lia," said the voice of Captain Lauren London. "What's going on?"

"We've been given a berth, Captain, and Ali is taking us there now. We were advised that a security detail will board the ship to perform a routine security scan," Lia replied.

"That seems odd. Please advise the Admiral and all ambassadors so they are prepared," Lauren said. "I'll be there in five minutes. London out." She rolled over and looked at Jon Lake, still asleep next to her. She leaned forward and kissed his lips. "Good morning, Jon," she smiled.

"I love you," he replied.

"I love you too, Jon. We're about to berth and they are sending in a security team for a sweep. You should probably not be here when that happens," she explained. "I've got to get to the bridge before we dock." They both rose and pulled on their clothes. Lauren went to the bathroom to freshen up.

Jon tapped his com-link and said, "Jake, it's time to go." The maklan popped into the room, flew over and landed on Jon's chest. "I'll talk to you later, Lauren," he shouted out. He patted Jake on the head. "Whenever you're ready, old friend." The two disappeared from Nightsky.

Nightsky approached the orbiting star port which had berths for fifty star ships. Landing lights pointed the way to bay E2. The E level bays were designed for colony ships and battle cruisers and it dwarfed the small vessel. The bays near E2 were all empty, which seemed odd with the long backlog to get accommodations on such a star port. Dave Brewster was standing at the large window in his ready room, sipping his morning coffee as the station took control of the ship for the last few hundred yards. A group of soldiers was already in the open bay looking for anomalies in the hull of the ship as it passed over them. Dave remembered docking inside Hive 1008 just a week ago. There had been no security scan then, and he wondered what had changed.

The vessel settled down on the floor of the bay. Machines and men flooded the bay connecting utilities and communications cables to the ship. Long enclosed tunnels stretched from the walls to the main external doors and locked in place. Nightsky had arrived. Dave sat at his table and took the chocolate croissant from its small plate and bit it. The game is on, he thought. A button flashed on his panel and he tapped it. "Yes, Lia," he said.

"Admiral, some visitors from Earth Prime wish to meet with you," she replied. "They are here on the bridge now." Dave tapped another button and the door to his ready room opened. Lauren London entered with two men and one woman. Dave rose and went to shake their hands. Lauren returned to the bridge and the door closed behind her.

"Admiral Brewster, I don't know if you remember me, but I am Councilor Nola Balee," the woman said as she shook his hand. These gentlemen are Admiral Pau Ongo and Brother Luka Nance."

"Of course I remember you, Councilor," Dave smiled. "I met you on Hive 1008 when you were reviewing the damage in the Balthazar community." He shook the men's hands. "Admiral, welcome to our ship. Brother? That is an interesting title. What does that mean on Earth Prime?"

"I don't know if you've heard of an organization here called the Brotherhood," Luka replied. "I serve as a leader of that group, hence the title. Admiral, may we sit and have some coffee with you? We have a few trifling matters to discuss before the more important meetings later this week."

"Of course, please sit down," Dave said as he walked to the door and opened it. "Lia, please have someone bring more coffee and pastry for our guests," he called out. He returned to the table and sat down. "Should I send for the ambassadors to join us? They speak for our planets. I am just an explorer."

"That's okay, Dave," Nola said. "We only need you for this meeting. The ambassadors will have ample opportunity to speak to more relevant leaders." Lia and Ali entered with trays of pastry and steaming coffee. They set them on the table and left, with the door closing behind them.

"I'm all ears," Dave smiled. "Please tell me what you want me to know."

"Please allow me to begin," Luka said. "I was concerned that your itinerary changed drastically after your visit to Narta Ela. When we learned you went to the Lagamar system, my concern level rose even more."

"Luka, as you know, we are hosting Wendo Balak and Antar Arrak. They changed the itinerary," Dave explained. "As you know, this is the only time we have been in the home galaxy. They chose the original itinerary. Then they changed it. I didn't see anything odd about that. This is their galaxy and I assumed they knew the best places to go."

"Pau, I told you it would be the old men," Luka said. "We never should have allowed them to come here."

"Not now, Brother," Pau said. "We do not need to draw Dave into our personal bickering." He turned to face Dave. "You must forgive Luka, Dave. He doesn't care for Wendo or Antar. But what did you think of the Lagamar system?"

"It was amazing," Dave said. "The people there are so warm and happy, even though their personal situations were very difficult."

"What did the Opa from your galaxy think of Lagamar Opa?" Nola asked. "We have all been waiting breathlessly to find out."

"That's probably a better question for Ambassador Mencius. It seemed to me everyone was very happy to make a connection from another galaxy," Dave said. He refilled his coffee cup and savored the flavor. "Mencius even gave his star ship to the people of Lagamar Opa. I thought that was very generous."

"Too generous in my mind," Luka said. "They have no right to get involved in the internal matters of this galaxy."

"You're wrong, Luka," Dave laughed. "We are all human. The people of Lagamar Opa and the Kalidean Federation are all Opa. They have as much right to help each other as the Society has to rule other planets."

"You should watch your words, Dave Brewster," Luka snarled. "You are still here in this galaxy, and we control what happens here."

"Be quiet, Brother!" Nola demanded. "Perhaps you should return to Earth Prime, Luka. This meeting is slipping out of control."

"I'll leave when I'm ready, Councilor," Luka scoffed. "Let me tell our cousin from the Ulagong Galaxy one final thing. Dave, I know what your Gallicean friends did to my agents on Lagamar 7. They will pay for their threats. I guarantee you of that." Luka rose and stormed out of the room.

"Dave, I am so sorry for that outburst," Nola said. "Please don't be bothered by him."

"Don't worry, Nola, I am not afraid of the Brotherhood," Dave smiled.

"I commend your bravery, Dave, but you should be careful here," she replied. She rose and walked behind Dave and pressed her lips to his ear. "Is this room safe?" she whispered.

Dave tapped his com-link and said, "Jake, can you and Mitch come here now?" The two maklans popped out of thin air and landed in the center of the table. Pau and Nola were stunned by the sudden appearance of the glass like flying spiders.

"What's up, Dave?" Jake asked.

"Jake, please check the room for listening devices," Dave thought. The two maklans glowed bright red and a moment. Jake flew up and then under the table. After a moment, he returned with a small device.

"Dave, the room is now clean," Jake said out loud, as he dropped the smashed device on the table. "It would seem one of your guests left you a present. We are sensing also several dozen devices on the security detail approaching the ship now. I'll have my team track and disable them immediately."

"That's too obvious, Jake," Dave said. "We should just move them to a secure place and provide simulated sounds."

"Aye-aye Admiral," Jake said as the two disappeared again.

"I suppose your friend Luka placed this device, right? That being said, the room is now clean, Councilor," Dave smiled.

"What kind of life forms were those creatures? I've never seen anything like them before," Nola said.

Dave smiled. "Those were maklans from the planet No-Makla in the Earth 47 system. They are an indigenous species from my galaxy. There are hundreds of sub-species throughout Ulagong. As you can tell, they have some unique abilities."

"Wow! They were incredible, but Dave, we don't have much time," Nola said. "Luka was with us by design. We are all being watched continuously while we are here. Brotherhood agents are everywhere. It is very dangerous for you and your passengers to be here."

"Okay, but we are here for a specific purpose, Nola," Dave replied. "If the High Council would approve our Free Society right now, I'd fly this ship out of here right now. But why are we in danger?"

"Your visit to the Lagamar system has sent shockwaves through this planet," Nola said. "Many of my fellow Councilors are terrified about that trip. Pau and I know the dirty secrets of that system, but the Brotherhood is hiding them from the people."

"But the circumstances of Lagamar are no different on other Opa, Vol or Ulu planets, are they?" Dave asked.

"No, but Lagamar is the only system where they live closely together," she replied. "And then there is the proximity to Nan. I hope and pray that Wendo did not take you there as well."

"Nan was the last planet we visited before returning here," Dave said.

"Then we are all lost," Pau sighed and dropped his head into his hands. "If the remainder of the High Council learns of this, the repercussions will bring down the Society."

"It's too late for that," Dave said. "We all know the Society is already crumbling. Nothing can save it now. The High Council is living in a fantasy world if they believe otherwise."

"Dave, the bloodbath that would follow the dissolution of the High Council will dwarf any wars ever fought by humans," Nola replied. "You must make an excuse to leave now and take your friends back to Ulagong."

"We can't do that Nola," Dave said. "We have too many enemies in our galaxy to return without a mandate to form a Free Society. That is the only way we can forestall a future of warfare. Besides, we have a few issues to take up with the High Council, and it is fortunate the Supreme Court is also in session. This is a matter for the courts as well."

"I believe you are suggesting a Grand Conclave, Dave," Pau said.

"What is that, Pau?" Dave replied.

"It is a joint meeting of the High Council, Supreme Court and Military High Command," Pau said. "There hasn't been one for hundreds of years, but there is precedent to demand one.

We have interracial and interspecies issues as well as an intergalactic treaty on the table. You know, that might just work, Nola."

"It's a huge risk, Pau," she replied. "But it is the only way I know to muzzle the Brotherhood and allow Dave and his friends to get a fair deal here. I'll make the request."

"I hope you two know what you're doing," Dave said.

"And we hope you and your friends are ready for this, Dave Brewster," Nola replied. "This is going to be a contentious meeting. Either you win everything, or there will be dire consequences for you and especially for your Gallicean friends."

Lia Lawson sat at a small table with Silva Odeen in a coffee shop on Earth Prime. The Narta neighborhood on the planet was home to most of the Ela who worked here. The shop fronted a wide boulevard where shuttles zipped by a few inches off the ground. The buildings rose several hundred stories over their heads, making the street a massive canyon of steel and glass. The Ela of Earth Prime managed trade routes throughout the Society. They also controlled traffic through the star ports and landing sites around the planet. That was why Silva Odeen had been the contact for Nightsky. A smaller group of Ela also managed the museums around the planet, which housed the finest collections in the Society.

The coffee shop was very large with two hundred tables and fifty baristas and waiters. At this late hour in the morning, only a few patrons were present. Silva had chosen a table near the front of the shop so they could watch the street and people passing by. "So, Lia, I heard your ship visited Narta Ela, the planet this neighborhood is named after. What did you think of it?" a very nervous Silva asked.

"Well, unfortunately, I did not have an opportunity to visit the surface, Silva," Lia said. "My dad told me it was magnificent though."

"Your father is on the Nightsky?" he asked. "That's interesting. What does he do?"

"He is Admiral Brewster's second in command," she smiled. "He and my dad were born more than a thousand years ago and came to this time to find new planets to settle and new cultures to engage."

"You're kidding, right?" Silva asked. "You people travel in time. That's amazing. Time travel is extremely rare here. There's too much danger of affecting the past."

"The same is true in my time. My mom and my stepmother were both in the Temporal Command. That's how they met my dad," she replied.

"So, you are not like other modern humans, since you have one parent from the past. Is that right?" Silva asked.

"Actually, I look very much like everyone else in my time, except for the blue eyes. That's the one obvious thing I got from my dad," she replied.

Silva reached over and put his hand on top of hers. "Lia, I must confess your eyes were one of the things I noticed most. I'm still sorry about embarrassing you the first time I saw you. I guess I got carried away."

She smiled and giggled. "What else did you notice, Silva?"

He pulled his hand away and withdrew a small tablet from his satchel. He tapped the screen for several seconds while Lia sipped her coffee. He turned the screen around and held it out to her. On the screen were images of several humans who looked as though they stepped off any street on Earth in the thirty-second century. "Isn't the resemblance uncanny, Lia?" he said. "The third from the left could be your twin sister, don't you think?"

"That is amazing, Silva. Which of the fifty species of human are they?" she asked.

"This is where it gets freaky, Lia. These are the Non-Ti, the original humans who went to the stars billions of years ago," Silva said. "That race disappeared a very long time ago. And now, here you are sitting with me. Doesn't that blow your mind?"

"So, I'm like a laboratory experiment to you, Silva, is that right?" Lia asked.

"Of course not!" he shouted. "Lia, you are a sweet and beautiful woman. Any man would be lucky to have you in his life, but I'm sure you are aware of the situation among the races here."

"I've heard the tension is high, Silva," she said. "Everyone tends to marry in their own race and each race has a defined role in the overall Society. Isn't that just an old caste system?"

Two men in black suits entered the shop and wandered slowly toward the counter. They gazed around the small crowd, looking to see who might be here. After a couple minutes, they stepped up to the counter to place their order. "You're right, Lia," Silva whispered, "but we can't talk here anymore. Let's just walk slowly toward the door now."

They rose and headed toward the door. As they reached it, two Ela men in similar black suits came in the door. One extended his hand to Silva and said, "If it isn't our friend, Lieutenant Silva Odeen? How have you been?"

"Agent Coos, I'm fine and how are you?" Silva replied. He shook hands with the other man. "Agent Loo, it's a pleasure to see you as well. We were just leaving."

"Silva, don't be impolite. You haven't introduced us to your acquaintance," Loo said. He turned to Lia and said, "How do you do? My name is Loo, what's yours?"

"I am Lieutenant Lia Lawson, Chief Communications Officer of the star cruiser Nightsky," she replied. "Is there a reason you are blocking our path, Agent?"

"Ah, that explains it," Coos laughed as the other two agents approached from the counter. "It's okay guys. Lieutenant Lawson is from the Earth 47 star cruiser. That's why Silva is here. He's just showing her around."

"What are you talking about?" Lia asked. "You idiots have nothing better to do than harass friends sharing a coffee. This is ridiculous. Come on, Silva, we're leaving."

Agent Loo blocked the door with his body. "Lieutenant, I know you are not accustomed to Earth Prime, so we'll excuse your insults this one time. You need to learn to respect the Brotherhood if your worlds want to be part of the Society." He grabbed Silva by the arm. "Lieutenant Lawson, go back to your ship now. My friends and I are going to have a word with Silva."

Lia tapped her com-link and said, "Jake, I need some help." Ten maklans popped into the shop.

"What are those things?" Loo said as he drew his blaster. "Is this some kind of trick, Lieutenant?" He leveled the blaster at Lia's head. The other agents drew their weapons as well.

Instantly, the maklans and agents were gone. The remaining people in the store rushed for the door and ran down the sidewalks, knowing more agents would respond quickly.

"Lia, what did you do?" Silva asked. "They'll just report and send a hundred more." He took her arm and led her out of the shop and down the sidewalk. "They think I'm involved in something now for sure. I've got to find a ship leaving here today. Once those four make their report, I'm in big trouble."

Jake and Mitch reappeared, floating in front of them. "Are you okay?" Mitch asked.

"We're fine, but what did you do with the agents?" Lia asked.

"We turned them over to Fa-a-Di," Jake chuckled. "He has plenty of room in his brig."

"I'm feeling faint," Silva said. "My life is ending and they're playing games with the Brotherhood."

"Don't worry, Silva," Lia said as she kissed him on the cheek. "Those four won't make a report until we allow them to. Mitch will jump you to your residence or your post, whatever you like. Just think about where you want to go, and you'll be there."

"But what happens when they do report? Who will protect me then?" Silva asked.

"I will," Lia said. "Trust us. Mitch, please take Silva to his house. Have a maklan keep an eye on him. If any others come after him, jump him onto Nightsky."

Mitch and Silva disappeared. "Okay, Lia, are you ready to go too?" Jake asked.

"Take me to see Dave and Darlene, Jake. I've got to tell them about this," she replied as they disappeared from the busy sidewalk.

Dave was listening intently as General Fa-a-Di reported on the progress in translating Zula and Boley telepathy. The general held a half-full glass of Gallicean whisky in his left hand and gestured wildly with his right. "Brother, I know that time is short," Fa-a-Di said. "Bill and No-o-Ka are confident that we'll be ready for the hearing tomorrow morning."

"It's okay, brother," Dave smiled. He picked up his glass of Scotch whisky and raised it to the view screen. "Here's to us, old friend." Both men took a drink and laughed. "Fa-a-Di, everything will work out tomorrow, one way or the other."

"I know that, Dave. It's "the other" that I'm worried about," Fa-a-Di replied. "I heard about Lia Lawson's encounter with the Brotherhood. I guess I should have dropped those bastards off the platform when I had the chance!"

"I really doubt they were the same agents, brother. Besides, they have no real crime to accuse you of committing, unless making an agent wet himself is a crime here," Dave laughed.

"Sending Charlie and Lia back to Nan to work with Bill and the Zula was a great idea too," the general said. "It gets her away from here, and her communications background will be crucial with the Zula. My men and I can tell the story of the Boley even if they cannot speak for themselves. They look like our smaller twins. The Zula are a different matter. Frankly, they look like food to me too."

"Except for the expressive eyes and telepathy, of course," Dave replied.

"Dave, just so you know, the Kong-Fa will arrive at Nan in less than one hour. We are carrying one hundred Boley, who continue to work with No-o-Ka and the maklans. God willing, we'll pick up Bill's team and some Zula and head directly to Earth Prime," Fa-a-Di explained. "What kind of reception can we expect there?"

"Cold, brother, very cold," Dave answered. "The Society doesn't like non-humans, as you have learned. They have become very isolated from the rest of this galaxy." He started laughing.

"What's so funny, brother?" Fa-a-Di asked. "It didn't sound like a laughing matter to my ears."

Dave wiped a few tears from his eyes. "It's not that, brother. I just had a picture in my mind of your team entering the meeting chamber with the Boley. I bet everyone will be freaking out and running for the exits."

"And how is scaring our jailors funny?" Fa-a-Di asked.

"Think about the High Council and Supreme Court, brother," Dave replied. "They are so confident in their superiority and leadership for the entire galaxy. The sight of you and your warriors will show them in that one moment they are not superior. They will see firsthand that other Beings can be ten times stronger and run huge interplanetary civilizations. That happened on my home world when we were fighting the War. Twenty Kalidean star ships flew into orbit and demanded we stop. Suddenly, we knew we were not that important in the grand scheme of things."

"If that happens, Dave, perhaps we will all survive tomorrow," Fa-a-Di said. He began to laugh. "I just had the picture in my mind too, Dave. I saw the Councilors sitting on their high bench when we walk in. All of us, and especially my brother-in-law will tower over their puny bench." He reached behind himself and grabbed a whisky bottle and refilled his glass and took a long drink. "You know, Dave, I am content now. We don't know what will happen tomorrow. Perhaps we win and perhaps we lose. We may survive or we may die. Either way, we will be together and that is what matters. I love you, my brother. Kong-Fa out."

Dave left the sitting room and walked quietly into the bedroom. Darlene was sleeping soundly. He changed into his pajamas and slid into bed. He reached over and kissed her on the cheek, whispering "Good night." He rolled over and instantly fell asleep. He dreamed his light was flying through space, surrounding by billions of others. His light flew over Nan, where a pink string of light shot forward and merged with his.

"Hi, Grandpa," the string said. "It's me, Bea, your future granddaughter."

"What are you doing here, Bea?" he asked.

"You already know that, Grandpa," she replied. "I haven't been born yet, but things are looking promising between my parents."

"That's great, Bea. I'm really looking forward to holding Baby Bea soon," Dave smiled warmly. Suddenly, Bea was gone and Dave felt his string being pulled away. He tried to think of Bea or his own body, but his string kept moving faster and faster. He did not know how to get back to Darlene and became very frightened. He wondered if this is what death felt like.

Dave sat up straight and opened his eyes. He was in a strangely familiar place. In the distance, he could see a sun peek over the heavily cloud-laden horizon. He heard footsteps behind him and turned to see High Priest Obu Neela of Lagamar Ulu approaching with a tray and two cups. "Obu, how did I get here? Why am I here? I have the hearing tomorrow and need to be with my crew."

"Please relax, Dave," Obu smiled as he handed Dave a cup of steaming coffee. "You will be back before you know it. Why you are here is another question. I'm just acting as host. You'll need to ask Odo Pak that question. Bring your coffee and come with me, Dave." Dave followed the High Priest to the large temple and climbed the twenty steps to enter the Great Hall. The High Priest held daily audiences in the Great Hall to answer the pilgrim's questions and offer prayers and blessings. They walked to the back of the hall, where Obu slid open a hidden door and led Dave into a private chamber. Sitting in a circle were twelve Beings of Light, who turned to face them as they entered. Dave immediately recognized Odo Pak. The others were also Nan, but he had never seen them.

"Welcome Obu and Dave," Odo said. "Please join our circle." He pointed to two empty chairs. The two sat down. "Dave, I know you are wondering why you are here now."

"Yes, I'd like to know why and how you took me from my bed," Dave replied.

"Dave, we did not take you from your bed," Odo replied. "We had intended to, but when we arrived, your light string was already gone. Fortunately, we were able to follow it to you."

"How did my light leave my body without the Hive, Odo?" Dave asked.

"That is a very good question, Dave," Odo replied. "We can do that if we are on Nan, even without the stone temple. But from a star ship over Earth Prime, that is unbelievable to us as well."

"I think it is clear that Dave has strong connections to Source," Obu said. "It is almost like the Source is reaching out to him and helping him."

"Are you suggesting Divine intervention, Obu?" one of the other Beings of Light asked.

"You tell me," Obu replied. "Odo, you know Dave's visit to the stone temple was unusual. You told me yourself."

"That is true," Odo said. He turned to face Dave. "Dave, when I took you to the temple, I was certain that I would have to bring Bill to Nan myself. It takes us many centuries to become grounded in the Source. I planned to use your light to guide me to him, nothing more. When you were able to morph, I was pleasantly shocked."

"I am totally confused now," Dave said. "Can I go back now?"

"Odo, perhaps you should explain our reason for this gathering," another Being of Light said.

"Of course, Ula," Odo said. "Dave, we are the twelve elders of Nan. We lead the Nan people and guard the secrets of our Hive. Do you know why they call us Elders?"

"I suppose because you are old and wise?" Dave surmised.

"That's one way to put it, Dave," Odo laughed. "The average human in the Society lives around one thousand years. Most Nan live six or seven hundred years. Our lives are difficult with long separations from our families and hard work. Dave, I am the senior Elder because of my age. I am nine thousand years old. Each of the other elders here are at least five thousand years old.”

“How is that possible?” Dave said. “Is that because the Hive is protecting you?”

“Of course,” Odo smiled. “Our simple lives and constant connection to the Hive gives the permanent residents of Nan great longevity and unique abilities, including the ability to morph into Beings of Light like you see before you now. Yet, a few nights ago you did the same thing on your first day on Nan. That is unbelievable and clearly not typical.”

“It’s as though Source is pushing Dave toward a goal,” Obu said. “The elders believe they know the goal and want to share it with you.”

“The only goal I have now is surviving the hearing on Earth Prime and getting my family and friends out of this galaxy,” Dave said. “Isn’t that enough?”

The elders chuckled softly. “Dave, your concern is touching and we share your desire to win the day on Earth Prime,” Odo said. “You have to know that we will not allow any harm to come to you or your friends. Even if you fail tomorrow, we will make certain that your people and ships return safely to your own galaxy. Please believe us.”

“But what happens here if I fail?” Dave asked.

“That’s very touching too, Dave,” Odo said. “It is not your concern what happens here after tomorrow, regardless of the events in the hearing. I already told you the events of this galaxy are not yours to bear. Have you forgotten already?"

"No, Odo, I remember perfectly well," Dave replied. "But when I think of the Zula and Boley becoming targets again, it makes my blood boil. I get very upset when I think about the plight of the Nan, Opa, Vol and Ulu as well."

"Please calm down, Dave," Obu said. "Everyone here has absolute confidence that you and your friends will do a wonderful job in the hearing. But even a perfect oratory may not sway the Council or the Court. Each one of them and each of us bear responsibility for our lives and our future. Your life and future are in your galaxy, not ours."

"Dave, you already know the Society is in ruins," Odo continued. "There is no risk that the Society will rise from its ashes like a phoenix and come after you and your friends. Unless an orderly break-up occurs, the planets of the former Society will spend the next ten thousand years fighting among themselves. Eventually, after we are all dead and forgotten, some may venture to your galaxy again. There, they will find a Free Society with many different races and species working together in peace. That will become the model for the rebuilding of a Free Society here. That will be your gift to our galaxy. But you have more important work to do in your own galaxy."

"I remember I must start a thousand new worlds," Dave said. "Is that what you mean?"

"Yes and no," Odo said. "You will found those new colonies. And you will partner with the tekkans to build more Hives to counter the advances of invading species, like the Donnaki and Paxran. However, there is another detail you need to consider."

"I thought my plate was already pretty full, Odo," Dave laughed. "What else am I supposed to do?"

"Dave, we have seen more than fifty natural Hives in your galaxy," Odo replied. "As you have seen from our mistakes, the culture holding such a planet gains incredible power. You must make certain that does not happen."

"How exactly do I do that?" Dave asked.

"We would like to send ten thousand Nan with the fleet returning to your galaxy," Odo said. "You're a smart man, Dave. Please tell us what you will do with them."

"I will take them to Nanda where they will educate the locals on their vital role in the galaxy," Dave said. "When we find a natural Hive, I will settle it with Nan, who will protect the secrets and power found there." He thought for a moment, then continued, "But what about other species who can learn from the natural Hive. It was an incredible experience for me, for example."

Odo smiled. "Dave, I told you the affairs of this galaxy are not on your shoulders. Likewise, the affairs of your galaxy are not ours to bear. You are a great man and a great elder, Dave Brewster. Trust your gut. Do what you think is right. We have faith in you to make it work. Please close your eyes, Dave."

He closed his eyes and felt his body dissolving. His stomach turned over and he felt his mind shattering into a million bits. After a moment, his head stopped spinning, and feeling better, he opened his eyes. He was sitting on the side of his bed on the Nightsky. He turned to Darlene who was just waking up. "Where have you been, honey?" she said. "I woke up a while ago and didn't see you in bed."

CHAPTER 48

The Great Hall had been set up for the hearing with the High Council of the Society of Humanity. The room was as large as a football field and the ceiling soared one hundred feet over the marble floor. The main entrances were on the south side of the room. All ten doors were open and the hundreds of spectators poured in and milled around the seating area, waiting for the meeting to begin. The high bench for the ten members of the High Council lined the northern end of the room. Dozens of staff members moved around the bench, placing tablets, water pitchers and glasses for their Councilors. The west side of the room was all glass, opening onto a large garden in the center of the Council District. The eastern wall contained two more high benches; one for the Supreme Court's eleven justices and a second for the five senior generals of the High Command. The justices and generals were already seated and looking at the materials placed before them. Their aides stood behind them and sent runners to obtain other materials they were asked for.

The first two rows of seats in the gallery will filled with agents of the Brotherhood. Guards kept the center aisle clear for those coming to speak before the Grand Conclave. The room became instantly quiet as Dave and Darlene Brewster entered along with Mencius, Zee and Jake. They walked quickly up the aisle and were escorted to a long table in front of the high bench of the Council. Almost no human had ever seen a sentient non-human and murmurs moved through the crowd at the site of the two maklans. It became quiet again as Wendo, Serena, Antar and Zina entered next. They were escorted to the same table where they joined the rest. Most people in the Society knew them immediately, but believed they had died in exile in the Ulagong Galaxy long ago.

A single person in a long black robe entered from behind the Council bench. The robe was hooded so no one could tell who it was. The person stopped at the front edge of the bench and pulled off her hood. She was a tall Ela woman. She picked up a large gavel and began to pound it on its base. The voices fell immediately silent and everyone rose to their feet. The ten High Councilors began to walk out the same door and moved to their respective chairs. The Ela took the gavel and presented it to the man in the center of the bench, who smiled at her and accepted it. Dave noticed that each of the Councilors were from a different race. He could recognize the man who accepted the gavel was also an Ela. He immediately recognized Councilor Nola Balee, and he saw a Zu in the group. He had never seen the other races though.

The Ela on the bench pounded the gavel three times to establish order. He wore brilliant white robes with gold ribbing. He wore golden rings on each finger with large gemstones. He smiled broadly at the group and said, "Welcome to the Grand Conclave, my friends and fellow members of the Society of Humanity. I am Passor Valka, current Presient of the High Council, and it is my honor to host the first Grand Conclave in many hundreds of years." He waved his arm at the people on the long table. "It is especially heartwarming for me to welcome our friends from the Ulagong Galaxy. Wendo and Antar, welcome back and thank you for bringing our other guests with you. We look forward to a lively discussion today." He motioned to the other high benches. "Would any of you care to make an opening remark before we begin?"

A Pa justice at the end of the Court panel rose. "I am Justice Vorto Nagee of the Supreme Court and I wish to join my friend, the President, in welcoming you all. This is a special day for the Court as well." He looked toward the High Command and they waved them off.

"Secretary Palam, you may state the agenda for today," Passor said.

The Ela woman who had first pounded the gavel said, "Thank you, Mr. President. The only item on the agenda today is the request from our visitors to establish a Free Society in the Ulagong Galaxy as a pilot."

"Point of order, Mr. President," said a voice behind the witness tables. Dave turned his head to see Brother Luka Nance come from the audience and walk up to the high bench. "Mr. President, we have the matter of the Gallicean incident on Lagamar 7 to discuss first. We cannot include violent thugs like them into our Society, even if they are in another galaxy. There is also the rumor about the disappearance of the Zula from Lagamar Vol and four agents who were kidnapped right here on this planet." The audience began to talk among themselves about kidnappers and violence. "It bears repeating that this is the reason we chose to exclude non-humans from the Society."

"Mr. President," said a voice from the High Command bench. A Pa general was standing and gesturing toward the bench. "To our guests, I am General Aon Barsu, Chief of the High Command. This is all meaningless. The agents were frightened by the size of the Galliceans and ran home to their mothers. There is a rumor of wild sea creatures suddenly disappearing. The Brotherhood can't keep track of their agents on this planet. Brother Vance is wasting the time of this conclave."

"Mr. President," said a second justice from their bench. "To our guests, I am Chief Justice Bool Nago. I respect the general's opinion and agree this is not something we can discuss right now. After all, the Galliceans have not arrived yet."

"Very good point, Bool," Passor said. "Luka, we will hold your concerns until after the Galliceans arrive." He looked at the witness table. "Admiral Dave Brewster, are the Galliceans coming?"

Dave stood and said, "Yes, Mr. President, they will be here. They had a slight delay on Nan but will arrive very shortly."

"You see, Mr. President," Luka said, "these Galliceans cannot be trusted. Why would they ever go to Nan?"

"I asked them to," Dave replied. Dave turned to face the audience. "Ladies and gentlemen, there is much more to discuss today than this treaty or some trifling offenses from my dear friends. Bear with us and you will learn more today than you imagined."

Palam shouted, "You will address your coments to the High Council, Admiral Brewster. You are here to see them, not pander to the audience." Dave smiled, turned around and sat down.

Passor laughed and looked at the other Councilors. "We have to look out for Admiral Brewster. He is a very good politician as well. He could take any of our places up here." He looked back at Dave and said, "We look forward to the fufullment of the promises you just made. Okay, who will speak to us about the request for a Free Society?"

Antar Arrak, Wendo Balak and Mencius stood and approached the bench. Mencius began, "Thank you for this audience today, Mr. President and the other Councilors. I am Mencius, Ambassador of the Kalidean Federation. Our society extends to over ten thousand planets. As you can tell, I am a descendent from the original Opa immigrants from the Society. The other ambassadors with me today represent just some of the worlds in our galaxy that are now living and trading together in peace. With me now are Ambassador Darlene Brewster representing the Earth 47 group of worlds, High Consul Zee Gongaleg of Tak-Makla and Ambassador Jacomofledes Benomafolays of No-Makla. High Commissioner Fa-a-Di and Ambassador De-o-Nu of Greater Gallia will join us shortly. There are many other planets and species in our galaxy who also will join our Free Society, but could not be here today." He took a sip of water. "But you can be certain there are others who want nothing more than to destroy us. Your Hive 1008 was recently attacked by the Donnaki Empire. All of us have recently defeated the Predaxian Alliance. The Hive on Tak-Makla, built with the aid of the Society, was recently heavily damaged by an unwarranted attack from the Maklakars. All of us are already joined together to fight any invaders. However, because most of us are human and our desire is to grow and find new civilizations to trade with, we need help from you. Lords Balak and Arrak have convinced us that as part of the greater Society of the universe; all of us will be safer and have better lives. That is why we want your approval for a Free Society. Thank you."

The room erupted in applause. Passor pounded his gavel lightly to allow the crowd to savor the moment. As the noise started to diminish, he pounded harder. "You are a very eloquent speaker, Mencius. Thank you for your empassioned remarks." He looked up and down the bench. "Shall we take a vote?"

"Point of order, Mr. President," said Chief Justice Bool Nago. "While I fully agree this is a wonderful idea, we still have to deal with Article 2, which clearly states that only human planets can join the Society."

"Bool, remind me of the protocol," Passor said. "How can we change an article?"

"It requires unanimous approval by the High Council and the Supreme Court, Mr. President," Bool replied.

"Okay, that's great! Let's vote. All in favor of allowing non-humans into the Society in the Ulagong Galaxy raise your right hand," Passor said. All the Councilors and Justices raised their hands. "Change approved!" The crowd erupted in cheers again. Passor loved the adoration from the crowd and waited patiently for the cheering to stop.

"Point of order, Mr. President," Luka called out again

"What is it this time, Brother?" Passor asked. "Can it wait until after the next vote?"

"No, Mr. President, it cannot," Luka sneared. "I suggest that the Galliceans only be allowed as provisional members in the new Free Society until they have answered for their crimes."

"Since they are coming soon, I guess that's reasonable," Passor said. "Wouldn't you agree Admiral Brewster?"

Dave stood and said, "Yes, Mr. President, that is fair. By the way, I've just been told they are arriving in the building as we speak."

"Excellent! Fellow Councilors please raise your right hand if you agree to establish the Free Society in the Ulagong Galaxy. That Society will allow non-humans, except the Galliceans are only provisional members until the hearing is complete." Everyone on the bench raised their hands. "Congratulations, you are all members of the Society now and can establish a Free Society in your galaxy!"

The audience went crazy, jumping up and down and cheering wildly. Wendo and Antar had tears in their eyes as they hugged the others at the witness bench. The justices were huddled together and the generals looked bored. The Brotherhood agents sat almost frozen. The Councilors shook each other's hands and were laughing.

The commotion continued for five minutes, until a Gallicean Marine walked through the entry door. His blood red battle armor was gleaming and his four daggers hung from his belt. He was followed by Doctor No-o-Ka and two other Marines pulling a small cage that held two Boley. The Boley looked frightened to death and were visibly trembling. Two more Marines entered pulling a tank with a Zula inside. Dave immediately recognized Ulook. At the end of the entourage came De-o-Nu who was five feet taller than the rest, followed by his brother-in-law. The two wore black battle armor and carried their three daggers on their belts. The Boley and Galliceans wore breathers.

"This is very irregular, Mr. President," Luka shouted. "These creatures should not bring weapons into this chamber."

"Wow!" Passor said. "You really know how to make an entrance. Which of you is the High Commissioner?"

Fa-a-Di walked up to the bench. Passor had to look up to see his face. "I am General Fa-a-Di, current High Commissioner of Greater Gallia. My tall colleage is my brother-in-law, Ambassador De-o-Nu. I have brought a few Marines to help me with these creatures which seem to be bothering some of you. I offer our apologies for the daggers, but we Galliceans are warriors. We do not go anywhere without these. Trust me, we have no desire to fight here. In fact, I would like to present my own daggers to you, Mr. President as a sign of our good faith." He gently pulled the three blades and laid them in front of Passor. "These are the Nak, Falon and Ullu. Every Gallicean warrior carries these. You might notice the Marines have a fourth blade, the Baloo. Only Marines are trained in that weapon. My blades were made for me by my personal blacksmith on Gallia. You will note the gold handles and inscriptions about my family tree. Please be careful though, they are extremely sharp."

Passor lifted the Falon, which while dagger sized to a Gallicean was almost two feet long. "This is very impressive indeed, General," he smiled. "I graciously accept your gift."

Enough of this diplomatic drivel, Mr. President," Luka said. "I demand answers to my questions."

"Be careful, Brother Nance," cautioned the Chief Justice. "As you know, the Brotherhood has no standing in our constitution. You have no right to make demands of the High Council or any of us."

"Relax, Bool," Passor said. "I'll alow it. After all, we just limited the Galliceans to provisional membership until they respond to the Brother's concerns. It's better to hear them out now and get it over with. Go ahead, Luka. You have the floor."

"General, you are charged with attacking a team of agents who visited a secret platform on Lagamar 7. How do you plead?" Luka asked.

Fa-a-Di walked over to Luka and placed his hand on his shoulder. "First of all, little man, I am a head of state. I am not going to plead to anything. As an honorable man, I will tell the truth about that day. You be quiet until I'm finished." He approached the high bench. "The brave leaders of Lagamar Vol, Mulwi and Bola Deka told my dearest friend, Admiral Dave Brewster about atrocities on Lagamar 7. He visited the planet and found a hospital facility had been built on a platform to care for wounded creatures. Apparently, some of your humans enjoy traveling there to kill unarmed creatures for sport. Now, many species hunt for food. I still do that today. However, there is no food motive here. It is just about killing. Okay, let's say I think killing unthinking creatures is not a horrible crime. But I visited the platform with Dave and found these Boley and many other creatures being treated in the hospital."

"Mr. President, this creature is wasting our time," Luka complained.

Fa-a-Di spun around, spread his wings and glowered at Luka. After a moment, he folded his wings and smiled. "Little man, what did I just tell you about interrupting a head of state? Do you have a brain in that tiny skull?" He turned to face the Councilors. "I learned something that day that caused me to send our ship's physician there to help. This is the renowned doctor, No-o-Ka. The agents came to the platform and forced the doctors to stop caring for their patients. They pointed a blaster at the head of this Boley and threatened to kill all of the creatures. Fortunately, my Marines and I were nearby and arrived at the correct moment to stop the carnage. I convinced them to stop. I found they had the Dekas held prisoner in their shuttle. I asked more than once to open the door and release them, but they refused. In a moment of anger, I may have slightly damaged their shuttle. But none of them were injured and they were returned.”

“What did you learn, General?” Councilor Nola Balee asked.

Fa-a-Di smiled broadly. “Let me have Fanon Ungo tell you,” he said. “Admiral Brewster’s son has been helping us with a project for the last few days. Bear with me a second.” He walked over to the cage and opened it. The audience held their breath at the release of the wild beast. Fa-a-Di took a translator and stuck onto the side of the breather.

“Greetings, I am Fanon Ungo,” the Boley said. “We have lived on the planet you call Lagamar 7 for all time. I am told that our ancestors were taken from our planet to the Ulagong Galaxy when the Society first tried to establish colonies there. It would seem some of us were left on Gallia where we eventually evolved into the Galliceans. It was a gift from God that Fa-a-Di and his people came to help us. We have lived in deathly fear of humans as long as we remember. Your people still come to our planet to kill us and the other creatures we share our world with. My village is on a large island several hundred miles below the platform. Too many of my neighbors and friends have been wounded or killed. I request that you stop this now. The Galliceans have provided us with our own weapons now, but we have no desire to fight you. We cannot survive in your atmosphere and you cannot breathe ours. Just leave us alone.” He walked back into the cage where the other Boley hugged him.

“There you have it,” Fa-a-Di said. “Your people have been slaughtering my cousins for pleasure. I hope you know why I was angry and did what I did. I'm sure you'll say you had no idea, but that is a joke. Dave Brewster knew it immediately. He is as human as you. As a warrior, I must sometimes go into battle and face other sentient creatures with weapons like mine. War is an abomination, but it is what can happen when cultures get greedy. But killing them for sport is murder."

"I am so sorry, General," Passor sighed. "Fanon, I don't know what to say, but this situation will be investigated as soon as possible. I think I can speak for the entire Council when I say there will be a moratorium on hunting on Lagamar 7, effective immediately. I hope that is an acceptable compromise. What is your next charge, Luka?"

The stunned agent said, "There is the rumor about the Zula being taken from Lagamar Vol, Mr. President. Since the Galliceans have brought a Zula with them, I suppose they want us to hear about them."

"Mr. President, I would like to speak about the Zula," Dave said as he stood next to Fa-a-Di. "First of all, I admit the Zula were taken from Lagamar Vol by the Galliceans on my order. I take full responsibility for this action and would do it again tomorrow."

"Finally, someone is taking responsibility for something," Luka said.

"That's right Brother, but you will soon wish I did not," Dave laughed. "In respect for the Councilors, I will not turn my back to them, but I want the Court, High Command and especially the audience to look closely at your Councilors." Several Councilors were looking at their papers and each other, including Passor. Dave walked over to the tank with Ulook swimming about. "You know, I love seafood," he said. "On

Tak-Makla, High Consul Zee held a feast for me with a crustacean for the main course. It was wonderful. Of course, that creature was nothing like this! Look at it. It's almost six feet long with those beautiful expressive eyes. I have no doubt the Zula tastes good too. Unfortunately for most people here, they are incredibly rare and expensive. The fishermen on Lagamar Vol tell me only Councilors can afford them. But there is a small problem with that. He walked to the cage and pulled the translator off Fanon's breather. He returned to the tank and placed it on the glass.

"Hello, everyone, my name is Ulook, and I am a Zula," she said. "Our species is native to the planet you call Nan. The Nan have been our friends for many generations. Some brought a few of us to Lagamar Vol to give luck and good fortune to the Vol. Unfortunately, that forced the Vol to hunt us and offer us for sale according to Society rules. As Dave mentioned, very few were purchased due to the price. The Vol even spent most of their money buying us back where they could. But if even a dozen were taken per year, this has been happening for a very long time. All of that changed when I met Dave Brewster. His dear friend and my rescuer, De-o-Nu took us all home to Nan where we hope we can live in peace."

"Once again, Admiral," Passor said. "We are sorry, but how could we know?"

"That is a lie, Mr. President," Dave said. "Anyone who has looked into a Zula's eyes immediately knows they are intelligent. I could see that in the fish market on Lagamar Vol. Anyone who touches the Zula can hear its thoughts. I bet if everyone in the gallery stepped up here, they could hear Ulook speak to them too."

Odo Pak and Obu Neela appeared in front of the bench as Beings of Light. The room became very quiet. Odo put his hand on Dave's shoulder. "That's enough, Dave," he smiled. "I know the rage you feel for these people, but you have accomplished your goal and so much more. You have exposed the barbarism of the Council and the stupidity of the Brotherhood."

"What is the meaning of this?" Passor shouted.

"Oh, be quiet, Passor," Obu laughed, "or I will expose your feet and those of your friends so everyone knows your Brotherhood past. Odo is right, Dave Brewster. We know what must happen here next. Everyone in this room knows the Society is dead. Wendo and Antar are back to lead us to a new future. The Zula and Boley are safe. Let us carry on with what needs to be done here."

"The elders are right, Dave," Councilor Nola Balee said. "You and your friends have done so much. Don't risk your future by trying to do more for us. Frankly, we don't deserve your help."

"I knew you were trouble, Councilor," Luka said. "We'll be watching you."

"Point of order, Mr. President," Nola said. "The Chief Justice has reminded us the Brotherhood has no standing in our constitution. I move the Brotherhood be disbanded and the High Command dismantles its infrastructure immediately. But before you vote, fellow Councilors, I want you to know that I've been following the Zula story for a long time. I know which of you have eaten them and that information can easily be shared."

"I object to this, Mr. President," Luka shouted.

"This is very unusual, Nola," Passor stammered. "Perhaps we can take this matter up at another meeting."

"Passor, please do the right thing. Take the vote," Nola begged.

He looked at the High Command and Supreme Court. All were smiling broadly and many were laughing. He looked at the other Councilors. More than half were smiling and nodding at him. The others had their heads buried in their hands. He wondered if he would be impeached when the people learned of his special taste for Zula and the tattoos on his feet. "All those in favor of abolishing the Brotherhood effective immediately, please raise your right hand." He looked at the audience who were smiling and laughing. Most of the Councilors raised their hands immediately. One by one, the others looked at their friends and put up their hands until Passor was the only one left. He raised his hand and said, "Motion carries unanimously. The Brotherhood no longer exists. General Barsu, I turn that operation over to you."

"This isn't over Passor," Luka said. "We will not go quietly, as he put his hand on his blaster."

Fa-a-Di walked over to Luka and grabbed him around the waist, pinning his arms to his sides. He held him over his head and waved him at the audience. "I agree with that comment, little man. You never go quietly anywhere." Fa-a-Di strode down the main aisle while the people on either side cheered. He reached two human guards and the door and set the man down, taking care to pull his blaster and crush it in his hand. "Guards, please take out this garbage. And put something over his mouth. He just won't shut up!" Fa-a-Di walked back down the aisle, where the people were cheering and reaching out to shake his hands.

Odo hugged Dave. "Okay, son, now even you have to agree your job is done," he smiled. "And I must admit your friend the general has a unique style about him. Most of the people in this room love you. The rest are scared to death. Don't worry about us anymore. We have given you even more aggressive goals in your own galaxy. You have plenty to do without fretting about us."

"I have to admit I'll miss this place," Dave said. "Odo, knowing you has been one of the best experiences in my life. What do we do now? I guess we go back to our ships and wait for a jump?"

"That won't be necessary, Dave," Odo replied. "While you've been here, we were calling many more Nan home. When you are ready, you'll be home. You don't need to go to the ship or gather your crew. Say the word and the Nan Hive will send you, your friends and your ships back to Tak-Makla. Don't worry about the Lagamar system or Nan anymore. When you see this display of power, you will know we are all right."

"Will I see you or any of this again?" Dave asked.

"Dave, you can do what Obu and I are doing now easily," Odo laughed. "You probably don't even need a Hive. I still haven't figured that out." Odo hugged him again. "Are you all ready?"

"Just a second," Dave said as he went back behind the table and held Darlene in his arms. "Are you ready, sweetheart?"

"As long as I'm with you, I'm ready for anything, babe," she replied as she kissed him.

"Okay, Odo, we're ready, and thank you again," Dave said.

Dave and Darlene were standing in each other's arms on the beach in front of their residence on Tak-Makla. Mencius, Jake, Zee, Fak, Fa-a-Di and De-o-Nu were standing next to them.

"That was pretty impressive," Fa-a-Di said. "And we're little again, so I suppose I don't need this." He pulled off his breather and dropped it onto the sand.

"General, Kong-Fa is in orbit and our Marines are on board," De-o-Nu said. "The four agents disappeared at the same moment we did."

"Dave, Jon Lake sends his regards from the Nightsky," Jake said. "He also advises that two Nan colony ships are in orbit as well."

"Wow! And I was impressed by the jump to Andromeda," Dave said as he released Darlene from the hug. "What did you think, honey?"

Darlene smiled. "Honestly, with that exit, it seems like a mutual dream that we all awoke from at the same moment. I think I could use some Gallicean whisky."

"That's my sister," Fa-a-Di laughed. "We should have several cases inside. What are we waiting for?" The group moved toward the house. After a moment, they could see Charlie and Aria Watson standing by the door. Each was smiling with two glasses of whisky in their hands.

"What took you guys?" Charlie laughed as the others came inside and sat on the large couches near the fireplace. "Kally is in the kitchen preparing some snacks. For some unknown reason, traveling two million light-years in an instant is affecting my appetite." Everyone laughed.

"Dave, Odo and Obu said you have a new mission. What was that about?" Zee asked as he sipped the whisky.

"Well, it's more of an expanded mission for all of us. If we do it well, we will be like the Nan and their amazing Hive," Dave replied.

"I wasn't aware the Nan built a Hive, Dave," Zee said, looking confused.

"They didn't build one, Zee," Dave chuckled. "The planet is a natural Hive. And our goal as members of the Free Society of the Milky Way is to find natural Hives here and protect the true power of the universe."

"That's amazing, Dave," Zee replied. "There are natural Hives? Unbelievable."

"Unbelievable but true," Dave smiled. "But none of that matters anymore." He held up his glass. "What matters most of all is us. Our love and friendship is the real power in the universe. That is what makes miracles happen. That is what Universal Power or the Source is made from."

"And that is why Odo said you don't need a Hive at all?" Zee asked.

"Apparently, none of us do," Dave sighed. "Zee, do you remember Engineer Nok?"

"How could I forget my favorite niece, Dave," Zee replied with a tear in his eye.

"I'm sorry, Zee. I didn't know," Dave said. "I want you to know that I met her while I was in the Source trying to retrieve Bill. She came to me and told me not to grieve for her. She is happy and at peace." He smiled and a tear trickled down his face. "Oddly, that's exactly how I feel right now."

ABOUT THE AUTHOR

Karl J. Morgan

Karl Morgan grew up fascinated by science fiction, beginning with Victor Appleton's Tom Swift novels that he read as a young boy. Later, he became enthralled with the works of his favorite author, Isaac Asimov, especially his Foundation series.

Those early experiences inspired his life-long love of science fiction and interest in hard science, focusing first on astronomy and later cosmology and quantum mechanics. Karl had the great honor to take his first astronomy course at the University of Iowa from the legendary scientist, Dr. James Van Allen. More recently, the brilliant works of Drs. Stephen Hawking, Brian Greene, and Michio Kaku helped him understand that our physical universe is still a magical and mysterious place.

It is that sense of magic and mystery that brings Karl to write about his alter ego, Dave Brewster, an unemployed accountant who finds himself a thousand years in the future with new friends and adventures far beyond anything he could have imagined. There, he can find answers to questions that befuddle mankind today. The truth he finds is no different from what we know today. Life is always about loving and caring for our family and friends.

Karl lives in San Diego with his wife, Aida and their beloved puppies. Their two grown children have fled the nest and started their own adventures in life.

OTHER BOOKS BY KARL J. MORGAN

Remembrances: Choose to Be Happy and Embrace the Possibilities
ISBN: 978-0-9826461-9-9

The David Brewster Series

The David Brewster Series: Showdown Over Neptune
(Book 1)
ISBN: 978-0-9860270-0-0

The Dave Brewster Series: Second Predaxian War
(Book 2)
ISBN: 978-0-9860270-1-7

The Dave Brewster Series: Tears of Gallia
(Book 4)
ISBN: 978-0-9860270-4-8
Available for purchase early Spring 2013

Heartstone

Heartstone: Sentinels of Far Sun
ISBN: 978-0-9860270-3-1
Available for purchase early Spring 2013

www.ingramcontent.com/pod-product-compliance
Lightning Source LLC
Chambersburg PA
CBHW070158120726
47909CB00001B/163